PENGUIN BOOKS

The Hanging Valley

Peter Robinson grew up in Leeds, Yorkshire. He emigrated to Canada in 1974 and attended university in Windsor and York University in Toronto. His first Chief Inspector Banks mystery, *Gallows View*, was shortlisted for the John Creasey Award in Britain and the Crime Writers of Canada first novel award. His next novel, *A Dedicated Man*, was nominated for the Arthur Ellis Award. *A Necessary End* and *The Hanging Valley*, his subsequent Banks mysteries, were both published to critical acclaim. Peter Robinson lives in Toronto and teaches at community colleges.

D0838965

THE HANGING VALLEY

An Inspector Banks Mystery

Peter Robinson

Penguin Books

PENGUIN BOOKS
Published by the Penguin Group
Penguin Books Canada Ltd, 2801 John Street, Markham,
Ontario L3R 1B4
Penguin Books Ltd, 27 Wrights Lane, London W8 5TZ, England
Viking Penguin, a division of Penguin Books USA Inc., 375
Hudson Street, New York, New York 10014, USA
Penguin Books Australia Ltd, Ringwood, Victoria, Australia
Penguin Books (NZ) Ltd, 182-190 Wairau Road, Auckland 10,
New Zealand

Penguin Books Ltd, Registered Offices: Harmondsworth,
Middlesex, England

First published in Viking by Penguin Books Canada Limited,
1989
Published in Penguin Books, 1990
1 3 5 7 9 10 8 6 4 2

*Publisher's note: This book is a work of fiction. Names,
characters, places and incidents either are the product of the
author's imagination or are used fictitiously, and any
resemblance to actual persons living or dead, events, or locales is
entirely coincidental.*

Manufactured in Canada

Canadian Cataloguing in Publication Data

Robinson, Peter, 1950-
The hanging valley

ISBN 0-14-011544-7

I. Title.

PS8585.025H36 1990 C813'.54 C88-094767-5
PR9199.3.R62H36 1990

British Library Cataloguing in Publication Data Available

For Jan

THE
HANGING
VALLEY

Part One:

MOTION IN CORRUPTION

1

I

It was the most exhilarating feeling in the world. His thighs ached, his calves throbbed and his breath came in short, sharp gasps. But he had made it. Neil Fellowes, humble wages clerk from Pontefract, stood at the summit of Swainshead Fell.

Not that it was an achievement comparable to Sir Edmund Hillary's; after all, the fell was only 1631 feet high. But Neil was not getting any younger, and the crowd at Baxwell's Machine Tools, where he worked, had taken the mickey something cruel when he told them he was going on a fell-walking holiday in the Yorkshire Dales.

"Fell?" taunted Dick Blatchley, one of the mail-room wags, "Tha'll a fell before tha's got started, Neil." And they had all laughed.

But now, as he stood there in the thin air, his heart beating deep in his chest like the steam-driven pistons in the factory, he was the one to laugh. He pushed his wire-rimmed glasses back up to the bridge of his nose and wiped off the sweat over which they had slid. Next he adjusted the straps of his rucksack, which were biting into his shoulders.

He had been climbing for well over an hour: nothing too dangerous—no sheer heights, nothing that required special equipment. Fell-walking was a democratic recreation: just plain hard work. And it was an ideal day for walking. The sun danced in and out between plump white clouds, and a cool breeze kept the temperature down. Perfect late May weather.

He stood in the rough grass and heather with nothing but a few sheep for company—and they had already turned their backs on him and scuttled a safe distance away. Lord of the whole scene, he sat on a weathered limestone boulder to savour the feeling.

Back down the fell he could just make out the northern tip of Swainshead village, from where he had come. He could easily pick out the whitewashed front of the White Rose across the beck, and the lichen-covered flagstone roof of the Greenock Guest House, where he had spent a comfortable night after the previous day's walking in Wharfedale. He had also enjoyed there a breakfast of sausage, bacon, black pudding, fried bread, grilled mushrooms, tomato, two fried eggs, tea, toast and marmalade before setting off that morning.

He stood up to take in the panorama, starting with the west, where the fells descended and rolled like frozen waves to the sea. To the north-west ranged the old, rounded hills of the Lake District. Neil fancied he could see the Striding Edge along Helvellyn and the occasional glint of sun on Windermere or Ullswater. Next he looked south, where the landscape hardened into the Pennines, the "backbone" of England. The rock was darker there, with outcrops of millstone grit ousting the glinting white limestone. Miles of wild, forbidding moorland stretched down as far as Derbyshire. South-east lay Swainsdale itself, its valley bottom hidden from view.

But what astonished Neil most of all was a small wooded valley down the eastern slope just below where he stood. The guide books hadn't mentioned anything of particular interest on the route he had chosen; indeed, one of his reasons for taking it was that nobody was likely to spoil his solitude. Most people, it seemed to Neil, would be off in search of stone circles, old lead mines and historic buildings.

In addition to its location and seclusion, the dale also had unusual foliage. It must have been a trick of the light, Neil thought, but when the trees everywhere else were fresh and green with spring, the ash, alders and sycamores below him seemed tinged with russet, orange and earth-brown. It seemed to him like a valley out of Tolkien's *Lord of the Rings*.

It would mean an extra mile or two and an unplanned climb back out again, but the sides didn't appear too steep, and Neil thought he might find some interesting wild flowers along the shaded banks of the beck. Balancing his pack, he struck out for the enchanted valley.

Soon, the rough tussocks underfoot gave way to springier grass. When Neil entered the woods, the leaves seemed much greener now the sunlight filtered through them. The smell of wild garlic filled his nostrils and made him feel light-headed. Bluebells swayed in the breeze.

He heard the beck before he saw it between the trees; it made a light, bubbling sound—joyful and carefree. From the inside, too, the valley clearly had a magical quality. It was more luxuriant than the surrounding area, its ferns and shrubs more lush and abundant, as if, Neil thought, God had blessed it with a special grace.

He eased off his rucksack and laid it down on the thick grass by the waterside. Taking off his glasses, he thought he would stay a while and relax, perhaps drink some coffee from his flask before carrying on. He rested his head on the pack and closed his eyes. His mind emptied of everything but the heady scent of the garlic, the song of the beck, the cool fingers of the wind that rustled through wild roses and honeysuckle, and the warbling of skylarks as they aimed themselves up at the sun and floated down like feathers, singing.

Refreshed—indeed, feeling as if he had been born anew—Neil wiped his eyes and put on his glasses again. Looking around, he noticed a wild flower in the woods across the water. It seemed, from where he was, to be about a foot high, with red-brown sepals and pale yellow petals. Thinking it might be a rare lady's slipper orchis, he decided to cross over and have a closer look. The beck wasn't very wide, and there were plenty of fortuitously placed stepping-stones.

As he neared the flower, he became aware of another smell, much more harsh and cloying than the garlic or loam. It clogged his nose and stuck to his bronchial passages. Wondering what it could be, he looked around, but could see nothing unusual. Near the flower, which was definitely a lady's slipper, some branches fallen from a tree lay on the ground and blocked his way. He started to pull them aside to get a better view.

But he didn't get very far. There, under a makeshift cover, lay the source of the smell: a human body. In the instant before he turned to vomit into the shrubs, Neil noticed two things: that it had no face, and that it seemed to be moving— its flesh was literally crawling.

Pausing only to wash his face and rinse out his mouth in the beck, Neil left his rucksack where it was and hurried as fast as he could back to Swainshead.

II

Disgusting, thought Katie Greenock, turning up her nose as she emptied the waste-bin of room three. You'd think people would be ashamed to leave such things lying around for anyone to see. Thank God they'd left that morning. There always had seemed something unwholesome about them anyway: the way they kissed and canoodled at the breakfast table, how it was always so long before they set off for the day and so early when they returned to their room. She didn't even believe they were married.

Sighing, Katie brushed back a strand of ash-blonde hair and emptied the bin into the black plastic bag she carried with her on her rounds. Already she was tired out. Her day began at six o'clock, and there were no easy rustic mornings of bird-song and dew for her, just sheer hard work.

First she had to cook the breakfasts and co-ordinate everything so that the eggs weren't cold when the bacon was ready and the tea was fresh for the guests as soon as they decided to come down. They could help themselves to juice and cereal, which she had put out earlier—though not too early, for the milk had to be chilled. The toast could get as cold as it liked—cold toast seemed to be a part of the tradition of an English breakfast—but Katie was pleased when, as sometimes happened, she succeeded in serving it warm at exactly the right time. Not that anyone ever said thank you.

Then, of course, she had to serve the meals and manage a smile for all the guests, whatever their comments about the quality of the food, and no matter what their sweet little children saw fit to drop on the floor or throw at the walls. She was also often asked for advice about where to go for the day, but sometimes Sam would help with that part, breaking off from his usual morning monologue on current events, with which he entertained the visitors daily whether they liked it or not.

Next, she had to clear the tables and wash the dishes. The machine Sam had finally bought her helped a lot. Indeed, it saved her so much time that she could hurry down to Thetford's Grocery on the Helmthorpe Road and take her pick of the morning's fresh produce. Sam used to do that before he had installed the machine, but now he had more time for the sundry business matters that always seemed to be pressing.

When Katie had planned the menu for the evening meal and bought all the ingredients, it was time to change the sheets and clean the rooms. It was hardly surprising, then, that by noon she was almost always tired. If she was lucky, she could sometimes find a little time for gardening around mid-afternoon.

Putting off the moment when she would have to move on to the next room, Katie walked over to the window and rested her elbows on the sill. It was a fine day in a beautiful part of the world, but to her the landscape felt like an enormous trap; the fells were boulders that shut her in, the stretches of moorland like deserts impossible to cross. A chance of freedom had offered itself recently, but there was nothing she could do about it yet. She could only wait patiently and see what developed.

She looked down on the grassy banks at each side of the fledgling River Swain, at the children sitting patiently with their home-made fishing-nets, a visiting couple having a picnic, the old men gossiping as usual on the small stone bridge. She could see it all, but not feel the beauty of any of it.

And there, almost dead opposite, was the White Rose, founded in 1605, as its sign proudly proclaimed, where Sam would no doubt be hob-nobbing with his upper-class chums. The fool, Katie thought. He thinks he's well in, but they'll never really accept him, even after all these years and all he's done for them. Their kind never does. She was sure they laughed at him behind his back. And had he noticed the way Nicholas Collier kept looking at her? Did Sam know about the times Nicholas had tried to touch her?

Katie shuddered at the thought. Outside, a sudden movement caught her eye and she saw the old men part like the Red Sea and stare open-mouthed as a slight figure hurried across the bridge.

It was that man who'd set off just a few hours ago, Katie realized, the mild-mannered clerk from Castleford, or Featherstone, or somewhere like that. Surely he'd said he was heading for the Pennine Way? And he was as white as the pub front. He turned left at the end of the bridge, hurried the last few yards and went running into the White Rose.

Katie felt her chest tighten. What was it that had brought him back in such a state? What was wrong? Surely nothing terrible had happened in Swainshead? Not again.

III

"Well," Sam Greenock was saying about the racial mix in England, "they have their ways, I suppose, but—"

Then Neil Fellowes burst through the door and looked desperately around the pub for a familiar face.

Seeing Sam at his usual table with the Collier brothers and John Fletcher, Neil hurried over and pulled up a chair.

"We must do something," he said, gasping for breath and pointing outside. "There's a body up on the fell. Dead."

"Calm down, mate," Sam said. "Get your breath, then tell us what's happened." He called over to the barman. "A brandy for Mr Fellowes, Freddie, if you please. A large one." Seeing Freddie hesitate, he added, "Don't worry, you bloody old skinflint, I'll pay. And get a move on."

Conversation at the table stopped while Freddie Metcalfe carried the drink over. Neil gulped the brandy and it brought on a coughing fit.

"At least that's put a bit of colour back in your cheeks," Sam said, slapping Neil on the back.

"It was terrible," Neil said, wiping off the brandy where it had dribbled down his chin. He wasn't used to strong drink, but he did approve of it in emergencies such as this.

"His face was all gone, all eaten away, and the whole thing was moving, like waves." He put the glass to his thin lips again and drained it. "We must do something. The police." He got up and strode over to Freddie Metcalfe. "Where's the police station in Swainshead?"

Metcalfe scratched his shiny red scalp and answered slowly. "Let me see ... There aren't no bobbies in T'Head itself. Nearest's Helmthorpe, I reckon. Sergeant Mullins and young Weaver. That's nigh on ten miles off."

Neil bought himself another double brandy while Metcalfe screwed up his weather-beaten face and thought.

"They'll be no bloody use, Freddie," Sam called over. "Not for something like this. It's CID business, this is."

"Aye," Metcalfe agreed, "I reckon tha's right, Sam. In that case, young feller mi'lad," he said to Neil, "it'll be that chap in Eastvale tha'll be after. T'one who were out 'ere last time we 'ad a bit o'bother. Gristhorpe, Chief Inspector Gristhorpe. Years back it was, though. Probably dead now. Come on, lad, you can use this phone, seeing as it's an emergency."

IV

"Chief Inspector" Gristhorpe, now Superintendent, was far from dead. When the call came through, he was on another line talking to Redshaw's Quarries about a delivery for the dry-stone wall he was building. Despite all the care he put into the endeavour, a section had collapsed during an April frost, and rebuilding seemed a suitable spring project.

The telephone call found its way, instead, to the office of Detective Chief Inspector Alan Banks, who sat browsing through the *Guardian* arts page, counting his blessings that crime had been so slack in Eastvale recently. After all, he had transferred from London almost two years ago for a bit of peace and quiet. He liked detective work and couldn't imagine doing anything else, but the sheer pressure of the job —unpleasant, most of it—and the growing sense of confrontation between police and citizens in the capital had got him down. For his own and his family's sake, he had made the move. Eastvale hadn't been quite as peaceful as he'd expected, but at the moment all he had to deal with were a couple of minor break-ins and the aftermath of a tremendous punch-up in The Oak. It had started when five soldiers from Catterick camp had taunted a group of unemployed miners from Durham. Three people ended up in hospital with injuries ranging from bruised and swollen testicles to a bitten-off earlobe, and the others were cooling off in the cells waiting to appear before the magistrate.

"Someone asking for the super, sir," said Sergeant Rowe, when Banks picked up the phone. "His line's busy."

"It's all right," Banks said, "I'll take it."

A breathless, slightly slurred voice came on the line. "Hello, is that Inspector Gristhorpe?"

Banks introduced himself and encouraged the caller, who gave his name as Neil Fellowes, to continue.

"There's a body," Fellowes said. "Up on the fells. I found it."

"Where are you now?"

"A pub. The White Rose."

"Whereabouts?"

"What? Oh, I see. In Swainshead."

Banks wrote the details down on his scrap pad.

"Are you sure it's a human body?" he asked. There had been mistakes made in the past, and the police had more than once been dragged out to examine piles of old sacks, dead sheep or rotten tree trunks.

"Yes. Yes, I'm sure."

"Male or female?"

"I . . . I didn't look. It was—"

The next few words were muffled.

"All right, Mr Fellowes," Banks said. "Just stay where you are and we'll be along as soon as possible."

Gristhorpe had finished his call when Banks tapped on the door and entered his office. With its overflowing bookcases and dim lighting, it looked more like a study than part of a police station.

"Ah, Alan," Gristhorpe said, rubbing his hands together. "They said they'll deliver before the weekend, so we can make a start on the repairs Sunday, if you'd care to come?"

Working on the dry-stone wall, which fenced in nothing and was going nowhere, had become something of a ritual for the superintendent and his chief inspector. Banks had come to look forward to those Sunday afternoons on the north daleside above Lyndgarth, where Gristhorpe lived alone in his farmhouse. Mostly they worked in silence, and the job created a bond between them, a bond that Banks, still an incomer to the Yorkshire Dales, valued greatly.

"Yes," he answered. "Very much. Look, I've just had a rather garbled phonecall from a chap by the name of Neil Fellowes. Says he's found a body on the fell near Swainshead."

Gristhorpe leaned back in his chair, linked his hands behind his head and frowned. "Any details?"

"No. He's still a bit shook up, by the sound of it. Shall I go?"

"We'll both go." Gristhorpe stood up decisively. "It's not the first time a body has turned up in The Head."

"The Head?"

"That's what the locals call it, the whole area around Swainshead village. It's the source of the River Swain, the head of the dale." He looked at his watch. "It's about twenty-five miles, but I'm sure we'll make it before closing time if I remember Freddie Metcalfe."

Banks was puzzled. It was unusual for Gristhorpe to involve himself so much in an actual field investigation. As head of Eastvale CID, the superintendent could use his discretion as regards his role in a case. Theoretically, he could, if he wanted to, take part in searches and house-to-house inquiries, but of course he never did. In part, his job was administrative. He tended to delegate casework and monitor developments from his office. This was not due to laziness, Banks realized, but because his talent was for thinking and planning, not for action or interrogation. He trusted his subordinates and allowed them far greater leeway with their cases than many superintendents did. But this time he wanted to come along.

They made an incongruous couple as they walked to the car-park out back: the tall, bulky Gristhorpe with his unruly thatch of grey hair, bristly moustache, pock-marked face and bushy eyebrows; and Banks, lean, slight, with angular features and short, almost cropped, black hair.

"I can't see why you keep on using your own car, Alan," Gristhorpe said as he eased into the passenger seat of the white Cortina and grappled with the safety belt. "You could save a lot of wear and tear if you took a department vehicle."

"Have they got tape-decks?" Banks asked.

"Cassettes? You know damn well they haven't."

"Well, then."

"Well, what?"

"I like to listen to music while I'm driving. You know I do. It helps me think."

"I suppose you're going to inflict some on me, too?"

It had always surprised Banks that so well-read and cultured a person as Gristhorpe had absolutely no ear for music at all. The superintendent was tone deaf, and even the most ethereal Mozart aria was painful to his ears.

"Not if you don't want," Banks said, smiling to himself. He knew he wouldn't be able to smoke on the way, either. Gristhorpe was a non-smoker of the most rabid kind—reformed after a twenty-year, pack-a-day habit.

Banks pulled into the cobbled market square, turned left onto North Market Street, and headed for the main Swainsdale road, which ran by the river along the valley bottom.

Gristhorpe grunted and tapped the apparatus next to the dashboard. "At least you've had a police radio fitted."

"What was it you said before?" Banks asked. "About this not being the first body in Swainshead."

"It was before your time."

"Most things were." Banks made the sharp westward turn, and soon they were out of the town, driving by the river meadows.

Gristhorpe opened his window and gulped in the fresh air. "A man had his skull fractured," he said. "It was murder, no doubt about that. And we never solved it."

"What happened?"

"Some Boy Scouts found the body dumped in an old mine shaft on the fell-side a couple of miles north of the village. The doc said it had been there about a week."

"When?"

"Just over five years ago."

"Was it a local?"

"No. The victim was a private-inquiry agent from London."

"A private investigator?"

"That's right. Name of Raymond Addison. A solo operator. One of the last of the breed, I should imagine."

"Did you find out what he was doing up here?"

"No. We had his office searched, of course, but none of his files had any connection with Swainsdale. The Yard asked around among his friends and acquaintances—not that he had very many—but they turned up nothing. We thought he might have been on holiday, but why choose Yorkshire in February?"

"How long had he been in the village?"

"He'd arrived fairly late in the day and managed to get a room in a guest house run by a chap named Sam Greenock, who told us that Addison said nothing except for some remarks about the cold. He wrapped up well and went out for a walk after the evening meal, and that was the last anyone saw of him. We made enquiries, but nobody had seen or heard him. It was dark when he went out, of course, and even the old men who usually hang about chatting on the bridge come rain or shine had gone in by then."

"And as far as you could find out he had no connection with the area at all?"

"None. And, believe me, we dug and dug. Either nobody knew or, more likely, someone wasn't talking. He was an ex-serviceman, so we checked up on old army pals, that kind of thing. We ended up doing a house-to-house of the entire village. Nothing. It's still unsolved."

Banks slowed down as he drove through Helmthorpe, one of the dale's largest villages. Beyond there, the landscape was unfamiliar to him. Though still broader than most of the dales, thanks to a glacier of particularly titanic proportions, the valley seemed to narrow slightly as they got closer to The Head, and the commons sloped more steeply up the fell-sides. There were none of the long limestone scars that characterized the eastern part of Swainsdale, but the hills rose to high, rounded summits of moorland.

"And that's not all," Gristhorpe added after a few moments of silence. "A week before Addison's body was found—the day after he was killed, as far as the doc could make out—a local woman disappeared. Name of Anne Ralston. Never been seen since."

"And you think there must have been a connection?"

"Not necessarily. At the time she went, of course, the body hadn't been discovered. The whole thing could have been a coincidence. And the doc admitted he could have been wrong about the exact day of death, too. It's hard to be accurate after a body's been buried that long. But we've no idea what happened to her. And you've got to admit it's damned odd to get a missing person and a murder in the same village within a week of each other. She could have been killed and buried, or maybe she simply ran off with a fellow somewhere. We'd hardly cause to block all the ports and airports. Besides, she could have been anywhere in the world by the time the body was found. At best we'd have liked her to answer a few questions, just to put our minds at rest. As it was, we did a bit more poking around the landscape but found no traces of another body."

"Do you think she might have murdered Addison and run off?"

"It's possible. But it didn't look like a woman's job to me. Too much muscle-work involved, and Anne Ralston wasn't one of those female body-builders. We questioned her boyfriend pretty closely. He's Stephen Collier, managing director of the company she worked for. Comes from a very prominent local family."

"Yes," Banks said. "I've heard of the Colliers. Did he cause any problems?"

"No. He was co-operative. Said they hadn't been getting on all that well lately, but he'd no idea where she'd gone, or why. In the end we'd no reason to think anything had happened to her, so we had to assume she'd just taken off. People do sometimes. And Anne Ralston seemed to be a particularly flighty lass, by all accounts."

"Still . . ."

"Yes, I know." Gristhorpe sighed. "It's not at all satisfactory, is it? We reached nothing but dead ends whichever direction we turned."

Banks drove on in silence. Obviously failure was hard for Gristhorpe to swallow, as it was for most detectives. But this murder, if that's what it really turned out to be, was a different case, five years old. He wasn't going to let the past clutter up his thinking if he could help it. Still, it would be well to keep Raymond Addison and Anne Ralston in mind.

"This is it," Gristhorpe said a few minutes later, pointing to the row of houses ahead. "This is Lower Head, as the locals call it."

"It hardly seems a big enough place to be split into two parts," Banks observed.

"It's not a matter of size, Alan. Lower Head is the newest part of the village, the part that's grown since the road's become more widely used. People just stop off there to admire the view over a quick cup of tea or a pint and a pub lunch. Upper Head's older and quieter. A bit more genteel. It's a little north-south dale in itself, wedged between two fells. There's a road goes north up there, too, but when it gets past the village and the school it gets pretty bad. You can get to the Lake District if you're willing to ride it out, but most people go from the Lancashire side. Turn right here."

Banks turned. The base of a triangular village green ran beside the main road, allowing easy access to Swainshead from both directions. The first buildings he passed were a small stone church and a village hall.

Following the minor road north beside the narrow River Swain, Banks could see what Gristhorpe meant. There were two rows of cottages facing each other, set back quite a bit from the river and its grassy banks. Most of them were either semis or terrace blocks, and some had been converted into shops. They were plain, sturdy houses built mostly of limestone, discoloured here and there with moss and lichen. Many had individualizing touches, such as mullions or white borders painted around doors and windows. Behind the houses on both sides, the commons sloped up, criss-crossed here and there by dry-stone walls, and gave way to steep moorland fells.

Banks parked the car outside the whitewashed pub, and Gristhorpe pointed to a large house farther up the road.

"That's the Collier place," he said. "The old man was one of the richest farmers and landowners around these parts. He also had the sense to invest his money in a food-processing plant just west of here. He's dead now, but young Stephen runs the factory and he shares the house with his brother. They've split it into two halves. Ugly pile of stone, isn't it?"

Banks didn't say so, but he rather admired the Victorian extravagance of the place, so at odds with the utilitarian austerity of most Dales architecture. Certainly it was ugly: oriels and turrets cluttered the upper half, making the whole building look top-heavy, and there was a stone porch at each front entrance. They probably had a gazebo and a folly in the back garden, too, he thought.

"And that's where Raymond Addison stayed," Gristhorpe said, pointing across the beck. The house, made of two knocked-together semis, was separated from the smaller terrace blocks on either side by only a few feet. A sign, Greenock Guest House, hung in the colourful, well-tended garden.

"'Ey up, lads," Freddie Metcalfe said as they entered, "t'Sweeney's 'ere."

"Hello again, Freddie," Gristhorpe said, leading Banks over to the bar. "Still serving drinks after hours?"

"Only to the select few, Mr Gristhorpe," Metcalfe replied proudly. "What'll you gents be 'aving?" He looked at Banks suspiciously. "Is 'ee over eighteen?"

"Just," Gristhorpe answered.

Freddie burst into a rasping, smoker's laugh.

"What's this about a body?" Gristhorpe asked.

Metcalfe pursed his fleshy lips and nodded towards the only occupied table. "Bloke there says he found one on t'fell. 'Ee's not going anywhere, so I might as well pull you gents a pint before you get down to business."

The superintendent asked for a pint of bitter and Banks, having noticed that the White Rose was a Marston's house, asked for a pint of Pedigree.

"'Ee's got good taste, I'll say that for 'im," Metcalfe said. "Is 'ee 'ouse-trained an' all?"

Banks observed a prudent silence throughout the exchange and took stock of his surroundings. The walls of the lounge-bar were panelled in dark wood up to waist height and above that papered an inoffensive dun colour. Most of the tables were the old round kind with cast-iron knee-capper legs, but a few modern square ones stood in the corner near the dartboard and the silent juke-box.

Banks lit a Silk Cut and sipped his pint. He'd refrained from smoking in the car in deference to Gristhorpe's feelings, but now that he was in a public place he was going to take advantage of it and puff away to his heart's, and lungs', content.

Carrying their drinks, they walked over to the table.

"Someone reported a death?" Gristhorpe asked, his innocent baby-blue eyes ranging over the five men who sat there.

Fellowes hiccuped and put his hand in the air. "I did," he said, and slid off his chair onto the stone floor.

"Christ, he's pissed as a newt," Banks said, glaring at Sam Greenock. "Couldn't you have kept him sober till we got here?"

"Don't blame me," Sam said. "He's only had enough to put some colour back in his cheeks. It's not my fault he can't take his drink."

Two of the others helped Fellowes back into his chair and Freddie Metcalfe rushed over with some smelling salts he kept behind the bar for this and similar exigencies.

Fellowes moaned and waved away the salts, then slumped back and squinted at Gristhorpe. He was clearly in no shape to guide them to the scene of the crime.

"It's all right, Inshpector," he said. "Bit of a shock to the syshtem, thass all."

"Can you tell us where you found this body?" Gristhorpe spoke slowly, as if to a child.

"Over Shwainshead Fell, there's a beautiful valley. All autumn colours. Can't mish it, just down from where the footpath reaches the top. Go shtraight down till you get to the beck, then cross it . . . easy. Near the lady's slipper."

"Lady's slipper?"

"Yes. The orchish, not the bird's-foot trefoil. Very rare. Body's near the lady's shlipper."

Then he half-twisted in his chair and stretched his arm up his back.

"I left my rucksack," he said. "Thought I did. Just over from my rucksack, then. Ruckshack marks the spot." Then he hiccuped again and his eyes closed.

"Does anyone know where's he staying?" Banks asked the group.

"He was staying at my guest house," Sam said. "But he left this morning."

"Better get him back there, if there's room. He's in no condition to go anywhere and we'll want to talk to him again later."

Sam nodded. "I think we've still got number five empty, unless someone's arrived while I've been out. Stephen?" He looked over to the man next to him, who helped him get Fellowes to his feet.

"It's Stephen Collier, isn't it?" Gristhorpe asked, then turned to the person opposite Greenock. "And you're Nicholas. Remember, I talked to you both a few years ago about Anne Ralston and that mysterious death?"

"We remember," Nicholas answered. "You knew Father too, if I recall rightly?"

"Not well, but yes, we bent elbows together once or twice. Quite a man."

"He was indeed," Nicholas said.

Outside, Banks and Gristhorpe watched Sam and Stephen help Neil Fellowes over the bridge. The old men stood by and stared in silence.

Gristhorpe looked up at the fell-side. "We've got a problem," he said.

"Yes?"

"It's a long climb up there. How the bloody hell are we going to get Glendenning and the scene-of-crime team up if we need them? Come to that, how am *I* going to get up? I'm not as young as I used to be. And you smoke like a bloody chimney. You'll never get ten yards."

Banks followed Gristhorpe's gaze and scratched his head. "Well," he said, "I suppose we could give it a try."

Gristhorpe pulled a face. "Aye," he said. "I was afraid you'd say that."

2

I

"Problem, gentlemen?" Nicholas Collier asked when he walked out of the White Rose and saw Banks and Gristhorpe staring up dejectedly at Swainshead Fell.

"Not at all," Gristhorpe replied. "Simply admiring the view."

"Might I suggest a way you can save yourselves some shoe-leather?"

"Certainly."

"Do you see that narrow line that crosses the fell diagonally?" Nicholas pointed towards the slope and traced the direction of the line with a long finger.

"Yes," said Gristhorpe. "It looks like an old track of some kind."

"That's exactly what it is. There used to be a farmhouse way up on the fell-side there. It belonged to Father, but he used to let it to Archie Allen. The place has fallen to ruin now, but the road that leads up is still there. It's not in good repair, of course, and you might find it a bit overgrown, but you should be able to get a car well above half-way up, if that's any help."

"Thank you very much, Mr Collier," Gristhorpe said. "For a man of my shape any effort saved is a blessing."

"You'll have to drive two miles up the road here to the next bridge to get on the track, but you'll see your way easily enough," said Nicholas, and with a smile he set off for home.

"Odd-looking sort of fellow, isn't he?" Banks remarked. "Not a bit like his brother."

Whereas Stephen had the elegant, world-weary look of a *fin-de-siècle* decadent, Nicholas's sallow complexion, long nose and prominent front teeth made him appear a bit horsy. The only resemblance was in their unusually bright blue eyes.

"Takes after his father, does Nicholas," Gristhorpe said. "And Stephen takes after his mother—as handsome a woman as I've seen around these parts. There's many a man drowned his sorrows in drink when Ella Dinsdale married Walter Collier. Didn't last long, though, poor lass."

"What happened?"

"Polio. Before inoculations came in. Come on, let's go and have a look at this body before it gets up and walks away."

Banks found the bridge and track easily enough, and though the the old road was bumpy, they managed to get as far as the ruined farmhouse without any serious damage to the car.

A little to the left, they saw the footpath Neil Fellowes had taken and began to follow it up the fell-side. Even though they had been able to drive most of the way, the path was steep and Banks soon found himself gasping for air and wishing he didn't smoke. Gristhorpe, for all his weight, seemed to stride up much more easily, though his face turned scarlet with the effort. Banks guessed he was more used to the landscape. After all, his own cottage was half-way up a daleside, too.

Finally, they stood at the top, where Fellowes had surveyed the scene a few hours earlier. Both were puffing and sweating by then, and after they'd got their breath back Gristhorpe pointed out the autumnal valley below.

"It looks enchanted, doesn't it," he said as they walked down the slope towards the woods. "Look, there's the rucksack."

They crossed the beck as directed and headed for the lady's slipper orchis by the fallen branches. When they smelled the corpse, they exchanged glances. Both had known that stench before; it was unmistakable.

"No wonder Fellowes was in such a state," Banks said. He took out a handkerchief and held it to his nose. Cautiously, Gristhorpe pulled more branches aside.

"By Christ, Glendenning's going to love this one," he said, then stood back. "By the look of that mess below the ribs there, we've got a murder case on our hands. Probably a knife wound. Male, I'd say."

Banks agreed. Though small animals had been at parts of the body, and maggots had made it their breeding ground, the dark stain just below the left rib-cage stood out clearly enough against the white shirt the man was wearing. Fellowes had been right about the movement. The way the maggots were wriggling under his clothes made it look as if the body were rippling like water in the breeze.

"'Motion in corruption,'" Gristhorpe muttered under his breath. "I wonder where the rest of his gear is. By the look of those boots he was a walker sure enough."

Banks peered as closely as he could at the cleated rubber Vibram treads. "They look new as well," he said. "Hardly worn at all."

"He must have had more stuff," Gristhorpe said, rubbing his whiskery chin. "Most walkers carry at least a rucksack with a few dried dates, compass, maps, torch, changes of clothing and what-have-you. Somebody must have taken it."

"Or buried it."

"Aye."

"He's not wearing waterproofs, either," Banks observed.

"That could mean he knew what he was doing. Only amateurs wear waterproofs all the time. Experienced walkers put their clothes on and off in layers according to the weather. If this is all he was wearing when he was killed, we might be able to get some idea of the date of death by checking weather records."

"It's been fairly constant these past few weeks," Banks pointed out. "We had a late spring, but now it looks like an early summer."

"True enough. Still, forensic might be able to come up with something. Better get the team up, Alan."

"The way we came? It's not going to be easy."

Gristhorpe thought for a moment. "There might be a better way," he said at last. "If my geography's correct."

"Yes?"

"Well, if I'm right, this'll be the beck that ends in Rawley Force on the Helmthorpe road about a mile east of Swainshead village. It's a hanging valley."

"Come again?"

"A hanging valley," Gristhorpe repeated. "It's a tributary valley running into Swainsdale at a right angle. The glacier here was too small to deepen it as much as the larger one that carved out the dale itself, so it's left hanging above the main valley floor like a cross-section. The water usually reaches the main river over a waterfall, like Rawley Force. I thought you'd been reading up on local geology, Alan."

"Haven't got that far yet," Banks mumbled. In fact, he'd put aside the geology book, after reading only two chapters, in favour of a new history of Yorkshire that his daughter, Tracy, had recommended. The trouble was that he wanted to know so much but had so little time for learning that he tended to skitter from one subject to another without fully absorbing anything.

"Anyway," Gristhorpe went on, "Rawley Force is only about ninety feet high. If we can get in touch with the Mountain Rescue Post at Helmthorpe and they're willing to rig up a winch, we'll be able to get the team up and down without much trouble. I can hardly see Glendenning, for one, walking the way we did. There'll be a lot of coming and going. And we'll have to get the body down somehow, too. A winch just might be the answer. It should be easy enough. The Craven and Bradford pot-hole clubs put one up at Gaping Gill for a few days each year to give the tourists a look—and that's a hell of a lot deeper."

"It sounds good," Banks said dubiously. He remembered swinging the three hundred feet down Gaping Gill, which opened into a cavern as huge as the inside of York Minster. It was an experience he had no wish to repeat. "We'd better get cracking, though, or it'll be dark before they all get here. Should we get Sergeant Hatchley in on this, too?"

Gristhorpe nodded.

"DC Richmond?"

"Not just yet. Let's see exactly what we've got on our hands before we bring in all our manpower. Richmond can hold the fort back at the station. I'll stay here while you go back to the car and radio in. You'd better let the doc know what state the body's in. He might need some special equipment."

Banks glanced towards the corpse, then back at Gristhorpe.

"Are you sure you want to stay here?"

"It's not a matter of wanting," Gristhorpe said. "Somebody should stay."

"It's been here alone long enough. I doubt that another half-hour will make any difference."

"Somebody should stay," Gristhorpe repeated.

Banks knew when to give up. Leaving the superintendent sitting like Buddha under an ash tree by the beck, he set off back through the woods to the car.

II

"What's wrong?" Katie Greenock asked as Sam and Stephen staggered in with Fellowes between them.

"He's had a bit too much to drink, that's all," Sam said. "Out of the way, woman. Is number five still vacant?"

"Yes, but—"

"Don't worry, he's not going to puke on your precious sheets. He just needs sleep."

"All right," Katie said, biting her lip. "Better take him up."

Stephen smiled apologetically at her as they passed by and struggled up the stairs. Finally, they dumped their burden on the bedspread and left Katie in the room with him. At first she didn't move. She just stood by the window looking at Fellowes in horror. Surely Sam knew how much she hated and feared drunks, how much they disgusted her. And Mr Fellowes had seemed such a nice, sober man.

She couldn't really picture her father clearly, for he had died along with her mother in a fire when Katie was only four, but he had certainly been a drunk, and she was sure that he was at the root of her feelings. The only vague image she retained was of a big, vulgar man who frightened her with his loud voice, his whiskers and his roughness.

Once, when they hadn't known she was watching, she saw him hurting her mother in the bedroom, making her groan and squirm in a way that sent shivers up Katie's spine. Of course, when she got older, she realized what they must have been doing, but the early memory was as firmly established and as deeply rooted as cancer. She also remembered once when her father fell down and she was afraid that he'd hurt himself. When she went to help him, though, he knocked her over and cursed her. She was terrified that he would do the same thing to her as he had done to her mother, but she couldn't remember any more about the incident, no matter how hard she tried.

The fire was a memory she had blocked out, too, though strange tongue-like flames sometimes roared and crackled in her nightmares. According to her grandmother, Katie had been in the house at the time, but the firemen had arrived before the blaze reached her room. Katie had been saved by the grace of God, so her granny said, whereas her parents, the sinners, had been consumed by the flames of hell.

The fire had been caused by smoking in bed, and her grandmother had seemed especially satisfied by that, as if the irony somehow marked it as God's special work, an answer to her prayers. It had all been God's will, His justice, and Katie was obliged to spend her life in gratitude and devoted service.

Katie took a deep breath, rolled Fellowes over carefully, and pulled back the sheets—they could be washed easily, but not the quilted spread. Then she unlaced his walking-boots and put them on some newspaper by the bed. They weren't muddy, but fragments of earth had lodged in the ribbed treads.

"Cleanliness is next to Godliness," her grandmother had drilled into her. And a lot easier to achieve, Katie might have added if she had dared. Apart from an unusually long list of its attributes—mostly "thou shalt nots," which seemed to include everything most normal people enjoyed—Godliness was an elusive quality as far as Katie was concerned. Lately, she had found herself thinking about it a lot, recalling her grandmother's harsh words and "necessary" punishments: her mouth washed out with soap for lying; a spell in the coal-hole for "swaying wantonly" to a fragment of music that had drifted in from next door's radio. These had all been preceded by the words, "This is going to hurt me more than it will hurt you."

Fellowes stirred and snapped Katie out of her reverie. For a second, his grey eyes opened wide and he grasped her hand. She could feel the fear and confusion flow from his bony fingers through her wrist.

"Moving," he mumbled, falling back into a drunken sleep again. "Moving . . ."

Spittle gathered at the edges of his lips and dribbled down his chin. Katie shuddered. Leaving him, she hurried back downstairs. There was still the evening meal to prepare, and the garden needed weeding.

III

Banks leaned over the edge of Rawley Force and watched Glendenning coming up in the winch. It was an amusing sight. The tall, white-haired doctor sat erect trying to retain as much dignity as he could. A cigarette dangled from the left corner of his mouth, as usual, and he clutched his brown bag tightly against his stomach.

Luckily, there had been hardly any rain over the past two weeks, so the waterfall to the doctor's right was reduced to a trickle. The staff at the Mountain Rescue Post had been only too willing to help and had come out and set up the winch in no time. Now, the police team were ready to come up slowly, one at a time, and Glendenning, as befit his status, was first in line.

Puffing as he struggled out of the harness, the doctor nodded curtly at Banks and straightened the crease in his suit trousers. Banks led him half a mile along the wooded valley to the scene, where Gristhorpe still sat alone.

"Thanks for coming so quickly," the superintendent said to Glendenning, getting up and dusting off his seat. Everyone in Eastvale Regional CID Headquarters had found it paid to be polite, even deferential, to the doctor. Although he was a crusty old bugger, he was one of the best pathologists in the country, and they were lucky he had chosen Eastvale as his home.

Glendenning lit another cigarette from the stub of his old one and asked, "Where is it, then?"

Gristhorpe pointed towards the pile of branches. The doctor cursed under his breath as he tackled the stepping-stones, and Gristhorpe turned to Banks and winked. "Everyone here, Alan?"

"Looks like it."

Next the young photographer, Peter Darby, came hurrying towards them, trying to head off Glendenning before the doctor could get to work. To Banks he always looked far too fresh-faced and innocent for his line of work, but he had never been known to bat an eyelid, no matter what they asked him to photograph.

After him came Sergeant Hatchley, red-faced after his short walk from Rawley Force along the hanging valley. The fair-haired sergeant was a big man, like Gristhorpe, and although he was twenty years younger, his muscle was turning quickly to fat. He resembled a rugby prop-forward, a position he had indeed played on the local team until cigarettes and beer took their toll on his stamina.

Banks filled him in on the details while Gristhorpe busied himself with the scene-of-crime team.

Glendenning, kneeling by the corpse, kept shooing the others away like flies. At last, he packed his bag and struggled back over the beck, stretching out his arms for balance like a tightrope-walker. With one hand he clung onto his brown bag, and in the other he held a test-tube.

"Bloody awkward place to go finding a corpse," he grumbled, as if the superintendent were personally responsible.

"Aye, well," Gristhorpe replied, "we don't get to pick and choose in our business. I don't suppose you can tell us much till after the post-mortem?"

Glendenning screwed up his face against the smoke that rose from his cigarette. "Not much," he said. "Looks like a stab wound to me. Probably pierced the heart from under the rib-cage."

"Then someone got very close to him indeed," Gristhorpe said. "It must have been someone he knew and trusted."

Glendenning sniffed. "I'll leave that kind of speculation to you boys, if you don't mind. There are lacerations and blows to the face, too. Can't say what did it at the moment, or when it was done. Been dead about ten days. Not more than twelve."

"How can you be certain?" Banks asked, startled by the information.

"I can't be certain, laddie," Glendenning said, "that's the problem. Between ten and twelve days doesn't count as accurate with me. I might be able to be more precise after the PM, but no promises. Those chappies over there have got a bag to put him in. He'll need to soak in a Lysol bath for a day or two." Glendenning smiled and held up his test-tube. "Maggots," he said. "*Calliphora erythrocephalus*, if I'm not mistaken."

The three detectives looked at the white, slow-moving blobs and exchanged puzzled glances.

Glendenning sighed and spoke as he would to a group of backward children. "Simple really. Bluebottle larvae. The bluebottle lays its eggs in daylight, usually when the sun's shining. If the weather's warm, as it has been lately, they hatch on the first day. Then you get what's called the 'first instar' maggot. That wee beauty sheds its skin like a snake after eight to fourteen hours, and then the second instar takes over and sheds after two to three days. The third instar, the one you use for fishing"—and here he glanced at Gristhorpe, a keen angler—"that one eats like a pig for five or six days before going into its pupa case. Look at these, gentlemen." He held up the test-tube again. "These, as you can see, are fat maggots. Lazy. Mature. And they're not in their pupa cases yet. Therefore, they must have been laid nine or ten days ago. Add on a day or so for the bluebottles to find the body and lay, and you've got twelve days at the outside."

It was the most eloquent and lengthy speech Banks had ever heard Glendenning deliver. There was obviously a potential teacher in the brusque chain-smoking Scot with the trail of ash like the milky way down his waistcoat.

The doctor smiled at his audience. "Simpson," he said.

"Pardon?" Banks asked.

"Simpson. Keith Simpson. I studied under him. Our equivalent of Sherlock Holmes, only Simpson's real."

"I see," said Banks, who had learned to tease after so long in Yorkshire. "A kind of real-life Quincy, you mean?" He felt Gristhorpe nudge him in the ribs.

Glendenning scowled and a half-inch of ash fell off the end of his cigarette. "Quite," he said, and put the test-tube in his bag. "I hope that glorified truss over there can get me back down safely."

"Don't worry," Gristhorpe assured him. "It will. And thank you very much."

"Aye. Now I have first-hand knowledge what it feels like to have my arse in a sling," Glendenning said as he walked away.

Banks laughed and turned back to watch the experts at work. The photographs had been taken, and the team were busy searching the ground around the body.

"We'll need a more thorough search of the area," Gristhorpe said to Hatchley. "Can you get that organized, Sergeant?"

"Yes, sir." Hatchley took out his notebook and pen. "I'll get some men in from Helmthorpe and Eastvale."

"Tell them to look particularly for evidence of anything recently buried or burned. He must have been carrying a rucksack. We're also looking for the weapon, a knife of some kind. And I think, Sergeant," Gristhorpe went on, "we'd better bring DC Richmond in on this after all. Get him to check on missing persons with the Police National Computer."

Vic Manson, the fingerprint expert, approached them, shaking his head. "It'll not be easy," he complained. "There might be prints left on three or four fingers, but I can't promise anything. I'll try wax injections to unwrinkle the skin, and if they don't work, it'll have to be formaldehyde and alum."

"It'll be a devil of a job finding out who he was," Banks said. "Even if we can get prints, there's no guaranteeing they'll be on record. And someone's gone to great lengths to make sure we can't recognize him by his face."

"There's always the clothes," Gristhorpe said. "Or teeth. Though I can't say I've ever had much luck with them myself."

"Me neither," Banks agreed. He always thought it amusing when he watched television detectives identify bodies from dental charts. If they really knew how long it would take every dentist in the country to search through every chart in his files. . . . Only if the police already had some idea who the body was could dental charts confirm or deny the identity.

"He might even be German," Hatchley added. "Or an American. You get a lot of foreigners walking the fells these days."

Across the beck, two men wearing face-masks slid the body into the large zip-up bag they had brought. Banks grimaced as he watched them brush off the maggots, shed in all directions, before they were finally able to secure the zip. They then started to carry their burden along the valley towards the winch.

"Let's go," Gristhorpe said. "It's getting late. There's nothing more to be done here till we can start a search. We'd better post a couple of men here for the night, though. If the killer knows we've discovered the body and if he's buried important evidence nearby, he might come back after dark."

Hatchley nodded.

"We'll arrange to send someone up," Gristhorpe went on. "You'd better stick around till they get here, Sergeant. See if you can persuade the rescue people to wait for them with the winch. If not, they'll just have to come the long way, like we did."

Banks saw Hatchley glance towards where the corpse had lain and shiver. He didn't envy anyone stuck with the job of staying in this enchanted valley after dark.

IV

Sam took Katie as roughly as usual in bed that night. And as usual she lay there and gave the illusion of enjoying herself. At least it didn't hurt any more like it had at first. There were some things you had to do, some sins you had to commit because men were just made that way and you needed a man to take care of you in the world. The important thing, Katie had learned from her grandmother, was that you must not enjoy it. Grit your teeth and give them what they want, yes, even cheat a little and make them think you like it—especially if they treat you badly when you don't seem enthusiastic—but under no circumstances should you find pleasure in it.

It never lasted long. That was one consolation. Soon Sam started breathing quickly, and she clung to him tighter and mouthed the sounds he liked to hear, told him the things he liked to know. At last he grunted and made her all wet. Then he rolled over on his side and quickly began snoring.

But sleep didn't come so easily for Katie that night. She thought about the body on the fell and pulled the sheets up tighter around her chin. Last time, it had been awful: all those questions, all the trouble there'd been—especially when the police tried to connect the dead man with the missing girl, Anne Ralston. They'd acted as if Stephen or one of his friends might have killed both of them. And what had they found out? Nothing. Raymond Addison seemed to have come from nowhere.

Katie had hardly known Anne, for she and Sam hadn't been in Swainshead long when all the trouble started five years ago. The only reason they had met her at all was because Sam wanted to seek out the "best people" in the village. He latched onto the Colliers, and Anne Ralston had been going out with Stephen at the time.

She hadn't been Katie's type, though, and they'd never have become good friends. Anne, she remembered, had seemed far too footloose and fancy-free for her taste. She had probably just run off with another man; it would have been typical of her to take off without a word and leave everyone to worry about her.

Katie turned on her side to reach for some Kleenex from the bedside table, dragging the sheets with her. Sam stirred and yanked back his half. Gently, she wiped herself. She hated that warm wetness between her legs. More and more every time she hated it, just as she had come to loathe her life with Sam in Swainshead.

And things had been getting worse lately. She had been under a black depression for a month or more. She knew it was a woman's place to obey her husband, to stay with him for better, for worse, to submit to his demands in bed and slave for him all day in the house. But surely, she thought, life shouldn't be so bleak. If there was any chance of escape from the drudgery that her life had become and from the beatings, would it really be such a sin to take it?

Things hadn't always been so bad. When they had met, Katie had been working as a chambermaid at the Queen's Hotel in Leeds, and Sam, an apprentice electrician, had turned up one day to check the wiring. It had hardly been love at first sight; for Katie, love was what happened in the romantic paperbacks she read, the ones that made her blush and look over her shoulder in case her granny could see her reading them. But Sam had been presentable enough—a cocky young bantam with curly chestnut hair and a warm, boyish smile. A real charmer.

He had asked her out for a drink three times, and three times she had said no. She had never set foot in a pub. Her granny had taught her that they were all dens of iniquity, and Katie herself held alcohol responsible for her father's wickedness and for the misery of her mother's life. Katie didn't realize at the time that her refusal of a drink was taken as a rejection of Sam himself. If only he would ask her to go for a walk, she had thought, or perhaps to the Kardomah for a coffee and a bite to eat after work.

Finally, in exasperation, he had suggested a Saturday afternoon trip to Otley. Even though Katie was over eighteen, she still had a difficult time persuading her grandmother to let her go, especially as she was to ride pillion on Sam's motorbike. But in the end the old woman had given in, muttering warnings about the Serpent in Eden and wolves in sheep's clothing.

In Otley they had, inevitably, gone for a drink. Sam had practically dragged her into the Red Lion, where she had finally broken down and blurted out why she had refused to go for a drink before. He laughed and touched her shoulder gently. She drank bitter lemon and nothing terrible happened to either of them. After that, she went to pubs with him more often, though she always refused alcohol and never felt entirely comfortable.

But now, she thought, turning over again, life had become unbearable. The early days, just after their marriage, had been full of hope after Katie had learned how to tolerate Sam's sexual demands. They had lived with his parents in a little back-to-back in Armley and saved every penny they earned. Sam had a dream, a guest house in the Dales, and together they had brought it about. Those had been happy times, despite the hours of overtime, the cramped living-quarters and the lack of privacy, for they had had something to aim towards. Now it was theirs, Katie hated it. Sam had changed; he had become snobbish, callous and cruel.

Like every other night for the past few months, she cried quietly to herself as she tried to shut out Sam's snoring and listen to the breeze hiss through the willows by the nameless stream out back. She would wait and keep silent. If nothing happened, if nothing came of her only hope of escape, then one night she would sneak out of the house as quiet as a thief and never come back.

V

In room five, Neil Fellowes knelt by the side of the bed and said his prayers.

He had woken from his drunken stupor in time to be sick in the wash-basin, and after that he had felt much better. So much so, in fact, that he had gone down and eaten the lamb chops with mint sauce that Mrs Greenock had cooked so well. Then he spent the rest of the evening in his room reading.

And now, as he tried to match the words to his thoughts and feelings, as he always did in prayer, he found he couldn't. The picture of the body kept coming back, tearing aside the image of God that he had retained from childhood: an old man with a long white beard sitting on a cloud with a ledger book on his lap. Suddenly, the smell was in his nostrils again; it was like trying to breathe at the bottom of a warm sewer. And he saw again the bloody, maggot-infested pulp that had once been a face, the white shirt rippling with corruption, the whole thing rising and falling in an obscene parody of breathing.

He tried to force his mind back to the prayer but couldn't. Hoping the Lord would understand and give him the comfort he needed, he gave up, put his glasses on the table, and got into bed.

On the edge of sleep, he was able to reconstruct the sequence of events in his mind. At the time, he had been too distraught, too confused to notice anything. And very soon his head had been spinning with the drink. But he remembered bursting into the pub and asking for help. He remembered how Sam Greenock and the others at the table had calmed him down and suggested what he should do. But there was something else, something wrong. It was just a vague feeling. He couldn't quite bring it to consciousness before sleep took him.

3

I

"What is it?" Banks asked, examining the faded slip of paper that Sergeant Hatchley had dropped on the desk in front of him.

"Forensic said it's some kind of receipt from a till," Hatchley explained. "You know, one of those bits of paper they give you when you buy something. People usually just drop them on the floor or shove them in their pockets and forget about them. They found it in his right trouser pocket. It'd been there long enough to go through the washer once or twice, but you know what bloody wizards they are in the lab."

Banks knew. He had little faith in forensic work as a means of catching criminals, but the boffins knew their stuff when it came to identification and gathering evidence. Their lab was just outside Wetherby, and Gristhorpe must have put a "rush" on this job to get the results back to Eastvale so quickly. The body had been discovered only the previous afternoon, and it was still soaking in a Lysol bath.

Banks looked closely again at the slip, then turned to its accompanying transcription. The original had been too faint to read, but forensic had treated it with chemicals and copied out the message exactly:

CHOOSE FRESH
CHOOSE WENDY'S
****************Store 006308****************
SNGL / CHZ
WITH . .
TOMATO
BACON   2.69
FRIES   .89
SMAL COKE   .85
Tax   .35
              Inside   4.78
              05.26PM 04/25

"Wendy's," Banks said. "That's a burger chain. There's a few branches in London. Look at those prices, though."

Hatchley shrugged. "If it was in London . . ."

"Come on! Even in London you don't pay two pounds sixty-nine pee just for a bloody hamburger. At least not at Wendy's you don't. You don't pay eighty-five pee for a Coke, either. What does that tax work out at?"

Hatchley took out his pocket calculator and struggled with the figures. "Eight percent," he announced finally.

"Hmm. That's an odd amount. You don't pay eight percent tax on food in England."

"I suppose it's an American company," Hatchley suggested, "if they sell hamburgers?"

"You mean our man's an American?"

"Or he could have just come back from a trip there."

"He could have. But that'd make it a bit soon for another holiday, wouldn't it? Unless he was a businessman. What about the labels on his clothes?"

"Torn off," Hatchley said. "Trousers and underpants seem to be ordinary Marks and Sparks cotton-polyester. Same with the shirt. The boots were Army and Navy Surplus. They could have been bought at any of their branches."

Banks tapped his ball-pen on the edge of the desk. "Why is it that somebody doesn't want us to know who he is or where he's from?"

"Maybe because if we knew that we'd have a good idea who the killer was."

"So the quicker we identify the body, the better our chances. Whoever did it was obviously counting on no-one finding it for months, then being unable to identify it." Banks sipped some lukewarm coffee and pulled a face. "But we've got a lead." He tapped the receipt. "I want to know where this Wendy's is located. It shouldn't take you long. There's a store code to go on."

"Where do I go for that kind of information?" Hatchley asked.

"Bloody hell!" Banks said. "You're a detective. At least I hope you are. Start detecting. First, I'd suggest you call Wendy's UK office. It's going to be a couple of days before we get anything from Glendenning and Vic Manson, so let's use every break we get. Did Richmond come up with anything from missing persons?"

"No, sir."

"I suppose our corpse is still supposed to be on holiday then, if no-one's reported him missing. And if he's not English it could be ages before he gets into the files. Check the hotels and guest houses in the area and see if any Americans have registered there lately. If they have, try and track them down."

Dismissed, Hatchley went to find Richmond, to whom, Banks knew, he would pass on as much of the load as possible. Still, he reasoned, the sergeant's work was solid enough once he built up a bit of momentum, and the pressure would serve as a test of Richmond's mettle.

Since passing his computer course with flying colours, the young detective constable looked all set for promotion. That would cause problems with Hatchley, though. There was no way, Banks reflected, that the sergeant could be expected to work with Richmond at equal rank. Things had been bad enough when Banks came from the Metropolitan force to fill the position Hatchley had set his own sights on. And Hatchley was destined to stay a sergeant; he didn't have the extra edge needed to make inspector, as Richmond did.

Grateful that promotion was not his decision, Banks glanced at his watch and headed for the car. Neil Fellowes was waiting in Swainshead, and the poor sod had already had to arrange for one extra day off work.

II

As he drove along the dale, Banks marvelled at how familiar some of its landmarks had become: the small drumlin with its four sick elms all leaning to the right like an image in one of those Chinese water-colours that Sandra, his wife, liked so much; the quiet village of Fortford with the foundations of a Roman fort laid bare on a hillock by the green; the busy main street of Helmthorpe, Swainsdale's largest village; and above Helmthorpe, the long limestone edge of Crow Scar gleaming in the sun.

The Kinks sang "Lola," and Banks tapped his fingers on the steering-wheel in time with the music as he drove. Though he swore to Sandra that he still loved opera, much to her delight he hadn't played any lately. She had approved of his recent flirtation with the blues, and now he seemed to be going through a nostalgic phase for the music he had listened to during his last days at school and first year at London Polytechnic: that idyllic, halcyon period when he hadn't known what to do with his life, and hadn't much cared.

It was also the year he had met Sandra, and the music brought it all back: winter evenings drinking cheap wine and making love in his draughty Notting Hill bed-sit listening to John Martyn or Nick Drake; summer boat-trips for picnics in Greenwich Park, lying in the sun below Wren's Observatory looking down on the gleaming palace, the Thames and London spread out to the west, the Beatles, Donovan, Bob Dylan and the Rolling Stones on the transistor radio. . . . All gone now, or almost all. He had lost interest in pop music shortly after the Beatles split up and the glitter boys took over the scene in the early seventies, but the old songs still worked their magic on him.

He lit a cigarette and rolled down the window. It felt good to be on his own in his own car again. Much as he loved the superintendent, Banks was glad that Gristhorpe had reverted to his usual role of planner and co-ordinator. Now he could smoke and listen to music as he drove.

More important still, he liked working alone, without the feeling that someone was always looking over his shoulder. It was easy enough to deal with Hatchley and Richmond, but with a superior heading the field investigation, it was difficult to avoid the sensation of being under constant scrutiny. That had been another reason for leaving London—too many chiefs—and for pinning his hopes on the Eastvale job after a preliminary chat with Superintendent Gristhorpe about the way he liked to run things.

Banks turned right at the Swainshead junction and parked his car in one of the spaces outside the White Rose. As he crossed the bridge, the old men stopped talking and he felt their eyes boring holes into his back as he walked down to the Greenock Guest House.

Though the door was open, he rang the bell. A young woman came rushing to answer it. She had a slender, dancer's body, but Banks also noticed an endearing awkwardness, a lack of self-consciousness about her movements that made her seem even more attractive. She stood before him drying her hands on her pinafore and blushed.

"Sorry," she said in a soft voice, "I was just doing some hand-washing. Please come in."

Though her accent was clearly Yorkshire, it didn't sound like the Swainsdale variety. Banks couldn't immediately place it.

Her eyes were brown—the kind of brown one sees in sunlight filtered through a pint of bitter, thought Banks, amused at just how much of a Yorkshireman he must have become to yoke beer and beauty so audaciously. But her hair was blonde. She wore it tied up at the back of her neck, and it fell in stray wisps around her pale throat and ears. She wore no make-up, and her light complexion was completely smooth, her lips full and strawberry red without any lipstick.

Between her lower lip and the curve of her chin was a deep indentation, giving her mouth a look somewhere between a pout and an incipient smile. She reminded him of someone, but he couldn't think whom.

Katie, as she introduced herself, led him into a hallway that smelled of lemon air-freshener and furniture polish, as clean and fresh as a good guest house should be. Neil Fellowes was waiting for him in room five, she said, and disappeared, head bowed, into the back of the house, where Banks guessed the Greenocks made their own living-quarters.

He walked up the thick-pile burgundy carpet, found the room and knocked.

Fellowes answered immediately, as if he had been holding the doorknob on the other side. He looked in much better shape than the previous day. His few remaining strands of colourless hair were combed sideways across his bald head, and thick-lensed wire-rimmed glasses perched on the bump near the bridge of his nose.

"Come in, please er . . ."

Banks introduced himself.

"Yes, come in, Chief Inspector."

Fellowes was obviously a man who respected rank and title. Most people automatically called Banks "Inspector," some preferred plain "Mister," and others called him a lot worse.

Banks glanced out of the window at the wide strips of grass on both sides of the Swain. Beyond the cottages and pub rose the overbearing bulk of a fell. It looked like a sleeping elephant, he thought, remembering a passage from Wainwright, the fell-walking expert. Or was it whale? "Nice view," he said, sitting down in the wicker chair by the window.

"Yes," Fellowes agreed. "It doesn't really matter which side of the house you stay in. Out back you can see Swainshead Fell, and over there it's Adam's Fell, of course."

"Adam's Fell?"

Fellowes adjusted his glasses and cleared his throat. "Yes.

After Adam and Eve. The locals do have a sense of humour
—of a sort."

"Do you visit the area often, Mr Fellowes?"

"No, not at all. I just like to research the terrain, so to
speak, before I embark. By the way, Chief Inspector, I do
apologize sincerely about yesterday. Finding that ... that
corpse was a great shock, and I never take liquor as a rule—
or tobacco, I might add. The brandy just seemed, well,
appropriate at the time. I wouldn't have thought of it myself,
but Mr Greenock was kind enough ..." He slowed and
stopped like an old gramophone winding down.

Banks, who had taken note of Fellowes's declaration of
abstemiousness and let go of the cigarette package he'd been
toying with in his pocket, smiled and offered a cliché of
consolation. Inwardly, he sighed. The world was becoming
too full of non-smokers for his comfort, and he hadn't yet
succeeded in swelling their ranks. Perhaps it was time to
switch brands again. He was getting tired of Silk Cut,
anyway. He took out his notebook and went on.

"What made you visit that spot in the first place?" he
asked.

"It just looked so inviting," Fellowes answered. "So
different."

"Had you ever been there before?"

"No."

"Did you know of its existence?"

"No. It's certainly not mentioned in my guide book."

Fellowes shrugged. "Locals would, I suppose. I really can't
say. Anyone could wander into it. It's on the maps, of course,
but it doesn't show up as anything special."

"But you do have to make quite a diversion from the
footpath to get there."

"Well, yes. Though I'd hardly say it's that much of a haul."

"Depends on what shape you're in," Banks said, smiling.
"But you reckoned it would be worthwhile?"

"I'm interested in wild flowers, Chief Inspector. I thought I
might discover something interesting."

"When did you arrive in Swainshead?"

"Three days ago. It was only a short break. I'm saving most of my holidays for a bicycle tour of Provence in autumn."

"I hope you have a less grim time of it there," Banks said. "Is there anything else you can remember about the scene, about what happened?"

"It was all such a blur. First there was the orchis, then that awful smell, and . . . No. I turned away and headed back as soon as I'd . . . as soon as I refreshed myself in the beck."

"There was nobody else in the valley?"

"Not that I was aware of."

"You didn't get a feeling of being followed, observed?"

"No."

"And you didn't find anything close to the body? Something you might have thought insignificant, picked up and forgotten about?"

"Nothing, Chief Inspector. Believe me, the feeling of revulsion was sudden and quite overwhelming."

"Of course. Had you noticed anything else before you found the body?"

"What do you mean?"

"The victim's rucksack was missing. We think he must have been carrying his belongings with him but we can't find them. Did you notice any signs of something being buried, burned, destroyed?"

"I'm sorry, Chief Inspector, but no, I didn't."

"Any idea who the victim was?"

Fellowes opened his eyes wide. "How could I have? You must have seen for yourself how . . . how . . ."

"I know what state he was in. I was simply wondering if you'd heard anything about someone missing in the area."

Fellowes shook his head.

Banks closed his notebook and put it back in the inside pocket of his pale blue sports jacket.

"There is one thing," Fellowes said hesitantly.

"Yes?"

"I don't like to cast aspersions. It's only a very vague impression."

"Go on."

"And I wasn't in full control of my faculties. It was just a feeling."

"Policemen have feelings like that, too, Mr Fellowes. We call them hunches and they're often very valuable. What was this feeling you had?"

Fellowes leaned forward from the edge of the bed and lowered his voice. "Well, Chief Inspector, I only really thought about it in bed last night, and it was just a kind of niggling sensation, an itch. It was in the pub, just after I arrived and, you know, told them what I'd seen. I sat at the table, quite out of breath and emotionally distraught. . . ."

"And what happened?"

"Nothing happened. It was just a feeling, as I said. I wasn't even looking, but I got the impression that someone there wasn't really surprised."

"That you'd found a body?"

"Yes."

"Was that all?"

Fellowes took off his glasses and rubbed the bridge of his nose. Banks noticed how small his eyes looked without the magnifying lenses. "More than that," Fellowes went on. "I was looking away at the time, but I felt an odd sort of silence, the kind of silence in which glances are exchanged. It was very uncomfortable for a moment, though I was too preoccupied to really notice it at the time. I've thought about it a lot since last night, and that's the only way I can put it, as if a kind of understanding look passed between some of the people at the table."

"Who was there?"

"The same people as when you arrived. There was the landlord, over at the bar, then Sam Greenock, Stephen and Nicholas Collier and John Fletcher. I'd met them the previous day when I was enquiring about the best places to search for wild flowers."

"Did it seem to you as if they were all in on some kind of conspiracy?"

"I'm not a paranoid, if that's what you're getting at, Chief Inspector."

"But you were upset. Sometimes our senses can over-react."

"Believe what you wish. I simply thought you ought to know. And in answer to your question, no, I didn't sense any gigantic conspiracy, just that someone at the table knew something."

"But you said you thought a glance was exchanged."

"That's what it felt like."

"So more than one person knew?"

"I suppose so. I can't say how many or how I received the impression. It just happened."

Banks took his notebook out again and wrote down the names.

"I don't want to get anybody into trouble," Fellowes said. "I could be wrong. It could have happened just as you said, an over-reaction."

"Let *us* worry about that, Mr Fellowes. We don't usually ask people to stand up in a court of law and swear to their feelings. Is that all you can tell me?"

"Yes. Will I be able to go home now? There'll be trouble at work if I'm not back tomorrow."

"Better give me your address and phone number in case we need to talk to you again," Banks said.

Banks made a note of Fellowes's address and left, thinking what a celebrity the man would be at work for a while. He went out of the open door without seeing Katie Greenock and breathed in the fresh air by the beck. A young man dangled his legs over the bank, eating a sandwich from grease-proof paper and reading a thick paperback; the old men still huddled around the eastern end of the stone bridge; and there were three cars parked outside the White Rose. Banks looked at his watch: twenty past one. With a bit of luck the same crowd as yesterday would be there. He read over the names Fellowes had given him again and decided to make a start.

III

First things first, Banks thought, and headed for the bar. He ordered Cumberland sausage, beans and chips, then paid, took his numbered receipt, and waited while Freddie Metcalfe poured him a pint of Pedigree.

"Is tha getting anywhere?" Metcalfe asked, his biceps bulging as he pulled down on the pump.

"Early days yet," Banks answered.

"Aye, an' it got to late days an' all last time, and still tha didn't find owt."

"That's how it goes sometimes. I wasn't here then."

"Thinks tha's better than old Gristhorpe, does tha, eh?"

"That's not what I meant."

"From down sahth, aren't tha?"

"Yes. London."

"London." Metcalfe placed the foaming brew on the cloth in front of Banks and scratched his hairy ear. "Bin there once. Full o' foreigners, London. All them A-rabs."

"It's a busy place," Banks said, picking up his beer.

"Don't get many o' them arahnd 'ere. Foreigners, that is. That why tha came up 'ere, to get shut on t'A-rabs, eh? Tha'll find plenty o' Pakis in Bradford, like, but I don't reckon as I've ever seed a darkie in Swainshead. Saw one in Eastvale, once."

Banks, growing quickly tired of Metcalfe's racist inanities, made to turn away, but the landlord grabbed his elbow.

"Don't tha want to ask me any questions then, lad?" he said, his eyes glittering.

Holding back his temper, Banks lit a cigarette and propped himself up against the bar. He had noticed that the three men he recognized from the previous day were only into the upper thirds of their pints, so he had enough time to banter with Metcalfe. He might just pick up some interesting titbit.

"What do you want me to ask you?" he opened.

"Nay, tha's t'bobby. Tha should know."

"Do you get many walkers in here?"

"Aye. We don't fuss 'em abaht rucksacks and boo-its and what-not like that stuck-up pillock on t'main road."

"But I understand this is the 'select' part of town?"

"Aye." Metcalfe laughed. "Tha could say that. It's t'oldest, anyroads. And t'Colliers drink 'ere, as did their father before them. Select, if tha likes, but dahn to earth, not stuck up." He shook his head slowly. "A right lad, were Walter Collier." Then he leaned forward and whispered, "Not like 'is sons, if tha knows what I mean. Wouldn't know a cratch from a gripe, neither on 'em. And they was brought up by a farmer, too."

Banks, who didn't know a cratch from a gripe either, asked why.

"Eddication," Metcalfe said, intoning the word as if it were responsible for most of the world's ills. "Fancy bloody Oxford eddication. Wanted 'em to 'ave a better chance than 'ee'd 'ad, did old Walter. Farming don't pay much, tha knows, an' Walter were sharp enough to get out 'imself." Metcalfe turned up his nose. "Well, tha can see what eddication does."

"What are they like, Stephen and Nicholas?" Banks asked.

Metcalfe sniffed and lowered his voice. He was clearly enjoying his role as dispenser of local opinion. "Right bloody useless pair, if y'ask me. At least yon Nicholas is. Mr Stephen's not so bad. Teks after old Walter, 'ee does. Bit of a ladies' man. Not that t'other's queer, or owt." Metcalfe laughed. "There were a bit o' trouble wi' a servant lass a few years back, when 'ee were still a young lad, living at 'ome, like. Got 'er up t'spout, Master Nicholas did. Old Walter 'ad to see 'er right, o' course, and I've no doubt 'ee gave t'lad a right good thrashing. But it's Mr Stephen that's t'ladies' man. One after t'other."

"What's the difference in their ages?"

"Nobbut a couple o' years. Stephen's t'eldest."

"What happened to the farm land?"

"Old Walter sold some on it," Metcalfe said, "and leased t'rest. T'Colliers are still t'biggest landowners in t'dale, mind thee. John Fletcher over there bought a goodly chunk on it."

He wagged his chin in the direction of the table. The drinkers were now into the last thirds of their drinks, and Banks decided it would be a good time to approach them.

"Tha still an't asked me no real questions," Metcalfe protested.

"Later," Banks said, turning. "I'd like to talk to these gentlemen here before they leave." Of the gentlemen in question, he recognized Nicholas Collier and Sam Greenock from the previous day; therefore, the third had to be John Fletcher.

"Wait on a minute," Metcalfe said. "Dun't tha want tha sausage and chips?"

And as if on cue, a freckled little girl in a red dress, her hair in pigtails, appeared from the kitchens and called out, "Number seventy-five! Sausage, beans and chips."

Banks gave her his receipt and took the plate, then he helped himself to condiments from the bar.

When he walked over to the table, the three men shifted around, scraping their chair-legs on the flagged floor, and made room for him.

"Do you mind if I eat at your table?" he asked.

"Not at all. Freddie been giving you a rough time, Inspector?" Nicholas Collier asked. His smile showed his prominent teeth to great disadvantage; they were discoloured with nicotine and crooked as a badly built dry-stone wall. His speech, Banks noticed, bore traces of the local accent under its assumed veneer of public-school English.

"No," he said, returning the smile. "Just entertaining me. Quite a fellow."

"You can say that again. He's been behind that bar as long as I can remember." Nicholas leaned forward and lowered his voice, "Between you and me, I don't think he quite approves of Stephen and myself. Anyway, have you met John, here?"

The squat man with the five-o'clock shadow was indeed John Fletcher, gentleman farmer. Stephen Collier, his brother said, was away dealing with some factory business.

"Is this just a social visit or do you have some questions for us?" Sam asked.

"Just one, really," Banks said, spearing a mouthful of sausage. "Have you any idea who it was we found up there?"

After a short silence, Nicholas said, "We get quite a lot of visitors in the area, Inspector. Especially when we're blessed with such a fine start to the year. There's nobody local missing, as far as I know, so it must be a stranger. Can't you check?"

"Yes," Banks said. "Of course we can. We can go through every name in every hotel and guest-house registration book and make sure everyone's accounted for. But, like you, I'm sure, we're all for anything that saves extra effort."

Collier laughed. "Naturally. But no, I can't think of anyone it might be."

"Your victim hadn't necessarily come through Swainshead, you know," Sam pointed out. "He could have been heading south from Swaledale or beyond. Even from the Lake District. He could have set off from Helmthorpe, too, or any number of other villages in the dale. Most of them have at least one or two bed-and-breakfast places these days."

"I know," Banks said. "Believe me, we're checking." He turned to Fletcher. "I hear that you own quite a bit of land?"

"Yes," Fletcher said, his dark eyes narrowing suspiciously. "Walter sold it me when he gave up farming and went into the food business." He glanced at Nicholas, who nodded. "Neither Nick here, nor his brother Stephen wanted to take over—in fact Walter hadn't wanted them to, he'd been preparing to sell for quite a while—so I thought I'd give it a go."

"How is it working out?"

"Well enough. I don't know if you understand much about Dales farming, Mr Banks, but it's a hard life. Old Walter himself had had enough, and he was one of those men—rare around these parts—with enough vision to get out and put what he'd got to better use. I'd never blame a farmer for wanting a different life for his sons. I've got no family myself," he said, and a hard look came into his eyes. "I'm not complaining, though. I make a living—the EEC and the National Parks Commission notwithstanding."

Banks turned to Nicholas. "What do you do?"

"I teach English at Braughtmore, just up the road here. It's only a small public school, of course, but it's a start."

"But you don't actually live there?"

"No. Hardly necessary, really. The house is so close. The pupils live in. They have to do; it's so damn far from civilization. And we have housemasters. Some of the teachers live in the grounds, but a couple of others have chosen to settle here in the village. The school's only five miles north, quite isolated. It's a good school, though I say so myself. Do you have any children, Inspector?"

"Yes. A boy and a girl."

"What school do they attend?"

"Eastvale Comprehensive."

"Hmm." The corner of Collier's lip twitched, giving just a fleeting hint of a sneer.

Banks shifted uneasily in his chair. "Your brother runs the family business, I gather."

"Yes. Managing Director of Collier Food Enterprises. It's over the Lancashire border, about ten miles west, just off the main road. The arrangement suits us both perfectly. Stephen never had a great deal of academic ambition, despite the excellent education he received, but he's bright and he's put his mind to good enough use—making money. It was one of father's wisest moves, buying up that old mill and setting up the food-processing operation. And as for me, I'm happy with my books and a few pliant young minds to work on." Again he bared his teeth in a smile.

They had all finished their drinks and Banks was wondering how to edge them gently towards the murder again, when Fletcher stood up and excused himself. Immediately, the others looked at their watches and decided they ought to leave and take care of various tasks.

"There's nothing else, is there, Inspector?" Nicholas asked.

"No," Banks said. "Not yet."

Freddie Metcalfe ambled over to the table to pick up the plate and the empty glasses as Banks was stubbing out his cigarette.

"Find owt aht yet?" he asked.

"No," Banks said, standing up. "Nothing."

"Early days, eh?"

And the deep, chortling laughter followed Banks out into the street.

IV

Back at Eastvale station things were quiet. Grabbing a cup of coffee from the filter-machine on the way, Banks walked upstairs to his office, a plain room furnished with nothing but filing cabinets, metal desk and a calendar of local scenes. The illustration for May showed the River Wharfe as it flowed among the limestone boulders of Langstrothdale. More recently, Banks had added, next to it, one more decoration: a broken pipe, which he had just rediscovered at the back of his drawer. It represented a vain attempt to project a rural image and wean himself from cigarettes at the same time, but he had cursed it constantly and finally thrown it at that very same wall in frustration over the Steadman case almost a year ago. It hung there like a piece of conceptual art to remind him of the folly of trying to be what one is not.

There were quite a few cars parked in the cobbled market square outside, and visitors walked in and out of the small Norman church and the shops that seemed to be built into its frontage. The gold hands of the clock stood at three-thirty against its blue face. Banks looked down on the scene, as he often did, smoking a cigarette and sipping his coffee. The police station itself was a Tudor-fronted building on narrow Market Street across from the Queen's Arms, which curved around the corner so that one of its entrances stood on the side of the square opposite the church. Looking to his right, Banks could see along the street, with its coffee-houses, boutiques and specialty shops, and out front was the busy square itself, with the NatWest bank, the El Toro coffee-bar and Joplin's newsagent's at the opposite side.

A knock at the door interrupted him. Sergeant Hatchley came in looking very pleased with himself. When he was excited about something he moved much faster than usual and seemed unable to stand still. Banks had come to recognize the signs.

"I've tracked it down, sir," Hatchley said. "That bit of paper he had in his pocket."

The two of them sat down and Banks told the sergeant to carry on.

"Like you said, I tried the London office. They said they'd check and get back to me. Anyway, they found out that that particular branch is in Canada."

"So our man's a Canadian?"

"Looks that way, sir. Unless, like I said before, he'd just been on holiday there. Anyway, at least we know there's a close connection."

"Anything else?"

"Yes. Once he'd discovered the outlet was in Canada, the bloke from Wendy's became very helpful."

Such helpfulness was a common enough occurrence, Banks knew from experience. He'd even invented a term for it: the Amateur Sleuth Syndrome.

"That particular branch is in Toronto, on Yonge Street, near Dundas Street, if that means anything."

Banks shook his head. "Never been over the Atlantic. You?"

Hatchley grunted. "Me? I've never been further west than Blackpool. Anyway, that narrows things down quite a bit, I'd say."

"It does," Banks agreed. "But it still doesn't tell us who he was."

"I got onto the Canadian High Commission and asked a bloke there to check if anyone from Toronto had been reported missing over here lately, but nobody has."

"Too early yet, I suppose. If he *is* from Toronto, obviously everyone back there still thinks he's on holiday."

"Aye, but that won't last forever."

"We haven't got forever. Who knows, he might have been a student and come over for the whole bloody summer. How's Richmond doing?"

"He's covered quite a few places already—Lyndgarth, Relton, Helmthorpe, Gratly."

"Well, his task ought to be a bit easier now we know it's a Canadian we're after."

"There's been quite a few Canadians staying locally," Hatchley said. "It's easy enough to call the B and Bs and make a list from their records, but it's damned hard to trace people's movements after they've left. They don't usually leave forwarding addresses, and it's only once in a while a landlady has been able to tell us where they said they were going next."

"There can't be that many men from Toronto travelling alone," Banks said. "I'm sure if he was a member of a group or a family somebody would have reported him missing by now. Better stick at it. At least you've narrowed the field considerably. Heard anything from Dr Glendenning?"

"The super called him a while ago. Still killing off those bloody maggots in disinfectant. Says he won't be able to make a start till tomorrow morning at the earliest."

Banks sighed. "All right. You'd better go help Richmond now. And thanks, Sergeant, you did a good job."

Hatchley nodded and left the office. They'd been working together for almost two years now, Banks realized, and he still couldn't bring himself to call the sergeant Jim. Maybe one day he would, when it came naturally to his lips. He lit another cigarette and went back to the window, where he watched the people wander about in the square, and drummed a tattoo on the sill.

V

"Sam's not in," Katie said that evening when she opened the back door to find Stephen Collier standing there. "He's having a night out with his old mates in Leeds."

"Can't I come in, anyway?" Stephen asked. "Just for a cup of tea?"

"All right," Katie said, and led him through to the spotless kitchen. "Just five minutes, mind you. I've work to be doing." She turned away from him and busied herself with the kettle and teapot. She felt her face burning. It wasn't right being alone in the house with a man other than her husband, even if it was someone as pleasant as Stephen. He had a reputation as a womanizer. Everybody knew that. Someone might even have seen him coming in.

"Nick tells me the police were around today," Stephen said.

Katie glanced at him over her shoulder. "It's to be expected, isn't it? One of our guests did find a dead body."

"He still here?"

"No. He left this afternoon."

"Well," Stephen said, "I just thought I'd drop by to see if you were all right. I mean, it can be a bit of a shock to the system, something like that happening right on your door-step, so to speak. Did the police ask a lot of questions?"

"Not to me, no. Why should they?"

"Just wondering," Stephen said. "How are things, anyway?"

"All right, I suppose," Katie answered. Though she had known him for over five years, and she certainly preferred him to his brother, Katie hadn't really spent much time alone with Stephen Collier before. Mostly, they had met socially at summer garden parties the Colliers liked to throw, in the pub and at occasional dinners. She liked Stephen. He seemed kind and thoughtful. Often at social functions she had caught him looking at her in an odd way. Not *that* way, not like Nicholas. It was a look she didn't quite understand, and she had never been able to return his gaze for long without lowering her eyes. Now she was alone with him she felt shy and awkward; she didn't really know how to behave. She brought the tea to the table and opened a box of Fox's Custard Creams.

"Come on, Katie," Stephen said. "You're not very convincing. You don't sound all right to me."

"I don't know what you mean."

"Yes, you do. I can tell. I've felt some sort of bond with you right from the start. I've been worried about you these past few months."

"Worried? Why?"

"Because you're not happy."

"Of course I'm happy. That's silly."

Stephen sighed. "I can't make you open up, can I? But you *can* talk to me if you want, if you need to. Everybody needs somebody to talk to now and then."

Katie bit her lower lip and said nothing. She couldn't talk to him. She couldn't tell anyone the things that went on in her mind, the sins she dreamed of, the desperation she felt. She couldn't tell him about her one chance of escaping from her miserable life, and what it had already cost her.

"Anyway," Stephen went on, taking a biscuit, "I might not be around here for much longer."

"What do you mean?"

"I've had enough of it, Katie. The plant, the house, the village. Lord, I'm nearly thirty. It's about time I got out and about, saw a bit of the world before I get too old."

"B-but you can't," Katie said, shocked. "Surely you can't just up and go like that? What about—"

Stephen slapped the table. "Oh, responsibilities be hanged," he said. "There's plenty of others willing and able to run Collier Foods. I'll take a long holiday then maybe try something else."

"Why are you telling me all this?" Katie asked.

Stephen looked at her, and she noticed that he suddenly looked old, much older than his twenty-eight years.

He ran his hand through his short brown hair. "I don't know," he said. "I told you, we're kindred spirits. You're the only person I've told. There's nobody else, really."

"But your brother . . ."

"Nicky? He wouldn't understand. He's too wrapped up in his own world. And don't think I haven't noticed the way he looks at you, Katie, even if Sam hasn't. I'd stay away from him if I were you."

"Of course I will," Katie said, blushing. "Why shouldn't I?"

"Oh, he can be very persuasive, Nicky can."

"What about John?" Katie asked. "Or Sam? Can't you talk to them?"

Stephen laughed. "Look, Katie," he said. "Nicky, Sam and the rest, they're all good drinking friends, but there are things I can't talk to them about."

"But why me?"

"Because I think it's the same for you. I think you're unhappy with your life and you've nobody to talk to about it. Why are you so afraid of talking to me? You've got all your problems bottled up inside you. Don't you like me?"

Katie traced rings on the table with her forefinger. "It's not that," she said. "I'm fine, really I am."

Stephen leaned forward. "Why don't you open up, show some feeling?" he urged her.

"I do."

"Not for me."

"It's not right."

"Oh, Katie, you're such a moralist." Stephen stood up to leave. "Would that I had your moral fibre. No, it's all right, there's no need to show me out."

Katie wanted to call after him, but she couldn't. Deep inside, she felt a thick darkness swirling and building in power, trying to force its way out. But it was evil and she had to keep it locked in. She had to accept her lot, her place in life. She was Sam's wife. That was her duty. There was no point talking about problems. What could she say to Stephen Collier? Or he to her? Why had he come? What did he want from her? "The thing that all men want," said a strong, harsh voice inside her. "The same thing his brother wants. Don't be fooled by talk of companionship. Satan has a sweet tongue."

"But he was reaching out to you," another, quieter voice said, "reaching out in friendship, and you turned him away."

Katie's chest tightened and her hands shook as she tried to bring the teacup to her mouth. "I'm lost," she thought. "I don't know what to do. I don't know what's right any more. Help me, someone, please help me!" And the cup rolled to the floor and smashed as Katie lay her head on the table and wept.

4

I

Two days later, on May 31, forensic information started
trickling in. During that time, Richmond and Hatchley had
tracked down all but two wandering Canadians who had left
local hotels or guest houses between ten and thirteen days
ago.

Events were moving too slowly for Banks. Most leads
appear during the first twenty-four hours after a murder has
taken place, but this body was about two hundred and forty
hours old by the time it was found. Still they had very little to
go on.

Therefore, when the first report from the forensic lab
landed on his desk at ten-thirty that morning, Banks drank
in the information like a man stranded in a desert without
water for three days.

Dr Glendenning had established that death was due to a
stab wound from a single-edged blade, probably a sheath-
knife about six inches long. One upward thrust had
penetrated the heart from beneath the ribs. After that, the
face had been slashed and then beaten with a rock until it
was unrecognizable. The victim was white, in his early
thirties, five feet eleven inches tall, ten and a half stone in
weight, and in good physical condition. That last part always
irritated Banks: how could a corpse ever be in good physical
condition? This one, certainly, had been about as far from it
as one could get.

Vic Manson had finally managed, through peeling the skin off and treating it with glycerine, to get three clear prints. He had already checked these against the Police National Computer and discovered that they weren't on record. So far no good, Banks thought. The forensic odontologist, a note said, was still working on his reconstruction of the dental chart.

Calling for Sergeant Hatchley on his way out, Banks decided it was time for a discussion over elevenses in the Golden Grill. The two men weaved their way through the local shoppers and parties of tourists that straggled along both pavement and the narrow street, and found a table near the window. Banks gave the order for coffee and toasted teacakes to Peggy, a plump girl with a bright smile, and looked across at the whitewashed front of the police station with its black timber beams. Black and white, he thought. If only life was as simple as that.

As they drank their coffee, Banks and Hatchley tried to add up what they had got so far. It wasn't much: a ten-day-old corpse of a white male, probably Canadian, found stabbed in an isolated hanging valley. At least cause of death had been established, and the coroner's inquest would order a thorough investigation.

"Perhaps he wasn't travelling alone," Banks said. "Maybe he was with someone who killed him. That would explain the need to disfigure him—to give the killer plenty of time to get back home."

"If that's the case," Hatchley said, "it'll be for the Canadian police to handle, won't it?"

"The murder happened on our turf. It's still our problem till the man at the top says different."

"Maybe he stumbled into a coven of witches," Hatchley suggested.

Banks laughed. "They're mostly bored accountants and housewives in it for the orgies. I doubt they'd go as far as to kill someone who walked in on them. And Glendenning didn't mention anything about ritual slaughter. How's the search for the elusive Canadians going?"

Hatchley reached slyly for another cigarette to prolong the

break. "I'm beginning to feel like that bloke who had to roll a rock up a hill over and over again."

"Sisyphus? Sometimes I feel more like the poor sod who had his liver pecked out day after day."

Hatchley lit his cigarette.

"Come on, then," Banks said, standing up to leave. "Better get back."

Hatchley cursed under his breath and followed Banks across the street.

"Chief Inspector Banks!" Sergeant Rowe called out as they passed the front desk. "Telephone message. You're to call a Dr Passmore at the lab. He's the odonto ... the odotol ... Oh, the bloody tooth fairy, or whatever they call themselves."

Banks smiled and thanked him. Back in his office, he picked up the phone and dialled.

"Ah, Chief Inspector Banks," said Passmore. "We've never met, but Dr Glendenning brought me in on this one. Interesting."

"You've got something for us?" Banks asked eagerly.

"It's a bit complicated. Would it be a great inconvenience for you to drop by the lab?"

"No, not at all." Banks looked at his watch. "If I leave now I can be there in about an hour. Can you give me some idea over the phone?"

"I think we'll be able to trace the identity of your corpse before too long, if I'm not mistaken. I don't think his dentist is too far away."

"With all due respect, I don't see how that can be, doctor. We're pretty sure he was a Canadian."

"That's as may be," Passmore replied. "But his dental work's as English as yours or mine."

"I'm on my way."

Still puzzled, Banks slipped a cassette into the deck and eased the Cortina out of the lot at the back of the station. At least something was happening. He drove slowly, dodging the tourists and shoppers who seemed to think Market Street was for pedestrians only. The breathy opening of Donovan's "Hurdy Gurdy Man" started on the tape.

He passed the new estate under construction on the town's southern edge, then he put his foot down once he got out of the built-up area. Leaving the Dales for the plain, he drove through a patchwork landscape of green pasture and fields of bright yellow rape, divided by hawthorn hedgerows. Bluebells and buttercups, about the only wild flowers Banks could put a name to, were in bloom among the long grass by the roadside. A frightened white-throat darted out in front of the car and almost ended up, like so many unfortunate rabbits and hedgehogs, splattered all over the tarmac.

The forensic lab was a square three-storey red-brick building just north of Wetherby. Banks identified himself at reception and climbed up to Passmore's second-floor office.

Dr Passmore gave new meaning to the term "egghead." The Lilliputians and the Blefuscudians could have had a fine war indeed over which end to open his egg-shaped skull. His bare, shiny dome, combined with circumflex eyebrows, a putty nose, and a tiny rosebud of a mouth, made him look more like an android than a human being. His mouth was so small that Banks wondered how there could be room for teeth in it. Perhaps he had chosen his profession out of tooth-envy.

Banks sat down as directed. The office was cluttered with professional journals and its one glassed-in bookcase was full to overflowing. The filing cabinets, also, bulged too much to close properly. On Passmore's desk, among the papers and pencil stubs, stood a toothless skull and several sets of dentures.

"Glad you could make it, Chief Inspector," Passmore said, his voice surprisingly rich and deep coming from such a tiny mouth. "I'm sorry to drag you all the way down here, but it might save time in the long run, and I think you'll find it worth the journey."

Banks nodded and crossed his legs. He looked around for an ashtray, but couldn't see one; nor could he smell any traces of smoke when he surreptitiously sniffed the air. Bloody hell, another non-smoker, he cursed to himself.

"The victim's teeth were very badly damaged," Passmore went on. "Dr Glendenning said that he was hit about the face with a rock of some kind, and I concur."

"He was found close to a stream," Banks said. "There were plenty of rocks in the area."

"Hmm." Passmore nodded sagely and made a steeple of his fingers on the desk. "Anyway, I've managed to make a rudimentary reconstruction for you." He pushed a brown envelope towards Banks. "Not that it'll do you much good. You can hardly have every dentist in the country check this against every chart he or she has, can you?"

Banks was beginning to wonder why he'd come when Passmore stood up with surprising energy and walked over to a cabinet by the door. "But," he said, pausing dramatically to remove something and bring it back to the table, "I think I might be able to help you with that." And he dropped what looked like a fragment of tooth and pink plastic on the desk in front of Banks. "A denture," he announced. "Upper right bicuspid, to be exact."

Banks stared at the object. "You got this from the body?"

Passmore nodded. "It was badly shattered, of course, but I've managed to reassemble most of it. Rather like putting together a broken teacup, really."

"How does this help us?"

"Well, in the first place," Passmore said, "it tells us that the deceased was more likely to be British than Canadian."

"How?"

Passmore frowned, as if Banks was being purposely obtuse. "Contrary to what some people believe," he began, "British dentists aren't very far behind their North American cousins. Oh, they might instigate new procedures over there before we do, but that's mostly because they have more money. Dentistry's private over there, you know, and it can be very expensive for the patient. But there are differences. Now, if your victim had come from Russia, for example, I could have told you immediately. They use stainless steel for fillings there. But in this case, it's merely an educated guess, or would be if it weren't for something else, which I'll get to in a moment."

Come on, Banks thought, fidgeting with the cigarette pack in his jacket pocket, get to the bloody point. Putting up with rambling explanations—full of pauses for dramatic effect—seemed to be the price he so often had to pay for information from specialists like Passmore.

"The mere fact that your corpse has denture work leads me to conclude that he's European rather than North American," the doctor continued. "The Americans go in for saving teeth rather than replacing them. In fact, they hardly do denture work at all."

"Very impressive," Banks said. "You mentioned something else—something important."

Passmore nodded. "This," he went on, holding up the false tooth, "is no ordinary denture. Well, it is, but there's one big difference. This is a coded denture."

"What do you mean?"

"A number of dentists and technicians have taken to signing their work, so to speak, like painters and sculptors. Look here."

Passmore prodded the denture with a pointed dental instrument, the one that always gave Banks the willies when he was in the chair. He looked closely at the pink plastic and saw a number of dark letters, which he couldn't quite make out.

"The code," Passmore said. "It's formed by typing the letters in a small print face on a piece of nylon, which you put between the mould and the plastic. During the manufacturing process, the nylon becomes incorporated into the denture and the numbers are clearly visible, as you can see."

"Why do they go to such trouble?" Banks asked.

Passmore shrugged. "For identification purposes in case of loss, or fire."

"And what does the code tell us?"

Passmore puckered his mouth into a self-satisfied smile. "Everything we need to know, Chief Inspector. Everything we need to know. Have a closer look."

Banks used a pair of tweezers to pick up the denture and looked at the code: 5493BKJLS.

"The last two letters give us the city code, the ones before that are the dentist's initials, and the rest is for identification of the owner."

"Amazing." Banks put the false tooth down. "So this will lead us to the identity of the victim?"

"Eventually. First, it'll lead us to his dentist."

"How can I find out?"

"You'd consult the directory in the library. But, luckily, I have a copy here and I've done it for you."

"And?"

Passmore smiled smugly again and held up a school-teacherly finger. "Patience, Chief Inspector Banks, patience. First, the city. Do you recognize that post-code?"

"Yes. LS is Leeds."

"Right. So the first thing we discover is that our man's dentist practises in Leeds. Next we look up the initials: BKJ. I found two possibilities there: Brian K. Jarrett and B.K. James."

"We'll have to check them both," Banks said. "Can I use your phone?"

Passmore rubbed his upper lip. "I, er, I already took the liberty. B.K. James doesn't do denture codes, according to his assistant, so I called Brian K. Jarrett."

"And?"

Passmore grinned. "The patient's name is Bernard Allen."

"Certain?"

"He's the one who was fitted with the denture. It was about four years ago. I'll be sending down the charts for official confirmation, of course, but from what we were able to compare over the phone, I'd say you can be certain, yes."

"Did you get an address?"

Passmore shook his head. "Apparently Allen didn't live in Leeds. Dr Jarrett did give me the sister's address, though. Her name's Esther Haines. Is that of any use?"

"It certainly is." Banks made a note of the first real lead so far. "You've done a great job, Dr Passmore." He stood up and shook hands.

Passmore inclined his head modestly. "If ever you need my help again . . ."

II

Katie walked down to the shops in Lower Head later than usual that day. There was no road on her side of the beck, just a narrow pathway between the houses and the grassy bank. At the junction with the main Helmthorpe road, where the River Swain veered left into the dale proper, a small wooden bridge, painted white, led over to the village green with its trees and benches, and the path continued to the row of shops around the corner from the church.

As she neared the road, a grey Jaguar passed by with Stephen Collier behind the wheel. He slowed down at the intersection, and Katie became flustered. She half raised her hand to wave, but dropped it quickly. Stephen didn't acknowledge her presence at all; he seemed to be looking right through her. At first she told herself he hadn't seen her, but she knew he had. Perhaps he was thinking of something else and hadn't noticed his surroundings. She often walked around in a daze like that herself. The blood ran to her face as she crossed the road and hurried on to the shops.

"Afternoon, Katie love," Mrs Thetford greeted her. "A bit late today, aren't you? Still, I've saved you some nice Brussels sprouts."

Katie thanked her and paid, her mind still on Stephen Collier. Why had he called last night when he knew Sam was out? Katie couldn't understand his desire to talk to her about his problems, or his apparent concern for her.

"Your change, dearie!" Mrs Thetford called after her.

Katie walked back to the counter and held out her hand, smiling. "I'd forget my head if it was loose."

She called at the butcher's and bought some pork loin chops, the best he had left, then turned back towards home. Stephen really had sounded as if he needed a friend. He had been tired, burdened. Katie regretted letting him down, but what else could she have done? She couldn't be his friend; she didn't know how. Besides, it wasn't right.

She noticed the speeding Mini just in time to dodge it and crossed the green again. A few people, mostly old women, sat on the benches nattering, and a light breeze rustled the new, pale green leaves on the trees. What Stephen had said about her being unhappy was true. Was it so obvious to everyone, or did he really sense a bond between them? Surely with all his money and success he couldn't be unhappy too.

Katie tried to remember when she had last been happy, and thought of the first weeks in Swainshead. It had been hard work, fixing up the house, but they had done it. And what's more, they had done it together. After that, though, when everything was ready, Sam left the running of it all to her. It was as if he'd finished his life's work and settled into early retirement.

"Ideas above his station," her granny had always said of Sam. And sure enough, no sooner were they in residence than he was off to the White Rose ingratiating himself with the locals. As soon as he found out that the Colliers, who owned the big house over the road, were the dale's wealthiest and most powerful family, there was no stopping him. But give him his due, Katie thought, he never fawned or lowered himself; he just seemed to act as if he'd found his natural place in the order at last. Why they accepted him, if indeed they did, she had no idea.

When she wasn't busy running the guest house, Katie became an adornment, something for Sam to hang on his arm at the summer garden parties. She was a kind of Cinderella for whom the ball was always ending. But unlike the fairy-tale character, Katie hated both her roles. She had no love for gowns and glass slippers. Finery, however stylish and expensive, made her feel cheap and sinful. Once, a workmate fortunate enough to go on holiday to Paris had brought her back a pretty green silk scarf. Her granny had snipped it into pieces and scattered them like spring leaves into the fire.

Perhaps, though Katie hated to admit it, she had last been truly happy when her grandmother died. She and Sam hadn't seen much of the old woman after they went to live with his parents in Armley. They visited her in hospital, though, where she lay dying of cancer of the colon, bearing all the pain and humiliation with the same hard courage as she had suffered life. She lay there, silver head against the white pillow, and would accept no comfort for what "God's Will" was gracing her with. It was almost, Katie thought, as if she had found true joy in the final mutiny of the flesh, of its very cells, as if dying was proof to her that life on earth really was nothing but a Vale of Tears. But that couldn't be true, Katie realized, for her granny had never taken pleasure in anything in her life.

Katie fainted at her funeral and then gagged on the brandy the minister gave her to bring her round. Now all she had left of granny was the heavy wooden cross on the living-room mantelpiece. A bare, dark cross, with no representation of the crucified Christ (for such things smelled too much of popish idolatry for granny), it symbolized perfectly the harsh, arid life the old woman had chosen for herself and her granddaughter. Katie hated the thing, but she hadn't been able to pluck up the courage to throw it out. Outbreaks of boils and plagues of locusts would surely follow such a blasphemous act.

So Stephen Collier was right—she was unhappy. There was nothing anyone could do about it, though, except perhaps . . . But no. She had a terrible feeling of apprehension about the future, certain that her only possible escape route was cut off now. Why she should feel that way she didn't know, but everyone was behaving oddly again— Stephen, Sam, John Fletcher. Could it really be a coincidence that Anne Ralston's name had been mentioned to her again so recently? And that so soon after it had come up, there had been another murder in the village?

Shuddering as if someone had just stepped over her grave, Katie walked back up the path and into the house to get on with cleaning the rooms.

III

After leaving the lab, Banks first drove into Wetherby and bought an *A to Z* street atlas of Leeds. He knew the city reasonably well, but had never been to Armley, where Allen's sister lived. He studied the area and planned a route over lunch in a small pub off the main street, where he ate a rather soupy lasagne, and drank an excellent pint of Samuel Smith's Old Brewery Bitter.

He listened to the Donovan tape as he drove. Those old songs certainly brought back memories. Why did the past always seem so much brighter than the present? Because he had been more innocent then? Surely every childhood summer couldn't have been as sunny as he recalled. There must have been long periods of rain, just as there always seemed to be these days. What the hell, he thought, humming along with "Teen Angel" as he drove—today's beautiful, enjoy the sun while it's here. Most of all, he wanted to put out of his mind for as long as possible what he would soon have to tell Bernard Allen's sister.

He lit a cigarette and turned onto the Leeds Inner Ring Road, which skirted the city centre by a system of yellow-lit tunnels affording occasional flashes into the open and glimpses of church spires, tower blocks and rows of dark terrace houses. It still felt warm, but the sun was now only a blurred pearl behind a thin grey gauze of cloud.

He came out onto Wellington Road, by the Yorkshire Post Building, then crossed the River Aire and, immediately afterwards, the Leeds and Liverpool Canal.

There had been a great deal of development in the area, and one or two very colourful red-and-gold barges stood moored by the waterside. But the river and canal banks were still very much of a wasteland: overgrown with weeds, littered with the tires and old prams people had dumped there.

Many of the huge Victorian warehouses still hung on, crumbling and broken-windowed, their red brick blackened by the industrial smoke of a hundred years or more. It was a little like Thameside, Banks thought, where old wharfs and warehouses, like the warrens where Fagin had run his band of child-thieves, were daily being converted into luxury apartment complexes, artists' studios and office space. Because Leeds was in the depressed and abandoned north, though, the process of regeneration would probably take quite a bit longer, if indeed it ever happened at all.

Skilfully manoeuvring the lanes of traffic and a huge roundabout, Banks managed to get on Armley Road. Soon he was at the bottom of Town Street, where the road swung right, past the park, to Bramley and Stanningley. He turned left up Crab Lane, a narrow, winding one-way street by a small housing estate built on a hill, and parked on the street near the library.

Banks soon found Esther Haines's house. It had a blue door, freshly painted by the look of it. In the garden was an overturned plastic tricycle, green with thick yellow wheels.

Banks pressed the bell and a thin-faced woman answered. She was perhaps in her late twenties, but she seemed haggard and tired. Judging from the noise inside the house, Banks guessed that the cares of motherhood had worn her down. She frowned at him and he showed her his identification card. Immediately, she turned pale and invited him in. For people on estates like this, Banks realized, a visit from the police always means bad news. He felt his stomach muscles tighten as he walked inside.

In the living-room, cluttered with children's toys, Mrs Haines had already sat down. Hands clasped in her lap, she perched at the edge of her seat on the sofa. A dark-haired man came through from the kitchen, and she introduced him as her husband, Les. He was wearing only vest and pants. His shoulders and chest were matted with thick black hair, and he had a tattoo of a butterfly on his right bicep.

"We were just having our tea," Esther Haines said. "Les is on the night shift at the yeast factory."

"Aye," her husband said, pulling up a chair and facing Banks aggressively. "What's all this about?"

A child with jam smeared all over his pale grinning face crawled through the open kitchen door and busied himself trying to tear apart a fluffy toy dog.

"I'm sorry," Banks said, "but I've got some bad news for you."

And the rest followed as it always did: disbelief, denial, shock, tears and, finally, a kind of numb acceptance. Banks was relieved to see that the first thing Mr Haines did was light a cigarette. He followed suit. Esther clutched a handkerchief to her nose. Her husband went to make tea and took the child with him.

After Mr Haines had brought in the teapot and cups, leaving the child to play in the kitchen, Banks leaned forward in his seat and said to Esther, "There are some questions I've got to ask."

She nodded. "Are you sure?" she said. "Are you sure it's our Bernie?"

"As sure as we can be at this point," Banks told her. He didn't want to have to tell her what state her brother's corpse had been in. "Your answers will help us a lot. When did you last see him?"

"It was a couple of weeks ago, now," she said. "He stayed with us a week."

"Can you find out the exact date he left here, Mrs Haines? It's important."

Her husband walked over to a calendar of Canadian scenes and ran a stubby finger along the squares. "It was the thirteenth," he said, then looked over at Esther: "Remember, love, that morning he went to the dentist's for that filling he needed?"

Mrs Haines nodded.

"Did he leave immediately after his visit to Dr Jarrett's?"

"Yes," said Les Haines. "He was heading for the Dales, so he had to be off about eleven. He was after taking one of them trains on the Settle–Carlisle route."

"And that was the last time either of you saw him, at eleven o'clock on May thirteenth?"

They both nodded.

"Do you know where he was headed?"

"Of course," Esther said. "He were off back to Swainshead."

"Going back? I don't understand. Is that where he was before he came to stay with you?"

"No, it's where he grew up, it's where we used to live."

Now Banks remembered where he'd heard the name before. Allen. Nicholas Collier had directed Gristhorpe and himself to the ruins of Archie Allen's old farmhouse high on the side of Swainshead Fell.

"Is your father Archie Allen?" he asked.

"Yes, that's right."

"And you lived on the fell-side, worked a farm?"

"Until it went belly-up," Mr Haines cut in.

"Did you live there too?" Banks asked him.

"Me? No. Leeds born and bred. But the missis grew up there."

"How long ago was this, Mrs Haines?" Banks asked Esther, who had started weeping quietly again.

"It's ten years since we moved, now."

"And you came straight here?"

"Not until Les and I got married. We lived in an old back-to-back off Tong Road. It's not far away. Dad got a job at Blakey's Castings. It were all he could get. Then they went to Melbourne—Australia, like—to go live with our Denny after they retired. Oh God, somebody'll have to tell Mum and Dad." She looked beseechingly at her husband, who patted her arm. "Don't worry about that, love," he said. "It'll keep a while."

"As far as I can gather," Banks said when Mrs Haines had regained her composure, "your brother had some connection with Toronto, in Canada. Is that right?"

She nodded. "He couldn't get a job over here. He was a bright lad, our Bernie. Got a degree. But there was no jobs. He emigrated eight years ago."

"What did he do in Toronto?"

"He's a teacher in a college. Teaching English. It's a good job. We was off out to see him next year."

Banks lit another cigarette as she wiped away the tears and blew her nose.

"Can you give me his address?"

She nodded and said, "Be a love, Les." Her husband went to the sideboard and brought out a tattered Woolworth's address book.

"How often did Bernard come home?" Banks asked, writing down the Toronto address.

"Well, he came as often as he could. This was his third trip, but he hadn't been for four years. Proper homesick he was."

"Why did he stay in Canada, then?"

She shrugged. "Money. No work for him here, is there? Not with Thatcher running the country."

"What did he talk about while he was with you?"

"Nothing really. Just family things."

"Did he say anything odd to you, Mr Haines? Anything that struck you as unusual?"

"No. We didn't talk a lot. We'd not much in common really. I'm not a great reader, never did well at school. And he liked his books, did Bernie. We talked about ale a bit. About what the boozers are like over there. He told me he'd found a nice pub in Toronto where he could get John Smith's and Tartan on draught."

"Is that all?"

Haines shrugged. "Like I said, we didn't have much in common."

Banks turned to Mrs Haines again. "What state of mind was he in? Was he upset about anything, depressed?"

"He'd just got divorced about a year ago," she said, "and he were a bit upset about that. I think that's what made him homesick. But I wouldn't say he were really depressed, no. He seemed to think he might be able to come back and live here again before too long."

"Did he say anything about a job?"

"No."

"How could he manage to move back here then?"

Esther Haines shook her head. "I don't know. He didn't say. He just hinted. Maybe it were wishful thinking, like, now he didn't have Barbara any more."

"That was his wife?"

"Yes."

"What happened between them?"

"She ran off wi' another man."

"Where had Bernie been before he visited you?"

Esther took a deep breath and dabbed at her red eyes. "He'd come to England for a month, all told," she said. "First off, he spent a week seeing friends in London and Bristol, then he came up here. He'd be due to go back about now, wouldn't he, Les?"

"Do you know how to get in touch with these friends?"
Banks asked.

She shook her head. "Sorry. They were friends of Bernie's
from university."

"Which university?"

"York."

"And you didn't know them?"

"No. They'd be in his notebook. He always carried a
notebook full of names and stuff."

"We didn't find it. Never mind, we'll find them somehow."
If necessary, Banks knew he could check with the university
authorities and track down Bernard Allen's contemporaries.
"Do you know where he was heading after Swainshead?"

"He were going to see another friend in Edinburgh, then
fly back from Prestwick. You can do that with Wardair, he
said, fly to London and go back from somewhere else." She
put her handkerchief to her nose again and sniffed.

"I don't suppose you have this person's address in
Edinburgh?"

She shook her head.

"So," Banks said, stubbing out his cigarette and reaching
for the tea, "he left here on May thirteenth to do some fell-
walking in the Dales, and then—"

Mrs Haines cut in. "No, that's not right. That's not the
reason he went."

"Why did he go, then? Sentimental reasons?"

"Partly, I suppose. But he went to stay with friends."

"What friends?"

"Sam and Katie. They run a guest house—Greenock's.
Bernie was going to stay with Sam and Katie."

Struggling to keep his excitement and surprise to himself,
Banks asked how Bernard had got to know Sam and Katie.
At first, Mrs Haines seemed unable to concentrate for
weeping, but Banks encouraged her gently, and soon she was
telling him the whole story, pulling at the handkerchief on
her lap as she spoke.

"They knew each other from Armley, from after we came
to Leeds. Sam lived there, too. We were neighbours. Bernie

was always going on about Swainshead and how wonderful it was, and I think it were him as put the idea into Sam's head. Anyways, Sam and Katie scrimped and saved and that's where they ended up."

"Did Bernie have any other close friends in Swainshead?"

"Not really," Esther said. "Most of his childhood mates had moved away. There weren't any jobs for them up there."

"How did he get on with the Colliers?"

"A bit above our station," Esther said. "Oh, they'd say hello, but they weren't friends of his, not as far as I know. You can't be, can you, not with the sons of the fellow what owns your land?"

"I suppose not," Banks said. "Was there any bitterness over losing the farm?"

"I wouldn't say that, no. Sadness, yes, but bitterness? No. It were us own fault. There wasn't much land fit for anything but sheep, and when the flock took sick . . ."

"What was Mr Collier's attitude?"

"Mr Walter?"

"Yes."

"He were right sorry for us. He helped out as much as he could, but it were no use. He were preparing to sell off to John Fletcher anyway. Getting out of farming, he were."

"How would that have affected you?"

"What do you mean?"

"The sale."

"Oh. Mr Walter said he'd write it into the terms that we could stay. John Fletcher didn't mind. He and Dad got on quite well."

"So there was no ill feeling between your family and John Fletcher or the Colliers?"

"No. Not to speak of. But I didn't think much of them."

"Oh?"

She pulled harder at the handkerchief on her lap, and it began to tear along one edge. "I always thought they were a pair of right toffee-nosed gits, but I never said nowt. Stephen thinks he's God's gift to women, and that Nicholas is a bit doolally, if you ask me."

"In what way?"

"Have you met him?"

"Yes."

"He's like a little kid, gets all over-excited. Especially when he's had a drink or two. Practically slavers all over a person, he does. Especially women. He even tried it on with me once, but I sent him away with his tail between his legs." She shuddered. "I don't know how they put up with him at that there school, unless they're all a bit that way."

"What about Stephen?"

Esther shrugged. "Seems a pleasant enough gent on the outside. Bit of a smoothie, really. Got a lot more class than his brother. Bit two-faced, though."

"In what way?"

"You know. All friendly one minute, then cuts you dead next time he sees you. But they can afford to do that, can't they?"

"Who can?"

"Rich folks. Don't have to live like ordinary people, like you and me, do they?"

"I don't imagine they have the same priorities, no," Banks said, unsure whether he approved of being called an ordinary person. "Did he try it on too?"

"Mr Stephen? No. Oh, he liked the girls, all right, but he was too much of a gentleman, for all his faults."

Mrs Haines seemed to have forgotten her grief for a few moments, so absorbed had she been in the past, but as soon as silence fell, her tears began to flow again and her husband put his arm around her. In the kitchen, something smashed, and the child ran wailing into the room and buried his jammy face in Esther Haines's lap.

Banks stood up. "You've been very helpful," he said. "I'm sorry to have been the bearer of such bad news."

Esther nodded, handkerchief pressed to her mouth, and Mr Haines showed him to the door. "What are we to do about . . . you know . . ."

"The remains?"

"Aye."

"We'll be in touch soon," Banks said. "Don't worry."

Upstairs, a baby started crying.

The first thing Banks did was look for a phonebox to call Sandra and tell her when he'd be back. That didn't prove as easy as it sounded. The first three he came across had been vandalized, and he had to drive almost two miles before he found one that worked.

It was a pleasant drive back to Eastvale through Harrogate and Ripon. In a quiet mood, he slipped in Delius's *North Country Sketches* instead of the sixties pop he'd been listening to. As he drove, he tried to piece together all the information he'd got that day. Whichever way he looked at it, the trail led back to Swainshead, the Greenocks, the Colliers and John Fletcher.

5

I

Only the cry of a distant curlew and the sound of water gurgling over rocks in the stream out back broke the silence.

Then Sam Greenock echoed the news: "Bernie? Dead? I can't believe it."

"Believe it," Banks said. It was the second time in two days that he had been the bearer of bad news, but this time it was easier. The investigation proper had begun, and he had more on his mind than Sam Greenock's disbelief, real or feigned.

They sat in the living-room at the back of the house: the Greenocks, Banks, and Sergeant Hatchley taking notes. Katie gazed out of the window, or sometimes she stared at the huge, ugly wooden cross on the mantelpiece. She had said nothing, given no reaction at all.

"It's true he was staying with you, then, is it?" Banks asked.

Sam nodded.

"Why didn't his name show up on the register? We went to a lot of trouble checking every place in Swainsdale."

"It's not my fault," Sam said. "He was staying with us as a friend. Besides, you know as well as I do that those guest books aren't legal requirements—they're only for people to write comments in if they want, show they've been here."

"When our man called and asked if you'd had any Canadians staying recently, why didn't you mention Bernard Allen?"

"He didn't ask me anything. He just looked at the register. Besides, I never thought of Bernie as a Canadian. Oh, I know he lived there, but that's not everything, is it? I've known people who lived in Saudi Arabia for a year working on the oil fields but I don't think of them as Saudis."

"Come off it, Sam. Bernard Allen had been in Canada for eight years, and you hadn't seen him for four. This was only his third trip back."

"Still . . ."

"Did you have any reason to lie about Bernie being here?"

"No. I told you—"

"Because if you did, we can charge you with concealment of information. That's serious, Sam. You could get two years."

Sam leaned forward. "Look, I never thought. That policeman who came, he didn't tell us what he was looking for."

"We can check, you know."

"Bloody check then. It's true."

Sam couldn't remember the officer's name, so Banks asked Hatchley to make a note of the time and date. It would be easy enough to find out who had made the visit and what approach he had taken. He still wasn't sure about Sam Greenock, though.

Banks sighed. "All right. We'll leave that for now. Which room did he stay in?"

Sam looked at Katie. She was staring out on the fell-side, so he had to nudge her and repeat the question.

"Five," she said, as if speaking from a great distance. "Room five."

"We'll need to have a look," Banks told her.

"It was two weeks ago," Sam said. "There's been other people in since then. That's where we took Fellowes after he'd found the body."

"We'll still need to look."

"Do you think he's hidden some secret message there, Inspector? Taped it to the bottom of the dresser drawer, maybe?"

"You've been reading too many espionage novels. And if I were you, I'd cut the bloody sarcasm. You might start me thinking that there's some reason you don't want me to look in Bernie Allen's room. And while we're at it, he's not the first person to get killed after leaving this guest house, is he, Sam?"

"Now wait a minute," said Sam. "If you're trying to imply—"

Banks held his hand up. "I'm not trying to imply anything. What was it the man said: once is happenstance, twice is coincidence? Let's just hope there's not a third time."

Sam put his head in his hands and rubbed his eyes. "I'm sorry," he said. "Really, I am. It's the shock. And now all these questions."

"Look at it from my point of view, Sam. Bernard Allen was killed after he left your guest house. That's given his killer about two whole weeks to cover his tracks, leave the country, arrange for an alibi, whatever. I need everything I can get, and I need it quick. And the last thing I need is for some clever bugger who just might have been withholding information to start playing the comic."

"Look, I've said I'm sorry. What more do you want?"

"First of all you can tell us when he left?"

"About two weeks ago."

"Can you be more specific?"

"Katie?"

Again, with great difficulty, Katie turned her attention to the people in the room. Banks repeated his question.

"It was a Friday," she said.

Hatchley checked the dates against his diary. "That'd be the seventeenth, sir," he said. "Friday, May seventeenth."

"What time?"

"Just after breakfast. About nine-thirty. He said he wanted to get an early start," Sam said.

"Where was he going?"

"He was heading for the Pennine Way, then up to Swaledale."

"Do you know where he was intending to stay?"

Sam shook his head. "No. He just said he'd find somewhere on the way. There are plenty of places; it's a very popular route."

"Did he say anything to you about visiting the hanging valley on his way?"

"No. I wouldn't have been surprised, though. He used to play there when he was a kid, or so he said."

"What did you do after he'd gone?"

"I drove to Eastvale to do some shopping. I always do on a Friday morning."

"What shops did you go to?"

"What is this? Are you trying to tell me I'm a suspect in the murder of my friend?"

"Just answer the bloody question."

"All right, Inspector, there's no—"

"It's Chief Inspector." Banks didn't usually push rank, but Sam Greenock had rubbed him up the wrong way.

"Chief Inspector, then. Where did I go? I went to Carter's for some seeds, peat moss and fertilizer. Katie's trying to get a vegetable patch going in the back garden. It'll save us a bit of money in the long run."

"Is that all?"

"No. But they'll remember me there. I called in at a newsagent's for some magazines—that one on King Street opposite the school road."

"I know it."

"I'm a regular there, too."

"Thanks, that'll do fine for a start. What kind of car do you drive?"

"A Landrover. It's in the garage."

"And you, Mrs Greenock, what did you do after Bernard Allen left?"

"Me? Housework. What else?"

Banks turned back to Sam: "You met Allen in Leeds about ten years ago, is that right?"

"Yes. In Armley. We lived just off Tong Road and the Allens came to live next door after they gave up the farm. Bernie and I were about the same age, so we palled up."

"What was he doing then?"

"Just finishing at university. It was only York, so he was home most weekends and holidays. We used to go for a jar or two every Saturday night."

"How did the family take the move?"

Sam shrugged. "They adapted. At first Mr Allen, Bernie's dad, went around as if he'd been kicked out of paradise. It must have been very hard for him, though, swapping farm work for a crummy factory job. Hard on the pride."

"Is that what he said?"

"Never in so many words, no. You could just tell. He's a tough old bird, anyway, so they survived."

"And Bernard?"

"He tried to fit in. But you know what it's like. He got his degree and all, but he couldn't get the kind of work he wanted. He lived at home and did all kinds of odd jobs— mushroom picking at Greenhill Nurseries, sweeping factory yards, production line . . . all dull routine work."

"Is that when he decided to go to Canada?"

"After a year or so of it, yes. He'd had enough. Someone he knew from university had already gone over and said it wasn't too hard to get teaching jobs in the colleges. He said they paid well, too."

"Who was this?"

"His name was Bob Morgan. I think he and Bernie taught at the same place, Toronto Community College."

"Was Bernie homesick?"

"I suppose so. I mean, you don't forget your roots, do you? But he stayed. One thing leads to another. He made friends over there, got married, divorced."

"What was his state of mind while he was staying here?"

"He was fine. Cheerful. Happy to be back."

"Did he talk about coming home to stay?"

Sam shook his head. "He knew better than that. There aren't any jobs for him."

"So he didn't seem unusually homesick or depressed, and he didn't say he was planning to come back."

"No."

Banks lit a cigarette and studied Katie's profile. She was a blank; he had no idea what she was thinking.

"How long have you been in Swainshead?" he asked Sam.

"Six years."

"And it's going well?"

Sam nodded. "Can't complain. We're hardly millionaires, but we like the life."

"And you, Mrs Greenock?"

Katie turned and focused on him. "Yes. It's better than cleaning rooms at the Queen's Hotel."

"Did Bernie have any other friends in the village apart from you?"

"Not really," Sam answered. "See, most of the kids he grew up with had moved away. A lot do these days. They see the good life on telly and soon as they're old enough there's no stopping them. Like Denny, Bernie's older brother. Off to Australia like a shot, he was."

"Was Bernie friendly with the Colliers?" Esther Haines had said not, but Banks thought she might have been prejudiced by her own opinions of Nicholas and Stephen.

"Well, I'd hardly say they were friends. Acquaintances, more like. But we had an evening or two in the White Rose together. I think Bernie was always a bit uncomfortable around Stephen and Nick, though, them having been his landlords, so to speak, the local gentry and all."

Banks nodded. "Can you think of anyone in the village who might have wanted him out of the way?"

"Bernie? Good Lord, no."

"He had no enemies?"

"None that I know of. Not here."

"What about in Leeds?"

"Not there either, as far as I know. Maybe somebody followed him over from Canada, an enemy he'd made there?"

"Mrs Greenock," Banks said, turning to Katie again, "do you know of anyone with a reason for getting rid of Bernard Allen?"

Katie hesitated before answering. "No. He was harmless. Just a friendly sort of person. Nobody would want to hurt him."

"One more thing: What was he carrying when he left here?"

"Carrying?" Sam said. "Oh, I see. His belongings. A big blue rucksack with his clothes, passport, money, a few books."

"And what was he wearing?"

"I don't really remember. Do you, Katie?"

Katie shook her head. "It was a warm day, though," she said. "That I do remember. I think he was just wearing an open-necked shirt. White. And slacks, not jeans. It's only the amateurs wear jeans for walking."

"They're too heavy, you see," Sam explained. "Especially if they get wet. We try to give a bit of advice to our guests sometimes, and we always make sure we know where they're going if they're due back in the evening. That way, if they don't return, we can let the Mountain Rescue Post know where they were heading."

Banks nodded. "Very sensible. Have you any vacancies at the moment?"

"I think so," Sam said.

"Six and eight," Katie added.

"Good, we'll take them."

"You're staying here?"

"There'll be quite a lot of questions to ask in Swainshead," Banks said, "and it's fifty miles to Eastvale and back. We'll be staying here tonight at least."

"One's a single," Katie said. "The other's a double."

Banks smiled at her. "Fine. Sergeant Hatchley will take the single." It was patently unfair, Banks knew. He was much more slightly built than the well-padded Hatchley, and a good four or five inches shorter. But rank, he reflected, did have its privileges.

"Don't sulk, Sergeant," he said as they walked over to the car to pick up their overnight bags. "My room might be bigger, but it's probably right next to the plumbing. What did you think of Mrs Greenock?"

"Not bad if you like those wand-like figures," Hatchley said. "Prefer 'em with a bit of meat on their bones, myself."

"I wasn't asking you to rate her out of ten on looks. What about her attitude?"

"Didn't say much, did she? Seemed in a bit of a daze to me. Think there might be more to her than meets the eye?"

"I think there might indeed," said Banks. "In fact, I got the distinct impression that she was holding something back."

II

The Greenocks ate their lunch in silence, then Sam dashed out. Katie, who had lost her appetite and merely played with her food, piled the dishes in the washer, set the controls and turned it on. There was still shopping to do and the evening meal to prepare, but she felt she could afford to relax for a few minutes.

As she lay down on the sofa and looked out on the slopes of Swainshead Fell beyond the back garden, she thought of Bernie helping her clear the dishes, talking about Toronto, watching cricket on the telly. She remembered the little presents he had brought each time—no doubt picked up at the airport at the last minute, for Bernie was like that—jars of pure maple syrup, a box of cigars or a bottle of malt Scotch for Sam, Opium perfume or Chanel No 5 for Katie. She'd never had the heart to tell him that she didn't wear perfume, that the one time she had tried she had felt like a tramp, even though it had been White Linen, and had scrubbed it off straight away. Now the three little bottles lay in the dark inside her dresser drawer, untouched.

Bernie had even helped her with the garden sometimes; he might not have had green fingers, but he could wield a trowel or a hoe well enough. Bernie: so considerate, so kind. But the dark images began to crowd out her thoughts. Frowning, she pushed them away. Instead she saw endless prairies of golden wheat swaying in the breeze, heard the sea beating against a rough coastline where redwood forests reared as tall as the sky. Bernie had told her all about Canada, all the places he'd been. She'd never get to see them now, she realized, because Bernie was dead.

Fellowes's words came back to her, what he'd said in his drunken stupor when he grasped her hand by the bed:

"Moving," he'd said. "Moving." And she hadn't understood at the time. Now she did. If Bernie had been lying up there for two weeks he would have been like that dead lamb she had seen on Adam's Fell last year. It didn't bear thinking about.

She'd given a bad impression to the police, she knew that, but at the time she had been unable to help herself. The lean, dark one, the one who seemed too short to be a policeman, would want to talk to her again, that was for sure. How could she keep her secret? She pictured her grandmother standing over her, lined face stern and hard, eyes like black pinheads boring into her: "Secrets, girl, secrets are the devil's doing. God loves a pure and open heart." But she had to keep this secret.

There were so many things, it seemed, one had to do in life that went against God's commandments. How could a person live without sinning? She was no longer even sure that she knew what was right or wrong. Sometimes she thought it was a sin to breathe, to be alive. It seemed you had to sin to survive in today's world. It was wrong to keep secrets and tell lies; but was it wrong to keep your word, your promise? And if you had broken it once for a special reason, was it all right to break it again?

Wearily, Katie got up and prepared to go to the shops down in Lower Head. Work and duty: they were the only constants in life. Everything else was a trap, a trick, a temptation to betrayal. The only way to survive was to shun pleasure. She picked up her purse and shopping basket and pulled a face at the nasty, soapy taste in her mouth as she left the house.

III

After Banks and Hatchley had carried their bags to their rooms, they walked over to the White Rose for lunch. The place was busy with Saturday tourists who had let their curiosity lead them to the northern part of Swainshead, but none of the regulars was present. Luckily, Freddie Metcalfe was too busy to chat. They both ordered gammon and chips and carried their pints over to a corner table.

"I want you to get onto Richmond after lunch," Banks said, "and have him check to see if anyone in Swainshead has connections with Canada, specifically with Toronto. I know it sounds like a big job, but tell him to start with the people we already know: the Greenocks, Fletcher, the Colliers. You might also add," he said, lowering his voice, "Freddie Metcalfe over there, and Neil Fellowes, too."

"The bloke who found the body? But he's from Pontefract."

"No matter. Remember, we thought Allen was from Canada at first, then from Leeds. And while we're on the subject, have him check on the brother-in-law, Les Haines. I want to know if he's made any trips to this area in the past few weeks. Ask him to get as much background as he can on all of them. I'm sure the superintendent will be able to get him some help from downstairs. And get someone to go to Carter's and that newsagent's to check Greenock's alibi. Tell them to make sure they get the times as exact as possible."

"Don't you believe him?"

Banks shrugged. "He could be telling the truth. He could also have driven to a convenient spot along the main road and approached the valley from the other side."

The little waitress brought over their food and they ate in silence. At the bar, they could hear Freddie Metcalfe enthralling visitors with examples of Yorkshire humour filched from *The Dalesman*, and at the next table, two middle-aged women from Lancashire were talking about lager louts: "They get right confident after a few drinks, young 'uns do."

When they had finished eating, Banks sent Hatchley to radio in to Richmond, then he stood outside the pub for a moment and took a deep breath of fresh air. It was June 1, another fine day. Nobody knew what the Dales had done to deserve such a long stretch of good weather, but according to a transistor radio Banks overheard, it certainly wasn't any thanks to Yorkshire Cricket Club, currently 74 for 6 at Somerset.

Banks wanted to talk to the Colliers, but first he returned to his room to change his shirt. On his way back down, he spotted Mrs Greenock in the hall, but she seemed to see or hear him coming and scuttled off into the back before he could catch her. Smiling, he walked back out into the street. He knew he could have followed her and confronted her with his suspicions there and then, but decided instead to let her play mouse to his cat until she tired of it.

There were plenty of people on the grassy banks of the River Swain that afternoon. Three children fished for tiddlers with nets at the end of cane rods while their parents sat and watched from lawn chairs, dad with a knotted handkerchief over his head reading the *Daily Mail* and mum knitting, glancing up occasionally to make sure the offspring were still in sight.

The Dales were getting as crowded and noisy as the coast, Banks thought as he crossed the bridge. There was even a small group of teenagers farther down, towards Lower Head, wearing cut-off denim jackets with the names of rock bands inked on the back. Two of them, a boy and a girl, Banks assumed, were rolling on the grass in an overtly sexual embrace while tinny music rattled out of a portable stereo placed close to one prostrate youth's ear.

Many of his colleagues, Banks knew, would have gone over and told them to move on, accused them of disturbing the peace and searched them for drugs. But despite his personal distaste for some gangs of youngsters and their music, Banks made it a rule never to use his power as a policeman to force his own will on the general public. After all, they were young, they were enjoying life, and apart from the noise, they were really doing no-one any harm.

Banks passed the old men on the bridge and made a mental note to have a chat with them at some point. They seemed to be permanent fixtures; maybe they had seen something.

He met Sergeant Hatchley at the car and they headed for the Collier house.

"Have you noticed," Banks said, "how Allen seemed to

have a different story for everyone he talked to? He was upset; he was cheerful. He was coming home; he wasn't."

"Maybe," said Hatchley, "it's just that all the people he talked to have a different story for us."

Banks gave the sergeant an appreciative glance. Thinking things out wasn't Hatchley's strong point, but there were times when he could be quite surprising.

"Good point," Banks said. "Let's see what the Colliers have to add."

Gristhorpe was right; the Collier house was a Victorian monstrosity. But it had its own grotesque charm, Banks thought as he walked up the crazy paving with Hatchley. Most Dales architecture was practical in nature and plain in style, but this place was for show. It must have been the great-grandfather who had it built, and he must have thought highly indeed of the Collier status.

Banks rang the bell on the panelled door and Stephen Collier answered, a frown on his face. He led them through a high-ceilinged hallway into a sitting-room at the back of the house. French windows opened onto the patio. In the centre of the large lawn stood an elaborate stone fountain. White dolphins and cherubim curled about the lip of the bowl.

The room itself contrasted sharply with the exterior of the house. Off-white walls created a sense of light and space on which the ultra-modern Swedish pine and chrome and glass furnishing made hardly any encroachment at all. Abstract paintings hung over a blue-tiled mantelpiece: bold and violent splashes of colour reminiscent, in their effect on Banks's eyes, of the Jackson Pollocks Sandra had insisted he look at in a London gallery years ago.

The three of them sat in white wicker chairs around a table on the patio. Banks half-expected a servant to arrive with a tray of Margaritas or mint juleps, but Collier himself offered them drinks. It was warm, so both men eagerly accepted a cold bottle of Beck's lager.

Before he went to fetch the drinks, Stephen Collier rapped on the French windows of the next room and beckoned to Nicholas. Banks had wanted to talk to them separately, but it wasn't important at this point. Stretching, he got up and walked over as Nicholas emerged onto his half of the patio. He was just in time to catch a glimpse of a much darker room, all oak panelling, leather-bound books and oil-paintings of ancestors gleaming on the walls.

Nicholas smiled his horsy yellow smile and held out his hand.

"It's an interesting set-up you've got here," Banks said.

"Yes. We couldn't bear to get rid of the house, however ugly it might seem from the outside. It's been in the family for years. Lord knows what prompted my great-great-grandfather to build such a folly—ostentatious display of wealth and position, I suppose. And it's so inappropriate for the area." Despite the deprecating tone, Banks could tell that Nicholas was proud of the house and the status of his family.

"Do you share the place?" Banks asked Nicholas after they had sat down at the tale.

"Sort of. It's divided into two halves. We thought at first that one of us could take the upstairs and the other the downstairs, but it's better like this. We've got the equivalent of two completely separate houses. Stephen and I have very different tastes, so the two halves make quite a contrast. You must let me show you around my half one day."

Stephen returned with the drinks. Dressed all in white, he looked like a cricketer breaking for tea. Nicholas, however, with his slight stoop, pale complexion, and comma of black hair over his forehead, looked more like an ageing umpire. It was hard to believe these two were brothers; even harder to accept that Stephen was the eldest.

After giving both of them time to register surprise and shock at the news of Bernard Allen's death, of which he was certain they knew already, Banks lit a cigarette and asked, "Did you see much of him while he was here?"

"Not a lot," Stephen answered. "He was in the pub a couple of times with Sam, so naturally we talked, but that's about all."

"What did you talk about?"

"Oh, just small talk, really. This and that. About Canada, places we'd both been to."

"You've visited Canada?"

"I travel quite a bit," Stephen said. "You might think a small food-freezing plant in the Dales isn't much, but there are other businesses, connected. Import, export, that kind of thing. Yes, I've been to Canada a few times."

"Toronto?"

"No. Montreal, as a matter of fact."

"Did you ever see Bernard Allen over there?"

"It's a big country, Chief Inspector."

"Did you get the impression that anything was bothering Allen while he was over here?"

"No."

"What about you?" he asked Nicholas.

"No, I can't say I did. I've always found it a bit awkward talking to Bernard, to tell you the truth. One always feels he has a bit of a chip on his shoulder."

"What do you mean?"

"Oh, come on," Nicholas said, grinning. "Surely you know what I mean. His father spent his life working on land rented from my father. They were poor. From where they lived they had a fine enough view of this place, and you can't tell me that Bernard never thought it unfair that we had so much and he had so little. Especially when his father failed."

"I didn't know Bernard Allen or his father," Banks said, peeling the foil from the neck of the Beck's, which he preferred to drink straight from the bottle. "Tell me about him."

"I'm not saying I knew him well, myself, only that he became a bit of a lefty, a socialist. Up the workers and all that." Nicholas grinned again, showing his stained teeth. His eyes were especially bright.

"Are you saying that Bernard Allen was a Communist?"

"I don't know about that. I don't know if he was a party member. All I know is he used to spout his leftist rot in the pub."

"Is this true?" Banks asked Stephen.

"Partly. My brother exaggerates a bit, Chief Inspector. It's a tendency he has. We sometimes had arguments about politics, yes, and Bernard Allen had left-wing views. But that's as far as it goes. I'd hardly say he was a proselytizer or that he toed some party line."

"His political opinions weren't particularly strong, then?"

"I wouldn't say so, no. He said he left the country partly because Margaret Thatcher came into office. Well, we all know about unemployment, don't we? Bernard couldn't find work in England, so he left. You could hardly say he was running from country to country to escape political tyranny, could you?"

"He just used to whine about it, that's all," Nicholas cut in. "Expected the government to do everything for him without him having to lift a finger. Typical socialist."

"As you can gather, Chief Inspector," Stephen said with a strained smile, "my brother's something of a young fogey. That hardly gave either of us reason to do away with Bernard, though."

"Of course not," Banks said. "And I was never suggesting it did. I just want to know as much about the victim as possible. Would you say that there was any real animosity between you—political arguments aside—over the farm?"

"Do you mean did he blame us?" Stephen asked.

"Yes."

"He blamed everyone but himself," Nicholas cut in.

Stephen turned on him. "Oh, shut up Nicky. You're being bloody awkward, you know."

"Did he?" Banks asked Stephen again.

"Not that I ever knew of. It was nothing to do with us, really. As you know, Father was preparing to give up farming anyway, and he certainly hadn't groomed us to take over. Nobody kicked Archie Allen off the land. He could have stayed there as long as he wanted to. It just wasn't financially viable any more. Ask any farmer, they'll tell you how things have changed over the past twenty years or so. If Bernard was holding a grudge, then it was a very unreasonable one. He didn't strike me as an unreasonable person. Does that answer your question?"

"Yes, thank you," Banks said. He turned to Nicholas again. "I understand you knew Mr Allen's sister, Esther."

Nicholas reddened with anger. "Who said that?"

"Never mind who said it. Is it true?"

"We all knew her," Stephen said. "I mean, we knew who she was."

"More than that," Banks said, looking at Nicholas, whose eyes were flashing. "Nicholas knows what I mean, don't you?"

"Don't be ridiculous," Nicholas said. "Are you trying to suggest that there was anything more to it than a landlord-tenant relationship?"

"Was there?"

"Of course not."

"Didn't you find her attractive?"

"She was hardly my type."

"Do you mean she was of a lower class?"

Nicholas bared his teeth in a particularly unpleasant smile. "If you want to put it that way, yes."

"And what about the servant girl? The one who used to work here."

"I insist you stop this at once, Chief Inspector," Stephen said. "I can't see how it's relevant. And I'm sure I don't have to remind you that the deputy chief constable is a good friend of the family."

"I'm sure he is," Banks said. He wasn't at all put out; in fact, he was enjoying their discomfort tremendously. "Just a couple of minor points, then we'll be on our way. When was the last time you saw Bernard?"

Nicholas said nothing; he appeared to be sulking. Stephen paused for a moment and answered in a business-like manner, "I'd say it was in the White Rose the evening before he left. Thursday. I remember talking to him about Tan Hill in Swaledale."

"Is that where he was heading?"

"Not specifically, no, but it's on the Pennine Way."

"Did he talk about the hanging valley at all, the place where his body was found?"

"No, not that I remember."

"Did either of you see him set off from Swainshead?"

Both the Colliers shook their heads. "I'm usually at the office before nine," Stephen said. "And my brother would have been at Braughtmore."

"So you saw nothing of him after that Thursday evening in the White Rose?"

"Nothing."

"Just one more thing: could you tell us where John Fletcher lives?"

"John? He's a couple of miles north of the village. It's a big farmhouse on the eastern fell-side. You can't miss it, it's the only one in sight."

"Fine, then." Banks nodded to Hatchley and they stood up to leave. Stephen Collier led them out and Nicholas followed, still sulking. As soon as the door closed, Banks could hear them start arguing.

Hatchley turned up his nose in disgust. "What a pair of wankers," he said.

"Aptly put," said Banks. "But we did learn a few things."

"Like what?"

"I never told them what time Allen left Swainshead, so why should Stephen Collier make a point of mentioning nine o'clock?"

"Hmm," said Hatchley. "I suppose he could have just been assuming that Allen would leave after breakfast. Or maybe it had been mentioned the night before?"

"It's possible," Banks said. "Come to that, Sam Greenock could have told them. Nicholas Collier seemed much more annoyed by my reference to Esther Haines than I thought he'd be. There could be much more to that than even she let on."

"I thought you were pushing it a bit there," Hatchley said. "I mean, the super did say to take it easy on them. They're important."

Banks sniffed. "The problem is, Sergeant, that it's all arse backwards, isn't it?"

"What do you mean?"

"Let's say Nicholas Collier might have been messing around with Allen's little sister, or Allen might have been bitter over losing the farm and eventually having to leave England. That gives him a motive for murder, but he's the one who ends up dead. Odd, that, don't you think?"

"Aye, when you put it like that," Hatchley said.

"Get on the radio and see if Richmond has turned up anything yet, will you? I want a word with these blokes here."

Hatchley carried on to the car. Banks neared the bridge and steeled himself for the encounter with the old men. Three of them stood there silently, two leaning on walking sticks. No flicker of interest or concern showed on their weather-beaten faces when Banks approached them. He leaned against the warm stone and introduced himself, then asked if they had been out as early as nine o'clock a couple of weeks ago.

No-one said a word at first, then one of them, a gnarled, misshapen man, turned to face Banks. With his flat cap and dark brown clothing, he looked like some strange plant with the power to uproot itself and walk among people.

He spat in the beck and said, "'Appen."

"Do you know Bernard Allen?"

"Archie Allen's lad? Aye, o'course."

"Did you see him that morning?"

The man was silent for a moment; he screwed up his eyes and contemplated Adam's Fell. Banks took out his cigarettes and offered them around. Only one of them, a man with a huge red nose, took one. He grinned toothlessly at Banks, carefully nipped off the filter and put the other end in his mouth.

"Aye," the spokesman said finally.

"Where did he come from?"

The man pointed towards the Greenock Guest House.

"Did he stop anywhere on his way?"

The man shook his head.

"Where did he go?"

"Up there." The man pointed with his stick to the footpath up Swainshead Fell.

"And that was the last you saw of him?"

"Aye."

"What was he wearing?"

"Nay, lad, I don't remember that. 'Ee was carrying one o'them there 'aversacks on 'is back, that's all I recollect. P'raps 'ee was wearing a shirt. I don't remember no jacket."

"Did you notice anyone go after him?"

The man shook his head again.

"Could someone have followed him without you seeing?"

"'Appen. There's plenty o'ways to get up t'fell."

"We know he went to the hanging valley over the fell-top," Banks said. "Are there many other ways to get there?"

"A few. Tha can go from t'main road, 'bout a mile past Rawley Force, and from further up t'valley."

"How could anyone know where he was headed?"

"That's tha job, bobby, in't it?"

He was right. Someone could easily have watched Allen set off up the side of Swainshead Fell then gone up by another route to head him off somewhere out of sight. And Sam Greenock had said he wouldn't have been surprised if Bernard had visited the hanging valley. Anyone else could have known that, too, and gone up earlier to wait for him there.

Typically, as more information came to light the case was becoming more and more frustrating. Clearly it would be necessary to do a house-to-house in the village and ask the people with an eastern view if they had noticed anything that morning. It would also be useful to know if anyone had seen a car parked off the Helmthorpe road near the other access point. The trouble was that May seventeenth was so long ago most people would have forgotten.

And those were only the most obvious ways in. Someone could surely have approached the hanging valley from almost any direction and lain in wait overnight if necessary, especially if he knew Bernard Allen was bound to pass that way. The break, if it came, didn't look so likely to come from establishing opportunity—just about everyone who had no alibi seemed to have had that—but from discovering a motive.

Banks thanked the old men and walked off to find Sergeant Hatchley.

6

Hatchley started the next day in a bad mood. He grumbled to Banks that not only was his bed too small but the noise of the plumbing had kept him awake.

"I swear there was some bugger in there for a piss every five minutes. Flushed it every time, too. The bloody thing took at least ten minutes to quieten down again."

Banks, who had slept the sleep of the truly virtuous, overlooked the sergeant's spurious arithmetic. "Never mind," he said. "With a bit of luck you'll be snug and warm in your own bed tonight."

"Not if I can help it."

"Carol Ellis?"

"Aye."

"How long's it been now?"

"Over eighteen months."

"It'll be wedding bells next, then?"

Hatchley blushed and Banks guessed he wasn't far from the truth.

"Anyway," Banks went on. "I'm sorry to keep you away from your love-life, but I think we'll be finished here today unless Richmond comes up with anything else."

Hatchley had been onto the detective constable back in Eastvale, but Richmond had discovered nothing of importance except that Sam Greenock's alibi seemed to hold.

There remained, however, some doubt about the exact times he had called at Carter's and the newsagent's, so he wasn't entirely out of the running.

Also, Richmond had spoken to PC Weaver, who had called at the Greenocks' to ask about Canadian visitors. Weaver said that in all cases he had both checked the register and made enquiries. It looked like Sam Greenock was lying. Weaver could have been covering himself, but he was a good officer, and Banks tended to believe him.

The previous evening, Banks and Hatchley had gone to interview John Fletcher, but he had been out. On the way back, they called in at the White Rose for a nightcap and had an early night. Mrs Greenock had still been skilfully managing to avoid them.

Breakfast seemed to cheer Hatchley up. Delivered by Katie, who blushed and ran as soon as she put, or almost dropped, the plates in front of them, the main course consisted of two fried eggs, two thick rashers of Yorkshire bacon, Cumberland sausage, grilled mushrooms and tomato, with two slices of fried bread to mop it all up. Before that they had drunk grapefruit juice and eaten cereal, and afterwards came the toast and marmalade. By some oversight, the toast was actually hot, and Hatchley, his equilibrium much restored, recoiled in mock horror.

"What's on after we've talked to Fletcher?" he asked.

"We've got to put it all together, write up the interviews, see what we've got. I'm due for lunch with the super, so as far as I'm concerned you can take the rest of the day off and make an early start in the morning."

Sergeant Hatchley beamed.

"I'll drop you off at home," Banks said. "I've got to go back to Eastvale to pick up Sandra and the kids, anyway."

They finished their tea and left the room to the quiet Belgian couple by the window and the young marrieds in the corner, who hadn't noticed anyone except each other. The Greenocks themselves were nowhere in sight.

Outside, the three men Banks had spoken with the previous day were on the bridge as usual. The one who had acted as spokesman gave him a curt, grudging nod of acknowledgement as he passed.

Hatchley nudged him as they got in the car. "It usually takes an incomer two generations to get any sign of recognition from those characters. What did you do, slip 'em a tenner each?"

"Southern charm, Sergeant," Banks said, grinning. "Sheer charm. That and a lot of luck."

About two miles up the valley, they crossed the low bridge and took a narrow dirt road up the fell-side. Fletcher's farmhouse was a solid, dark-stone construction that looked as if it had been extruded from the earth like an outcrop of rock. Around the back were a number of pens and ditches for dipping and shearing. This time, he was at home.

"I'm sorry I wasn't in," he said when Banks mentioned their previous visit. "I was doing a bit of business over in Hawes. Anyway, come in, make yourselves comfortable."

They followed him into the living-room, a spartan kind of place with bare plastered walls, stiff-backed chairs and a solid table on which rested an old wireless and precious little else. Whatever money Fletcher had in the bank, he certainly didn't waste any on luxurious living. The small window looked out across the valley. With a view like that, Banks thought, you'd hardly need paintings or television.

One thing in particular caught Banks's eye immediately, partly because it just didn't seem to fit in this overtly masculine environment. Propped on the mantelpiece was a gilt-framed photograph of a woman. On closer inspection, which Banks made while Fletcher went to brew tea, the photo proved doubly incongruous. The woman, with her finely plucked eyebrows, gay smile and long, wavy chestnut hair, certainly didn't look as if she belonged in Fletcher's world. Banks could imagine her cutting a fine figure at society cocktail parties, sporting the latest hat at Ascot or posing elegantly at fashion openings, but not living in this godforsaken part of the world with a dark, squat, rough-cheeked sheep-farmer.

When Fletcher came back, Banks pointed to the photograph and asked who she was.

"My wife," he said. "She's been gone two years now." There was a distinct chill in his tone that harmonized with the lonely, brooding atmosphere Banks sensed in the house.

He didn't like to ask, but curiosity, as it often did, got the better of him. "I'm sorry," he said. "Is she dead?"

Fletcher looked sharply at him. "Not dead, no. If you must know, she left me."

And you're still in love with her, Banks thought. At least that explained something of the heaviness that Fletcher seemed to carry around inside himself.

"We've come about Bernard Allen," Banks said, accepting a cup of tea and changing tack quickly.

"Aye, I heard," Fletcher said. "Poor sod."

"Did you know him well?"

"Not really, no. Just used to pass an evening or two in the White Rose when he dropped by for a visit."

"Did you know him before he went to Canada?"

"I met him a few times. Hard not to when I was dealing with Walter Collier. Archie Allen worked some of his land."

"So I heard. What were you going to do about that?"

Fletcher shrugged. "I wasn't going to evict them, if that's what you're getting at. They were quite welcome to stay as far as I was concerned."

"But they couldn't make a go of it?"

"That's right. It's tough, sheep-farming, like I said before. I felt sorry for them, but there was nothing I could do."

"So you only knew Bernard through his father at first?"

"Aye. He was off at university around then, too. And his brother had emigrated to Australia. There was only the young lass left."

"Esther?"

"Aye. How is she? Have you seen her?"

"Yes," Banks said. "She's well. Married. Lives in Leeds. Did you ever hear anything about her and Nicholas Collier?"

Fletcher frowned. "No, I can't say as I did. Though I wouldn't put it past him. She were a nice lass, young Esther. I've often thought things might've worked out different if the others had stuck around, kept the family together, like."

"You mean Bernard and Denny going away might have caused their father's problems?"

"Some of them, perhaps. Not all, mind you. But it costs money to hire men. If you've got a family, there might be more mouths to feed, but there's more hands to help, too."

"Did you have any connection with Bernard other than his father? There can't have been much of an age difference between you."

"Nay, I'm older than I look," Fletcher said, and grinned. "Like I said, we'd pass the time of day in the White Rose now and then. Him and his girlfriend were in there often enough."

"Girlfriend? Who was that, Mr Fletcher?"

"The one who disappeared. Anne Ralston, her name was."

Banks felt a tremor of excitement. "She was Bernard Allen's girlfriend?"

"Aye. Childhood sweethearts. They grew up together. I don't think it was owt serious later, like, or he wouldn't have gone off to Canada and left her. But they were thick as thieves, them two—more like brother and sister, maybe, as they got older."

"And after he'd gone, she took up with Stephen Collier?"

"Aye. Got a job at Collier Foods and, well . . . Stephen's got a way with the women."

"Did Bernard Allen ever say anything about this?"

"Not in my hearing he didn't. You're thinking maybe he was jealous?"

"Could be."

"Then the wrong one got himself killed, didn't he?"

Banks sighed. "It always seems to look that way in this case. But if Allen thought Stephen Collier had harmed her, he might have been out for revenge."

"Waited long enough, didn't he?" Fletcher said.

"I'll be frank with you, Mr Fletcher," Banks said. "We've no idea why Bernard Allen was murdered, none at all. At the moment I'm gathering as much information as I can. Most of it will probably turn out to be useless. It usually does. But right now there's no way of telling what's of value and what isn't. Can you think of any reason why someone in Swainshead would want him out of the way?"

Fletcher paused to think for a few moments, his dark eyebrows knitting together. "No," he said finally. "It's nothing to do with the farming business, I'm sure of that. There's not enough money in it to make murder worthwhile. And there was no animosity between myself and the Allens. Like I said, I don't think there was bad feeling between Bernard and the Colliers, but I couldn't swear to it. I know he baited them a bit about being capitalist oppressors, but I don't think anyone took that seriously enough to kill for."

"What was your impression of Bernard Allen?"

"I liked him. As I said, I didn't know him well, and I can't say I agreed with his politics—with him on one side and Nicholas on the other, it was hardly my idea of a peaceful evening's drinking. But he was bright, thoughtful, and he loved the land. He knew he wasn't cut out to be a farmer—few are—but he loved The Head."

"When was the last time you saw him?"

"The evening before he left. We were all in the White Rose. He was getting quite maudlin about coming home. Said if only he could get a job, however little it paid, or maybe a private income, then he'd be back like a shot. Of course, Nicholas jumped on that one—a socialist wanting a private income!"

"Were there any serious arguments?"

"No. It was all playful. The only serious bit was Bernard's sentimentality. He really seemed to convince himself that he was coming back here to live. But he'd had a few too many, of course. Sam had to help him back to the house. I'm sorry I can't be more useful, Mr Banks. I'd like to, but I don't know anything. I had no reason to harm Bernard and, as far as I know, nor did any of the others. If there are motives, they're hidden from me."

"Did he mention his divorce at all?"

"Oh aye," Fletcher said grimly. "I could sympathize with him over that."

"Did he seem upset about it?"

"Of course. His wife had run off with another man. Wouldn't you be upset? I think that's what set him thinking about coming back home to stay. You get like that when you lose whatever it is that keeps you away."

"Did Mr Allen know your wife?"

Fletcher's face hardened. "What do you mean 'know'? 'Know' in the biblical sense? Are you suggesting there was something between them and I killed him in a fit of jealousy?"

"No," said Banks, "I'm simply trying to get a grasp on the web of relationships."

Fletcher continued to eye him suspiciously. "She didn't know him," he said. "Oh, I'm not saying their paths never crossed, that they wouldn't say hello if they passed one another in the street, but that's all."

"Where is your wife?"

Fletcher looked at the picture. "In Paris," he said, his voice shaking with grief and anger. "In Paris with that bastard she ran off with."

The silence that followed weighed on them all. Finally, Banks gestured to Hatchley and they stood up to leave. "I'm sorry if I upset you," he said. "It wasn't intentional, believe me, but sometimes in a murder investigation . . ."

Fletcher sighed. "Aye, I know. You've got to ask. It's your job. No offence taken." And he held out his square, callused hand.

Driving down the fell-side, Banks and Hatchley said very little. Banks had been impressed by Fletcher's solidity; he seemed a man with great integrity and strong foundations. But such a man, he knew, could kill when pushed too far. It was easier to push an earnest man too far than it was a more frivolous one. Although he was inclined to believe Fletcher, he nonetheless made a mental note of his reservations.

"Ideal place, isn't it?" Hatchley said, looking back at Fletcher's farm as they crossed the bridge.

"In a way," Banks answered. "A bit dour and spartan for my tastes, though."

"I didn't mean that, sir." Hatchley looked puzzled. "I meant it's an ideal location for approaching the hanging valley unseen."

Banks slowed down on the narrow road as Sam Greenock's Landrover passed them going in the other direction. Sam waved half-heartedly as he drove by.

"Yes," Banks said absently. "Yes, I suppose it is. I'd just like to stop off at the Greenocks' before we go back to Eastvale. There's something I'd like to do. You use the radio and get onto Richmond. See if anything's come up."

II

Katie flinched and backed towards the wall when she saw Banks appear in the doorway of the room she was cleaning.

"It's all right, Katie," he said. "I'm not going to hurt you. We've got to have a little talk, that's all."

"Sam's out," Katie said, clutching the yellow duster tight over her breast.

"I know he is. I saw him drive off. It's you I want to talk to. Come on, Katie, stop playing games. You've been trying to avoid us ever since we got here. What is it? What are you afraid of?"

"I don't know what you're talking about."

Banks sighed. "Yes you do." He sat down on the corner of the bed. "And I'm prepared to wait until you tell me."

Now, as she stood cringing by the window, Banks realized who she reminded him of: Hardy's Tess Durbeyfield. Physically, she resembled Nastassia Kinski, who had played Tess in the film version, but the similarity went deeper than that. Banks had a sense of Tess as a child in a woman's body, not fully aware of her own beauty and sexuality, or of the effect she might have on men. It wasn't entirely innocence, but it was close—a kind of innocent sensuality. He made a note to look up the description of Tess in the book when he got home.

"Look," he went on, "we can either talk here, or we can go to CID headquarters in Eastvale. It's up to you. I don't really mind at all."

"You can't do that," Katie said, thrusting out her bottom lip. "You can't just take a person away like that. I haven't done anything. I've got my work to finish."

"So have I. You're withholding evidence, Katie. It's a crime."

"I'm not withholding anything."

"If you say so." Banks stood up with exaggerated slowness. "Let's go, then."

Katie stepped back until she was flat against the wall. "No! If you take me away Sam . . . Sam'll . . ."

"Come on, Katie," Banks said, more gently, "don't be silly." He pointed to the chair. "Sit down. Tell me about it."

Katie flopped into the chair by the window and looked down at the floor. "There's nothing to tell," she muttered.

"Let me try and make it a bit easier for you," Banks said. "Judging by the way you behaved when we talked to you and Sam yesterday, I'd guess that something happened between you and Bernard Allen while he was staying here. Maybe it was personal. You might think it's your business and it has nothing to do with his death, but I'm the one to be the judge of that. Do you understand?"

Katie just stared at him.

"You'd known him a long time, hadn't you?"

"Since he came to Leeds. We lived next door."

"You and Sam?"

"With his parents."

"What happened to your own parents?"

"They died when I was a little girl. My grandmother brought me up." Katie lowered her gaze down to her lap, wringing the yellow duster in her hands.

"Did you ever go out with Bernie Allen?"

She looked up sharply, and the blood ran to her cheeks. "What do you mean? I'm married."

"Well, something happened between you, that's clear enough. Why won't you tell me what it was?"

"I've told you," Katie said. "Nothing happened. We were friends, that's all." She went back to twisting the duster on her lap. "I'm thirsty."

Banks brought her a glass of water from the sink.

"Were you lovers, Katie?" he asked. "Did you sleep with Bernard Allen while he was staying here?"

"No!" Tears blurred Katie's clear brown eyes.

"All right." Banks held up his hand. "It's not important. I believe you." He didn't, but he often found it useful to pretend he believed a lie. It was always clear from the teller's obvious relief that it had been a lie. Afterwards it was easier to get at the information that really mattered. And he had a feeling she was hiding something else.

"But you spent some time together, didn't you? Time alone, like friends do?"

Katie nodded.

"And you must have talked. What did you talk about?"

Katie shrugged. "I don't know, just things. Life."

"That's a broad subject. Anything in particular?"

She was chewing on her bottom lip now, and Banks could sense that she was on the verge of talking. He would have to tread carefully to avoid scaring her off again.

"It might be important," he said. "If he was a friend of yours, surely you want his killer caught?"

Katie looked at him as if the idea was completely new to her. "Yes," she said. "Yes, of course I do."

"Will you help me, then?"

"He talked about Canada, his life in Toronto. What it was like there."

"What about it?"

"How wonderful and exciting it was."

It was like drawing a confession out of a naughty child. "Come on," Banks prompted her. "There was something special, wasn't there? You'd have no reason to hide any of this from me, and I know you're hiding something."

"He told me in confidence," she said. "I wasn't to tell anyone. Sam'll kill me if he finds out."

"Why?"

"He doesn't like me talking to people behind his back."

"Look, Katie. Bernard is dead. Somebody murdered him. You can't keep a secret for a dead man, can you?"

"Life doesn't end with death."

"Maybe not. But what he said might be important."

There was a long pause while Katie seemed to struggle with her conscience; each phase of the skirmish flashed across her flawless complexion. Finally, she said, "Annie was there. That's what he told me. Annie was in Toronto."

"Annie?"

"Yes. Anne Ralston. She was a friend of Bernie's from years ago. She disappeared when we had all that trouble here five years back."

"I've heard of her. What exactly did Bernard say?"

"Just that she was living in Toronto now. He'd heard from her about three years ago. She was in Vancouver then. They'd kept in touch, and now she'd moved."

"Did he say anything else about her?"

Katie looked at him blankly. "No. She just asked him not to go telling everyone in Swainshead that he'd seen her."

"This is what Bernard told you?"

"Yes."

"Why did he tell you, do you think, when Anne had told him not to tell anyone?"

"I . . . I . . . don't know," Katie stammered. "He trusted me. He was just talking about people leaving, finding a new life. He said she was happy there."

"Were you talking about wanting a new life for yourself?"

"I don't know what you mean."

Her words lacked conviction. Banks knew he was right. Katie had probably been telling Bernard Allen that she wanted to get away from Swainshead. Why she should want to leave he didn't know, but from what he'd seen and heard of Sam so far, she might have one good reason.

"Never mind," Banks said. "Did he say anything about coming home to stay?"

Katie seemed surprised. "No. Why should he? He had a wonderful new life out there."

"Did he tell you this on the morning he left or before?"

"Before. Just after he arrived."

"And you were the only one he told?"

"Yes."

"You're hesitating, Katie. Why?"

"I . . . I don't know. You're confusing me. You're making me nervous."

"Were you the only one he told?"

"As far as I know, yes."

"And who did you tell?"

"I didn't tell anyone."

"You're lying, Katie."

"I'm not. I—"

"Who did you tell? Sam?"

Katie pulled at the duster so hard it tore. "All right, yes! I told Sam. He's my husband. Wives aren't supposed to keep secrets from their husbands, are they?"

"What did Sam say?"

"Nothing. He just seemed surprised, that's all."

"Did he know Anne Ralston?"

"Not well. It was only about a year after we arrived that she disappeared. We met her with Bernie, and she was going out with Stephen, but Sam didn't know the Colliers as well then."

"Are you sure you told no-one else?"

"No-one," Katie whispered. "I swear it."

Banks believed her.

Sam Greenock, he reflected, was quite a one for passing on news, especially to his cronies in the White Rose, with whom he seemed intent on ingratiating himself. Socially, he was beneath them all. The Colliers were cocks of The Head, and Fletcher owned quite a bit of land. Stephen Collier, as Katie said, had been going out with Anne Ralston around the time she disappeared, which had also been coincidental with the murder of Raymond Addison, the London private-enquiry agent. Somewhere, somehow, Sam Greenock was involved in it all.

What if Sam had told Stephen that Bernard Allen had been in touch with Anne? And what if she was in a position to tell Allen something incriminating about Collier, something to do with the Addison murder? That would certainly give Stephen a motive. And if that was what had happened, to what extent was Sam Greenock an accessory? For the first time, there seemed to be the strong possibility of a link between the murders of Raymond Addison and Bernard Allen. This would certainly interest Superintendent Gristhorpe, who had withdrawn into his usual role because the two cases hadn't seemed connected.

"Thank you, Katie," Banks said, walking to the door. "You'd better keep our rooms for us. I think we'll be back this evening."

Katie nodded wearily. Pale, slumped in the chair, she looked used and abused like a discarded mistress.

III

"Anne Ralston?" Gristhorpe repeated in disbelief. "After all these years?"

He and Banks knelt beside the pile of stones. Usually, when they worked on the wall together they hardly spoke, but today there was pressing police business to deal with. Sandra had taken Brian and Tracy down into Lyndgarth after lunch to see a local craft exhibition, so they were alone with the twittering larks and the cheeky wagtails on the valley-side above the village.

"You can see how it changes things," Banks said.

"I can indeed—if it had anything to do with Bernard Allen's murder."

"It must have."

"We don't even know that Anne Ralston's disappearance was connected with Addison's killing, for a start."

"It's too much of a coincidence, surely?" Banks said. "A private detective is killed and a local woman disappears on practically the same day. If it happened in London, or even in Eastvale, I'd be inclined to think there was no link, but in a small village like Swainshead . . . ?"

"Aye," said Gristhorpe. "Put like that . . . But we need a lot more to go on. No, not that one—it's too flat." Gristhorpe brushed aside the stone Banks had picked up.

"Sorry." Banks searched the pile for something better. "I'm working on the assumption that Anne Ralston knew something about Addison's murder, right?"

"Right. I'll go along with that just for the sake of argument."

"If she did know something and disappeared without telling us, it means one of two things—either she was paid off, or she was scared for her own life."

Gristhorpe nodded. "Or she might have been protecting someone," he added.

"But then there'd be no need to run."

"Maybe she didn't trust herself to bear up under pressure. Who knows? Go on."

"For five years nobody hears any more of her, then suddenly Bernard Allen turns up and tells Katie Greenock he's been seeing the Ralston woman in Toronto. The next thing we know, Allen's dead before he can get back there. Now, Katie said that Bernard had been told not to spread it around about him knowing Anne. Was she protecting him, or herself? Or both? We don't know. What we do know, though, is that she didn't want her whereabouts known. Allen tells Katie, anyway, and she tells her husband. I think we can safely assume that Sam Greenock told everyone else. Allen must have become a threat to someone because he'd met up with Anne Ralston, who might have known something about Addison's murder. Stephen Collier was closely associated with her, so he looks like a good suspect, but there's no reason to concentrate on him alone. It could have been any of them—Fletcher, Nicholas, Sam Greenock, even Katie—they were all in Swainshead at the time both Addison and Allen were killed, and we've no idea what or who that private detective was after five years ago."

"What about opportunity?"

"Same thing. Everybody knew the route Allen was taking out of Swainshead. He'd talked all about it in the White Rose the night before. And most of them also knew how attached he was to that valley. The killer could easily have hidden among the trees up there and watched for him."

"All right," Gristhorpe said, placing a through-stone. "But what about their alibis?"

"We've only got Fletcher's word that he was at home. He could have got to the valley from the north without anyone knowing. He lives alone on the fell-side and there are no other houses nearby. As for the Colliers, Stephen says he was at the office and Nicholas at school. We haven't checked yet, but if Nicholas wasn't actually teaching a class and Stephen wasn't in a meeting, either of them could have slipped out for a while, or turned up later. It would have been easy for Nicholas, again approaching from the north, and Stephen could have got up from a half a mile past Rawley Force. It's not much of a climb, and there's plenty of cover to hide the car off the Helmthorpe road. I had a look on my way over here."

"The Greenocks?"

"Sam could have got there from the road too. He went to Eastvale for supplies, but the shopkeepers can't say exactly what time he got there. Carter's doesn't open till nine, anyway, and the chap in the newsagent's says Sam usually drops in at about eleven. That gives him plenty of time. He might have had another motive, too."

Gristhorpe raised his bushy eyebrows.

"The woman denies it, but I got a strong impression that something went on between Katie Greenock and Bernard Allen."

"And you think if Sam got wind of it . . . ?"

"Yes."

"What about Mrs Greenock?"

"She says she was home cleaning, but all the guests would have gone out by then. Nobody could confirm that she stayed in."

"Have you checked the Colliers' stories?"

"Sergeant Hatchley's doing it tomorrow morning. There's no-one at the factory on a Sunday."

"Well maybe we'll be a bit clearer when we get all that sorted out."

"I'm going back to Swainshead for another night. I'll want to talk to Stephen Collier again, for one."

Gristhorpe nodded. "Take it easy, though, Alan. I've already had an earful from the DCC about your last visit."

"He didn't waste any time, did he? Anyway, I could do with a bit of information on the Addison case and the Ralston woman's disappearance. How did the alibis check out?"

Gristhorpe put down the stone he was weighing in his hand and frowned. Banks lit a cigarette—at least smoking was allowed in the open, if not in the house. He looked at the sky and noticed it had clouded over very quickly. He could sniff rain in the air.

"Everyone said they were at home. We couldn't prove otherwise. It was a cold, dark February evening. We pushed Stephen Collier as hard as we dared, but he had a perfect alibi for the day of the girl's disappearance: he was in Carlisle at a business meeting."

"Was Walter Collier around in those days?"

"No. He was dead by then."

"What was he like?"

"He was quite an impressive man. Complex. He had a lot of power and influence in the dale, some of which has carried over to the sons, as you've already found out. Now, you know how I feel about privilege and such, but you had to respect Walter—he never really abused his position. He was proud, especially of the family and its achievements, but he managed to be kind and considerate without being condescending. He was also a regular church-goer, a religious man, but he liked the ladies and he could drink most villagers under the table. Don't ask me how he managed to square that with himself. It's rare for a Dales farmer, especially one from a family as long-established as the Colliers, to sell up. But Walter was a man of vision. He saw what things were coming to, so he shifted his interests to food processing and encouraged his sons to get good educations rather than strong muscles."

"What was he like as a father?"

"I'd imagine he was a bit of a tyrant," Gristhorpe answered, "though I can't say for certain. Used to being obeyed, getting his own way. They probably felt the back of his hand more than once."

Banks held out his palm and felt the first, hesitant drops of rain. "When Anne Ralston disappeared," he asked, "were there no signs at all of what might have happened to her?"

"Nothing. There were a few clothes missing, that's all."

"What about money, bank accounts?"

"She didn't have one. She got a wage-packet every two weeks from Collier Foods. What she did with the cash, I've no idea. Maybe she hid it under the mattress."

"But you didn't find any in the cottage?"

"Not a brass farthing."

"So she could have packed a few things, a bit of money, and simply run off?"

"Yes. We never found out what happened to her, until now." Gristhorpe stood up and scowled at the grey sky. A flock of rooks wheeled above the valley-side. "Better go inside."

As they walked round to the side door, they saw Sandra and the children come hurrying up the drive with their coats thrown over their heads. Banks waved to them.

"It would be very interesting to have a chat with Anne Ralston, wouldn't it?" he said.

Gristhorpe looked at him and narrowed his eyes. "Aye, it would. But I'm not sure the department would be able to justify the expense."

"Still . . ."

"I'll see what I can do," Gristhorpe said. Then Sandra, Brian and Tracy came racing into the house.

7

I

Katie finished her cleaning in a daze when Banks had gone, and she was so distracted she almost forgot to put the roast in on time. The Greenock Guest House always served a traditional Yorkshire Sunday dinner, both for guests and non-residents, at two o'clock. It was Sam's idea. Thank God he was in the pub, his usual Sunday lunch-time haunt, Katie thought. He'd be bending elbows with the wonderful Colliers.

Perhaps Sam needn't know what the policeman had made her tell. But the inspector would be sure to question him, she knew, and he would find out; he was bound to accuse her of betraying him.

With a start, she realized she was in room five, where the talk had taken place on the second morning of Bernie's stay. But it wasn't his words she thought of now. The rush of images almost overwhelmed her at first, but she forced herself to re-examine what had happened. Perhaps it hadn't been such a sin, after all? Of course it was, she told herself; it was a double sin, for she was a married woman. But it had happened, she couldn't deny that. The first time in all her married life.

That morning she had been cleaning the rooms as usual, when Bernie had come back to put on his walking-boots. The sky had brightened, he said, and he had decided to go for a good long walk after all. They'd talked for as much time as she dared take off from her chores, then he had sat on the bed while she washed the windows. All the time she had been aware of him watching her. Finally, when she felt his arms around her waist, she told him no. She had her back to him and he bent to kiss her neck where the wisps of blonde hair were swept up and tied while she worked. She struggled, but he held her tight and his hands found her breasts. She dropped the chamois and it fell in the bucket and splashed water on the carpet.

Why did she let him? She had always liked him, but why this? Why let him do what she hated most? She thought perhaps it was because he offered her a chance of escape, and that this was the price she would have to pay. He was gentler than Sam. His mouth moved over her shoulder and his hands slid down along her stomach and over her thighs. She didn't have the heart or the courage to put up a fight; men were so strong. Surely, she thought, it could do no harm as long as she didn't feel pleasure. She couldn't tell Sam. That would mean she'd have to lie, too. She would have to wash her mouth out with soap.

Then he said he loved her, that he'd always wanted her, as his hands unfastened her skirt. She struggled again, but less violently this time, and he backed her towards the bed. There, he finished undressing her. She was trembling, but so was he; even body language speaks ambiguously at times. She held onto the bedposts tightly as he bore down on her, and she knew he thought her groans were sounds of pleasure. Why did men want her like this? Why did they want to do these things to her?

He kissed her breasts and said he would take her back to Canada with him, and suddenly that seemed like the answer. She wanted to get away, she needed to. Swainshead and Sam were stifling her.

So she didn't struggle any more. Bernard talked of the vast prairie skies and of lakes as boundless as oceans as his hands caressed her still body. Yes, he would take her with him, he said, he had always wanted her. Urgently, he drew himself along the length of her body and entered her. She bit her tongue in loathing and self-disgust, and he looked into her eyes and smiled as she made little strangled cries that must have sounded like pleasure.

After, as they dressed, Katie had tried to hide the shame of her nakedness from his gaze. He had laughed and told her he found her modesty very appealing. She said he'd better go, that Sam would be back, and he reminded her about Canada.

"I'll send for you when I get back," he promised. "I'll find a place for us and I'll send for you. Anne's there, too. She wanted to get away, just like you. She's happy now."

"Yes," she had said, anxious to get rid of him. "I'll come with you." Then he had kissed her and left the room.

After that morning, they had hardly spoken to one another—mostly because Sam had been around or Katie had contrived to avoid Bernie—but he kept giving her meaningful glances whenever nobody was looking. She believed him. He would send for her.

Not any more. All for nothing. All gone. All she had left was the guilt. "As ye sow, so shall ye reap," her granny had always said. She had behaved wantonly, like that time she had swayed to the distant music. It didn't matter that she hadn't enjoyed it; now everything was a mess, Bernie was dead, and the police were all over the place. She was reaping what she had sown.

II

Stephen Collier sat in his spacious living-room reading a thick, leather-bound report when Banks and Hatchley called that evening. The French windows were open onto the patio and lawn, and the fountain played against a backdrop of dry-walled fell-side. A brief, heavy shower had cleansed the landscape and in the gentle evening light the grass was lush and green, the limestone outcrops bright as marble.

Stephen seemed surprised and annoyed at a second visit from the police so close on the heels of the first, but he quickly regained his composure and offered drinks.

"I'll have a Scotch, please," Banks said.

"Sergeant Hatchley?"

"Don't mind if I do, sir." Hatchley glanced towards Banks, who nodded his permission. After all, he had spoiled the sergeant's weekend. Hatchley took out his notebook and settled in a corner with his drink.

"What can I do for you this time?" Stephen asked. "Do you want to see my brother, too?"

"Not at the moment," Banks said. "I want to talk to you about Anne Ralston."

Collier frowned. "Anne Ralston? What about her? That was years ago."

"I'd like to know what happened."

"Aren't I entitled to know why?"

"Will you just bear with me for a while?"

"Very well."

"As far as I know," Banks began, "she disappeared the day after the private detective, Raymond Addison, was killed. Am I right?"

"I wouldn't know when he was killed," Stephen said. "Though I do remember Superintendent Gristhorpe saying something about a post-mortem report."

"But it was around that time she disappeared?"

"Yes."

"And she was an employee of Collier Foods?"

"Yes. Your superintendent already knows all this. Please get to the point, Chief Inspector." He tapped the book on his lap. "I have an important report to study for a meeting in the morning."

"I won't keep you long, sir," Banks said, "if you'll just answer my questions. Were you going out with Anne Ralston at the time of her disappearance?"

"Yes. You know I was. But I don't see—"

Banks held up his hand. "Let me finish, please. Can you think of any reason why should she disappear?"

"None."

"What do you think happened to her?"

Collier walked over to the cocktail cabinet and refreshed his drink. He offered Banks and Hatchley cigarettes from a box on the glass-topped coffee-table.

"I thought she might have taken off to see the world," he answered. "It was something she'd often talked about."

"Didn't it worry you?"

"Didn't what worry me?"

"Her disappearance."

"I must admit, in some of my darker moments I thought something might have happened to her—a wandering psychopath or something—especially with the Addison business. But I decided it wasn't so out of character for Anne to just up and go."

"Weren't you bothered that she never got in touch with you. Or did she?"

Collier smiled. "No, Chief Inspector, she didn't. And, yes, it was a bit of a blow to the ego at first. But I got used to it. It wasn't as if we were engaged or living together."

"I noticed you mentioned a moment ago that you linked her disappearance with the Addison killing—a wandering psychopath. Did it occur to you to link the two events in any other way?"

"What do you mean?"

"Could Anne Ralston have had something to do with Addison's visit to Swainshead? He was private-enquiry agent, after all."

"Yes, I know. But nobody here had any idea why he was in the area. If it was anything to do with Anne, she certainly kept quiet about it. Maybe he was just on holiday. I'm sure private eyes have holidays too."

"Would she have been likely to tell you?"

"I don't know. I don't imagine she told me everything about her life. Ours was a casual relationship. I'd never have expected her to bare her soul."

"Are you sure it wasn't more serious on her part?"

"Not at all. She'd been around."

"And you?"

Stephen smiled. "I wasn't new to the wily ways of the fair sex, no. Another drink?"

Hatchley passed his empty glass and Banks nodded. He lit a Silk Cut and looked out onto the lawn. Two sparrows were taking a bath in the fountain. There was plenty of room, but each defended its territory with an angry flapping of wings, splashing water all over the place. A shadow fell over the patio and Nicholas Collier popped his head around the French windows.

"Hello," he said, stepping into the room. "I thought I heard voices."

"If you don't mind sir . . ." Sergeant Hatchley stood up and blocked the entrance, a task for which he might have been specially designed.

Nicholas tilted his head back and looked down his long nose at Hatchley. "What's going on?"

"I'm just having a little chat with your brother," Banks said. "You're perfectly at liberty to stay, but I'd be obliged if you'd refrain from interrupting."

Nicholas raised his black eyebrows. He seemed to have forgotten his sulking, but he clearly wasn't used to being told what to do. For a moment, anger flashed in his eyes, then he simply nodded and sat by the windows.

"Look," Stephen said, frowning at his brother and coming back with the drinks. "Where on earth is all this leading? Anne Ralston is history now. I haven't seen or heard from her in five years. Quite frankly, it was embarrassing enough at the time having our relationship, such as it was, plastered all over the local papers. I wouldn't like to relive that."

"You mean you didn't know?" Banks said, sipping his Scotch.

"Didn't know what?"

"About Anne Ralston."

"Look here. If this is some kind of a game . . ."

Did he or didn't he? Banks couldn't be sure. Sam Greenock would know the answer to that—when he got home, and if he could be persuaded to talk.

"Anne's turned up again."

"But . . . where?"

"Bernard Allen knew where she was. He told the Greenocks. Surely Sam told you?"

"No. No, I'd no idea. How is she? What happened?"

"I don't know all the details," Banks said. "Just that she's alive and well and living in Canada. Are you sure nobody told you?"

"I've already said so, haven't I? This is a complete surprise to me. Though I was sure she'd turn up somewhere, some day." He went over and poured himself another drink; his hand was shaking. Banks glanced sideways at Nicholas, who sat impassively in his chair. There was no way of telling what he knew or didn't know.

Banks and Hatchley finished their drinks and stood up.

"I'm sorry it came as such a shock, Mr Collier," Banks said. "I just thought you ought to know."

"Yes, of course," Stephen said. "I'm very grateful to you. If you do hear anything else . . ."

"We'll let you know."

"There is just one thing," Stephen said, standing in the doorway. "What has this to do with Bernard Allen's death? Do you see any connection?"

"I don't know, Mr Collier," Banks said. "I really don't know. It does seem like a bit of a coincidence, though— Anne disappearing the day after Addison's killing, then turning up again, so to speak, around the time of Allen's murder. It makes you wonder, doesn't it?"

And they walked back over the bridge, where the three men stood like shadows in the soft light. On impulse, Banks sent Hatchley on ahead and stopped.

"Do you remember Anne Ralston?" he asked the gnarled spokesman.

As was his custom, the man spat in the fledgling River Swain before answering. "Aye. Alus in and out o'there." He nodded over at the Collier house.

"Have you seen her at all over the last few years?"

"Nay. She flitted."

"And she hasn't been back?"

He shook his head.

"Have you seen either Mr or Mrs Greenock go over to the Collier house this afternoon?"

"Aye," the man said. "Sam Greenock went over about three o'clock."

"To see Stephen or Nicholas?"

"It were Mr Stephen's door he knocked on."

"And did Stephen Collier answer it?"

The man scowled. "Aye, course he did."

"How long was Mr Greenock in there?"

"'Baht ten minutes."

"Thank you," Banks said, heading for the guest house. "Thank you very much."

He heard his reluctant informant hack into the beck again, then the murmur of their voices rose up behind him.

III

Katie Greenock hurried away when she saw Banks coming, but he couldn't help noticing that she moved with some difficulty.

"Katie!" he called, hurrying down the hall after her and grasping her elbow.

She spun around and faced him, one hand over her stomach. Her face was white and tense with suppressed pain. "What do you want?" she asked angrily. "Haven't you caused enough trouble?"

"There'll be a lot more before this business is over, Katie. I'm sorry, but there it is. You'll just have to learn to face the world. Anyway, that's not why I called you. What's wrong? You look ill."

"Nothing's wrong."

"You're white as a ghost. And what's wrong with your stomach? Does it ache?"

"What do you care?" she asked, breaking away.

"Is it Sam? Has he hurt you?"

"I don't know what you mean. I've got a tummy-ache, that's all."

"Did you tell Sam you'd told me about Anne?"

"I had to, didn't I? He knew there was something wrong. I'm not good at hiding things."

"And what did he do, beat it out of you?"

"I told you, I've just got a tummy-ache. Leave me alone, I feel sick."

"Where is he?"

She gestured with her head. "In back."

"Will you stay out here for a few minutes, Katie, while I talk to him?"

Katie nodded and edged into the dining-room.

Banks walked down the hall and knocked on the door that separated the Greenocks' part of the house from the rest. Sam let him in.

"Chief Inspector Banks," he said. "What a surprise. I hope nothing's wrong?"

"Has your wife told you we had a little talk earlier today?"

Greenock sat down. "Well, yes. She did right, too. I'm her husband."

"Why didn't you tell me about the Ralston woman earlier, as soon as we found out it was Bernard Allen feeding the maggots up in the hanging valley? This is the second time you've obstructed our investigation, and I'm having serious thoughts about taking you in."

"Now hold on a minute." Sam stood up again and puffed out his chest. "You can't come around here making accusations like that."

"She said she told you that Bernard had met up with Anne Ralston in Canada."

"So?"

"So you should have told me."

"You never asked."

Banks glared at him.

"I didn't think it was relevant. Dammit, Chief Inspector, the woman's been gone for five years."

"You know bloody well how important she is. She's important enough for you to dash out and tell Stephen Collier that Katie had told me what Bernie said. What's going on, Greenock? Just what is your involvement in all this?"

"Nothing," Sam said. "There's nothing going on. I don't know what you're talking about."

"But you did go over to Stephen Collier's this afternoon?"

"So what? We're friends. I dropped by for a drink."

"Did you also dash over a few weeks ago and tell him what

Bernie said about Anne Ralston turning up?"

"I didn't tell anyone."

"I think you did. I also think you told him this afternoon that your wife had let the cat out of the bag to me about Anne Ralston. Didn't you?"

"I did no such thing. And you can't prove it either."

"I will prove it," Banks said. "Believe me, I will. And when I do, your feet won't touch the ground."

"You don't scare me," Sam said.

Banks drew closer and Greenock backed towards the wall. They were both about the same size, though Sam was heavier.

"I don't?" Banks said. "Well I bloody well should. Where I come from, we don't always do things by the book. Do you know what I mean?" It was Hatchley's line, Banks knew, but it wasn't as if he was intimidating some scared kid. Sam was a villain, and Banks knew it. His dark eyes glittered with pent-up energy and Sam flinched as he felt his shoulder-blades make contact with the wall.

"Leave me alone!" Sam shouted. "I'll bloody report you, I will."

Banks sneered. "That's a laugh." Then he backed away. "Keep out of my sight, Greenock," he said. "If I want you, I'll know which rock to look under. And when I do, I'll have proof. And if I see or hear any more evidence—even the merest hint—that you've been hurting your wife again, I'll make you bloody sorry you were ever born."

IV

"Will there be anything else, Miss?" the waitress asked, clearing away the empty plate.

"What? Oh, yes. Yes. Another cup of tea, please." Katie Greenock had to pull herself back from a very long way. It would be her third cup, but why not? Let it simply be another part of her little rebellion.

She sat at a table with a red-checked cloth—very clean, she noticed—by the window of the Golden Grill in Eastvale.

The narrow street outside was busy with pedestrians, even in the thin drizzle, and almost directly opposite her was the whitewashed building with the black beams and the incongruous white-on-blue sign over the entrance: POLICE.

It was early Monday afternoon, and she didn't know what she was doing in Eastvale. Already she was beginning to feel guilty. It was simply a minor gesture, she tried to convince herself, but her conscience invested it with the magnitude of Satan's revolt.

That morning, at about eleven o'clock, she had felt so claustrophobic cleaning the rooms that she just had to get out—not only out of the house, but out of Swainshead itself for a while. Walking aimlessly down the street, she had met Beryl Vickers, a neighbour she occasionally talked gardening with, and accepted her offer of a ride into Eastvale for a morning's shopping. Beryl was visiting her sister there, so Katie was left free to wander by herself for a few hours. After buying some lamb chops and broccoli at the indoor market for that evening's dinner, she had found the Golden Grill and decided to rest her feet.

She had only been sitting there for fifteen minutes when she saw three men come out of the pub next door and hurry through the rain back into the police station. Two of them she recognized—the lean, dark inspector and his fair, heavy sergeant—but the young athletic-looking one with the droopy moustache and the curious loping walk was new to her. For a moment, she thought they were sure to glance over their shoulders and see her through the window, so she covered the side of her face with her hand. They didn't even look.

As soon as she saw the inspector, she felt again the bruises that Sam had inflicted on her the previous afternoon. She knew it wasn't the policeman's fault—in fact, he seemed like a kind man—but she couldn't help the association any more than she could help feeling one between room five and what she had let Bernie do to her.

"What's wrong with you?" Sam had asked when he came home.

Katie had tried to hide her red-rimmed eyes from him, but

he grasped her chin between his thumb and forefinger and asked her again. That was when she told him the police had been back and the inspector had interrogated her so hard she couldn't hide it from him any more.

Sam had hit the roof.

"But it's not that important," Katie protested. "It can't be!"

"That's not for you to say," Sam argued. He threw up his hands. "You stupid bloody bitch, have you any idea what trouble you might have caused?"

Though she was scared, Katie still felt defiant. "What do you mean, trouble?" she asked, her lower lip trembling. "Trouble for who?"

"For everyone, that's for who."

"For your precious Colliers, I'll bet." As she said it, her image was of Nicholas, not Stephen.

And that was when Sam hit her the first time, a short sharp blow to the stomach. She doubled up in pain, and when she was able to stand again he thumped her left breast. That hurt even more. She collapsed on the sofa and Sam stood over her. His face was red and he was breathing funny, in short gasps that seemed to catch in his throat. "If we make something of ourselves in this place," he said, "it won't be any thanks to you."

He didn't hit her any more. He knew when enough was enough. But later that night, in bed, the same cruel hands grasped the same wounded breast. He pulled her roughly to him, and there was nothing she could do about it. Katie shuddered, trying to shake off the memory.

"Will that be all?" the waitress asked, standing over her again.

"Oh, yes. Yes, thank you," Katie said, paying the bill. Awkwardly, aware of the ache in her breast and the Black Forest gâteau sitting uneasily in her sore stomach, she made her way out into the street. She had one more hour of freedom to wander in the rain before meeting Beryl near the bus station at two-thirty. Then she would have to go home and face the music.

V

After a pub lunch in the Queen's Arms and a chat with Hatchley and Richmond about the case, Banks was no further ahead. Back in his office, he sat down, sent for some coffee, and put his feet up on the desk to think things out. When PC Craig arrived with the coffee—looking very put out, no doubt because Susan Gay had coerced him into carrying it up—Banks lit a Silk Cut and went over what he'd got.

Richmond had discovered that Les Haines, Bernie Allen's brother-in-law, had done a brief stretch in Armley Jail for receiving stolen goods (i.e. two boxes of Sony E-120 video cassette tapes). It was his second offence, hot on the heels of an assault charge against a man in the alley outside a Leeds bier-keller. But Haines had been at work on the day of Allen's murder, so he would have had no opportunity to get to Swainshead and back, even if there had been some obscure family motive. Besides, as Banks well knew, just because a man has a record as a petty thief, it doesn't make him a murderer. Esther had been home with the kids, as usual, and Banks could hardly visualize her trailing them up to the hanging valley and knocking off her brother.

Most interesting of all were the Colliers' alibis, or lack of them. Nicholas never taught classes on Friday mornings, but he usually went in anyway and used the time for paperwork. On the Friday in question, however, the headmaster's administrative assistant remembered seeing him arrive late—at around eleven o'clock. This was nothing unusual—it had happened often enough before—but it did leave him without a valid alibi.

Stephen Collier, it turned out, had no meetings scheduled for that day, again quite normal in itself, and nobody could remember whether he had been in or not. Work days, the world-weary secretary had explained to Sergeant Hatchley, are so much the same that most office workers have difficulty remembering one from another. Mr Collier was often off the premises anyway, and the people who actually ran the business never saw much of him.

PC Weaver from Helmthorpe, who had been questioning people in Swainshead that morning, reported that nobody remembered seeing Bernard Allen out there on the morning in question, let alone noticed anyone follow him.

At about two o'clock, Richmond popped his head around the door. He'd been using the computer to check with various business agencies and immigration offices, but so far he'd found no-one in Swainshead with Canadian connections. Except for Stephen Collier, who dealt with a Montreal-based food-products corporation.

"What's a food product, do you think?" Banks asked Richmond.

"I wouldn't know, sir. Something that's not real food, I'd imagine."

"And I thought he was trading Wensleydale cheese for maple syrup. That reminds me: what time is it in Toronto?"

Richmond looked at his watch. "It'll be about nine in the morning."

"I'd better phone the Mounties."

"Er ... they won't be Mounties, sir. Not in Toronto." Richmond stroked his moustache.

"Oh? What will they be?"

"The Toronto Metropolitan Police, sir. The RCMP's federal. These days they mostly do undercover work and police the more remote areas."

Banks grinned. "Well, you learn something new every day."

When Richmond had left, he lit a cigarette and picked up the phone. There was a lot of messing about with the switchboard, but after a few minutes of clicks and whirrs, the phone started ringing at the other end. It wasn't the harsh and insistent sound of an English telephone, though; the rings were longer, as were the pauses between them.

When someone finally answered, it took Banks a while to explain who he was and what he wanted. After a few more clicks, he finally got through to the right man.

"Chief Inspector Banks? Staff Sergeant Gregson here. And how's the old country?"

"Fine," said Banks, a little perplexed by the question.

"My father was a Brit," Gregson went on. "Came from Derbyshire." He pronounced the "e" as in "clergy," and "shire" came out as "sheer." "Do you know it?" he asked.

"Oh, yes. It's just down the road."

"Small country."

"Right."

Gregson cleared his throat and Banks could hear papers rustling three thousand miles away. "I can't say we've got any good news for you," the Canadian said. "We've had a look around Allen's apartment, but we didn't find anything unusual."

"Was there an address book?"

"Address book ... let me see ..." More paper rustled. "No. No address book. No diary."

"Damn. He must have taken them with him."

"Makes sense, doesn't it? If he was going on vacation he'd be sure to want to send pretty postcards to all his buddies back home."

"What about his friends? Have you seen any of them?"

"We talked to his colleagues at work. There's not many of them around. College finishes in early May, so teachers are pretty thin on the ground at this time of year. Nice work if you can get it, eh? Now they're all off swimming in the lake and sunning themselves on the deck up at their fancy summer cottages in Muskoka."

"Is that like a villa in Majorca?"

"Huh?"

"Never mind. What did they have to say?"

"Said he was a bit aloof, stand-offish. Course, a lot of Brits over here are like that. They think Canada's still part of the Empire, so they come on like someone out of 'The Jewel in the Crown.'"

"Did you find his ex-wife?"

"Yup. She's been in Calgary for the past six months, so you can count her out."

"Apparently, there was a lover," Banks told him. "Someone at the college. That's why they got divorced."

"Have you got a name?"

"Sorry."

Gregson sighed. "I'd like to help you, Chief Inspector, I really would," he said. "But we can't spare the men to go tracking down some guy who ran off with Allen's wife. We just don't have the manpower."

"No, of course not."

"Besides, people don't usually steal a man's wife and then kill him."

"They might if he was causing them problems. But you're right, it's not likely. Did he have any girlfriends?"

"As I said, his colleagues thought he was a bit stuck-up. One of them even thought he was gay, but I wouldn't pay much mind to that. Sometimes, with their accents and mannerisms and all, Brits do seem a bit that way to us North Americans."

"Yes," Banks said, gritting his teeth. "I think that just about covers it all. I can see now why they say you always get your man." And he hung up. Nothing. Still nothing. He obviously couldn't expect any help from across the Atlantic.

Still feeling a residue of irrational anger at Gregson's sarcasm, he stalked over to the window and lit a cigarette. The drizzle had turned into steady rain now and the square below was bright with open umbrellas. As he gazed down on the scene, one woman caught his eye. She walked in a daze, as if she wasn't sure where she was heading. She looked soaked to the skin, too; her hair was plastered to her head and the thin white blouse she wore was moulded to her form so that the outline of her brassiere stood out in clear relief. It took Banks a few moments to recognize Katie Greenock.

He grabbed his raincoat and made a move to go down and make sure she was all right, but when he looked out for her one last time, she was nowhere in sight. She had disappeared like a phantom. There was no sense in searching the town for her just because she was walking in the rain without an umbrella. Still, he was strangely disturbed by the vision. It worried him. For the rest of the wet afternoon he felt haunted by that slight and sensuous figure staring into an inner distance, walking in the rain.

Part Two:

THE
THOUSAND-
DOLLAR CURE

8

I

The powerful jet engines roared and Banks felt himself pushed back in his seat. It was his first time in a Jumbo. The plane lumbered along the runway at Manchester International Airport, fixtures and fittings shaking and rattling, as if defying anyone to believe that a machine of such bulk could fly. But it did. Soon, Lancashire was a checkerboard of wet fields, then it was lost completely under the clouds. The NO SMOKING sign went off and Banks lit up.

In a few moments, the blue-uniformed flight-attendant with her shocking pink lipstick and impossibly white teeth— the same one who had managed to put such drama into the routine demonstration of the use of the life-jacket—came around with more boiled sweets and personal headphones in plastic bags. Banks took a set, as he knew there would be a film later on, but he gave the designer music a miss and took out his own Walkman. Soon the plane was over Ireland, an occasional flash of green between the clouds, the Beatles were singing "Dear Prudence," and all was well with the world.

Banks ordered Scotch on the rocks when the trolley came around and relaxed with his miniature Johnny Walker Red. Closing his eyes, he settled back to reconsider the events that had led to his present unnatural position—about 35,000 feet above the Atlantic Ocean, hurtling at a speed of roughly 600 miles an hour towards a strange continent.

It was Saturday, July 3, almost a month since the Bernard Allen case had stalled. Banks had visited Swainshead once or twice and found things relatively quiet. Stephen and Nicholas Collier had remained polite in their arrogant way; Sam Greenock had been surly, as usual; Katie Greenock still seemed troubled and distracted; and John Fletcher had expressed passing interest in the progress of the case.

The problem was that there really wasn't a case any more. Enquiries had turned up neither new witnesses nor motives. A number of people had the opportunity to kill Bernard Allen, but no-one had a clear reason. As long as the suspects stuck to their stories, it didn't matter whether they were lying or telling the truth; there was no solid evidence to break the case. That was why it was vital for Banks to find Anne Ralston—she was the link between the Addison and Allen murders—and he had convinced Gristhorpe he could do it in a week.

"How?" the superintendent had asked. "Toronto's a strange city to you. A big one, too."

"Where would you head if you were an Englishman living abroad?"

Gristhorpe rubbed his chin. "I'd seek out the expatriate community, I suppose. The 'club.' I'd want to be among my own."

"Right. So, given we're not dealing with the gentry, I'd expect Allen to hang around the English-style pubs. Every big city has them. His brother-in-law, Les Haines, told me Allen liked his ale and had found a pub where he could get imported British beer. There can't be all that many of them in Toronto.

"But it's Anne Ralston we're looking for, remember that."

"I know. I'm just assuming that if Allen was a bit standoffish with his mates at work, he had a crowd of fellow *émigrés* he hung around with in his spare time. The odds are they'd meet up in a pub and stand at the bar quaffing pints. They might know the Ralston woman."

"So you want to go on a pub-crawl of Toronto?"

"Looks like it, doesn't it?"

"Better not tell Jim Hatchley or you'll get nowt out of him for a month or more. Why can't you get the Toronto police to find her?"

"For a start, I got the impression on the phone that they didn't have time or didn't give a damn, or both. And anyway, they wouldn't know how to question her, what to ask. Someone would have to brief them on two murder investigations, the sociology of the Yorkshire village, the history of—"

Gristhorpe held up his hand. "All right, all right, I get the point."

"And I think they'd scare her off, too," Banks added. "She was nervous enough about what she knew to warn Allen not to spread it around, so if she thinks the police are after her, the odds are she'll scarper."

"Have you considered that she might not be using her own name?"

"Yes. But I've got her photograph from our missing person files—it's a bit old, but it's all we've got—and I think I know where to look. Being English myself gives me an advantage in that kind of environment, too. Do you think it makes sense?"

"It's all a bit iffy, but yes, yes I do, on the whole. If you can track down Allen's drinking companions, there's a good chance he'll have told them about Anne Ralston. She might even drop in at his local herself from time to time, if she's the kind that likes to be among her own."

"So you'll see what you can do about getting me over there?"

Gristhorpe nodded. "Aye. I'll see what I can do."

About a week later, on a Thursday morning, the superintendent had asked Banks to drop by his office. Banks stubbed out his cigarette and carried his full coffee mug carefully along the corridor. As usual, Gristhorpe's door was slightly ajar. Banks nudged it open with his shoulder and entered the cosy, book-lined room. He took his usual seat and put his coffee on the desk in front of him.

Gristhorpe pushed a long envelope over the blotter.

"You've done it?"

"Open it."

Inside was a return ticket on a charter flight from Manchester to Toronto.

"There's an important international conference on policing the inner city in London, Ontario. I thought you ought to go."

"But this ticket's for Toronto."

"Aye, well, there isn't an international airport in London."

"And Eastvale doesn't have an inner city."

Gristhorpe scratched his hooked nose. "We might have, one day. We did have a riot a few months ago, didn't we? It pays to be prepared."

"Will you be expecting a report?"

"Oh, a brief verbal account will do."

Banks grinned.

"There's one catch, though."

"Oh?"

"Money. All I could scrounge was the ticket and a bit of loose change for meals. You'll have to supply most of your own pocket money."

"That's all right. I'm not likely to be spending a fortune. What about accommodation, though?"

"You'll be staying with my nephew—at least, you can stay in his apartment. He's off to Banff or some such place for the summer. Anyway, I've been in touch and he says he'll be happy to meet you at the airport. I described you to him, so just stand around and look lost. He's rather a lanky lad, as I remember. His hair's a bit too long and he wears those silly little glasses—granny-glasses, I think they're called. He's a nice enough lad—graduate student, organic chemistry or some such thing. He says he lives downtown, whatever that means. You told me a week, Alan. I'm depending on you."

"I'll do my best," Banks said, pocketing the ticket.

"Find Anne Ralston and discover what she knows. I don't care how you do it, outside of torture. And for Christ's sake keep away from the local police. They wouldn't appreciate your trespassing on their patch. You're a tourist, remember that."

"I've been wondering why you're sending me," Banks said. "You're very much concerned with this case yourself, especially the connection with the Addison murder. Why don't *you* go?"

"I would," Gristhorpe said slowly. "Believe me, I would." He looked sideways towards the open window. "I did my National Service in the RAF. I'd always hero-worshipped fighter pilots in the war and I suppose, in my folly, I wanted to be just like them. First time up one of the engines caught fire. If the pilot hadn't been so damn good we'd have both been dead. Even so . . . I've never fancied the idea since."

"I can't say I blame you," Banks said. "I'll find her, don't worry. At least I've an idea where to look."

And that was that. Sandra and the children were excited and, of course, disappointed that they couldn't go with him. Sergeant Hatchley acted as if Banks had been given a free holiday in an exotic place. And now here he was, high above the Atlantic Ocean, the pink lips and white teeth leaning over him with a tray of cling-wrapped food.

Banks took off his headphones and arranged the tray in front of him. The main course appeared to be a small, shrivelled chicken leg with pale, wrinkled skin, accompanied by tiny potatoes and carrots covered in gravy. On further inspection, Banks discovered that one-half of the meal was piping hot and the other still frozen solid. He called the attendant, who apologized profusely and took it away. When she delivered it again, the frozen side was warm and the other overcooked. Banks took a few mouthfuls and gave up in disgust. He also felt no inclination to investigate the mound of jelly-like substance with a swirl of cream on its top, or the limp, wet lettuce leaves that passed for a salad. Instead, he turned to his cheese and crackers which, being wrapped in cellophane, were at least fresh, and washed them down with a small plastic bottle of harsh red wine.

Feeling the onset of heartburn, Banks declined the offer of coffee and lit a cigarette. After the trays had been cleared, more drinks came. They really were very generous, Banks thought, and wondered what havoc a plane full of drunks might wreak—especially if the booze ran out. But it didn't.

He was kept well supplied with Johnny Walker Red—a kind of sedation, he guessed, insurance against restless and troublesome passengers—and soon people were asked to pull down their blinds against the blazing sunlight in preparation for the movie. This turned out to be a dreadful cops-and-robbers affair full of car chases and shoot-outs in shopping precincts. After about ten minutes, Banks put his headset aside, closed his eyes and went over in his mind the questions he wanted to ask Anne Ralston. The jet engines were humming, the Scotch warmed his veins, and soon he fell into a deep sleep. The last thing he remembered was the crackly voice of the pilot saying they were soon going to reach the tip of Newfoundland and would then fly along the St Lawrence River.

II

While Banks was asleep somewhere over Quebec City, Detective Superintendent Gristhorpe sat hunched over a pint of Theakston's bitter and a veal-and-egg pie in the Queen's Arms, waiting for Sergeant Hatchley.

Frowning, he looked at his watch. He'd told Hatchley to arrive no later than seven-thirty. He glanced out of the window at the market square, but saw no sign of the sergeant. It was still raining. That very morning the clouds had closed in again, draining the valley-sides of their lush greens and flattening the majestic perspective of fells and moors.

At last Hatchley burst in and looked anxiously around for the superintendent. His hair was slicked down by the rain, emphasizing the bullet shape of his head, and the shoulders of his beige trench coat were splotched dark with wet patches.

"Sorry, sir," he apologized, sitting opposite Gristhorpe. "The damn weather's slowing traffic down all along the dale."

Gristhorpe could smell the beer on his breath and guessed that he'd probably stopped for a quick one in Helmthorpe on his way—or maybe he had even made a minor diversion to the Black Sheep in Relton, where the landlord brewed his own prize-winning beer on the premises. He said nothing, though. Without Banks around, Hatchley and Richmond were all he had, and he had no wish to alienate the sergeant before putting his plan into action.

Gristhorpe accepted Hatchley's offer of another pint and leaned back in his seat to avoid the drift of smoke when the sergeant lit a cigarette.

"Did you tell them?" Gristhorpe asked.

"Aye, sir. Found them all in the White Rose."

"I hope you weren't too obvious."

Hatchley looked offended. "No, sir. I did it just like you said. When Freddie Metcalfe started probing and prodding about why I was there, I just told him it was a few loose ends I had to tie up, that's all."

"And then?"

"Ah, well. Then, sir, I got myself invited over to the table. It was all very casual, like, chatting about the cricket and the local markets as if we was old mates. Then Sam Greenock asked me where my boss was."

"What did you say?"

"Just what you told me, sir. I said he'd gone off to Toronto to talk to Anne Ralston."

"And?"

"And what, sir?"

"What happened next, man? How did they react?"

Hatchley took a long pull at his beer and wiped his lips with the back of his hairy hand. "Oh, they just looked at one another and raised their eyebrows a bit."

"Can you be a bit more specific, Sergeant? What did Sam Greenock say?"

"He didn't really say anything. Seemed excited to hear the news. I got the impression it made him a bit angry. And Stephen Collier went distinctly a bit pale. That poncy brother of his just looked down his nose like I was something the cat dragged in."

"Who else was there?"

"Only John Fletcher."

"Did he react in any way?"

Hatchley scratched his ear. "I'd say he got a bit tight-lipped. You wouldn't really say he reacted, but it was as if it rang a bell somewhere and sent him off in his own world. More puzzled and worried than anything else."

Gristhorpe thought over the information and filed it away in his mind. "Good work, Sergeant," he said finally. "You did well."

Hatchley nodded and started casually rocking his empty pint glass on the table. "What now, sir?" he asked.

"We keep an eye on them. Tomorrow I'm going to send DC Richmond to stay at the Greenock Guest House for a few days. I don't think his face is well known in Swainshead." Gristhorpe turned up his nose and leaned forward to grind out Hatchley's cigarette butt, which still smouldered in the ashtray. "We keep an eye on them," he repeated. "And we watch very carefully for one of them to make a slip or try and make a run for it. All right, Sergeant. You don't have to break the bloody glass on the table. I know it's my round. Same again?"

III

Somewhere, with maddening metronomic regularity, a bell was ringing. Banks rubbed his eyes and saw the seat-belt sign was lit up. The NO SMOKING sign was still out, so he lit a cigarette immediately to clear his head. Looking out of the window, he saw a vast urban area below. It was too far down to distinguish details, but he could make out the grid system of roads and fancied he could see cars flash in the sun.

The attendant said something over the PA system about a final descent, and passengers were then asked to extinguish their cigarettes. Banks's ears felt funny. He swallowed and yawned to clear them, and the noise of the plane roared in again. All the way down he had to keep repeating the process every few seconds.

The plane banked to the left and now individual buildings and moving vehicles stood out quite clearly. After a long turn, a great expanse of water came into sight on the right and a cluster of tall buildings appeared on the waterside. The plane was dropping quickly now, and within moments it touched the runway smoothly. The loud retro-jets kicked in. They felt like ropes tied to the back of the plane, dragging it to a halt. Several nervous passengers applauded.

After some delay, the doors slid open and the slow line of people left the aircraft, running a gauntlet of fixed smiles from the attendants. Banks negotiated the stairs and corridors, then found himself in a long queue at Immigration. After that, there was another wait until the baggage came around on the carousel. Clutching his small suitcase, duty-free Scotch and cigarettes, he walked past the customs officers, who paid him no mind, and out into the throng of people waiting to welcome friends and relatives. As Gristhorpe suggested, he stood to one side and looked lost. It was easy.

Soon he noticed an Adam's apple the size of a tennis ball stuck in a long skinny neck below a head covered with long brown hair making its way through the crowd. As the head also wore a pair of ridiculously old-fashioned granny-glasses, Banks risked a wave of recognition.

"Gerry Webb," the man said, shaking hands. "Are you Chief Inspector Banks?"

"Yes. Just call me Alan. I'm not here officially."

"I'll bet," Gerry said. "Come on, let's get out of here."

They pushed their way through the crowds of relatives embracing long-lost children or parents, and took a lift to the multi-storey car-park.

"This is it," Gerry said, pointing proudly to a saffron Volkswagen bug. "I call her 'Sneezy' because she's a bit of a dwarf compared to most of the cars here, and she makes a funny noise when I try to start her in mornings, especially during winter. Still, she gets me around." He patted Sneezy on the bonnet and opened the boot at the front. Case and duty-free securely stored, Banks got in the passenger door after a false start on the left.

"It always happens when people visit from England," Gerry said, laughing. "Without fail. Just wait until you try and cross the road."

The first things Banks noticed as Gerry drove out onto the expressway were the huge cars and the stifling heat. It was like trying to breathe at the bottom of a warm bath. In no time, his shirt was stuck to his skin. He took off his jacket and tossed it on the back seat. Even the draught through the open window was hot and wet.

"You've come in the middle of a heat wave, I'm afraid," Gerry explained. "It's been between thirty-three and thirty-six degrees for the past three days now. Above ninety percent humidity, too."

"What's a hundred like?"

"Funny, that," Gerry said. "We never get a hundred. Not even during a thunderstorm. Summer can be a real bitch here. Toronto's a city of extremes as far as climate is concerned. In winter it's bloody cold, real brass-monkey weather, and in summer it's so hot and humid it's unbearable, as you can tell. Pollution count goes way up, too."

"What about spring?"

"We don't have one. Just a lot of rain and then the sun. Fall's the best. September, October. Warmish days, cool evenings. Beautiful." He glanced sideways at Banks. "I suppose you were expecting icicles and snowmen?"

"Not exactly. But I didn't expect the heat to be this bad."

"You should see the Americans," Gerry said. "I lived in Windsor for a while when I was doing my MSc, and I worked for customs during summer. They'd come over the border from the Detroit suburbs in the middle of July with skis on top of their cars and fur coats on the back seats. What a laugh that was. Americans know bugger all about Canada."

"I can't say I know much, myself," Banks admitted.

"Worry not. Keep your eyes and ears open and all will be revealed." Gerry had an odd accent, part Yorkshire and part North American, with a mixed vocabulary to match.

They swung eastwards around a bay. For a moment, Banks thought they were on the wrong side of the road. He tensed and the adrenalin prickled in his veins. Then, again, he realized he was in Canada.

On the right was Lake Ontario, a ruffled blue sheet with

millions of diamonds dancing on it. The white triangular sails of yachts leaned at sharp angles. There seemed to be at least a cooler breeze coming from the water and Banks envied the idle rich who could spend their days sailing like that.

"Those are the Islands over there," Gerry said, pointing towards a low hazy blur of green. "They're just a long sandbar really, but everyone calls them islands. People live on the far ones, Ward's and Algonquin, but the politicians want to chuck them off and make a heliport or a mini golf-course."

"That sounds typical," Banks said, recalling the various schemes for developing adventure playgrounds and safari parks in the Dales.

"A lot of trouble over it," Gerry said. "At first, the islanders even got themselves a Home Guard organized— hard hats, the lot. They were prepared to fight off an invasion."

"What happened?"

"It's still going on really. Oh, various bright sparks come up with ideas for long-term leases and what-not, but there's always trouble brewing. It's jealousy, I think. Most of the people who live there now are academics or artists and a lot of people stuck in the city envy them their lives. They think only the filthy rich ought to be able to afford such a pleasant environment."

"What about you?"

"I don't envy anyone who survives winter after winter out there in not much more than a wooden shack. Look." He pointed ahead.

In front of them a cluster of tall buildings shimmered in the heat like a dot-matrix block-graph. A few were black, others white, and some even reflected the deep gold of the sun. Close to the lake, dominating them all, was a tapering tower with a bulbous head just below its long needle-point summit. It was a phallic symbol of such Olympian proportions that it made the London Post Office Tower look like it had a serious sexual dysfunction.

"The CN Tower," Gerry said. "Toronto's pride and joy.

Tallest free-standing structure in the world—or at least it will
be until the Japanese build a bigger one. See those elevators
going up the outside?"

Banks did. The mere thought of being in one made him
feel dizzy. He wasn't afraid of heights up to a certain point,
but he'd never felt like risking a meal in a revolving
restaurant at the top of a tower.

"What's it for?" he asked.

"Well may you ask. For show really."

"What's at the top?"

"A restaurant, what else? And a disco, of course. This is
the height of western civilization. A feat on a par with the
great pyramids and Chartres Cathedral."

"A disco?"

"Yes. Honest. Oh, I suppose I'm being flippant. They do
use the place as a radio- and TV-signal transmitter, but it's
basically just one of man's muscle-flexing exercises. This is
downtown."

The expressway, on a kind of elevated ramp, rolled past
the backs of warehouses and billboards. Because the buildings were so close, the speed the car was travelling at was
exaggerated and Banks felt as if he was on a roller coaster.

Finally, Gerry branched off, drove through an industrial
wasteland of dirty old factories with external plumbing, then
turned onto a busy street. Most of the buildings seemed quite
old and run-down, and Banks soon noticed that nearly all
the shop-signs were in Chinese. Roast ducks hung by their
feet in shop windows and teeming stalls of colourful fruit and
vegetables blocked the pavements in front of grocery stores.
One shop displayed a handwritten sign offering a mysterious
combination of "LIVE CRABS & VIDEOS." The street was
bustling with people, mostly Chinese, pushing and shoving
to get to the best deals, picking up and examining wares. The
rich smell of food gone bad in the heat, mingled with the
aroma of exotic spices, drifted into the car along with the
suffocating air. A red- and cream-tram rattled along its track
beside them.

"Chinatown East," Gerry said. "Not far to go now."

He continued up the street past a prison and a hospital. To

the left was a broad green valley. Beside the road, it sloped like a huge lawn down to the broad bottom, where a busy expressway ran beside the brown river. Above the trees on the far side, the downtown towers shimmered, greyish blurs in the heat-haze. Gerry turned right into a tree-lined street and pulled up in the driveway of a small brick house with a green-and-white porch.

"Home," he announced. "I've got the bottom floor and there's a young couple upstairs. They're generally pretty quiet, so I wouldn't worry too much about noise." He put his key in the lock and opened the door. "Come on in. I'm dying for a cold beer."

The place was small and sparsely furnished—apparently with cast-offs bought from second-hand shops—but it was clean and comfortable. Books stuffed every possible shelf and cavity. The Gristhorpe clan certainly seemed to be great readers, Banks thought.

Gerry led him into the small kitchen and took two cans of Budweiser from the fridge. Banks pulled the tab and poured the iced, slightly malty beer down his throat. When Gerry tipped back his can to drink, his Adam's apple bobbed wildly.

"That's better," he said, wiping his lips. "I'm sorry it's so hot in here, too, but I can't afford an air-conditioner. Actually, I've lived in worse places. There's a good through-draft, and it does cool down a bit at night."

"What's this area of town called?" Banks asked.

"Riverdale. It's gone very yuppie in the past few years. Property values have shot up like crazy. You'll see the main drag, the Danforth, if you walk or take a streetcar up to the corner. It used to be all Greek cafés, restaurants and twenty-four-hour fruit-and-vegetable stores. Now it's all health foods, late-night bookshops, and bistros with long-stemmed wineglasses and coral pink table-cloths. All right if you like that kind of thing, I suppose."

"And if you don't?"

"There's a few unpretentious places left. You get some good blues at the Black Swan on Saturday afternoons. And then there's Quinn's, not a bad pub. Some of the old Greek places are still around, but I can't say I've ever been fond of Greek food myself—it's all greasy lamb, eggplant and sticky desserts as far as I'm concerned."

They sat down on the sofa, an overstuffed, maroon fifties monstrosity with arms like wings, and finished their beers.

"Your uncle said you had to go to a conference some-where," Banks said. "I hope I'm not driving you out?"

"Not at all. Actually, the conference isn't so important, but Banff is a great place—right on the edge of the Rockies—so I'll get a bit of hiking and partying done too."

"How are you getting there?"

"Sneezy."

"How far is it?"

"A couple of thousand miles. But you get used to distances like that here. Sneezy's done it before. She quite likes long journeys. I'll take my tent and camp out on the way. If you need a car . . ."

Banks shook his head. "No. No, I wouldn't dare drive on the wrong side of the road. What's the public transport like?"

"Very good. There's a subway, buses, and the streetcars you've seen. We don't call them trams here."

"I was surprised," Banks said. "I haven't been on one of them since I was a kid."

"Well now's your chance to make up for lost time. I use them a lot myself to get around the city. Often it's not worth the bother of parking in town, and the cops can be pretty sticky about drinking and driving. Oops, sorry."

Banks laughed.

"Anyway," Gerry went on, delving into a drawer and bringing out a couple of maps. "This is the city—easy to find your way about as it's mostly an east-west, north-south grid system. And here's the transit map. It's not as complicated as the London Underground, so you shouldn't have much trouble."

And Gerry went on giving information about subway tokens and free transfers from one mode of transport to another. But after the journey and in the sweltering heat, Banks felt his eyes closing. He could do nothing about it.

"Here," Gerry said, "I'm boring you to death. I don't suppose you're taking any of this in."

"Not much."

"Do you want to go to bed?"

"I wouldn't mind a nap."

Gerry showed him the bedroom.

"Isn't this your room?" Banks asked.

"It's okay. I'll bed down on the couch tonight."

"I can do that."

"Not necessary. I'm off early in the morning anyway. This'll be your room for the next week."

Too tired to argue more and, frankly, grateful for a bed, Banks undressed, sank onto the mattress and fell asleep within seconds.

When he woke he was disoriented at finding himself in an unfamiliar bed. It took him a few moments to remember where he was. It was hot and dark, and the sheets felt moist with sweat. Hearing sounds in the front room, Banks rubbed his eyes, pulled on his pants and walked through. He found Gerry stuffing clothes into a huge backpack. For a moment, it made him think of Bernard Allen.

"Hi," Gerry said. "I thought you were out for the count."

"What time is it?"

"Ten o'clock. Three in the morning, your time."

"I just woke up suddenly. I don't know why."

"Jet lag does funny things like that. It's much worse going the other way."

"Wonderful."

Gerry grinned. "Beer?"

"Any chance of a cup of tea?"

"Sure. We're not all coffee-drinking barbarians out here, you know."

Gerry switched on the TV set and went into the kitchen. Banks sank into the sofa and put his feet up on a battered pouffe. A pretty woman was talking very intensely about a debate in the House of Commons. Again Banks felt the shock of being in a foreign land. The TV newscaster spoke with an odd accent—less overbearing than the Americans he had heard—and he knew none of the politicians' names.

Gerry brought the tea and sat beside him.

"There might be a couple of things you can help me with," Banks said.

"Shoot."

"Where can I find Toronto Community College?"

"Easy. The subway's the quickest." And Gerry told him how to get to Broadview station by streetcar or on foot, where to change trains, and where to get off.

"There's another thing. Do you know anything about the English-style pubs in town? Somewhere that sells imported beer."

Gerry laughed. "You've certainly got your work cut out. There's dozens of them. The Madison, The Sticky Wicket, Paupers, the Hop and Grape, the Artful Dodger, The Jack Russell, The Spotted Dick, The Feathers, Quigley's, not to mention a whole dynasty of Dukes. I'll try and make a list for you. What's it all about, by the way, if that's not top secret?"

"I'm looking for a woman. Her name's Anne Ralston."

"What's she done?"

"Nothing, as far as I know."

"How very secretive. You're as bad as Uncle Eb, you are."

"Who?"

"Uncle Eb. You mean you don't know . . . ?"

Banks shook his head. Gristhorpe had never mentioned his first name, and his signature was an indecipherable scrawl.

"Well maybe I shouldn't tell you. He won't thank me for it, if I know him."

"I won't tell him I know. Scout's honour. Come on."

"It's short for Ebenezer, of course."

Banks whistled through his teeth. "No wonder he never lets on."

"Ah, but that's not all. His father was a grand champion of the labouring man, especially the farm workers, so he called his oldest son Ebenezer Elliott—after the 'Corn Law Rhymer.'"

Banks had never heard of Ebenezer Elliott but made a mental note to look him up. He was always interested in new things to read, look at or listen to.

"Ebenezer Elliott Gristhorpe," he repeated to himself. "Bloody hell."

"Thought you'd like that," Gerry said, grinning. "It does have a certain ring to it, doesn't it? My poor mum got lumbered with Mary Wollstonecraft. Very progressive Grandad was, respected the rights of women, too. But my dad was plain old George Webb, and thank the Lord he'd no hobbyhorse to tie his kids to."

On the news, a gang of street kids in Belfast threw stones and tossed Molotov cocktails at police in riot gear. It was night, and orange flames blossomed all along the street. Black smoke rose from burning tires. The world really was a global village, Banks thought, feeling his attention start to slip. Consciousness was fading away again. He yawned and put down his teacup on the low table.

"You can tell me something now," Gerry said. "Where did you get that scar?"

Banks fingered the white scar by his right eye. "This? I passed out from lack of sleep and hit my head on the corner of a table."

Gerry laughed. "I get the point. I'm keeping you up."

Banks smiled. "I'm definitely falling asleep again. See you in the morning?"

"Probably not," Gerry said. "I've got a long way to go and I'm setting off at the crack of dawn. There's coffee and sugar in the cupboard above the sink. Milk and stuff's in the fridge. Here's a spare door-key. Make yourself at home."

Banks shook his bony hand. "Thanks," he said. "I will. And if you're ever in England . . ."

"I'll be sure to visit Uncle Ebenezer. I always do. And we'll have a jar or two in the Queen's Arms. Goodnight."

Banks went back into the bedroom. A light breeze had sprung up to ease the suffocating heat a little, but it was still far from comfortable. He flopped down on the damp sheets. Outside, a short distance away, he heard a streetcar rattle by and remembered exciting childhood trips to big cities when the trams were still running. He thought of the Queen's Arms on the edge of sleep, and pictured the pub on the corner of

Market Street and the cobbled square. He felt very far from
home. The Queen's Arms was a long, long way away, and
there was a lot to do if he was to track down Anne Ralston
before the week was over.

9

I

They were going to church: the women smiling in their wide-brimmed hats and cotton-print dresses, the men ill at ease in tight ties and pinching waistcoats.

Every Sunday morning Katie watched them as she cleaned the rooms, and every week she knew she should be with them, dragging Sam along with the promise of an hour in the pub for him later while she cooked dinner. But he went to the pub anyway, and she cooked dinner anyway. The only thing missing was the hour in church. And that she couldn't face.

All through her childhood, Katie had been forced to go to the Gospel with her grandmother, and the icy devotion of the congregation had scared her half to death. Though they were praising God, they hardly dared sing so loud for fear He would think they were taking pleasure in the hymns. Katie could never understand the readings or the lessons, but she understood the passionate menace in the tones of those who spoke; she understood the meaning of the spittle that sometimes dribbled over their lips, and the way their eyes glazed over. As she grew older, all her fear affixed itself to the sights, sounds and smells of the church: the chill mustiness rising from worn stone flags; the pews creaking as a bored child shifts position; the unearthly echo of the minister's voice; the wooden board announcing the hymn numbers; the stained glass fragmenting colour like broken souls. Just thirty seconds in a church meant panic for Katie; she couldn't breathe, she started trembling, and her blood turned to stone.

But she knew she should go. It was, after all, God's Mansion on Earth, and she would never escape this Vale of Tears if she didn't give herself to Him completely. Instead, she watched the rest of the village go off in their finery and listened to the hymns on the radio as she dusted, tidied and swept, humming along very quietly under her breath. Surely, surely, He would approve? She was working, doing her duty. It was the Sabbath, of course, but there were still guests to take care of, and she suspected deep in her heart that the Sabbath was only meant for men anyway. Surely He would approve. Her work would count in her favour. But it was a sin, she remembered vaguely, to court His favour, to say, "Look what I've done, Lord." It was the sin of Pride. At least some said it was. She couldn't remember who, or whether she had been told to believe or disbelieve them—there were so many heresies, traps awaiting those impure in body and mind—but words such as Faith, Works and Elect circled one another in her thoughts.

Well, Katie concluded dismally, working on Sundays could only add to the weight of sin she carried already. She picked up the black plastic bag. There were still three more rooms to do, then there was dinner to see to. When, she wondered, was it all going to end?

She went downstairs to put the roast in and immediately recognized the new guest standing over the registration book in the hallway. He signed himself in as Philip Richmond, from Bolton, Lancashire, and he told Sam, who was dealing with the details, that he was simply after a few relaxing days in the country. But Katie remembered the moustache and the athletic spring in his step; it was the man she had seen with Chief Inspector Banks and Sergeant Hatchley the day she had run away to Eastvale.

Seeing him there brought back the whole day. Nothing had come of it, really, except that she had caught a minor cold. The housework got done. Not on time, but it got done.

Sam never even found out, so there was no retribution at his hands. Nor were there any outbreaks of boils, thunderbolts from heaven, plagues of locusts or other such horrors her grandmother had assured her would happen if she strayed from the path.

She felt as if she had lost sight of the path completely now. That was all she really knew about what was happening to her. The conflicting voices in her mind seemed to have merged into one incomprehensible rumble, and much of the time she felt as if she had no control over her thoughts or deeds.

There were clear moments, though. Like now. Outside, the landscape was fresh after the previous few days' rain, which was now rising in sun-charmed wraiths of mist from the lower fell-sides and the valley bottom. And here, in their hall, stood a man she recognized as having a close association with the police.

She hadn't seen what all the fuss was about the previous evening, when Sam had stumbled home from the White Rose in a very bad mood.

"He's gone to find her," he had said, scowling. "All the way to bloody Canada. Just to find her."

"Who?" Katie had asked quietly, confused and frightened of him. In moods like this he was likely to lash out, and she could still feel the pain in her breast from the last time.

"Anne Ralston, you silly bitch. That copper's taken off to Toronto after her."

"Well, what does it matter?" Katie had argued cautiously. "If she killed that man all those years ago, they'll put her in jail, won't they?"

"You don't know nothing, woman, do you? Nothing at all." Sam hit out at her and knocked the wooden cross off the mantelpiece.

"Leave it," he snarled, grabbing Katie by the arm as she bent to pick it up. "Can't you think of anything but bloody cleaning up?"

"But I thought you wanted me—"

"Oh, shut up. You don't know nothing."

"Well, tell me. What is it? Why does it matter so much that

he's gone chasing after Anne Ralston in Canada? You hardly knew her. Why does it matter to us?"

"It doesn't," Sam said. "But it might to Stephen. She might make things difficult for him."

"But Stephen hasn't done anything, has he? How could she harm him?"

"She was his fancy woman, wasn't she? Then she ran off and left him. She could tell lies about his business, about— hell, I don't know! All I know is that it's all your bloody fault."

Katie said nothing. Sam's initial rage was spent, she could tell, and she knew she would remain fairly safe if she kept quiet. It was tricky, though, because he might get mad again if she didn't give the proper response to his ranting.

Sam sat heavily on the sofa and turned on the television. There was an old black-and-white film about gangsters on. James Cagney shot Humphrey Bogart and ran for it.

"Get me a beer," Sam said.

Katie got him a can of Long Life from the fridge. She knew it was no good telling him he'd had enough already. Besides, on nights like this, when he'd had a bit more than usual, he tended to fall asleep as soon as he got to bed.

"And don't forget the Colliers' party next week," he added, ripping open the can. "I want you looking your best."

Katie had forgotten about the garden party. The Colliers had two or three every summer. She hated them.

In the morning, Sam had a thick head and remembered very little about the night before. He sulked until after breakfast, then managed a welcome for the new guest before disappearing somewhere in the Landrover. Katie showed Richmond his room, then went to get on with her work.

So there was a policeman in the house. She wondered why he was there. Perhaps he was on holiday. Policemen must have holidays too. But if he was from Eastvale, he was hardly likely to travel only twenty-five miles to Swainshead for his yearly vacation. Not these days. He'd be off to Torquay, or even the Costa del Sol. Katie didn't know how much policemen got paid, so she couldn't really say. But he wouldn't come to Swainshead, that was for sure. He was a spy, then. He thought nobody would recognize him, so he could keep an eye on their comings and goings while the little one with the scar was in Toronto and the big one was God knows where.

And Katie knew who he was. The problem now was what to do with her knowledge. Should she tell Sam, put him on his guard? He'd spread the word then, like he always did, and maybe he'd be grateful to her. But she couldn't remember anything about Sam's gratitude. It just didn't stand out in her memory like the other things. Did she need it? On the other hand, if Sam had done something wrong—and she didn't know whether he had or not—then the policeman, Richmond, if that was his real name, might find out and take him away. She'd be free then. It was an evil thought, and it made her heart race, but ...

Katie paused and looked out of the back window at the gauze of mist rising like breath from the bright green slopes of Swainshead Fell. It would take a bit of thinking about, this dilemma of hers. She knew she mustn't make a hasty decision.

II

"I'm afraid there's hardly anybody here to talk to, Mr ... er ... ?"

"Banks. Alan Banks. I was a friend of Bernard Allen's."

"Yes, well the only person I can think of who might be able to help you is Marilyn Rosenberg." Tom Jordan, head of the Communications Department at Toronto Community College, looked at his watch. "She's got a class right now, but she should be free in about twenty minutes, if you'd like to wait?"

"Certainly."

Jordan led him out of the office into a staff lounge just big enough to hold a few chairs and a low coffee-table littered with papers and teaching journals. At one end stood a fridge and, on a desk beside it, a microwave oven. The coffee-machine stood on a table below a connecting window to the secretary's office, beside a rack of pigeon-holes for staff messages. Banks poured himself a coffee and Jordan edged away slowly, mumbling about work to do.

The coffee was strong and bitter, hardly the thing to drink in the thirty-three-degree heat. What he really needed was a cold beer or a gin and tonic. And he'd gone and bought Scotch at the duty-free shop. Still, he could leave it as a gift for Gerry Webb. It would surely come in handy in winter.

It was Monday morning. On Sunday, Banks had slept in and then gone for a walk along the Danforth. He had noticed the signs of yuppification that Gerry had mentioned, but he had found a pleasant little Greek restaurant, which had served him a hearty moussaka for lunch. Unlike Gerry, Banks enjoyed Greek food.

After that, he had wandered as far as Quinn's. Over a pint, he had asked around about Bernie Allen and shown Anne Ralston's photograph to the bar staff and waitresses. No luck. One down, two dozen to go. He had wandered back along the residential streets south of Danforth Avenue and noticed that the small brick house with the green-and-white porch fence and columns was a sort of Toronto trademark.

Too tired to go out again, he had stayed in and watched television that evening. Oddly enough, the non-commercial channel was showing an old BBC historical serial he'd found boring enough the first time around, and—much better— one of the Jeremy Brett "Sherlock Holmes" episodes. The only alternatives were the same American cop shows that plagued British TV.

He had woken at about nine o'clock that Monday morning. Still groggy from travel and culture-shock, he had taken a shower and had had orange juice and toast for breakfast. Then it was time to set off. He slipped a sixties anthology tape of Cream, Traffic and Rolling Stones hits in the Walkman and put it in the right-hand pocket of his light cotton jacket. In the left, he placed cigarettes and Hardy's *Tess of the D'Urbervilles*, the only book he'd brought with him.

Jacket slung over shoulder, he set off, following Gerry's directions. A rolling, rattling streetcar ride took him by the valley-side, rife with joggers. The downtown towers were hazy in the morning heat. Finding the westbound platform at Broadview subway station was every bit as straightforward as Gerry had said, but changing trains at Yonge and getting out to the street at St Clair proved confusing. All exits seemed to lead to a warren of underground shopping malls—air-conditioned, of course—and finding the right way out wasn't always easy.

Still, he'd found St Clair Avenue after only a momentary diversion into a supermarket called Ziggy's, and the college was only a short walk from the station.

Now, from the sixth floor, he looked out for a while on the office buildings opposite and the cream tops of the streetcars passing to and fro below him, then turned to the pile of journals on the table.

Half-way through an article on the teaching of "critical thinking," he heard muffled voices in the corridor, and a young woman with a puzzled expression on her face popped around the door. Masses of curly brown hair framed her round head. She had a small mouth and her teeth, when she smiled, were tiny, straight and pearly white. The greyish gum she was chewing oozed between them like a new gum disease. She carried a worn, overstuffed leather briefcase under her arm, and wore grey cords and a checked shirt.

She stretched out her hand. "Marilyn Rosenberg. Tom tells me you wanted to talk to me."

Banks introduced himself and offered to pour her a cup of coffee.

"No thanks," she said, grabbing a Diet Coke from the fridge. "Far too hot for that stuff. You'd think they'd do something about the air-conditioning in this place, wouldn't you?" She pulled the tab and the Diet Coke fizzed. "What do you want with me?"

"I want to talk about Bernard Allen."

"I've been through all that with the police. There wasn't really much to say."

"What did they ask you?"

"Just if I thought anyone had a reason to kill him, where my colleagues were over the last few weeks, that kind of thing."

"Did they ask you anything about his life here?"

"Only what kind of person he was."

"And?"

"And I told them he was a bit of a loner, that's all. I wasn't the only one they talked to."

"You're the only one here now."

"Yeah, I guess." She grinned again, flashing her beautiful teeth.

"If Bernard didn't have much to do with his colleagues here, did he have a group of friends somewhere else, away from college?"

"I wouldn't really know. Look, I didn't know Bernie that well. . . ." She hesitated. "Maybe it's none of your business, but I wanted to. We were getting closer. Slowly. He was a hard person to get to know. All that stiff-upper-lip Brit stuff. Me, I'm a simple Irish-Jewish girl from Montreal." She shrugged. "I liked him. We did lunch up here a couple of times. I was hoping maybe he'd ask me out sometime but . . ."

"It never happened?"

"No. He was too damn slow. I didn't know how much clearer I could make it without ripping off my clothes and jumping on him. But now it's too late, even for that."

"How did he seem emotionally before he went to England?"

Marilyn frowned and bit her bottom lip as she thought. "He hadn't quite got over his divorce," she said finally. "So I guess he might have been off women for a while."

"Did you know his ex-wife?"

"No, not really."

"What about her lover?"

"Yeah, I knew him. He used to work here. He's a louse."

"In what way?"

"Every way. Strutting macho peacock. And she fell for it. I don't blame Bernie for feeling bad, but he'd have been well rid of her anyway. He'd have got over it."

"But he was still upset?"

"Yeah. Withdrawn, sort of."

"How did he get on with his students?"

"Well enough, considering."

"Considering what?"

"He cared about literature, but most of the students don't give a damn about James Joyce or George Orwell. They're here to learn about business or computers or electrical engineering—you know, useful stuff—and then they think they'll walk into top, high-paying jobs. They don't like it when they find they all have to do English, so it makes our job a bit tough. Some teachers find it harder than others to adjust and lower their expectations."

"And Bernie was one?"

"Yeah. He complained a lot about how ignorant they were, how half of them didn't even know when the Second World War was fought or who Hitler was. And, even worse, they didn't care anyway. Bernie couldn't understand that. He had one guy who thought Shakespeare was a small town in Saskatchewan. That really got to him."

"I don't understand," Banks said. "How could someone like that get accepted into a college?"

"We have an open-door policy," Marilyn said. "It's a democratic education. None of that elitist bullshit you get in England. We don't send our kids away to boarding schools to learn Latin and take a lot of cold showers. All that *Jane Eyre* stuff."

Banks, who had not attended a public school himself, along with, he suspected, the majority of English children, was confused. "But don't a lot of them fail?" he asked. "Doesn't it waste time and money?"

"We don't like to fail people," Marilyn said. "It gives them a poor self-image."

"So they don't need to know much to get in, and they aren't expected to know much more when they leave, is that it?"

Marilyn smiled like a nurse with a particularly difficult patient.

"What did Bernie think about that?" Banks hurried on.

She laughed. "Bernie loved youth, young people, but he didn't have much respect for their intelligence."

"It doesn't sound like they had much."

"There, you see. That's exactly the kind of thing he'd say. You're so sarcastic, you Brits."

"But you liked him?"

"Yeah, I liked him. We might have disagreed on a few things, but he was cute. And I'm a sucker for an English accent. What can I say? He was a nice guy, at least as far as I could tell. I mean, he might not have thought much of his students, but he treated them well and did his damnedest to arouse some curiosity in them. He was a good teacher. What are you getting at, anyway? Do you think one of his students might have killed him over a poor grade?"

"It sounds unlikely, doesn't it?"

"Not as much as you think," Marilyn said. "We once had a guy come after his English teacher here with a shotgun. Luckily, security stopped him before he got very far. Still," she went on, "I shouldn't think an irate student would go to all the trouble of following him over to England and killing him there."

"What did Bernie do when he went home after work? Did he ever mention any particular place he went to?"

Marilyn shook her head and the curls danced. "No. He did once say he'd had a few pints too many in the pub the night before."

"The pub?"

"Yeah."

"He didn't say which pub?"

"No. He just said he'd had six pints when five was his limit these days. Look, what is all this? What are you after? You're not one of those private eyes, are you?"

Banks laughed. "No. I told you, I'm a friend of Bernie's from England. Swainsdale, where he grew up. I want to piece together as much of his life here as I can. A lot of people over there are hurt and puzzled by what happened."

"Yeah, well . . . me too. He wasn't the kind of guy who gets himself killed. Know what I mean?"

Banks nodded.

"Swainsdale, you said?" she went on. "Bernie was always going on about that place. At least the couple of times we talked he was. Like it was some paradise on earth or something. Especially since the divorce, he started to get homesick. He was beginning to feel a bit lost and out of place here. It can happen, you know. So he took the thousand-dollar cure."

"The what?"

"The thousand-dollar cure. I guess it's gone up now with inflation, but it's when Brits take a trip back home to renew their roots. Used to call it the thousand-dollar cure. For homesickness."

"Did he ever talk of going back to Swainsdale to stay?"

"Yeah. He said he'd be off like a shot if he had a job, or a private income. He said there was nothing for him here after he split up with Barbara. Poor guy. Like I said, he got withdrawn, dwelled on things too much."

Banks nodded. "There's nothing else you can tell me? You're sure he didn't name any specific pub or place he used to hang out?"

"Sorry." Marilyn grinned. "I'd remember if he had because I'd have probably dropped in there one evening. Just by chance, you know."

Banks smiled. "Yes. I know. Thanks anyway. I won't waste any more of your time."

"No problem." Marilyn tossed her empty can into the waste-paper basket. "Hey!" she called, as Banks left the staff lounge. "I think your accent's cute, too."

But Banks didn't have time to appreciate the compliment. Coming along the corridor towards him were two very large police officers.

"Mr Banks?" the taller one asked.

"Yes."

"We'd like you to come with us, if you don't mind."

"What for?"

"Just a few questions. This way, please."

There was hardly room for them to walk three abreast down the hallway, but they managed it somehow. Banks felt a bit like a sardine in a tin. As they turned the corner, he noticed from the corner of his eye Tom Jordan wringing his hands outside his office.

Banks tried to get more out of the officers in the lift, but they clammed up on him. He felt a wave of irrational fear at the situation. Here he was, in a foreign country, being taken into custody by two enormous uniformed policemen who refused to answer his questions. And the feeling of fear intensified as he was bundled into the back of the yellow car. The air smelled of hot vinyl upholstery; a strong wire mesh separated him from the men in the front; and the back doors had no inside handles.

III

"What does tha write, then?" Freddie Metcalfe asked, expertly refilling the empty pint glass with Marston's Pedigree Bitter.

"Science fiction," said Detective Constable Philip Richmond. In his checked Viyella shirt and light-brown cords, he thought he looked the part. Posing as a writer would make him less suspicious, too. He would be expected to spend some time alone in his room writing and a lot of time in the pub, with perhaps the occasional constitutional just to keep the juices flowing.

"I knew a chap used to write books once," Freddie went on. "Books about t'Dales, wi' pictures in 'em. Lived down Lower 'Ead." He placed the foaming pint in front of Richmond, who paid and drained a good half of it in one gulp. "I reckon one of them there detective writers would 'ave a better time of it round 'ere these days."

"Why's that?"

Freddie leaned forward and lowered his voice. "Murder, that's why," he said, then laughed and picked up a glass to dry. "Right baffled, t'police are. It's got that southron—little chap wi' a scar by 'is eye—it's got 'im running around like a blue-arsed fly, it has. And t'old man, Gristhorpe—well, we all know he durst hardly show his face around 'ere since t'last one, don't we?"

"Last what?"

"Murder, lad! What's tha think I'm talking about? Sheep-shagging?"

"Sorry."

"Think nowt on it. I'm forgetting tha's a foreigner. Tha sounds Yorkshire to me. Bit posh, mind you, but Yorkshire."

"Lancashire, actually," Richmond lied. "Bolton."

"Aye, well, nobody's perfect. Anyroads, as I were saying— blue-arsed flies, t'lot of 'em."

An impatient customer interrupted Freddie's monologue, and Richmond took the opportunity to sip more beer. It was eight-thirty on Monday evening, and the White Rose was about half full.

"Keep your eyes skinned, lad," Sergeant Hatchley had instructed him. "Watch out for anybody who looks like doing a bolt." The orders couldn't have been more vague. What on earth, Richmond wondered, did someone about to do a bolt look like? Would he have to sit up all night and watch for the culprit stealing down by the fledgling Swain with his belongings tied in a bag on the end of a stick slung over his shoulder, faithful cat at his heels, like Dick Whittington? Richmond had no idea. All he knew was that all the suspects had been told Banks had gone to Toronto.

Richmond also had strict instructions not to identify himself and not to push himself forward in any way that might make the locals suspicious. In other words, he wasn't to question anyone, no matter how casually. He could keep his ears open though, he was relieved to hear, especially for anything Sam Greenock might let slip over breakfast, or some titbit he might overhear in the White Rose. At least he'd pack away a few pints of Marston's tonight. Maybe even smoke a panatella.

"Where was I?" Freddie asked, leaning on the bar again.

"Murder."

"Aye, murder." He nodded in the direction of the table in the far corner and whispered again. "And them there's all t'suspects."

"What makes them suspects?" Richmond asked, hoping he was not exceeding his brief by asking the question.

"'Ow would I know? All I know is that t'police 'ave spent a lot of time wi' 'em. An' since yesterday they've all been on hot coals. Look at 'em now. You wouldn't think they 'ad a big party coming up, would you?"

It was true that the group hardly seemed jolly. John Fletcher chewed the stem of his stubby pipe; his dark brows met in a frown. Sam Greenock was staring into space and rocking his glass on the table. Stephen Collier was talking earnestly to Nicholas, who was trying very hard not to listen. Nicholas, in fact, seemed the only unconcerned one among them. He smiled and nodded at customers who came and went, whereas the other two hardly seemed to notice them.

Richmond wished he could get closer and overhear what they were saying, but all the nearby tables were full. It would look too suspicious if he went and stood behind them.

He ordered another pint. "And I'll have a panatella, too, please," he said. He felt like indulging in a rare treat: a cigar with his beer. "What party's this?" he asked.

"A Collier do. Reg'lar as clockwork in summer."

"Can anyone go?"

"Tha must be joking, lad."

Richmond shrugged and smiled to show he was, indeed, jesting. "What's wrong with them all, then?" he asked. "You're right. They don't look like they're contemplating a booze-up to me."

Metcalfe scratched his mutton-chops. "I can't be certain, tha knows, but it's summat to do wi' that London copper taking off for Canada. Talk about pale! Ashen, they went. But I'll tell tha summat, it were good for business. Double brandies all round!" Freddie nudged Richmond and laughed. "Aye, there's nobody drinks like a murder suspect."

Richmond drew on his cigar and looked over at the table. Outside some enemy back in Toronto, it came down to these four. Come on, he thought to himself, make a bolt. Run for it, you bugger, just try it!

IV

"I don't know what people do where you come from, but over here we like a bit of advance warning if some foreigner's come to invade our territory."

Banks listened. There was nothing he could say; he had been caught fair and square. Fortunately, Staff Sergeant Gregson of the Toronto Homicide Squad was nearing the end of what had been a relatively mild bollocking, and even more fortunately, smoking was allowed—nay, encouraged—in his office.

It was an odd feeling, being on the carpet. Not that this was the first time for Banks. There had been many occasions at school, and even one or two in his early days on the Metropolitan Force, and they always brought back those feelings of terror and helplessness in the face of authority he had known as a working-class kid in Peterborough. Perhaps, he thought, that fear of authority might have motivated him to become a policeman in the first place. He knew he didn't join in order to inflict such feelings on others, but it was possible that he did it to surmount them, to conquer them in himself.

And now here he was, tongue-tied, unable to say a word in his own defence, yet inwardly seething with resentment at Gregson for putting him in such a position.

"You've got no power here, you know," Gregson went on.

Finally, Banks found his voice. Holding his anger in check, he said, "I wasn't aware that I needed any special power to talk to people—either in England or in Canada."

"You won't get anywhere being sarcastic with me," Gregson said, a smile tugging at the corners of his tightly clamped mouth.

He was a round man with a square head. His grey hair was closely cropped, and a brush-like wedge of matching moustache, nicotine-yellow around the ends of the bristles, sprouted under his squashed nose. As he spoke, he had a habit of running his fingers under the collar of his white shirt as if it was too tight. His skin had a pinkish, plastic sheen, like a balloon blown up too much. Banks wondered what would happen if he pricked him. Would he explode, or would the air hiss out slowly as his features folded in on themselves?

"What have you got against irony, Sergeant?" Banks asked. That felt odd, too: being hauled up before a mere Sergeant.

"You know what they say about sarcasm being the lowest form of wit, don't you?" Gregson responded.

"Yes. But at least it is a form of wit, which is better than none at all."

"I didn't bring you here to bandy words."

"Obviously."

Banks lit another cigarette and looked at the concrete-and-glass office blocks out of the window. His shirt was stuck with sweat to the back of the orange plastic chair. He felt his anger ebb into boredom. They were somewhere downtown in a futuristic, air-conditioned building, but the office smelt of burning rubber and old cigar smoke. That was all he knew.

"What are you going to do, then?" Banks asked. "Arrest me?"

Gregson shrugged. "For what? You haven't done anything wrong."

Banks leaned forward. "Then why the bloody hell did you get Laurel and Hardy out there to bundle me in the back of a car and bring me here against my will?"

"Don't be like that," Gregson said. "When Jordan phoned me and said there was a suspicious Englishman asking questions about Bernard Allen, what the fuck else could I do? What would you have done? Then it turned out to be you, a goddamn police inspector from England. And I hadn't even been advised of your visit. I considered that an insult, which it is. And I didn't find your remark on the phone about getting my man particularly funny, either. I'm not a Mountie."

"Well, I'm sorry for any inconvenience I've caused you, Sergeant," Banks said, standing up, "but I'd like to enjoy the rest of my holiday in peace, if you don't mind."

"I don't mind," Gregson said, making no move to stop him

walking over to the door. "I don't mind at all. But I think you ought to bear a few things in mind before you go storming off."

"What things?" Banks asked, his palm slippery on the doorknob.

"First of all, that what I said to you on the phone before is true: we don't have the resources to work on this case. Secondly, yes, you can talk to as many people as you wish, providing they want to talk to you. And thirdly, you should have damn well asked for permission before jumping on that fucking jet and flying here half-cocked. What if you find your killer? What are you going to do then? Have you thought about that? Smuggle him out of the country? You could be getting yourself into a damn tricky legal situation if you're not very careful." Gregson rubbed his moustache with the back of his hand. "All I'm saying is that there are things you can't do acting alone, without authority."

"And you don't have the resources. I know. You told me. Look, this is where I came in, so if you don't mind—"

"Wait!" Gregson jumped to his feet and reached for his jacket.

"Wait for what?"

Gregson pushed past him through the door. "Come on," he said, half-turning. "Just come with me."

"Where?"

"You'll see."

"What for?"

"I'm going to save you from yourself."

Banks sighed and followed the sergeant down the corridor and down the lift to the car-park.

There was enough room for a soccer team on the front seat of Gregson's car. With the open windows sucking in what hot wet air they could, the staff sergeant drove up Yonge Street and turned right at the Hudson's Bay building. On the crowded street-corner, vendors sold ice-cream, T-shirts and jewellery; one man, surrounded by quite a crowd, was drawing large portraits in coloured chalk on the pavement.

Farther along, Banks recognized the stretch of the Danforth he'd walked the previous day: the Carrot Common shopping centre; the little Greek restaurant where he'd eaten lunch; Quinn's pub. They came to an intersection called Coxwell, and Gregson turned left. A few blocks up, he pulled to a halt outside a small apartment building. Sprinklers hissed on the well-kept lawn. Banks was tempted to run under one for a cold shower.

They walked up to the third floor, and Banks followed Gregson along the carpeted corridor to apartment 312.

"Allen's place," the staff sergeant announced.

"Why are you helping me?" Banks asked, as Gregson fitted the key in the door. "Why are you bringing me here? You said your department didn't have the resources."

"That's true. We've got a hunt on for a guy who sodomized a twelve-year-old girl, then cut her throat and dumped her in High Park. Been looking for leads for two months now. Twenty men on the case. But this is personal time. I don't like it that a local guy got killed any more than you do. So I show you where he lived. It's no big deal. Besides, like I said, I'm saving you from yourself. You'd probably have broken in, and then I'd have had to arrest you. Embarrassing all around."

"Thanks anyway," Banks said.

They walked into the apartment.

"Building owner's been bugging us to let him rent it out again, but we've been stalling. He knows he's sitting on a gold mine. We've got a zero vacancy rate in Toronto these days. Still, Allen paid first and last month when he moved in, so I figure he's got a bit of time left. To tell you the truth, we don't know who's gonna take care of the guy's stuff."

There wasn't much: just a lot of books, Swedish assemble-it-yourself furniture, pots and pans, a few withered houseplants, and a desk and typewriter by the window. Bernard Allen had lived simply.

The room was hot and stuffy. There was no sign of an air-conditioner, so Banks went over and opened a window. It didn't make much difference.

"What kind of search did your men do?" Banks asked.

"Routine. We didn't open up every book or read every letter, if that's what you mean. The guy didn't keep much personal stuff around, anyway. It was all in that desk drawer."

Banks extracted a messy pile of bills and letters from the drawer. First, he put aside the bills then examined the sheaf of personal mail. They were all dated within the last six months or so, which meant that he threw his letters out periodically instead of hoarding them like some people. There were letters from his parents in Australia and one brief note from his sister acknowledging the dates of his proposed visit. Banks read these carefully, but found nothing of significance.

It was a postcard from Vancouver dated about two weeks before Allen set off for England that proved the most revealing, but even that wasn't enough. It read:

Dear Bernie,
　　Wrapping things up nicely out here. Weather great, so taking some time for sunbathing on Kitsilano Beach. It'll be a couple more weeks before I get back, so I'll miss you. Have a great trip and give my love to the folks in Swineshead! (Only joking—best not tell anyone you know me!) See you in the pub when you get back.

　　　　Love,

　　　　Julie.

It was perfectly innocent on the surface—just a postcard from a friend—so there was no reason why Gregson or his men should have been suspicious about it. But it was definitely from Anne Ralston, and it told Banks that she was going under the name of Julie now.

"Looks like you've found something," Gregson said, looking over Banks's shoulder.

"It's from the woman I'm looking for. I think she knows something about Allen's murder."

"Look," Gregson said, "are we talking about a criminal here? Are there charges involved?"

Banks shook his head. He wasn't sure. Anne Ralston could certainly have murdered Raymond Addison and run for it, but he didn't want to tell Gregson that and risk the local police scaring her off.

"No," he said. "They used to know each other in Swainshead, that's all."

"And now they've met up over here?"

"Yes."

"So?"

Banks told him about Ralston's disappearance and the Addison murder, stressing that she wasn't seriously implicated in any way.

"But she might have known something?" he said. "And told Allen. You think that's what might have got him killed?"

"It's possible. We know that she asked him to keep quiet about meeting her over here, and we know he didn't."

"Who did he talk to?"

"That's the problem. Someone who makes it his business to make sure that everyone who counts knows."

"It won't be easy."

"What?"

Gregson tapped the postcard. "Finding her. No address. No phone number. Nothing."

Banks sighed. "Believe me, I know. And all we've got is her first name. I'm just hoping I can dig out some of the spots she might turn up. She mentioned the pub, so at least I was right about her drinking with him there."

"Know how many pubs there are in Toronto?"

"Don't bother to tell me. I'd only get discouraged. It's the kind of job I should have sent my sergeant on." Banks explained about Hatchley's drinking habits and Gregson laughed.

"Can I have a good look around?" Banks asked.

"Go ahead. I'll be down in the car. Lock up behind you."

After the staff sergeant left, Banks puzzled over him for a moment. He was beginning to warm to Gregson and get some understanding of Canadians, especially those of distant British origin. They behaved with a strange mixture of patronage and respect towards the English. Perhaps they'd had British history rammed down their throats at school and needed to reject it in order to discover themselves. Or perhaps the English had simply become *passé* as far as immigrants went, and had been superseded by newer waves of Koreans, East Indians and Vietnamese.

The next item of interest Banks found was an old photograph album dating back to Allen's university days. There were pictures of his parents, his sister, and of the Greenocks standing outside a typical Armley back-to-back. But the most interesting was a picture dated ten years ago, in which Allen stood outside the White Rose with a woman named as Anne in the careful white print under the photo on the black page. The snap was a little blurred, an amateur effort with a Brownie by the look of it, but it was better than the one he'd got from Missing Persons. Anne looked very attractive in a low-cut T-shirt and a full, flowing Paisley skirt. She had long light-brown hair, a high forehead and smiling eyes. Her face was heart-shaped and her lips curved up slightly at the corners. That was ten years ago, Banks thought, carefully taking the photo from its silver corners and pocketing it. Would she look like that now?

He went on to make a careful search of the rest of the apartment, and he did take out every book and flip through the leaves, but he came up with nothing else. The postcard signed "Julie" and the old photograph: those were all he had to go on. By the time he'd finished, his shirt was stuck to his back.

Outside, Gregson seemed quite at ease smoking in his hot car.

"Find anything?" he asked.

"Only an old photograph. Probably useless. What time is it?"

"Ten after four."

"I suppose I'd better make my way home."

"Where are you staying?"

"Riverdale."

"That's not far. How about a beer first?"

"All right." It was impossible to resist the thought of an ice-cold beer.

Gregson drove back downtown and pulled into a car-park behind a grimy cinder-block building with a satellite dish on the roof.

Despite the warm gold sunlight outside, the bar was dark and it took a while for Banks's eyes to adjust. He did notice, though, that it was cold, gloriously cold. There wasn't any sawdust on the floor, but he got the feeling there ought to be. It was a high-ceilinged room as big as a barn, peppered with black plastic tables and chairs. At one end was the bar itself, a feeble glimmer of light in the distance, and at the other was a stage littered with amps and speakers. At the moment a rather flat-chested young girl was dancing half-naked in a spotlight to the Rolling Stones' "Jumpin' Jack Flash." The volume was way too loud. Against a third wall was a huge TV screen on which a game of baseball was in progress.

A waitress sashayed over, shirt-ends tied in a knot under her ample breasts, and took their orders with a weary smile. Shortly, she returned with the drinks on a tray. As Banks looked around, other figures detached themselves from the gloom and he saw that the place was reasonably full. Smoke swirled and danced in the spot beam. Whatever this bar was, it wasn't one of the English-style pubs where Bernard Allen went for his pint. The four glasses of draft beer in front of them were tiny and tapered to thick heavy stems.

"Cheers." Gregson clinked glasses and practically downed his in one.

"If you have to order two each at a time," Banks asked, leaning over and shouting against the music, "why don't they switch to using bigger glasses?"

Gregson shrugged and licked foam off his moustache. "Tradition, I guess. It's always been like this long as I can remember." He offered Banks a cigarette. It was stronger than the ones he usually smoked.

The music ended and the girl left the stage to a smattering of polite applause.

Gregson nodded towards the TV screen. "Get baseball back home?"

Banks nodded. "We do now. My son likes it, but I'm a cricket man myself."

"Can't figure that game at all."

"Can't say I know much about baseball, either." Banks caught the waitress's attention and put in another order, changing his to a bottle of Carlsberg this time. She smiled sweetly at him and made him repeat himself.

"Likes your accent," Gregson said afterwards. "She heard you the first time. You'll be all right there, if you're interested."

"Married man."

"Ah. Still, while the cat's away ... And you are in a foreign country, a long way from home."

Banks laughed. "The problem is, I have to take myself with me wherever I go."

Gregson nodded slowly. "I know what you mean." He tapped the side of his square head. "There's a few pictures stuck in here I wish I could throw out, believe me." He looked back at the screen. "Baseball. Greatest game in the world."

"I'll take your word for it."

"Listen, if you've got a bit of time, how about taking in a game next Saturday? I've got tickets. Jays at home to the Yankees."

"I'd like that," Banks said. "Look, don't get me wrong, but I got the impression you were distinctly pissed off with me a few hours ago. Now you're inviting me to a baseball game. Any reason?"

"Sure. You were out of line and I did my duty. Now I'm off duty and someone's got to show you there's more to Canada than snow, Mounties, beavers and maple trees."

"Fair enough. Don't forget the Eskimos."

"Inuit, we call them now."

Banks finished his beer and Gregson ordered more. The spot came on again and an attractive young woman with long, wavy black hair and brown skin came onto the stage.

Gregson noticed Banks staring. "Beautiful, eh? She's a full-blooded Indian. Name's Wanda Morningstar."

She certainly was beautiful, in such an innocent, natural way that Banks found himself wondering what the girl was doing taking her clothes off for a bunch of dirty old men in the middle of a summer's afternoon. And, come to think of it, what the hell was he doing among them? Well, blame Gregson for that.

More drinks came, and more strippers walked on and off the stage, but none could hold a candle to Wanda Morningstar. It was after ten when they finally left, and by then Banks felt unusually merry. Because the beer was ice-cold, it had very little taste and, therefore, he had assumed, little strength. Wrong. It was stronger than what he was used to, and he felt light-headed as he followed Gregson to the car.

Gregson paused as he bent to put his key in the door. "No," he said to himself. "Time to take a cab. You've been leading me astray, Alan. It'd be damned embarrassing if I got done for drunken driving in my own city, wouldn't it?"

They walked out onto the street. It was still busy, and many of the shops were open—all-night groceries and the ubiquitous Mac's Milk. Or was this one Mo's, Mc's or Mick's? You'd never get anything but an off-licence open past five-thirty in Eastvale, Banks reflected.

Gregson waved and a cab pulled up. They piled in the back. The driver, an uncommunicative West Indian, nodded when he heard the directions. He dropped Banks off first outside Gerry's house, then drove on with Gregson waving from the back.

Banks walked into the hot room and slumped in front of the TV. A rerun of "Perry Mason" came on. Finally, a little dizzy and unable to keep his eyes open any longer, he went into the bedroom and lay down. The events of the day spun around chaotically in his mind for a while, but the last image, the one that lulled his consciousness to sleep, was of Wanda Morningstar dancing naked, not on a stage in a seedy bar, but in a clearing somewhere in the wilderness, her dark skin gleaming in firelight.

But the scene shifted, as it does in dreams, and it was no longer Wanda Morningstar dancing, but Anne Ralston running ahead of him in her long Paisley skirt. It was a typical policeman's dream, too, for try as he might, he just couldn't run fast enough. His feet felt as if they were glued to the earth. Every so often, she would pause and beckon him, smiling indulgently when she saw him try to drag himself along. He woke at six, covered with sweat. Outside, the birds were singing and an early-morning streetcar clattered by. He got up and took a couple of Gerry's aspirins with a pint of water, then drifted off to sleep again.

10

I

The sun had just gone down behind Adam's Fell, silhouetting the steep hillside against its deep crimson glow. The guests milled around in the Colliers' large garden. Doors to both parts of the house were open, allowing access to drinks and a huge table of cheeses, pâtés, smoked salmon and fresh fruit. Music drifted out from Stephen's stereo. Now it was Mozart, but earlier there had been Motown and some ersatz modern pop. The crowd was mostly early to mid thirties, apart from one or two older landowners and friends of the family. There were a couple of bright young teachers from Braughtmore, several members of Stephen's management staff, and a great assortment of entrepreneurs, some with political ambitions, from all over the dale. The parties were a fairly regular affair; they helped maintain the social status of the Colliers and introduce those who had something to those who might be willing and able to pay for it.

Katie stood alone by the fountain, with a glass of white wine in her hand. She had been holding it so long it was warm. Occasionally a well-dressed young man would approach her and begin a conversation, but after a few minutes of her averted looks, blushes and monosyllabic answers, he would make an excuse to get away.

As usual, Sam had insisted she come.

"I didn't buy you those bloody expensive dresses for nothing, you know," he had railed when she told him at the last minute that she didn't want to go.

"I didn't ask you to buy them," Katie said quietly. "I don't even want them." And it was true. She felt uncomfortable in finery, full of pride and vanity.

"You'll damn well do as I say. There'll be some important people there and I want you to make a good impression."

"Oh, Sam," she pleaded, "you know I never do. I can't talk to people at parties. I get all tongue-tied."

"Have a few drinks like everyone else, for a change. That'll loosen you up. For Christ's sake, can't you let your hair down for once?"

Katie turned away.

Sam grasped her arm. "Look," he said, "you're coming with me and that's that. If you're so worried about talking to people, then just stand around and look decorative. At least you can do that. But you are coming. Got it?"

Katie nodded and Sam let go of her. Rubbing her arm, she went up to her room and picked out a cotton print dress just right for the occasion, gathered at the waist and cut low down the back. It looked particularly good if she tied her hair up. She decided to take a fringed woollen shawl, too; sometimes, even in July, the evenings got chilly. After Sam had approved of her appearance and suggested a bit more eye make-up, they left.

She could see Sam in his white suit talking and laughing with a couple of local businessmen. He had a glass of wine too, though she knew he hated the stuff. He only drank it because that was the thing to do at the Colliers' parties.

Katie looked around for John Fletcher, but she couldn't see him. John was always kind and, of all of them, she found him the easiest to talk to, or even to be silent with. She liked Stephen Collier, but felt more comfortable with John Fletcher. He was a sad and haunted man since his wife ran off—but at least she hadn't gone because he mistreated her. Maureen Fletcher, Katie remembered, had been beautiful, vain, haughty and foolhardy. The small community of Swainshead couldn't hold her. Katie thought John ought to be glad to be rid of her, but she never said anything to him. They never discussed anything personal, but he seemed, beyond the depths of his sadness, a good man.

Katie shivered. The sunset had faded, leaving the sky above Adam's Fell a deep, dark violet colour. Even over the clinking glasses and the Motown music, which had started up again because some people wanted to dance, she could hear the eerie, mournful call of a curlew high on the fell. She began to make her way into Nicholas's part of the house to pick up her shawl where Sam had left it, then decided she wanted to go to the bathroom, too. Pausing on the way, she admired the oak panelling and the old-fashioned style of his living-room, with its water-colours of Nelson and Wellington on the walls, and its rows of leather-bound books. She wondered if he ever read them. On a small teak table by the Adam fireplace stood a bronze bust. Looking closer, Katie saw the name "Oscar Wilde" scratched into the base. She'd heard the name before somewhere, but it didn't mean very much to her. What a beautiful place for a monster like Nicholas Collier to live. It would be difficult to clean, though, she thought, taking in all the nooks and crannies with a professional eye.

Finally, she found the toilet, which was more modern than the rest of the house. There, she poured her drink down the bowl and hid for a while, idly glancing at one of the copies of *Yorkshire Life* so thoughtfully set out by the bathtub. Then she got worried that Sam might be looking for her.

On her way back down the hall, she met Nicholas coming up. He was walking unsteadily, and his bright eyes were glassy. A stubborn lock of hair near his crown stood straight up. He looked like a naughty public schoolboy.

"Ah, Katie my dear," he said, reaching out and holding her shoulders. His voice was slurred and his cheeks were flushed with drink. "Come to me, for thy love is better than wine."

Katie blushed and tried to wriggle free, but Nicholas only tightened his grip. He looked behind him.

"Nobody around," he whispered. "Time for a little kiss, my rose of Sharon, my lily of the valley."

Katie struggled, but he was too strong. He held her head

still, brought his mouth closer to hers and seemed to suffocate her with a long, wet kiss. His breath tasted rank with wine, garlicky pâté and Stilton cheese. When he stopped, she gulped in the air. But he didn't let her go. One hand was on her bare back now and the other was feeling her breasts.

"Ah, thy breasts are like two young roes that are twins," he said, breathing hard. "Come on, Katie. In here. In the bedroom."

"No!" Katie shouted. "If you don't let me go I'm going to scream."

Nicholas laughed. "I like a girl with a bit of spirit. Come on, I'll make you scream, sure enough. But not yet." He put one hand over her mouth and started dragging her along the hallway. Suddenly, she heard a familiar voice behind them and Nicholas's grip loosened. She shook herself free and turned to hear John Fletcher tell Nicholas to take his hands off her.

"You go to hell!" Nicholas said, clearly too far gone in temper to pull back. "Who are you to tell me what to do? You're nothing but a jumped-up farm boy."

And suddenly, John hit him. It was a quick, sharp blow to the mouth, and it stopped Nicholas in his tracks. He glared at John as the blood welled to his lips and a thin line trickled down his chin. Out in the garden, a glass smashed and somebody giggled loudly above Mary Wells's "My Guy." Nicholas bared his teeth at John, put his hand over his mouth and stalked off to the bathroom.

Fletcher rubbed his knuckles. "Are you all right, Katie?" he asked.

"Yes, yes, thank you." Katie stared down at the patterned carpet as she spoke. "I—I'm sorry . . . I'm so embarrassed. It's not the first time he's tried to touch me, but he's never been that rough before."

"He's drunk," Fletcher said, then smiled. "Don't worry. I've been wanting to do that for a long time."

"But what will he do? He looked so angry."

"He'll cool off. Come on, let's get back to the others."

Katie picked up her shawl, and they walked back into the

garden, which was lit now by strategically placed antique
lanterns. Katie excused herself, thanking John again, and
sneaked around the side of the house into the street. She felt
she needed to be out of there for a while, at least until her
heart stopped beating so wildly and she could catch her
breath again. Her flesh felt numb where Nicholas's hands
had touched her. She shuddered.

There was no-one on the street. Even the old men had
gone from the bridge. The lights were on in the White Rose,
though, and Katie heard the sound of laughter and talk from
inside. She thought the young policeman would be in there,
the one nobody knew about but her. He hadn't been invited
to the party, of course, so he wouldn't get the chance to spy
on them that night. She wondered why he was really in the
village. He hadn't asked any searching questions of anyone;
he just seemed to be there, somehow, always in sight.

Sighing, Katie crept back into the garden. A slow song
was playing and some of the couples held each other close.
Suddenly, she felt a hand on her back and flinched.

"It's only me. Dance?"

"B-but I . . . can't. . . ."

"Nonsense," Stephen Collier said. "It's easy. Just follow
what I do."

Katie had no choice. She saw Sam looking on and smiling
with approval from Stephen's doorway. She felt like she had
two left feet, and somehow her body just wouldn't respond to
the music at all. It felt like wood. Soon, she began to feel
dizzy and everything went dark. At the centre of the darkness
was a biting, sooty smell. She stumbled.

"Hey, I'm not as bad as all that." Stephen supported her
with one arm and led her to the fountain.

Katie regained her balance. "I'm sorry," she said. "I told
you I was no good."

"If I didn't know better," Stephen said, "I'd say you'd had
too much to drink."

Katie smiled. "About one sip of white wine. It's too much
for me."

"Katie?" Stephen suddenly seemed earnest.

"Yes?"

"I enjoyed our little chat in your kitchen that time. It's good to have someone . . . someone outside to talk to."

"Outside what?"

"Oh, business, family . . ."

The occasion seemed so long ago that Katie could hardly remember. And Stephen had ignored her ever since. She certainly hadn't imagined it as an enjoyable occasion for either of them. But there was something so little-boyish about Stephen, especially now when he seemed so nervous and serious. The muscle in the corner of his left eye had developed a tic.

"Remember what we talked about?" he went on.

Katie didn't, but she nodded.

He looked around and lowered his voice. "I think I've made my mind up. I think I'm going to leave Swainshead."

"But why?"

Stephen noticed a couple of his senior executives heading in their direction. "We can't talk here, Katie. Not now. Can I see you on Friday?"

"Sam goes to—"

"Yes, I know Sam goes to Eastvale on Fridays. I don't want to see Sam, I want to see you. We'll go for a walk."

"I—I don't know."

His tone was urgent and his eyes were pleading with her. The two men had almost reached them. "All right," she said. "A walk. A little one."

Stephen relaxed. Even the tic in his eye seemed to disappear.

"Ah, Stephen, here you are," one of the executives, a plump, florid man called Teaghe, said. "Trust you to corner the prettiest filly at the party, eh?" He cast a lecherous glance at Katie, who smiled politely and made an excuse to leave.

She poured herself another glass of wine for appearance's sake and leaned by the side of the French windows, watching the lantern-lit dancers in relief against the huge black mass of Adam's Fell. The garden was a tangled web of shadows, crossing and knotting like an enormous cat's cradle. As the warm light caught their features at certain angles, some of the dancers looked positively Satanic.

So, although she had never thought of herself as a
sympathetic listener—so bound up in her own shyness and
discomfort was she—Stephen had asked her to be his
confidante and she had agreed to go for a walk with him, to
listen to his problems. It was more than Sam ever asked her
to do. There were only two things he wanted from her: work
and sex.

She trusted Stephen as far as she could trust any man. He
hadn't tried anything last time, when he could have, and he'd
been distinctly cool towards her since. But why did he want
to leave Swainshead? Why did he seem so on edge? Was he
running away from something? Still, she thought, if he was
going away, and he really liked her, then there was just a
chance he might take her with him.

She suspected that it might be a sin to desert her husband,
but she had thought so much about it, she decided it was
worth the risk. Surely God would forgive her for leaving a
man with such vile and lascivious appetites as Sam
Greenock? She could make amends, do good works. She
might have to give Stephen her body, too, she knew that. If
not on Friday, then later, if he took her away with him. But
that was one sin nobody could catch her out on. She had
learned how to comply with all the things men wanted, but
she got no pleasure from them herself. She thought it was
just because of Sam, her only lover for years, but when
Bernie had forced himself on her and she hadn't had the
energy or the power to fight him off, she knew that she could
never enjoy the act with any man. Bernie had at least been
kind and gentle when he got her where he wanted her, but it
made no difference to the way she felt about what he was
doing.

She looked at the lantern-lit guests again. Sam was
dancing with an attractive brunette, probably from Collier
Foods, and Nicholas was back in circulation, talking and
laughing by the fountain with a group of commuters who
lived in Swainsdale and made their money elsewhere. His
lower lip was swollen as if he'd been stung by a bee. When he
caught her glance, he glared at her with such lust and hatred

that she shivered and pulled her shawl up more tightly around her shoulders.

II

In Toronto, Banks combined sightseeing with his search for Anne Ralston in the English-style pubs. The weather remained uncomfortably hot and humid, and a window-rattling thunderstorm one night only seemed to make things worse the next day.

Banks gave the CN Tower a miss, but he walked around the Eaton Centre, a huge shopping mall with a glass roof and a flock of sculptured Canada geese flying in to land at one end, and he visited Yonge and Dundas after dark to watch the hookers and street kids on the neon strip. He took a ferry to Ward's Island and admired the Toronto skyline before walking along the boardwalk on the south side. Lake Ontario glittered in the sun, as vast as an ocean. He went to Harbourfront, where he sipped Carlsberg on a waterfront patio and watched the white sails of the yachts cut slow as knives through treacle in the haze.

One morning he took a bus to Kleinburg to see the McMichael collection. Sandra, he thought, would love the Lawren Harris mountain-scapes and the native art. Also in the collection was a painting by Emily Carr that he associated with Jenny Fuller, a psychologist friend who sometimes helped with cases in Eastvale. She had a print of it on her living-room wall, and it was at her suggestion that he had made the visit.

Nor could he bear to miss Niagara Falls. If anything, it was even more magnificent than he had expected. He went out on the Maid of the Mist, wrapped up in oilskins, and the boat tossed like a cork when it reached the bottom of the falls. From a certain angle, he could see a rainbow cut diagonally across the water. When the boat got closer, the spray filled his eyes like a mist and he could see nothing; he could hear only the primeval roar of the water.

The rest of the time, he visited pubs. Allowing an hour or so in each, he would sit at the bar, show the photographs and ask after Bernard Allen and Anne Ralston of bar staff and customers.

This part of the job was hard on his liver and kidneys, so he tried to slow down his intake and pace himself. To make the task more interesting—for solo pub-crawling is hardly the most exciting pastime in the world—he sampled different kinds of draft beer, both imported and domestic. Most of the Canadian beers tasted the same, and they were uniformly gassy. The English beers, he found, didn't travel well. Double Diamond and Watney's he determinedly ignored, just as he did back home. By far the best were the few local brews that Gerry Webb had told him about: Arkell Bitter, Wellington County Ale, Creemore Springs Lager and Conner Bitter. Smooth and tasty, they had body and, when required, boasted fine heads.

Despite good beer, he was heartily sick of pubs. He was smoking too much, drinking too much and eating too much fried food. On Tuesday, after getting back from Kleinburg, he had tried The Sticky Wicket, the Madison and the Duke of York, all close to the university. No luck. On Wednesday, after his return from Niagara Falls, he had started out at The Spotted Dick, then made his way down busy Yonge Street among the shoppers and pleasure-seekers to the Hop and Grape, via the Artful Dodger and The Jack Russell. He had sat in the Hop and Grape, on the ground floor of an office block near Yonge and College, and watched long-haired heavy-metal fans in the street flock towards a rock concert at Maple Leaf Gardens. His clothes were soaked with sweat and his feet hurt. The pub was quiet at that time, as the office workers had gone home and the evening crowds hadn't yet turned up. There were only two days left, and he was very much conscious of time's winged chariot at his rear. Fed up, he had gone back to the house for an early night.

He knew he had to be right, though; Bernard Allen had frequented an English-style pub, and he must have had drinking companions who would be mourning his loss.

On Thursday at about three-fifteen, Banks got off a streetcar outside The Feathers, in the east end of the city. The inside door opened opposite a small darts area: two boards against a green baize backing, pock-marked with miss-shots. To his left was the pub itself, all darkly gleaming wood, polished brass and deep red velvet upholstery. And it was cool.

The wall opposite the bar was covered with framed photographs, mostly of English and Scottish scenes. Banks recognized a pub he knew in York, Theakston's brewery in Masham, a road sign he'd often passed on the way to Ripon and, most surprising of all, a photo of the Queen's Arms in Eastvale's cobbled market square. It was an odd sensation, seeing that. He was in a pub over three thousand miles from home looking at a photo of the Queen's Arms. Eerie.

The place was almost empty. Near the door sat a group of four or five people listening to a silver-haired man with a lived-in face and a Lancashire accent complain about income tax.

Banks stood at the bar close to a very tall man with short, neat hair. He was smoking a pipe and staring abstractedly into space as if musing about the follies of mankind. Behind the bar, above the till, was a small Union Jack.

"I'll have a pint of Creemore, please," Banks said, noticing the logo on one of the pumps.

The barmaid smiled. She had curly auburn hair and brown eyes full of humour and mischief. When she walked over to the end of the bar to fill a waitress's order, Banks noticed she was wearing a very short skirt. It did more than justice to a fine pair of legs.

"Quiet," Banks commented, when she placed the ice-cold pint in front of him.

"It usually is at this time," she said. "We get busy around five when people drop in after work."

Banks took a deep breath and reached for the photographs in his jacket pocket. They were getting dog-eared. He was so used to disappointment that he put hardly any enthusiasm into his question: "I don't suppose you had a regular here by the name of Bernard Allen, did you?"

"Bernie?" she said. "Bernie who got killed over in England?"

Banks could hardly believe his ears. "Yes," he said. "Did you know him?"

The barmaid's eyes turned serious as she spoke. "He was a regular here," she said. "I wouldn't say I really knew him, but I talked to him now and then. You know, like you do when you're waitressing. He was a nice guy. Never made any trouble. It was terrible what happened."

"Did he drink alone?"

"No. There was a group of them—Bernie, Glen, Barry and Ian. They always sat in that corner over there." She pointed to a round table opposite the far end of the bar.

"Was there ever a woman with them?"

"Sometimes. But I never talked to her. Why do you want to know all this? Are you a cop or something?"

Banks decided on honesty. "Yes," he said. "But I'm here unofficially. We think Bernie met an old friend over here who might have some information for us. It could help us find out who killed him."

The barmaid rested her elbows on the bar and leaned forward.

Banks showed her the photographs. "Is this her?"

She looked closely and frowned. "It could be. The shape of the face is the same, but everything else is different. These must be old photos."

"They are," Banks said. "But it could be her?"

"Yes. Look, I'm sorry, I can't stand here talking. I honestly don't know much more. Jack over there used to talk to Bernie sometimes. He might be able to help."

She pointed to a man on the periphery of the group near the entrance. He was a solidly built man with a moustache and a fine head of greyish hair, in his mid to late thirties, Banks guessed. At the moment, he seemed to be poring over a crossword puzzle.

"Thank you." Banks picked up his half-finished pint and walked over to the table. He introduced himself and Jack told him to pull up a chair. The Lancastrian at the next table lit a cigarette and said, "I'll just have another gin and tonic, then I'll go."

"We weren't really close friends," Jack said when Banks had asked about Bernie, "but we had some decent conversations." He had a Canadian accent, which surprised Banks. He'd assumed that apart from the bar staff all the regulars were British.

"What did you talk about?"

"Books, mostly. Literature. Bernie was about the only other guy I knew who'd read Proust."

"Proust?"

Jack gave him a challenging look. "Greatest writer who ever lived. He wrote *Remembrance of Things Past*."

"Maybe I'll give him a try," Banks answered, not sure what he was letting himself in for. He tended to follow through on most of his self-made promises to read or listen to things other people recommended, though time constraints always ensured he had a huge backlog.

"Do that," said Jack. "Then I'll have someone to talk to again. Excuse me." He got up and went to the washroom.

The Lancastrian belched and said to the waitress, "Gin and tonic please, love. No fruit."

Banks observed the other people at the table: a small, slim youth with an earring and a diamond stud in his left ear; a taller thin-faced man with a brush-cut and glasses; a soft-spoken man with a hint of an Irish accent. They were all listening to a Welshman telling jokes.

Jack sat down again and ordered another pint of Black Label. The waitress, a nicely tanned blonde with a beautiful smile, took Banks's order for another Creemore, too, and delivered both drinks in no time. Banks paid, leaving her a good tip—one thing he'd soon learned to do on his pub-crawl of Toronto.

"Did you know any of Bernie's friends?" he asked.

Jack shook his head. "Self-important Brits, for the most part. They tend to pontificate a bit too much for my liking. But Bernie seemed to have transcended the parochial barriers of most English teachers."

Marilyn Rosenberg, at Toronto Community College, had said much the same thing in a different way. Whether it was a plus or a minus in her eyes, Banks hadn't been sure.

"When do they usually come in?"

"About five, most days."

Banks looked at his watch; it was just after four.

"Thanks a lot," he said. "By the way, six across is sculls. 'Rows—of heads, we hear!' Head ... skull. To row ... to scull." Jack raised his eyebrows and filled in the answer.

They worked at the crossword together for the next hour as the place filled up. At quarter past five, they were puzzling over "Take away notoriety and attack someone (6)" when two men in white shirts and business suits walked in.

"That's them over there," Jack said. "Excuse me if I don't join you."

Banks smiled. "Thanks for your help, anyway."

"Nice meeting you," Jack said, and they shook hands. "Defame. Of course!" he exclaimed just before Banks moved away. "'Take away notoriety and attack someone.' Defame. Amazing how you get so much more done when there are two minds working at it."

Banks agreed. It was the same with police work. He could certainly have done with some help on this trip. Not Sergeant Hatchley—he hadn't the self-control to separate work from a pub-crawl—but DC Richmond would have been fine.

When he got to their table, the two men had already taken the opportunity to loosen their ties, take off their suit jackets and roll up their sleeves. One was tall and skinny with a bony face and fine blond hair plastered flat against his skull to cover the receding hairline; the other, who only came up to his friend's shoulders, was pudgy and also balding. What little hair he had stood out like a kind of mist or halo around his head. He wore a fixed smile on his lips, and his dark eyes darted everywhere.

Banks walked over to them and told them why he was in Toronto.

"I'm Ian Grainger," said the tall blond one. "Sit down."

"Barry Clark," the other said, still smiling and looking everywhere but at Banks.

"Glen should be along in a while," Ian said. "How can we help you?"

"I'm not sure if you can. I'm looking for Anne Ralston."

For a moment, both men frowned and looked puzzled.

"You might know her as Julie."

"Oh, Julie. Yes, of course," Barry said. "You lost me there for a second. Sure we know Julie. But what could she have to do with Bernie's murder?" His accent was English, as was Ian's, but Banks couldn't place either of them exactly.

"I don't honestly know if she had anything to do with it," Banks said. "But she's the only real lead we've got." He explained about her disappearance just after the Addison murder.

The drinks arrived just before Glen Tadworth, a dark-bearded, well-padded young man with a pronounced academic stoop and a well-developed beer belly, walked over to join them. His red shirt seemed glued to his skin, and there were wet patches under the arms and across the chest. He carried a battered black briefcase stuffed with papers, which he plonked on the floor as he sat down and sighed.

"Bloody students," he said, running his hand through his greasy black hair. "'Dover Beach'—a simple enough poem, you'd say, wouldn't you?" He looked at Banks as he talked, even though they hadn't been introduced. "One bright spark came up with the theory that it was about Matthew Arnold's hangover. Quite elaborate, it was, too. The 'grating roar' was the poet being sick. And as for the 'long line of spray'.... Well, I suppose one should be grateful for their inventiveness, but really ..." He threw his hands up, then reached over and took a long swig from Ian's pint.

"Don't mind him," Barry said, managing to keep his eyes on Banks for a split second as he spoke. "He's always like this. Always complaining." And he introduced them.

"From Swainsdale, eh?" Glen said. "A breath of fresh air from the old country. Lord, what I'd give to be able to live back there again. Not Swainsdale in particular, though it'd do. I'm from the West Country myself—Exeter. The accent's flattened out a bit over the years here, I'm afraid."

"Why can't you go back if you want to?" Banks asked, reaching for another cigarette. "Surely you weren't sent into permanent exile?"

"Metaphorically, my dear Chief Inspector, metaphorically. You know, some people have got hold of the idea that we expatriates, scattered around the ex-colonies and various watering-holes of Europe and Asia, are all pipe-puffing Tories enjoying life without income tax."

"And aren't you?"

"Far from it. Where is that waitress? Ah, Stella, my dear, a pint of Smithwick's please. Where was I? Exile. Yes. If the government really did seek our proxy votes in the next election, I think they'd bloody well regret it. Most of us feel like exiles. We have skills that no-one back home seems to value any more. It's hard enough getting jobs here, but at least it's possible. And they pay well. But I, for one, would be perfectly happy to do the same work back home for less money. There's hardly a day goes by when I don't think about going back."

"What about Bernie?"

"He was as bad as Glen, if not worse," Barry said. "At least recently he was. Full of nostalgia. It's time-travel they're after really, you know, not just a flight across the Atlantic. All of us baby boomers are nostalgic when it comes down to it. That's why we prefer the Beatles to Duran Duran."

Banks also liked the Beatles better than Duran Duran, a group that his son, Brian, had inflicted on him once or twice before moving on to something new. He thought it was because of the quality of the music, but maybe Barry Clark was right and it was more a matter of nostalgia than anything else. His own father had been just the same, he remembered, going on about Glenn Miller, Nat Gonella and Harry Roy when Banks had wanted to listen to Elvis Presley, The Shadows and Billy Fury.

"The longer you're away, the more you idealize the image of home," Barry went on, eyes roving the room. The place was packed and noisy now. People stood three deep at the bar. Jack, Banks noticed, had been joined by a small, pretty woman with short, dark hair laid flat against her skull. The Lancastrian and his friends had left. "Of course, what people don't realize is that the country's changed beyond all recognition," Barry continued. "We'd be foreigners there now, but to us home is still the Queen's Christmas message, the last night of the Proms, Derby Day, the Test Match at Lords, the FA Cup Final—without bloodshed!—leafy lanes, a green and pleasant land. Ordered and changeless. Bloody hell, even the dark Satanic mills have some sort of olde worlde charm for homesick expatriates."

"Damn right," Glen said. "I'd work in a bloody woollen mill in Bingley if it meant being back home. Well, maybe. . . . It's the wistfulness of the exile, you see, Chief Inspector. You get it a lot in poetry. Especially the Irish."

Banks was beginning to see what Jack had meant.

"Bernie was just the same," Ian said. "You should have heard him going on about Yorkshire. It was bloody Dales this and bloody Dales that. You'd think he was talking about paradise. You'll never catch me going back to live over there. Canada's a great place as far as I'm concerned."

"That's because you're in real estate," Glen said. "You're making a bloody fortune. Is that all you care about—the material things? What about your soul, your roots?"

"Oh, shut up, Glen. You're getting tiresome."

"If he could have got a job over there," Banks asked, "do you think he would have gone back?"

"Like a shot," Ian answered. The others agreed.

"Did he ever mention anything about a job?"

"He did say there was a chance of getting back to stay," Glen said. "Lucky bastard. But I didn't know whether to believe him or not."

"What was this chance?"

"He didn't say. Very hush-hush, apparently."

"Why?"

Glen scratched his shoulder and tried to unstick the shirt from his armpit. "Dunno. It was just one of those nights when you've had a few too many, if you know what I mean. Bernie said something about a plan he had to get himself back home."

"But he gave you no details?"

"No. Said he'd let us know after he got back."

"Was it a job he mentioned?"

"Not specifically, no. Just a chance to get back. I assumed it must have been some possible job offer. How else would he be able to live?"

"How attached was he to teaching?"

"He liked it up to a point," Glen answered. "It was something he was good at. He should have been teaching university. He was good enough, but there aren't any jobs. Like most of us, though, he hated the conditions he had to work in and he despised the students' wilful ignorance. They don't know anything and they don't want to know—unless it's in a ballpark or on video. They expect you to spoon-feed them knowledge, then ask them to regurgitate it in a test. For that they expect to be given an A-plus, no matter how bad their writing or how inaccurate their answers. I could go on—"

"You usually do, Glen," Barry cut in, "but I don't think Mr Banks wants to hear it."

Banks smiled. "Actually, I am running out of time," he said. "I need to find Julie as quickly as possible. Do you know where she lives?"

"No," said Ian. "She just comes in on a Friday after work for a couple of drinks."

"It's somewhere near here, I think," Barry added. "She mentioned sunbathing in Kew Gardens once."

"Have you any idea what surname she's using?"

"It's Culver, isn't it?" Barry said. "Or Cleaver, Carver, something like that."

None of the others could improve on Barry's contribution.

"Do you know where she works?"

"In one of those towers near King and Bay," Ian answered. "The TD Centre or First Canadian Place. She complained that the elevators made her ears go funny."

"That's a lot of help," Glen said. "Do you know how many businesses operate from those places?"

Ian shrugged. "Well, that's all I know. What about you?"

Glen and Barry both shook their heads.

"She should be in here at about six tomorrow, though," Barry said. "She hasn't missed a week yet."

"Fine. Look, would you do me a favour? If she turns up early or if I'm late, please don't tell her I want to see her. It might scare her off. You know how some people react to the police."

"Are you sure you're not after her for something?" Glen asked suspiciously.

"Information. That's all."

"All right," Glen agreed. "If it's going to help catch Bernie's killer, we'll do whatever you want." He paused to pick up his pint glass and raise it for a toast. "There is one good thing in all this, you know. At least Bernie died in the place he wanted to live."

"Yes," Banks said. "There is that."

And they all drank to dying where they wanted to live.

11

I

"John told me about Nick's behaviour at the party the other night," Stephen Collier said. "I'm sorry. I warned you to stay away from him."

Katie looked down at the stony path and blushed. "I didn't go seeking him," she said. "He's an animal, a filthy animal."

"But he is my brother, Katie. He's the only family I've got left. I know he acts outrageously sometimes, but ... I promise it won't happen again."

Katie remembered a phrase from the Bible: "Am I my brother's keeper?" Could Stephen keep Nicholas like an animal in a zoo? He looked strained, she thought. He poked at the stones and sods with his ashplant stick as they walked; his face was pale and the tic in his eye was getting worse.

It was fine walking weather: warm but not hot, with a few high, white clouds and no sign of rain. Sam was in Eastvale for the day—not that Katie's walking out with Stephen would have mattered to him, she thought; he practically threw her at the Colliers as if she were his membership ticket to some exclusive club.

They took the diagonal path up the side of Swainshead Fell, heading for the source of the river. The air was clear, and after a few minutes walking even Stephen's pallid cheeks began to glow like embers.

At last they reached their destination. The source of the

River Swain was an unspectacular wet patch on the side of Swainshead Fell. All around it, the grass was greener and grew more abundantly than anywhere else. Only yards away was the source of another river, the Gaiel, which, when it reached the valley below, perversely turned north towards Cumbria.

Stephen had brought a flask of coffee and some dark chocolate. They sat down to eat on the dry grass above the source and looked back on Swainshead. A tewit went into his extended "pee-wit" song as he wove through the air, plummeted and levelled out just before hitting the ground. His wings beat like sheets flapping in a gale.

"He must be trying to attract a mate," Stephen said.

"Or scare us away."

"Perhaps. Coffee? Chocolate?"

Katie accepted the plastic cup of black coffee. She usually liked hers with plenty of cream and a spoonful of sugar, but she took it as it came without complaint. The dark, bitter chocolate puckered her taste buds.

"I shouldn't be here, you know," she said, pushing back a stray wisp of fair hair behind her ear.

"Relax," Stephen said. "Sam's in Eastvale."

"I know. But that's not the point. People will talk."

"Why should they? There's nothing to talk about. Everybody knows we're all friends. You're so old fashioned, Katie."

Katie flushed. "I can't help it. I wish I could," she added in a whisper.

"Look," Stephen went on in a soothing voice, "we've just gone for a short walk up the fell-side, as many people do. Where's the harm in that? We're not hiding from anyone, we're not sneaking off. You act as if we're guilty of something terrible."

"It just feels wrong," Katie said, managing a brief smile. "Oh, don't mind me. I'm trying, I really am. I'm just not very good with people."

"Don't you feel comfortable with me?"

Katie fidgeted with the silver paper from the chocolate wrapper, folding it into a neat, shiny square. "I don't know," she said. "I don't feel afraid."

Stephen laughed. "At least that's a start. But seriously, Katie, sometimes it's necessary to talk. I told you the other night I've got nobody. Nick's hardly the type to make a good listener, and the people at work are just that: employees, colleagues, not friends."

"What about all those guests at the party?"

"Nick's people, most of them. Or from work, business acquaintances. Don't you ever need to talk to someone real, Katie? Don't you ever have problems you want to let out and share?"

Katie frowned and stared at him. "Yes," she said. "Yes, of course I do. But I'm no good at it. I don't know where to start."

"Start with your life, Katie. Are you happy?"

"I don't know. Am I supposed to be?"

"That's what life's for, isn't it, to be enjoyed?"

"Or suffered."

"Are you suffering?"

"I don't think I'm happy, if that's what you mean."

"Why don't you do something about it?"

"There's nothing I can do."

"But there must be. You must be able to change things if you want."

"I don't see how. What would I do? Without the guest house I've got nothing. Where would I go? I don't know anywhere outside Leeds and Swainsdale." She toyed with a stray tress of hair. "I could just see me down in London or somewhere like that. I wouldn't last five minutes."

"Cities aren't quite as bad as you think they are. You only see the worst on television. Many people live happy lives there."

"Still," Katie said, "I'd be lost." She finished the coffee and wiped her lips with the back of her hand.

"Perhaps by yourself you would be."

"What do you mean?"

Suddenly Stephen seemed closer, and somehow he seemed to be holding her hand. Katie tensed. She didn't want to upset him. If he wanted to touch her she would have to let him, but her stomach clenched and the wind roared in her ears. His touch was oddly chaste, though; it didn't seem to threaten her at all.

"I don't know, Katie," he said. "I'm not sure what I'm saying. But I've got to go away. I can't stay around here any longer."

"But why not?"

She felt him trembling as he moved even closer and his grip tightened on her hand. "There are things you don't know anything about, Katie," he said. "Dear, sweet Katie." And he brushed his fingers down her cheek. They felt cold.

Katie wanted to move away, but she didn't dare struggle. "I don't know what you mean," she burst out. "Sam's always telling me I know nothing, too. What is it? Am I so blind or so stupid?" There were tears in her eyes now, blurring her vision of the valley below and the water that bubbled relentlessly from the source.

"No," Stephen said. "No, you're not blind or stupid. But things aren't always what they seem, people aren't what they pretend to be. Listen, let me tell you . . ."

II

The woman who sat opposite Banks in the dining section of The Feathers had changed considerably from the one in Bernard Allen's photograph, but it was definitely the same person. She wore her hair cut short and tinted blonde now, and dressed in a cream business suit. When she sat down and fished in her bag for a cigarette, Banks also noticed that the carefree laughter in her eyes had hardened into a wary, suspicious look. Her long cigarette had a white filter which soon became blotched with lipstick; she had a habit of tapping it on the edge of the ashtray even when there was no ash, and she held it straight out between the V of her first two fingers like an actress in an old movie, pursing her lips to inhale. Her nails were long and painted red.

She had turned up at six, as Glen had said, and she and Banks had left the others to go and talk privately over dinner. There wasn't much separation between the two areas of the pub except for the way the seating was arranged, and they could still hear the conversations at the bar and the tables.

The waitress, a petite brunette with a twinkle in her eye and a cheeky smile, came up and gave them menus. "Something to drink?" she asked.

Julie ordered a White Russian and Banks a glass of red wine, just for a change.

"I need to know why you left Swainshead in such a hurry," he said, when the waitress had gone for the drinks.

"Can't a woman do as she pleases? It's not a police state, you know. Or it wasn't when I was last there."

"Nor is it now. It was your timing that interested us."

"Oh? Why?"

"We tend to be suspicious of someone who disappears without a trace the day after a murder."

"That was nothing to do with me."

"Don't play the innocent. What did you expect us to think? You could have been in danger yourself, or you could have been the killer. For all we knew you could have been buried down a disused mine shaft. You didn't stop to let anyone know what had happened to you."

"Well, I'm telling you now. That killing had nothing to do with me."

"How do you know about it? You don't seem at all surprised at my mentioning it, but the body wasn't discovered until after you'd left."

Julie ground her cigarette into the ashtray. "Don't try your tricks on me," she said. "I read the papers. I know what happened."

The waitress arrived with the drinks and asked if they were ready to order. Banks asked for a few more minutes and she smiled and went away. Julie turned to her menu.

"What would you recommend?" Banks asked.

She shrugged. "The food's always good here. It depends what you fancy. The prime-rib roast and Yorkshire pudding on special is excellent, if you don't mind being reminded too much of home."

Banks looked around at the decor and the photos on the walls. "Not at all," he said, smiling.

This time a different waitress came for their orders, an attractive woman with reddish blonde hair and a warm manner. Banks hoped he hadn't offended the other.

"Where did you go?" he asked Julie, as soon as they'd ordered their meals.

"None of your damn business." She sipped her White Russian.

"A week after you left," Banks pressed on, "the body of a London private-enquiry agent called Raymond Addison was discovered in Swainshead. He'd been murdered. Did you know anything about that?"

"No."

"We've got good reason to think you did. Listen, if you want to make things difficult Miss Ralston—"

"It's Culver, Mrs. Mrs Julie Culver. And it's quite legal. Julie's my middle name and Culver is my husband's. Ex-husband's, I should say."

"Why change your name if you've nothing to hide?"

She shrugged. "It was a new start. Why not a new name?"

"Not very convincing. But Mrs Culver it is. We're on good terms with the Canadian government. We have extradition arrangements and a mutual help policy. If I wanted to, I could make enough fuss to have you sent back to England to answer my questions. This is the easy way."

Julie lit another cigarette. "I don't believe you. I'm a Canadian citizen now. You can't touch me at all."

"That doesn't matter," Banks said. "You're connected to a murder in England. Don't expect your government to protect you from that."

"But you can't prove I had anything to do with it. It's just a coincidence I went away then."

"Is it? What about your involvement with Stephen Collier?"

Julie paled. "What about it? What's he been telling you?"

"Nothing. What does he know?"

"How should I know?"

Banks sighed. "A few weeks ago a friend of yours, Bernard

Allen, was murdered in the hanging valley just over Swainshead Fell."

"I know the place," Julie said sadly. "I've been there with
him. It always looked like autumn. But what makes you
think his death had anything to do with me? I wasn't even in
the country. I was here. It could have been a thief or a psycho
... or a ... a ..."

There was something in her tone that let Banks know she
was interested now, no longer so hostile. "In the first place,"
he said, "we know that you told him not to let anyone know
he'd met you here, which is suspicious enough in itself. And
in the second place, he did tell someone: a woman called
Katie Greenock. Her heart seems to be in the right place, but
she told her husband, Sam, who soon broadcasted it to the
whole White Rose crowd. In the third place, Bernard had
been talking about going home to stay, and there's no
evidence he had a job lined up. Then Bernard got killed
before he had a chance to leave the dale. What does all that
indicate to you?"

"You're the sleuth. You tell me." Julie blew cigarette
smoke down her nose.

Banks leaned forward. "The way I read it," he said, "is that
you knew something about Raymond Addison's murder.
Something incriminating. I'm not sure who else was involved, or why, but it had to be someone with money. I'd
guess that Stephen Collier played a large part. I think you
told Bernard what you knew and he intended to use that
knowledge to blackmail his way to what he wanted most—
his return to Swainshead."

"My God! I ... Are you trying to say I'm responsible for
Bernie's death?"

"I'm not placing any blame, Mrs Culver. I simply want to
know what happened. I want to nail Bernie's killer."

Julie seemed to be thinking fast. Conflicting emotions
flashed across her face. "I'm not guilty of anything," she said
finally. "I've nothing to be afraid of. And I don't believe you.
Bernie could never have been a blackmailer."

The waitress brought their food. Before she left, they
ordered another round of drinks, then Banks tucked into his

roast, while Julie picked at a Caesar salad. They remained silent while they ate. It wasn't until they both pushed their plates aside and reached for their cigarettes that Julie started to talk again.

"It's been such a long time, you know," she began. "A lot's happened. There's been long stretches when I haven't thought about Swainshead at all."

"Not homesick?"

"Me? I'm at home anywhere. Almost anywhere. Though I can't say I cared for the Middle East much."

"Bernie was homesick."

"He was the type, though, wasn't he? If you'd known him you'd have understood. The place was in his blood. He couldn't even really settle down in Leeds. Yes, Bernie wanted to go back. Which was a shame. I'd kind of been hoping . . ."

"You and Bernie? Again?"

She raised a thin, dark-pencilled eyebrow. "You know about that?"

"It was hardly a state secret."

"True. Anyway, why not? We were both free agents again."

"Tell me what happened five years ago that sent you running off around the world."

The waitress came to pick up their plates. Banks ordered a pint of Creemore this time and Julie asked for a coffee and a double Cognac. All the spaces were occupied now. Next to them, a group of about eight people had pulled two tables together.

"It seems more like a million years ago," Julie said when she got her drink. "I suppose I was a naïve young thing back then. My education really began after I left."

She was stalling for time, Banks thought, telling the story her own way. Perhaps she wasn't sure yet whether she was going to tell him the truth or not. The best thing for now, he decided, was to let her go with it and subtly steer her in the right direction. "Where did you go?" he asked.

"First I went to Europe. I'd been saving up for quite a long time—kept my money under the mattress, believe it or not—just waiting for the day when I knew I would take off and never come back. I took a boat over to Holland and ended up in Amsterdam for a while. Then I bummed around France, Italy, Germany. To cut a long story short, I met a man. A Canadian. This'd be about a year later. He took me back to Vancouver with him and we got married." Julie blew out a steady stream of smoke. "Life was fine for a while . . . then he decided I wasn't enough for him. Two can play at that game, I thought. . . . Anyway, it ended."

"When did you first get in touch with Bernie?"

"About eighteen months ago. That was after I split up with Charles. Bernie was having marriage problems of his own, I soon found out, and he seemed happy enough to hear from me. I might have got in touch with him earlier, but I'd been wary about doing so. I knew he was here, of course. He left Swainshead before I did. But I felt that I'd burned all my bridges."

"What made you contact him, then?"

"Circumstances, really. I'm a freelance publicity agent. I started the business in Vancouver because I liked the idea and it gave me something to do while my husband was . . . not around." She tapped her cigarette against the glass ashtray. "It turned out I had a knack, a flair, so I decided to open an office in Toronto as well. I don't know how much you understand about Canada, but Toronto is pretty much the centre of the universe here. I knew Bernie lived in the city, so I thought what the hell. Any trouble I might have caused would have blown over by now anyway."

"Trouble?"

She narrowed her eyes and looked at him closely. "I had thought Bernie might not want to see me."

"I don't understand."

"I went out with Stephen Collier."

"But Bernard was over here by then. What was that to him?"

"It's not that. Bernie and I were never much more than childhood sweethearts anyway. But we were close friends, like brother and sister. I was hoping that might change here . . ." She sighed. "Anyway, it's just that Stephen . . . well . . . he's a Collier."

"And Bernie was very class conscious?"

"Yes."

"So he'd feel betrayed."

"Something like that."

"And did he?"

"He wrote me some pretty nasty letters at the time. Then, when I went away, we lost touch for a while. But when we met up again here it had all blown over. Bernie was compassionate. He understood. That's why I can't believe he was a blackmailer."

"He might not have been. I can't be sure. He might just have opened his mouth out of turn."

Julie smiled. "That sounds more like him."

"What about Nicholas Collier?" Banks asked. "Were you ever involved with him?"

Julie raised her eyebrows. "What on earth do you think I am?" she asked, smiling. "I didn't get around that much. And credit me with some taste. Nicky really did nothing for me, though I caught him giving me the eye once or twice."

"Sorry," Banks said. "I'm not trying to insinuate you're a—"

"Tart? Slut? Harlot? Jezebel? Loose woman? Believe me, I've been called much worse." The old laughter lit up Julie's eyes for a moment. "Do you know the difference between a slut and a bitch?"

Banks shook his head.

"A slut is a woman who sleeps with anyone; a bitch is a woman who sleeps with anyone but you."

Banks laughed. "That's from the man's point of view, of course."

"Of course."

"So what happened?" he asked. "What made you leave when you did?"

"You're a persistent man, Mr Banks," Julie said, lighting another long, white cigarette. "Even my tasteless jokes don't seem to deflect you for very long. But I'm still not sure I ought to tell you."

Banks caught her eyes and held them. "Mrs Culver," he said quietly, "Bernard Allen—your childhood sweetheart, as you called him—was murdered. All murders are cruel and vicious, but this one was worse than many. First he was stabbed, and then his face was slashed and beaten in with a rock so nobody could recognize him. When we found him he'd been hidden away in the hanging valley for nearly two weeks and there were maggots crawling out of his eye sockets."

Julie turned pale and gripped her Cognac glass so tightly Banks thought she was going to shatter it. Her jaw was clenched and a muscle just below her ear twitched. "Bastard," she whispered.

The silent tension between them seemed to last for hours. Banks could hear the aimless chatter around him as if it were from a distant movie soundtrack: snippets of conversation about marathon running, beer, cricket and teaching native children up north, all in a medley of Canadian, Yorkshire, London and Scottish accents. Julie didn't even seem to realize he was there any more. She was staring at the wall just to the left of him. He half-turned and saw a photograph of a wooded valley. The leaves were russet, yellow and orange.

He lit a cigarette. Julie finished her Cognac and a little colour returned to her cheeks. The waitress came by and they ordered another round.

When they had their drinks, Julie shook her head and regarded Banks with something close to hatred. "For Bernie, then," she said, and began: "The night before I left I was supposed to see Stephen. We'd arranged to go to dinner at the Box Tree in Ilkley. He picked me up about half an hour late and he seemed unusually agitated—so much so that he pulled into a lay-by after we'd not gone more than four or five miles. And then he told me. He said there'd been some trouble and someone had got hurt. He didn't say killed at that time, just hurt. He was in a terrible state. Then he said something about the past catching up, that it was connected with something that had happened in Oxford."

"When he was at university there?"

"I suppose so. He did go to Oxford. Anyway, this man, a private investigator, had turned up out of the blue and was intent on causing trouble. Stephen told me that Sam Greenock called and said there was someone looking for a

Mr Collier. Sam was a bit suspicious about the newcomer asking questions and didn't give anything away. The man said he was going for a short evening walk up the valley. Stephen said he went after him and they talked and the man was going to blackmail the family."

"About this event that had occurred in Oxford?"

"Yes. According to Stephen, tempers were raised, they fought and the man was hurt—badly hurt. I told Stephen he should call an ambulance.

"He got angry then and told me I didn't understand. That was when he said the man was dead. He went on to say there was nothing to connect them. Sam would keep quiet if they humoured him and let him play the local squire. Stephen just had to tell someone, to unburden himself, and he didn't really have anyone else he felt he could talk to but me."

"What was your reaction?"

Julie lit a fresh cigarette from the stub of her old one. "You have to understand Stephen," she said. "In many ways he's a kind, considerate, gentle man. But he's also a businessman and he can be ruthless when he feels the need. But more than all that, he's a Collier. There are few things more important to him than the good name of his family and its history. I wouldn't say I was in love with him, but I thought a lot of him and I didn't want to see him suffer. Needless to say, we didn't have dinner that night. We stopped at the nearest pub and had a bit too much to drink, then we—" Julie stopped. "The rest is of no interest. I never saw him again after that night."

"Why did you leave the next day? Did he suggest it to you?"

"No. I think he trusted me. He knew I was on his side."

"So why did you go?"

"For my own reasons. First, and perhaps least, I'd been thinking about making a break for a while. I've no family. My parents died ten years ago and I just kept on the cottage. I had no real ambitions, no plans for my life. I was getting bored with my job and I was realistic enough not to see myself as the future Mrs Stephen Collier. Stephen wasn't going to propose, and I'd had hints from him that Nicholas

didn't consider me to be of the right class, as if I wasn't aware
of that already. These new events just hurried me along a bit.
Secondly, I didn't trust myself. I thought if the police came
around and started asking me questions, they'd know something was wrong and they'd keep pressuring me until I gave
Stephen away. I didn't want to let that happen. I'm not a
good liar, Mr Banks, as you can see."

"And third?"

"Fear."

"Of Stephen?"

"Yes. As I said, he's a complex man. There's a dark side to
him. He's vulnerable in some ways, but very practical in
others. Sentimental and pragmatic. It can sometimes make
for a frightening combination. Didn't someone once say that
Mafia dons are very sentimental people? Don't they send
flowers to the widow when they've killed someone? And
weren't the Nazis sentimental too? Anyway, he'd done it
before, confided in me one day then cut me dead the next—
no pun intended—just pretended we'd never been intimate at
all. Basically, Stephen couldn't get close to anyone. He'd try,
and one of the ways he did it was by confiding. But then he'd
regret it the next day and turn cold. What worried me was
the importance of this confidence. It was the kind of thing he
might not be able to live with, someone as weak as me
knowing his secret."

"In other words, you were worried you might become his
next victim."

"I know it sounds a horrible thing to say about someone
you basically like and respect—even loved, perhaps, once—
but yes, it did cross my mind. Much easier to disappear, as
I'd been thinking of it anyway. And there was no-one to
make a fuss about my going."

"What kind of things did he confide in you about before?"

"Oh, nothing much. Perhaps a slightly shady business deal
—he was pleased if he'd put one over on somebody. Or an
income-tax fiddle. He hated the inland revenue."

"Nothing more?"

"No. Not until that time."

They sipped their drinks and let the conversations flow

around them. Julie seemed more relaxed now she had told her story, and Banks could see no traces of that hateful look left in her eyes.

"Did he say anything else about this incident in Oxford?" he asked.

Julie shook her head. "Nothing."

"So you don't know what happened there, or who else might have been involved?"

"No. I'm sorry. At the time I never even thought to ask. It was all hard enough to take in as it was."

Banks sighed. Still, even if he hadn't uncovered the whole story yet, he'd done well. The trip had been worthwhile. Julie rejoined the others. Banks said his farewells and left. It was about nine o'clock, a hot, humid evening. Instead of taking the bus, he crossed Kingston Road and started walking towards the lake. The road sloped steeply at one point, crossed another main street with tram rails, then a hundred yards or so farther on ended at a beach.

Couples walked hand in hand along the boardwalk or sat on benches and stared out at the water. Some people jogged by, sweating, and others ambled along with dogs on leashes. Banks made his way over the soft sand to where a group of rocks stuck out into the lake. He clambered as far forward as he could and sat down on the warm stone. Water slopped around just below his feet. The horizon was a broad mauve band; above it, the sky's pink was tinged with misty grey. Banks lit a cigarette and wondered if it was the United States he could see in the distance or just a low, narrow layer of mist.

He'd got what he came for, though he still couldn't put everything together. At least when he got back he would be able to question Stephen Collier more thoroughly, no matter what the man's influence with the deputy chief constable. Collier had killed Raymond Addison, and he might even have killed Bernard Allen too. There was no proof as yet, but Banks would find some if it took him a lifetime. Collier wasn't going to escape justice because of influence or social position; of that Banks would make sure.

By the time he had finished his cigarette, the sun had gone

down much lower and the sky had changed. The horizon was now grey, and the mauve band much higher in the sky. The lake seemed scattered with pink, as if the colour had transformed itself into raindrops and shattered the ice-blue surface of the water. Carefully, Banks got to his feet on the angled rock and made his way back towards a streetcar stop.

III

Earlier that day, back in Swainsdale, Detective Constable Philip Richmond had sat on a knoll high on Adam's Fell and unwrapped his cheese-and-pickle sandwiches. He flicked away the flies that gathered and poured some coffee from his flask. Up there, the air was pure and sharp; below, the sun glinted on the steel kegs in the backyard of the White Rose and flashed in the fountain playing in the Colliers' huge garden behind the ugly Gothic mansion. The old men stood on the bridge, and the Greenocks' front door was closed.

Sam had driven off on one of his regular jaunts to Leeds or Eastvale, and Katie had gone for a walk with Stephen Collier up Swainshead Fell. He thought he could see them across in the north-east, near a patch of grass that was greener than that around it, but it could have been someone else.

Sipping the bitter, black coffee, Richmond had reminded himself that tomorrow was his last day in Swainshead. He was expected back at the station with a report on Sunday morning. Not that he hadn't enjoyed himself—it had been very much like a week's holiday—but he longed to get back to his Eastvale mates. Tomorrow the rugby team was playing Skipton, a game he would have to miss. There was always a good booze-up and sing-song after the match, and it would be a shame to miss that too. Jim Hatchley was usually there for the booze, of course. An honorary member they called him now he wasn't fit enough to play any more. But even the sergeant's presence didn't spoil Richmond's fun: a few jars, a good sing-song, then, with a bit of luck, a kiss and a cuddle with Doreen on the way home. He prided himself on being a man of simple tastes, yet he also liked to think that nothing else about him was simple.

Finishing his sandwich, he unwrapped a Kit-Kat and picked up *The Three Stigmata of Palmer Eldritch*, the last of the four Philip K. Dick books he'd brought along. But he couldn't concentrate. He began to wonder why nothing had happened during Banks's absence. Was the killer certain that the chief inspector would find out nothing in Toronto? Or was there, perhaps, no connection at all between the Addison and Allen murders?

Certainly there had been a bit of a fuss or flap, as Freddie Metcalfe had said, earlier in the week. But it had soon died down and everyone carried on as normal. Was it a false sense of security? The lull before the storm. Perhaps they knew who Richmond was and were being especially careful? He certainly couldn't keep an eye on all of them.

He stroked his moustache and turned back to his book. Not ours to reason why ... But still, he thought, an arrest would have helped his career. A thrilling car chase, perhaps, or a cross-country marathon. He pictured himself bringing in the killer, arm twisted up his back, and throwing him in Eastvale nick under Banks's approving smile. Then he laughed at himself, brushed a persistent wasp away and went back to Philip K. Dick.

IV

That Saturday, the afternoon of his last day in Toronto, Banks went to his first baseball game. The retractable roof was open, and a breeze from the lake relieved some of the humidity at the SkyDome, where the Toronto Blue Jays were playing the New York Yankees, but the temperature was still almost thirty degrees. In England, people would have been fainting from the heat.

Banks and Gregson sat in the stands, ate hotdogs and drank beer out of flimsy plastic cups.

"Lucky to be drinking it at all," Gregson said when Banks complained. "It took a lot of doing, getting drinking allowed at ball games."

A fat boy of about twelve sitting next to Banks stopped shovelling barbecue-flavoured potato crisps into his maw to stand up and hurl obscene death-threats at the Yankees' pitcher. His equally obese mother looked embarrassed but made no attempt to control him.

Banks wished his son, Brian, could be there. Unlike Banks, he had watched enough baseball on Channel 4 to be able to understand the game. When Banks first took his seat, the only baseball term he knew was "home run," but by the end of the third inning, Gregson had explained all about RBIs, the tops and bottoms of the innings, designated hitters, knuckle balls, the bullpen, bunting, the balk rule, pinch hitters and at least three different kinds of pitches.

The game mounted to an exciting conclusion, and the boy next to him spilled his crisps all over the floor.

Finally, the home crowd went wild. Down five-four at the bottom of the ninth, with two out, the sixth Blue Jay up drove one home with all the bases loaded—a grand slam, Gregson called it. That made the score eight-five, and that was how the game ended.

They pushed their way out of the stadium, and Gregson negotiated the heavy traffic up Spadina to Bloor, where they stopped in at the Madison for a farewell drink.

"Are you planning to do anything about the Culver woman?" Gregson asked.

Banks sipped his pint of Conner bitter. They were out on the patio, and the late afternoon sun beat down on his shoulders.

"No," he answered. "What did she do, after all?"

"From the sound of it, she withheld evidence. She was a material witness. If she'd spoken up, this new homicide might never have happened."

Banks shook his head. "She didn't have much choice really. I know what you mean, but you've got to understand what things are like around Swainshead. It's not like Toronto. She couldn't tell what she knew. There was loyalty, yes, but there was also fear. The Colliers are a powerful family. If she'd stayed we might have got something out of her, but on the other hand something might have happened to her first."

"So she left under threat?"

"That's the way I'd put it, yes."

"And you think this Collier guy killed Allen because he knew too much?"

"I think it was more to do with what Allen intended to do with his knowledge. I can't prove it, but I think he was going to blackmail Stephen Collier. Julie Culver disagrees, but from what one of Allen's boozing buddies told me, he had some plan to get back home to England. I think he asked Collier for the money to come home and live in Swainshead again, or maybe to fix him up with a job. Collier's brother teaches at a small public school, and Allen was a teacher. Maybe he suggested that Stephen tell Nicholas to get him a job there. Instead, Stephen decided to get rid of Allen the same way he did with Addison."

"Shit," said Gregson, "I'd no idea Toronto was so bad that people would stoop to blackmail to get out of here."

Banks laughed. "Maybe it's just that Swainsdale is so beautiful people would do anything to get there. I don't know. Allen was seriously disturbed, I think. A number of things took their toll on him: the divorce, the distance from home, the disappointment of not getting the kind of job that would really challenge his mind. Someone told me that he had gone beyond the parochial barriers of most English teachers, but he found himself in a system that placed no value on the exceptional, a system that almost imposed such barriers. The teaching he was doing was dreary, the students were ignorant and uninterested, and I think he tended to blame it on the local educational system. He thought things would be better in England. He probably remembered his own grammar-school days when even poor kids got to learn Latin, and he thought things were still like that. Perhaps he didn't even think he was doing anything really bad when he approached Collier. Or maybe he did. He had plenty of cause to resent him."

"That old British class system again?"

"Partly. It's hard to figure Allen out. Mostly, he seems like a decent person gone wrong, but he also had a big chip on his shoulder all along. I don't suppose we'll ever know what really motivated him."

"But you do have your killer."

"Yes—if he hasn't done a bunk. But we've no proof yet."

"He knows you're here, onto the girl?"

"The whole village knows. We've got a man there."

"Well, then . . . What time's your flight?"

"Nine o'clock." He looked at his watch. "Christ, it's six now. I'd better get back and pick up my stuff."

"I'll drive you," Gregson said. "I'm off duty all day, and it can be a real hassle getting to the airport."

"Would you? That's great."

At the house, Banks packed his meagre belongings and the presents he had bought for his family, then left a thank-you note with the bottle of Scotch for Gerry. In a way, he felt sad to leave the house and neighbourhood that had become familiar to him over the past week: the sound of streetcars rattling by; the valley with its expressway and green slopes; the downtown skyline; the busy, overflowing Chinese shops at Broadview and Gerrard.

The traffic along Lakeshore Boulevard to the airport turn-off wasn't too heavy, and they made it with plenty of time to spare. The two policemen swapped addresses and invitations outside the departures area, then Gregson drove straight off home. Banks didn't blame him. He'd always hated hanging around airports himself if he didn't have a plane to catch.

After the queue at the check-in desk, the trip to the duty-free shop, and the passage through security and immigration, it was almost time to board the plane. As they took off, Banks looked out of the window and saw the city lit up in the twilight below him: grids and figure-eights of light as far as he could see in every direction except south, where he could pick out the curve of the bay and the matt silver-grey of Lake Ontario.

Once in the air, it was on with the Walkman—Kiri te Kanawa's soaring arias seemed most appropriate this time—down the hatch with the Johnny Walker, and away with the food. A seasoned traveller already. This time even the movie was tolerable. A suspense thriller without the car chases and special effects that so often marred that type of film for Banks, it concentrated on the psychology of policeman and victim.

He slept for a while, managed to choke down the coffee and roll that came for breakfast, and looked out of the window to see the sun shining over Ireland.

It was going on for ten o'clock in the morning, local time, when he'd cleared customs and reclaimed his baggage. Among the crowd of people waiting to welcome friends and relatives stood Sandra, who threw her arms around him and gave him a long kiss.

"I told Brian and Tracy they should come, too," she said, breaking away and picking up the duty-free bag, "but you know what they're like about sleeping in on Sunday mornings."

"So it's not that they don't love me any more?"

"Don't be silly. They've missed you as much as I have. Almost."

She kissed him again, and they set off for the car.

"It's a bloody maze, this place," Sandra complained, "and they really fleece you for parking. Then there's roadworks everywhere on the way. They're still working on Barton bridge, you know. It was misty, too, high up in the Pennines. Oh, I am going on, aren't I? I'm just so glad to see you. You must be tired."

Banks stifled a yawn. "It's five in the morning where I am. Where I was, rather. And I can't sleep on planes. Anything interesting happen while I was away?"

Sandra frowned and hesitated. "I wasn't going to tell you," she said, loading the small case and the duty-free bag into the boot of the white Cortina, "at least not until we got home. Superintendent Gristhorpe called this morning just before I set off."

"On a Sunday morning? What about?"

"He said he wants to see you as soon as you get back. I told him what state you'd be in. Oh, he apologized and all that, but you've still got to go in."

"What is it?" Banks lit cigarettes for both Sandra and

himself as she drove down the spiral ramp from the fourth floor of the multi-storey car-park out into the sunlit day.

"Bad news," she said. "There's been another death in Swainshead."

Part Three:

THE DREAMING
SPIRES

12

I

"Accidental death! Don't you think that's just a bit too bloody convenient?"

Sergeant Hatchley shrugged as if to imply that perhaps if Banks didn't go gallivanting off to the New World such things might not happen. "Doc says it could have been suicide," he said.

Banks ran his hand through his close-cropped black hair. It was twelve-thirty. He was back in his office only an hour after arriving home, jet-lagged and disoriented. So far, he hadn't even had a chance to admire his favourite view of the cobbled market square. The office was smoky and a cup of black coffee steamed on the desk. Superintendent Gristhorpe was keeping an appointment with the deputy chief constable, whose personal interest in events was a measure of the Colliers' influence in the dale.

"And where the hell was Richmond?" Banks went on. "Wasn't he supposed to be baby-sitting the lot of them while I was away?"

"Yes, sir."

"Where was he then?"

"Asleep at the Greenocks', I suppose. He could hardly invite himself to spend the night with the Colliers, could he?"

"That's not the point. He should have known something was wrong. Send him in."

"He's just gone off duty, sir."

"Well bloody well bring him back again!"

"Yes, sir."

Hatchley stalked out of the office. Banks sighed, stubbed out his cigarette and walked over to the window. The cobbled market square was still there, a bit rain drenched, but still there. Tourists posed for photographs on the worn plinth of the ancient market cross. The church door stood open and Banks could hear the distant sound of the congregation singing "Jerusalem."

So he was home. He'd just had time to say hello to Brian and Tracy, then he'd had to hurry down to the station. He hadn't even given them their presents yet: a Blue Jays sweatshirt for Brian, the *Illustrated History of Canada* for his budding historian daughter, Tracy, and a study of the Group of Seven, with plenty of fine reproductions, for Sandra. They were still packed in his suitcase, which stood next to the duty-free cigarettes and Scotch in the hall.

Already Toronto was a memory with the quality of a dream—baseball, the community college, Kleinburg, Niagara Falls, the CN Tower, and the tall downtown buildings in black and white and gold. But Staff Sergeant Gregson, the Feathers crowd and Anne Ralston/Julie Culver weren't a dream. They were what he had gone for. And now he'd come back to find Stephen Collier dead.

There was no suicide note; at least nobody had found one so far. According to Nicholas Collier, John Fletcher and Sam Greenock, who had all been with Stephen on his last night at the White Rose, Stephen, always highly strung and restless, had seemed excessively nervous. He had got much more drunk than usual. Finally, long beyond closing time, they had had to help him home. They had deposited Stephen fully clothed on his bed, then adjourned to Nicholas's half of the house, where they had a nightcap. John and Sam then left, and Nicholas went to bed.

In the morning when he went to see how his brother was, Nicholas had discovered him dead. The initial findings of Dr Glendenning indicated that he had died of suffocation. It appeared that Stephen Collier had vomited while under the influence of barbiturates and been unable to wake up. Such things often happened when pills and booze were mixed, Glendenning had said. All that had to be determined now was the amount of barbiturate in Stephen's system, and that would have to wait until the post-mortem. He had suffered from insomnia for a long time and had a prescription for Nembutal.

So what had happened? According to Hatchley, Stephen must have got up after the others left and taken his sleeping pills as usual, then gone downstairs and played a record— Mozart's *Jupiter* symphony was still spinning on the turntable—had another drink or two of Scotch from a tumbler, which was still half full, gone back upstairs, taken some more sleeping pills and passed out. By that time, given how much he'd had to drink, he probably wouldn't have remembered taking the first lot of pills. The only question was, did he do it deliberately or not—and the only person who could answer that was Stephen himself.

It was damned unsatisfactory, Banks thought, but it looked like an end to both the Addison and Allen cases. Stephen Collier had certainly confessed to Anne Ralston. He knew that Banks would find her and that when she heard Bernie had been killed, she would pass on the information. He must have gone through a week of torment trying to decide what to do—make a run for it or stay and brazen it out. After all, it was only her word against his. The strain had finally proved too much for him, and either accidentally or on purpose—or accidentally on purpose—he had put an end to things, perhaps to save himself and the family name the ignominy of a trial and all the publicity it would bring down on them.

Feeling calmer, Banks lit another cigarette. He finished his coffee and determined not to haul Richmond over the coals. After all, as Hatchley had said, the constable couldn't be everywhere at once. He still felt restless, though; his nerves were jangling and his eyes ached. He had that strange and disturbing sensation of wanting to sleep but knowing he couldn't even if he tried. When he rubbed his chin, he could feel the bristles. He hadn't even had time for a shave.

When Richmond arrived, they walked over to the Queen's Arms. After the morning sunshine, it had turned cool and rainy: a wonderful relief after the hellish steam-bath of Toronto, Banks thought as he looked up and let the rain fall on his face. Cyril, the landlord, rustled them up a couple of ham-and-tomato sandwiches. They found an empty table in a corner, and Banks got the drinks in.

"Look, I'm sorry for dragging you back, Phil," he said, "but I want to hear your version of what happened."

"In the White Rose, sir?"

"The whole week. Just tell me what you saw and thought."

"There's not very much to tell, really," Richmond said, and gave Banks his version of the week's events in as much detail as he could.

"Katie Greenock went off with Stephen Collier on Friday afternoon, is that right?"

"Yes, sir. They went for a walk up Swainshead Fell. I took a walk up Adam's Fell and I could see them across the dale."

"Did they go towards the hanging valley?"

"No, sir, they didn't go over the top—just diagonal, as far as the river's source. It's about half-way up and a bit to the north."

Banks wondered if anything had gone on between Katie and Stephen Collier. It seemed unlikely, given the kind of woman she seemed, but he was sure that she had surrendered to Bernard Allen. And in her case, the old-fashioned term "surrendered" was the right word to use. Banks recalled the image of Katie standing in the market square, soaked to the skin, just before he'd left, and he remembered the eerie feeling he'd had that she was coming apart at the seams. It would certainly be worth talking to her again; at the very least she would be able to tell him something more about Collier's state of mind on the day before he died.

"What about Saturday night in the White Rose? How long were you there?"

"From about nine till closing time, sir. I tried to pace myself, not drink too much."

Banks grinned, remembering his own nights in the

Toronto pubs. "A tough job, eh? Never mind. Notice anything?"

"Like I told the super and Sergeant Hatchley, sir, it seemed pretty much of a normal night to me."

"You didn't think Stephen Collier was drinking more than usual?"

"I don't know how much he usually drank, sir. I'd say from the other three nights I saw him in the White Rose during my stay, he did drink more on Saturday. But it was Saturday night. People do overdo it a bit then, don't they? No work in the morning."

"Unless you're a copper."

Cyril called last orders and Banks hurried to the bar for another two pints.

"What was the mood like at the table?" he asked when he got back.

"A bit festive, really."

"No arguments, no sullen silences?"

"No. Everyone seemed to be enjoying themselves. There was one thing . . ."

"Yes?"

"Well, I couldn't hear anything because Sam and Stephen were talking quite loudly, but I got the impression that at one point John Fletcher and Nicholas Collier were having a bit of a barney."

"What do you mean?"

"I'm just going by the expressions on their faces, sir. It looked like Nicholas was mad at Fletcher for some reason and Fletcher just brushed him aside."

"Did the others appear to notice?"

"No. Like I said, sir, they were talking, arguing about politics or something."

"And this was Nicholas Collier and John Fletcher, not Stephen?"

"Yes, sir."

"Odd. How did Stephen seem?"

"I'd say he was a fairly happy drunk. Happier than he ever seemed sober."

"What was he drinking?"

"They were all drinking beer."

"How many pints would you say Stephen had?"

Richmond flushed and fiddled with his moustache. "I wasn't really counting, sir. Perhaps I should have been ... but ..."

"You weren't to know he'd be dead in the morning. Don't worry. It's the bane of our lives. If we all had twenty-twenty hindsight our job'd be a lot easier. Just try and remember. Picture it as clearly as you can."

Richmond closed his eyes. "At a guess, I'd say about five or six, sir."

"Five or six. Not a lot, really, is it? Not for a Yorkshireman, anyway. And he was practically legless?"

"Yes, sir. Maybe he was drinking the vodka as well."

"What vodka?"

"I'm not clear on it, but I remember Freddie Metcalfe, the landlord, muttering something about having to change the bottle after one of them had been up and bought a round. It was busy and he said he needed eight hands to do his job."

"But you never saw Stephen put a shorts glass to his lips?"

"No, sir."

"Did anyone?"

"Not that I remember."

"Odd, that, isn't it? What happened to the vodka, then?"

"Perhaps whoever bought it just drank it down at the bar."

"Hmm. It's possible. But why? Let's leave it for the moment, anyway. Did you hear any mention at all of Oxford during the week?"

"You mean the university, sir?"

"Any mention at all. The name: Oxford."

Richmond shook his head.

"All right, that'll do for now." Banks rubbed his eyes.

They drifted out into the street with the others as Cyril prepared to lock up for the afternoon. There was a lot more to think about now. Nothing that Banks had heard since he got back had been at all convincing. Something was wrong, he felt, and the case was far from over. Sending Richmond back home, he decided on a short walk in the rain to freshen himself up before returning to the station.

II

Katie watched the rain swell the becks that rushed down Swainshead Fell as it got dark that night. The rhythmic gurgle of water through the half-open window calmed her. All day she had been agitated. Now it was after ten; Sam was still at the pub, and Katie was brooding over the day's events.

If only she had told Sam that their guest was a policeman, probably sent to spy on them. Then he'd have informed all and sundry, and maybe things would have been different. But now Stephen had to die, too: another escape route cut off. Had the policeman noticed anything? Katie didn't think so. There had been nothing really to notice.

Ever since morning, when Stephen's body had been discovered, Upper Head had been stunned. Women gathered in the street after church and lowered their voices, looking over at the Gothic house and shaking their heads. The Colliers were, when all was said and done, still regarded as lords of the manor.

All the curtains of their spooky Victorian mansion across the river had been drawn since morning, when the police and doctors had finished and taken Stephen's body away. One or two people had dropped by to offer condolences, including John Fletcher, who'd have got a rude reception from Nicholas, Katie thought, under any other circumstances. Sam, of course, had been one of the first, keen to establish himself with the new squire now that the more approachable Stephen was gone. Now Sam and John were no doubt getting maudlin drunk in the White Rose. Katie hadn't gone across to the house; she couldn't face Nicholas Collier alone again after the incident at the party.

Rain spilled in over the window-sill. Katie dipped a finger in it and made patterns on the white paintwork. The water beaded on the paint no matter what she tried to make it do. A breeze had sprung up and it brought the scent of summer rain indoors; shivering, she pulled her grey lamb's-wool cardigan around her shoulders.

"Be sure your sins will find you out," another of her grandmother's favourite maxims, sprang into her mind.

With it came the dim and painful memory of a tell-tale boy's hair on her collar when she had come home from her one and only visit to the church-run youth club. It must have got there in the cloakroom, somehow, but her grandmother had thrust it forward as irrefutable evidence of Katie's lewd and lascivious nature before making her stand "naked in her shame" in the corner of the cold, stone-flagged kitchen all evening. She had been supposed to repeat "Be sure your sins will find you out" under her breath all the time she stood there, but she hadn't. That was another sin: disobedience. The vicar had got an earful, too, about running a house of ill-repute and corrupting local youth. That had pleased Katie; she didn't like him anyway because his breath smelled like the toilet when he came close, which he always did. Taking pleasure in the misfortunes of others was another sin she had been guilty of that day.

Katie closed the window and turned to get into bed. It was after ten-thirty. Sam would probably be back soon. There was a chance that if she pretended to be asleep . . .

But sleep didn't come easily. She thought of Stephen again, of his chaste touch. Life might not have been so bad if he had taken her away with him. She knew he would want to have her eventually—it would be part of the price—but he seemed a gentle person, like Bernard had been, and perhaps he wouldn't be too demanding. The images blurred in her mind as sleep came closer: her grandmother brandishing the hair, black eyes flashing, Bernard breathing hard as he pulled at her clothes. . . . She heard the back door open and close noisily. Sam. Quickly, she turned over and pulled the covers up to her ears. Her feet were cold.

III

"What do you think, then, Alan?"

Banks and Gristhorpe sat at the dining-room table later that night and sipped duty-free Bell's. The children were in bed and Sandra was leafing through the book Banks had brought her from Toronto. Banks felt better after the short nap he had taken late in the afternoon.

"It stinks. I track down Anne Ralston in Toronto and she tells me Stephen Collier practically confessed to killing Addison because of some scandal he was involved in at Oxford. Then, when I get back I find Collier's conveniently dead—accidental death. It's too pat."

"Hmm." Gristhorpe sipped his Scotch. "It could be true. But let's suppose it's not. What else could have happened? I'm sorry, I know you're still tired, Alan. Maybe tomorrow would be better?"

Banks lit a cigarette. "No, it's all right. What do I think happened? I don't know. I thought I'd got it all worked out but now everything's gone haywire. I know it makes sense that Collier killed himself rather than face the trouble he knew he'd be in for when I got back. Maybe the pressure built in him over the week. On the other hand, what if he didn't kill Allen? What if he knew who did, and whoever it was was afraid he'd crack under pressure and give it away. That would have given someone enough motive to get rid of him, wouldn't it? We still don't have a clear connection between Addison and Allen, though."

"Except the Ralston girl."

"What if there's something else? An angle we haven't really considered."

"Such as?"

"That's the trouble. I've no idea."

Gristhorpe swirled the Bell's in his glass. "Then it has to be connected with Addison and Ralston."

"I'd like to go down to Oxford as soon as possible and dig around. Ted Folley's in the local CID there. We were at training school together."

Gristhorpe nodded. "That's no problem."

"Maybe Addison found something out and was going to blackmail Collier."

"He had a clean record."

"True. But you know as well as I do what private investigators are like—especially solo operators. We can also assume that Bernard Allen had the same information, or part of it, and that he too was blackmailing Collier."

Gristhorpe rubbed his whiskery chin. "Aye. But if Collier did kill Allen for that reason, who killed Collier—and why?"

"That's what we have to find out."

"So we're still looking at the lot of them?"

"It seems that way. Any one of them could have gone back to the house—the French windows at the back weren't locked—and given him another drink with the barbiturates. Or someone could have mixed a few nembies with his drinks earlier. He was so far gone he probably wouldn't have noticed."

"Risky, though."

"Yes. But what murder isn't?"

"Aye."

"And then there's the matter of the vodka. I want to talk to Freddie Metcalfe about that."

"What vodka?"

"Someone in the party was buying vodka that night, but Richmond never actually saw anyone drink it."

"So you think someone was spiking Collier's drinks with vodka, making sure he got really drunk?"

"It's a strong possibility, yes. Vodka's pretty much tasteless in a pint."

"Aye, in more ways than one," Gristhorpe said.

"The trouble is," Banks went on, "it was such a busy night that I can't rely on anyone remembering. It could have been Sam Greenock, John Fletcher or Nicholas Collier—any one of them. I'm assuming they all bought rounds."

"What about the Greenock woman?"

Banks saw again in his mind's eye the image of Katie standing soaked to the skin in the market square. "Katie? I suppose she could play some part in all this. As far as I can tell, though, she's in a world of her own. There's something not quite right about her. I thought it was just her marriage. Sam's a real bastard—thrashes her every now and then—but I think there's more to it than that. According to Richmond, though, she wasn't in the White Rose that night."

Gristhorpe looked at his watch and stood up. "Good Lord, is that the time? I'd better be off. Don't worry about being in early tomorrow."

"I probably will be," Banks said. "I want to go to Swainshead and see a few people. Then I'll go to Oxford. Mind if I take Sergeant Hatchley? There might be a bit of legwork, and I'd rather have Richmond up here taking care of business."

"Aye, take him. He'll feel like a fish out of water in Oxford. Do him good, though. Broaden his horizons."

Banks laughed. "I'm afraid Sergeant Hatchley's horizons are firmly fixed on beer, idleness, sports and sex—in that order. But I'll try."

Gristhorpe drained his glass and left. Banks sat beside Sandra and looked at some of the pictures with her, but his eyes began to feel suddenly prickly and heavy. He'd been wondering whether to let the superintendent know that Gerry Webb had revealed his full name, but decided against it. Names were, after all, a kind of power. He would tell no-one at the station, but it was too good to keep to himself.

"Do you know," he said, slipping his arm around Sandra's shoulders, "I found out a very interesting thing about Superintendent Gristhorpe in Toronto."

"It sounds like you discovered a lot of interesting things there," Sandra said, raising an arched black eyebrow. Her eyebrows contrasted sharply with her natural blonde hair, and that was one of the features Banks found sexy about her. "Go on," she urged him. "Give."

"I've missed you," Banks said, moving closer. "I'll tell you in bed, later."

"I thought you were tired."

"Only my eyes."

"Is it worth knowing?"

"It's worth it."

"Right, then." Sandra turned towards him. "Let's not waste time and energy climbing upstairs. It has been a whole week, after all."

IV

It was good to be home, Banks thought, as he drove the white Cortina along the dale. The sun was out, the water glittered silver, the valley sides shone vibrant green, and the Beatles were singing "And Your Bird Can Sing" on the cassette. He lit a cigarette and slowed down to pass a colourful group of hikers. They clustered together in the deep grass by the dry-stone wall and waved as he drove by.

Who to visit first? That was the question. It was still only ten-thirty, so perhaps he'd best leave Freddie Metcalfe till the White Rose opened at eleven and call on Nicholas Collier— the interview he was least looking forward to.

Accordingly, he carried on past the pub and pulled up on the verge outside the Collier house. Nicholas opened the door at the first ring of the bell.

"Chief Inspector Banks," he said. "Long time, no see. Come in." He looked tired; his usually bright eyes had lost their sparkle and there were dark pouches under them. "Please, sit down." He pointed towards a leather upholstered armchair by the open French windows. "I'm not in a mood to sit in the sun today, but I feel I must remind myself of its presence."

"I'm sorry about what happened," Banks said. "I'd been hoping to talk to Stephen when I got back."

Nicholas turned to look at the fountain outside and said nothing. Banks thought he could see a fading bruise at the side of his mouth.

"I hope you're not going to ask me to go through it all again," Nicholas said at last, taking a cigarette from the porcelain box on the low table beside him. "Policemen always seem to be asking people to repeat their stories."

"There's a good reason for that," Banks said. "Sometimes people remember things. Little things they thought insignificant at the time."

"All the same, I very much doubt that I can help you."

"I was wondering if you had any knowledge of your brother's problems?"

"Stephen's problems? No, I can't say I did. Though he seemed a bit edgy this past week or two, as if he had something on his mind."

"Did you ask him what it was?"

"No. Does that surprise you? Well, it shouldn't. Stephen

wasn't the most forthcoming of people. If he wanted to talk, he would, to whoever struck his fancy at the moment. But if you asked him, you got nowhere. Certainly I never did."

"I see. So you've no idea what he was worried about?"

"Not at all. I take no interest in the business, so I wouldn't know about that side of things. Did he have business problems? Trouble at t'mill?"

"Not that I know of, no, Mr Collier. His problem was that we think he may have killed a man over five years ago because of something that happened at Oxford. We also think he might have been responsible for the murder of Bernard Allen more recently."

"Stephen! You're joking, Chief Inspector, surely?"

Banks shook his head. "When was Stephen at Oxford?"

"He went there nine years ago. But nothing untoward happened to him in Oxford as far as I know." He paused and his eyes turned hard. "You're not joking, are you?"

"I'm afraid not."

"Well, what can I say? Your wording would seem to indicate that this is mere supposition, that you have no proof."

"Only the testimony of Anne Ralston."

"That woman Stephen was seeing all those years ago?"

"Yes. I found her in Toronto."

"And you'd take a slut's word that Stephen was a murderer?"

"She'd no reason to lie. And I don't believe she's a slut."

Nicholas shrugged dismissively. "As you like. She certainly wasn't the type of woman I'd want for a sister-in-law. But haven't you considered that she might have been the guilty party? As I remember, she disappeared the morning after the man was killed."

"Yes, she did."

"So she'd have everything to gain by trying to put the blame on Stephen."

"It's possible, yes. But there's Bernard Allen's murder to take into account, too. She wasn't in Swainshead at the time. She was in Toronto."

"So?"

"So she couldn't have killed Allen."

"I'm sorry but I don't see the connection. You admit she could have killed the other man, but not Bernard Allen. What I don't see is why you should even think the same person killed both of them. What had Allen and that private detective chappie got in common?"

"Nothing, as far as we can tell. Except that they were both killed in Swainshead." Banks lit a cigarette. "There are too many coincidences, Mr Collier. One of the most interesting ones is that Bernard Allen was friendly with Anne Ralston in Toronto. That would make him the only person from Swainshead to see her since she disappeared. And the whole village was aware of that, thanks to Sam Greenock. It's also a coincidence that Stephen was going out with Anne Ralston at the time she left Swainshead, and that she told me he confessed to her about killing Addison. It's another coincidence that Stephen is dead when I return."

"I can't argue with your logic, Chief Inspector. There certainly are a lot of coincidences. But they *are* coincidences, aren't they? I mean, you've no real evidence to link them or to back up your suppositions, have you?"

"Are you sure you knew nothing about your brother's problems?" Banks asked.

"I've told you," Collier sighed. "We just weren't that close. You can see for yourself how we've split the house—into two very different halves, I might add. All we had in common was family. Even if he had been a murderer, which I don't believe for a moment, Stephen would have hardly told me."

"But he told Anne Ralston."

"So you say. I can only repeat that the woman must be lying to save her own skin." He leaned forward to stub out his cigarette but didn't slouch back in the chair again. "Chief Inspector," he said, folding his hands on his lap, "I hope you're not going to spread these accusations about my brother around the dale. After all, you admit you've no proof. You could do untold damage to the family name—not to mention my career."

"Rest assured, Mr Collier. I'm not in the habit of spreading unfounded accusations."

"And might I suggest," Nicholas added, "that even if Stephen had been guilty, he's certainly suffered adequate penalty for his sin, and no useful purpose would be served by going poking around in his past affairs."

"Ah, that's where we differ," Banks said. "I'm not judge or jury, Mr Collier. I just try to dig out the truth. And until there are answers to a number of questions, Stephen's file remains open—wherever Stephen himself may be." Nicholas opened his mouth to protest but Banks ignored him and went on. "I don't care who you are, Mr Collier. You can threaten, you can pull strings, you can do what you bloody well want. But I'm going to get to the bottom of this." He stood up and walked over to the door. Nicholas sat where he was and stared coldly at him.

"One more question," Banks said. "Which one of you was drinking vodka in the White Rose on Saturday night?"

"Vodka?" Nicholas grunted. "None of us, I shouldn't think. Can't stand the stuff, myself."

"Did you see your brother drink any?"

Nicholas walked over to the door and grasped the handle. "No, I didn't. Stephen never drank vodka." He opened the door. "Now would you mind leaving? And you can be damn sure you haven't heard the last of this."

Was he lying? Banks found it hard to tell. People of Nicholas Collier's class had so much self-confidence bred into them that they could carry most things off.

"What was your argument with John Fletcher about?" he asked, leaning against the open door.

"What argument?"

"You didn't have words?"

Nicholas flicked his wrist. "We may have done, but I can't remember why. A trifle, I should imagine. Now . . ." he nodded towards the path.

Banks set off.

It hadn't been satisfactory at all. Banks swore under his breath as he headed down the path. He should have pushed Nicholas even harder. Still, there would be time later. Plenty of time. There was still Oxford. And Katie Greenock and Freddie Metcalfe. He looked at his watch and walked into the White Rose.

"I understand tha's been globe-trotting," Freddie Metcalfe said, pouring out a pint of Marston's Pedigree.

"That's right," Banks answered. "Been to visit the New World." He counted out his change and put it on the damp bar-towel.

"I don't 'old wi' Americans," Freddie said, screwing up his face. "Get plenty on 'em in 'ere, tha knows. Alus asking for fancy drinks—bourbon and branch water and t'like. Can't understand none on 'em. And Perrier. Bloody Perrier wi' a twist o' lemon them purple-haired old women want. Mutton dressed up as lamb, if y'ask me." He sniffed and carried the money to the till.

Banks thought of pointing out that Canada was not the same as the USA, but he didn't want to miss a good opening. "Not get a lot of fancy drinks orders in here, then? Not many drink shorts?" he asked.

"Nah," said Freddie, ambling back. "Most tourists we get's fell-walkers, and they like a good pint, I'll say that for 'em. T'lasses sometimes ask for a brandy and Babycham, like, or a Pony or Cherry B. But mostly it's ale."

"What about vodka?"

"What about it?"

"Get through much?"

"Nah. Bloody Russkie muck, that is. Can't taste it. We get through a good bit o' single malt Scotch, but vodka . . . nah."

"I understand you had a vodka drinker on Saturday night?"

"What makes tha think that? Tha weren't 'ere then."

"Never mind that. Did you?"

Freddie scratched his mutton-chop whiskers. "Aye, come to think on it, I do remember 'aving to change t'bottle, so somebody must've been at it."

"Who, Freddie, who?"

"I can't rightly say. It might not've been me who served 'im. I don't recollect as I did. Lot o' strangers in last weekend 'cos t'weather brightened up, like. It were a busy night, Sat'day, and that gormless lass from Gratly never showed up. S'posed to give me an 'and behind t'bar. No, I'm sorry, lad.

It's no good. I know I changed t'bottle, but I were alus serving four orders at once. Need eight bloody arms on this job, specially on a Sat'day night. And I only 'ad young Betty to 'elp me."

"Were there any arguments in the pub that night?"

Freddie laughed. "Well, it'd 'ardly be a Sat'day night wi'out a few 'eated words, would it?"

"I suppose not. What about at the Collier table?"

"I don't recollect owt. Billy Black and Les Stott were barneying about whippets, and Wally Grimes—Wally's a local farmer, like—'ad a little disagreement wi' some walkers about National Trust footpaths. But that's all I can remember."

"You don't remember anything between Nicholas Collier and John Fletcher?"

"Nah. But that wouldn't be nowt new. Now John and Mr Stephen, they understood each other. But John Fletcher never did 'ave time for young Nicholas, even when 'e were a lad."

"But you heard nothing on Saturday?"

"Nay. Too much bloody noise. I only 'eard t'others because they were standing at t'bar right a-front o'me."

"Did you clear the tables later?"

"Nay, Betty did that." He pointed towards a buxom rosy-cheeked girl washing glasses.

"Can I talk to her?"

"Aye. Betty, lass, come over 'ere. T'Inspector wants a word wi' thee."

The roses quickly spread over Betty's entire complexion, and down as much of her throat and chest as was exposed. She lowered her big brown eyes and stood in front of Banks like a schoolgirl before the head.

"It's all right, Betty," Banks said, "I just want to ask you a couple of questions about Saturday night when you worked here."

She nodded but still didn't look up.

"Do you remember serving Mr Collier's group at all?"

"Aye," she said. "Well . . . no . . . I mean, I did serve them, but it were that busy I don't remember nothing about it."

And you collected all the glasses later?"

"Aye."

"Do you remember picking up any shorts glasses from Mr Collier's table?"

Betty thought for a moment—a process Banks fancied he could almost hear—and then shook her head. "I remember picking up some shorts glasses off t'bar," she said, "but I can't say who drank 'em."

"Is this the part of the bar the Collier group came to for their orders?"

"Aye, it would've been," Freddie said.

"But neither of you can say which member of the Collier group was ordering vodka?"

They both shook their heads glumly.

Banks sighed, then finished his pint philosophically and lit a cigarette.

"What's it all about, then?" Freddie asked.

"Eh? Oh, never mind for now," Banks said. "Probably nothing."

"They were all a bit merry, like."

"The Collier group?"

"Aye. All on 'em. But Mr Stephen were t'worst."

"Did he drink more than the rest?"

Freddie shook his head. "I can't say. Shouldn't think so, though. They was drinking rounds. Unless . . ." Then comprehension dawned on his round red face. "Unless 'e were drinking vodka as well as pints."

"And was he?"

Again, Freddie shook his head. "I can't say."

Suddenly Betty, who had remained standing there as if she were waiting to be dismissed, raised her head. Brown curls bobbed around her chubby cheeks. "I can tell yer!" she said excitely. "I can tell yer."

"What?" Banks asked.

"It can't've been Mr Stephen buying vodka."

"Why on earth not, lass?" Freddie said.

"Well, yer know," Betty spluttered, "'e alus used to say, 'ello, like, Mr Stephen. Proper gentleman. And 'e'd ask me 'ow I was. Well once on Sat'day night 'e were on 'is way to t'loo and 'e nearly bumped into me, and me carrying a trayful o'—"

"Get on wi' it, lass!" Freddie bellowed. "T'Inspector dun't want to know what tha et for breakfast an' all, tha knows."

Betty cast him a dark glance and announced, "'E'd forgotten 'is wallet."

"'E'd what?"

"'E sometimes slips me a quid—a tip, like," she added proudly. "But on Sat'day 'e patted 'is pockets and said 'e was sorry 'e 'ad no change and 'e'd left 'is wallet at 'ome. 'E was 'aving to depend on t'generosity of 'is friends." She turned to Banks. "Those were 'is very words, 'the generosity of my friends.' 'E'd 'ad a few, like, when 'e said it. . . ."

"Thank you, Betty," Banks said. "I don't suppose you overheard Nicholas Collier and John Fletcher having an argument?"

Betty's face dropped. "No. Not while I were picking t'glasses up. Is it important?"

"It might be. But it's not as important as what you've just told me."

It wasn't a great help, but if Stephen Collier hadn't been up to the bar to buy rounds, and if Freddie had found empty shorts glasses at the spot where the orders had been placed, then one of the party might have been spiking Stephen's beer with vodka. Of course, he realized, anyone could have left the glasses there, and any member of the group could have tipped back a quick shot while waiting for Freddie to pull the pints. But it was a start.

Betty beamed as if she'd solved the case. Freddie sent her back to her glass-cleaning and turned to face Banks.

"There," he said, "Any 'elp?"

"I hope so."

"Well, so do I. Tha's taking tha bloody time, I'll say that about thee. Does tha know, t'last Yankee we 'ad in 'ere . . ."

Banks left Freddie mid-sentence and almost bumped into Katie Greenock as he was leaving the pub.

"Ah," he said, holding the door for her, "just the person I want to see."

But she turned and started to hurry away.

"What is it?" Banks asked after her. He could sense her fear; it was more than just the adrenalin produced by a shock.

"It's nothing," she said, half-turning. "I was just looking for Sam, that's all." He could see a tear streaking down her flushed cheek.

"Katie, have you got something to tell me?" Banks asked, approaching her.

She carried on walking away. Banks put his hand gently on her shoulder. "Katie?"

"No!" she recoiled and started running down the empty street. Banks dashed after her and soon she slowed, dazed, to a halt.

"Come on, Katie," he said. "Let's talk." He offered his hand, but she wouldn't take it. Instead, she walked obediently beside him back to the car. She was shaking.

"A drink?" Banks suggested.

She shook her head. Her fair hair was tied back, but a few strands freed themselves and stuck to her damp cheeks.

"Let's go for a ride, then."

She got in the Cortina beside him and he drove north out of Swainshead. Thinking it might help her relax, he took out the Beatles cassette and put on Vivaldi's *Four Seasons*, turning the volume low.

"I was lying," Katie blurted out as they passed the bridge to John Fletcher's farmhouse. Then she said something else that Banks didn't quite catch. It sounded like "wash my mouth out with soap."

"What about?" he asked.

"I wasn't looking for Sam. I saw you go in there. I saw you leave Nicholas Collier's, too. I was trying to get my courage up."

"For what? Are you sure a drink wouldn't help?"

"No, I don't take alcohol."

"What is it, Katie?"

"You've got to help me," Katie said, staring down into her lap and twisting her hands. "I did it . . . I killed them . . . I killed them all."

13

I

Looking at the ornate limestone building, Banks realized he had never seen Braughtmore school before. Built in the mid-nineteenth century after the previous building had burned down, it had oriels projecting from the first floor, then two floors of tall sash windows topped by dormers and a red pantile roof. It stood at the mouth of a small valley which a tributary had carved on its way down to the Gaiel, and enough flat ground had been cleared around it for rugby and cricket fields.

Banks pulled into a lay-by across the road, lit a cigarette and turned to Katie.

"Tell me about it," he said.

"I did it," Katie repeated. "I killed them."

"Who did you kill?"

"Bernie and Stephen."

"Why?"

"Because I . . . because they . . . It was God's judgment."

"God's judgment for what, Katie?"

"My sins."

"Because you made love to them?"

Katie turned and glared at him through her tears. "Not love," she said. "They were going to take me away, take me away from here, from my husband."

"But you made love with Bernard Allen. Did you sleep

233

with Stephen, too?"

"Bernie took me in his room. It was the price. I found no pleasure in it. He said he'd send for me when he got back."

Banks didn't have the heart to tell her that Bernie was bent on returning to Swainshead, not staying in Canada.

"And Stephen?" he asked.

"He . . . he kissed me. I knew I would have to pay, but later. And now . . ."

"Did you kill him so that you wouldn't have to pay?"

Katie shook her head. "He was going to take me away, like Bernard. He had to die."

"How did you kill him?"

"Everyone who wants to help me dies."

"But how did you kill him?"

"I don't know, don't remember."

"Katie, you didn't kill Stephen Collier or Bernard Allen, did you?"

"They died because of me. The Lord's vengeance. Nicholas was the Lord's vengeance, too. Against me. To show me my vile nature."

"Nicholas? What happened with Nicholas?"

"He put his hands on me. His filthy hands. The Hands of the Beast."

"When was this? Where?"

"At his house. The party Sam made me go to. I didn't want to go, I told him. I knew it would be bad."

"What happened?"

"John came and they fought."

"John and Nicholas?"

"Yes."

At least that explained their argument in the White Rose, Banks thought. "Did Sam know? Did you tell Sam?"

Katie shook her head. "Sam doesn't care anyway. Not where his precious Colliers are concerned."

"But you didn't kill anyone, did you?"

She put her head in her hands and wept. Banks moved to put his arm around her, but she stiffened and jerked away towards the door. She rested her cheek against the window and stared ahead up the dale.

"Are you protecting Sam, Katie? Is that what you're doing? Do you think Sam killed them because they were going to take you away?"

"I killed them. I told you."

"Maybe you think you're responsible, Katie, but you didn't kill anyone. There's a big difference between feeling guilty and taking someone's life, you know. You haven't done anything wrong."

"I wanted to escape my husband, didn't I?"

"He beats you. He's not a good man."

"But he's my husband." She started to sob again. "I must serve him. What else can I do? I can't leave him and go away by myself. I don't know how to live."

Banks wound down his window and tossed out his cigarette end.

"Do you want to walk a while?" he asked.

Katie nodded and opened her door.

There was a pathway worn in the hillside opposite the school, and they set off slowly up towards the ridge. About half-way, they sat on warm grass among limestone boulders and gazed down on the scene. The building glowed like mother-of-pearl, and the red S-shaped tiles shone bright in the sun. Some pupils dressed in whites were practising in the cricket nets by one of the mowed fields, and a group in shorts and vests were running around the cinder track. Plenty of exercise and cold showers, Banks thought. Cross-country runs and Latin unseens to keep their minds off sex—and perhaps a bit of masturbation in the dorms, a little buggery in the bushes, sodomy in the cycle sheds. It was every outsider's version of public-school life. Probably the reality was much more innocent. After all, these people were being groomed to run the country, the government. Still, look how many of them ended up on the front pages of the tabloid press. Perhaps the outsider's version wasn't so far from the truth.

Katie plucked blades of grass and scattered them on the light breeze.

"Tell me what happened with Stephen," Banks said.

"We walked up to the source. He said he was going away. I

thought he would take me with him if I let him kiss me. That's all."

"What else did he say? You must have talked about things."

"Oh, yes." Katie's voice sounded like it was coming from a great distance.

"Why was he going away?"

"He said he'd had enough, he couldn't stand being here any longer. He said something about getting away from the past and from who he was."

"What did he want to get away from?"

For the first time, Katie looked directly at him. Her eyes were red-rimmed with crying but still shone warm brown in the sunlight. Banks could feel her attraction. The desire to protect her merged with the impulse to touch her. She made him want to reach out and brush the blonde hairs away from her cheeks, then kiss her white throat and explore the gentle curves and mounds of her body. And he also knew that she was largely unaware of the effect she had; it was as if she couldn't understand the natural sexual instinct that draws people to one another. She knew what men wanted, yes, but she didn't know why or what it was all about. She was innocent, a unique and vulnerable wild flower growing here at the edge of the moorland.

"What did he want to get away from?" she echoed, shattering his illusion. "What we all want to get away from. The traps we make for ourselves. The traps God makes for us."

"It's not such a terrible thing to want to escape a bad marriage, Katie," Banks said. But he felt he couldn't get the tone right, couldn't find the way to talk to this woman. What he said came out as patronizing when he didn't intend it to.

"It's a woman's duty," Katie answered. "Her cross to bear."

"What was Stephen running away from? Was it me? Did he mention me?"

Katie seemed surprised. "No," she said. "Not you. His past, the life he led."

"Did he mention anything in particular?"

"He said he'd been bad."

"How?"

"I don't know. He just talked. I didn't understand it all. I was thinking about something else. The river bubbling up from the grass, how green and shiny the grass was where the water always flowed over it and in it."

"Can you remember anything? Anything at all?"

"He talked about Oxford. Something bad happened at Oxford."

"Did he say what it was?"

"A girl. A girl died."

"Is that all he said?"

"Yes. That's how it started, he said. The nightmare."

"With a girl dying at Oxford?"

"Yes."

"How was he involved with this girl?"

"I don't know. Just that she died and it was bad."

"And now he'd had enough and he was going away to escape the past, the consequences?"

Katie nodded, then she stared at him sharply. "But you can't escape consequences, can you? Bernie couldn't. Stephen couldn't. I can't."

"Was Stephen unhappy?"

"Unhappy? I don't think so. He was worried, but not unhappy."

"Do you think he would have harmed himself?"

"No. Stephen wouldn't have done that. He had plans for the future. He was going to take me with him. But his future killed him."

"I thought it was his past?"

"It was me," she said calmly. "Whatever you say, I know it was me who killed him."

"That's not true, Katie. I wish I could get you to believe it." Banks took out his cigarettes and offered her one. She said no and carried on plucking blades of grass and rubbing them between her fingers.

"Why didn't he go away before?" Banks asked. "He had plenty of time, plenty of opportunity."

"I don't know. He said it was hard for him—the family name, the house, the business. He seemed to be trying to find the courage to make a break, like me. I didn't tell him, if that's what you're thinking."

"Didn't tell him what?"

"About the policeman you sent to spy on everyone. I saw him with you one day in Eastvale, but I didn't tell Stephen."

"Did you tell Sam?"

Katie shook her head slowly. "No," she said. "Not this time."

So Stephen had been struggling with himself over whether to run or whether to stay and brazen it out. After all, he probably knew that the police could have no real proof of his guilt, just hearsay—Anne Ralston's word against his.

"If he'd gone," Katie said, as if she'd been reading his mind, "it would have been like admitting his guilt, wouldn't it?"

"Perhaps." Banks stood up and brushed the grass from his pants. "Come on." He held out his hand and Katie took it. As soon as she'd stood up, though, she let go and followed him back to the car in silence.

II

"What else did she say?" Sergeant Hatchley asked, as the white Cortina, with Banks at the wheel, hurtled down the M1.

"Nothing," Banks answered. "I told her to get in touch with us if she remembered anything else at all, then I drove her home. She went in without a word. To tell you the truth, I'm worried about her. She's so bloody fragile and she's close to breaking-point. The woman needs help."

Hatchley shrugged. "If she doesn't like her nest she can always change it."

"It's not as easy as that for some people. They get stuck, they don't know where to turn, how to take care of themselves. Katie Greenock's like that."

They passed Sheffield's cooling towers, shaped like giant whalebone corsets by the motorway. Even with the windows and many of the factories closed, the sulphurous smells of steelworks seeped into the car.

"What exactly will we be doing in Oxford?" Hatchley asked.

"We'll be trying to track down an incident involving the death of a girl about nine years ago, maybe two or three years later. Undergraduate courses are usually three years long, so that's a welcome limit."

"Unless Collier wasn't actually a student when it happened."

"That's bloody helpful," Banks said. "We'll deal with that if we draw a blank on the other."

"What kind of incident?"

"It strikes me we're looking for an unsolved crime, or a freak accident. Could have been hit and run, drug overdose, anything."

"Then what? Whoever this lass was, she won't be doing much talking now."

"I don't know," Banks admitted. "We try and link her to Stephen Collier."

"And what if we come up blank?"

Banks sighed and reached for a cigarette. He swerved quickly to avoid a Dutch juggernaut meandering on the centre lane. "You're being bloody negative today, Sergeant," he said. "What's the matter, did you have something planned for tonight? A date with Carol, maybe?"

"No. Carol understands my job. And I like a nice ride out. I'm just trying to cover all the angles, that's all. I find the whole damn thing confusing. I'm not even sure we've got a case. After all, Collier is dead, whether he died accidentally or offed himself."

"It is confusing," Banks agreed. "That's why I don't believe we're at the bottom of it yet. That's why we're off to Oxford, to try and make it simpler."

"Oh, I see." Hatchley wound down his window a couple of inches. With the two of them smoking, the fug in the car was making his eyes water. "I suppose it's full of silly-looking buggers in caps and gowns, Oxford?"

"Maybe so," Banks said. "Never been there, myself. They say it's a working town, though."

"Aye. It might have been at one time. But there's not many

left making cars these days. Some nice buildings there, though. I saw those on telly as well. Christopher Wren, Nicholas Hawksworth."

"Bloody hell, Jim, have you been watching BBC2 again? We'll not have much time for sightseeing. Except for what you can take in on the job. Anyway, it's Hawksmoor. Nicholas Hawksmoor."

He realized with a shock that it was the first time he had called Sergeant Hatchley by his first name. It felt strange, but Hatchley said nothing.

Banks drove on in silence and concentrated on the road. It was after five o'clock and the stretches of motorway that passed close to urban areas were busy with rush-hour traffic. By the time they got to Oxford they wouldn't have time to do much but check in at the police station, say hello to Ted Folley, and maybe discuss the case over a pint—which would certainly appeal to Hatchley—before bed. Banks had booked them in at a small hotel recommended by Ted on the phone. In the morning the real work would begin.

Holding the wheel with one hand, Banks sorted through the cassettes. "Do you like music?" he asked. It was odd; he knew Gristhorpe was tone deaf—he couldn't tell Bach from the Beatles—but he had no idea what Hatchley's tastes ran to. Not that it would affect his choice. He knew what he wanted to hear and soon found it—the Small Faces' greatest hits.

"I like a good brass band," Hatchley mused. "A bit of country-and-western now and then."

Banks smiled. He hated country-and-western and brass bands. He lit another cigarette and edged up the volume. The swirling chords of "All or Nothing" filled the car as he turned off near Northampton onto the road for Oxford. The music took him right back to the summer of 1966, just before he started in the sixth form at school. Nostalgia. A sure sign he was pushing forty. He caught Hatchley looking at him as if he were mad.

III

There weren't many caps and gowns in evidence on High Street in Oxford the following morning. Most of the people seemed to be ambling along in that lost but purposeful way tourists have. Banks and Hatchley were looking for somewhere to eat a quick breakfast before getting down to work at the station.

Hatchley pointed across the street. "There's a McDonald's. They do quite nice breakfasts. Maybe . . ." He looked at Banks apprehensively, as if worried that the chief inspector might turn out to be a gourmet as well as a southerner and a lover of sixties music. Despite all the times they'd enjoyed toasted teacakes and steak pies together, maybe Banks would insist on frogs' legs with anchovy sauce for breakfast.

Banks glanced at his watch and scowled. "At least they're fast. Come on, then. Egg McMuffin it is."

Astonished, Hatchley followed him through the golden arches. Most of the places Banks had eaten in on his trip to Toronto had provided quick, friendly service—so much so that it had been one of the things that had impressed him—but it seemed that even McDonald's could do nothing to alter the innate sloth and surliness of the English catering industry. The look they got from the uniformed girl behind the counter immediately communicated that they were being a bloody nuisance in placing an order, and, of course, they had to wait. Even when she slung the food at them, she didn't say, "Thank you, please come again."

Finally, they sat by the window and watched people walk in and out of W.H. Smith's for the morning papers. Hatchley ate heartily, but Banks picked at his food, then abandoned it and settled for black coffee and a cigarette.

"Nice bloke, that Ted Folley," Hatchley said with his mouth half full of sausage. "Not what I expected."

"What did you expect?"

"Oh, some toffee-nosed git, I suppose. He's real down-to-earth, though. Dresses like a toff, mind you. They'd have a bit of a giggle over him in The Oak."

"Probably in the Queen's Arms, too," Banks added.

"Aye."

They had found time for a few drinks with Folley before returning to their hotel for a good night's sleep, and Banks wondered whether it was Ted's generosity that won Hatchley over, or his store of anecdotes. Either way, the sergeant had managed to down a copious amount of local ale (which he pronounced to be of "passable" quality) in a very short time.

They had stood at the bar of a noisy Broad Street pub, and Ted—a dapper man with Brylcreemed hair and a penchant for three-piece pin-stripe suits and garish bow-ties —had regaled them with stories of Oxford's privileged student classes. Hatchley had been particularly amused by the description of a recent raid on an end-of-term party: "And there she was," Folley had said, "Deb of the Year with her knickers round her ankles and white powder all over her stiff upper lip." The sergeant had laughed so much he had got hiccups, which kept returning to haunt him for the rest of the evening.

"Come on," Banks said. "Hurry up. It can't be so bloody delicious you need to savour every mouthful."

Reluctantly, Hatchley ate up his food and slurped his coffee. Ten minutes later they were in Ted Folley's office on St Aldates.

"I've got the files out already," Ted said. "If you can't find what you're after there, come and see me. I think you will, though. They cover all unsolved crimes, including hit and runs, involving women during the three-year period you mentioned."

"Thank God there aren't many," Banks said, picking up the slim pile.

"No," Folley said. "We're lucky. The students keep us busy enough but we don't get all that many mysterious deaths. They're usually drug related."

"These?"

"Some of them. Use that office over there." Folley pointed across to a small glass-partitioned area. "Doug's on holiday, so you won't be disturbed."

Most of the cases were easily dealt with. Banks or Hatchley would phone friends or parents of the deceased, whenever phone numbers appeared in the files, and simply ask if the name Stephen Collier meant anything. On the off chance, they also asked if anyone had hired a private investigator named Raymond Addison to look into the unsolved crime. In the cases where no numbers were given, or where people had moved, they made notes to follow up on later. In some of those cases, the phone directory told them what they needed to know, and Ted also proved as helpful as ever.

By mid-afternoon, after a short lunch-break, they had only three possibilities left. Folley was able to rule one of those out—the girl's parents had died tragically in a plane crash less than a year after their daughter's death—which left one each for Banks and Hatchley. They tossed for it, and Banks drew the phoneless family in Jericho, Hatchley the paraplegic father in Woodstock.

Wedged between Walton Street and the canal, Jericho is a maze of small nineteenth-century terraced houses, originally built for the foundry workers and navvies of the city. Most of the streets are named after Victorian battles or military heroes. It is as far away in spirit and appearance from the magnificent architectural beauty of the old university city as is Eastvale's East End Estate from its cobbled market square and Norman church.

Banks drove slowly down Great Clarendon Street until he found the turning he wanted. His car attracted the attention of two scruffy children playing jacks on the pavement, and he was manoeuvred into paying them fifty pee to "protect" it for him.

At first no-one answered the cracked blue door, but eventually, Banks heard someone move inside and when the door opened, an old, haggard face stared out. He couldn't tell whether it was male or female until a deep man's voice asked him roughly what he wanted.

"It's about your daughter, Cheryl," he said. "May I come in?"

The man blinked and opened the door a bit wider. Banks could smell boiled turnip and stale pipe smoke.

"Our Cheryl's been dead six years or more," the man said. "Nobody did anything then; why should they bother now?"

"If I could just come in . . . ?"

The man said nothing, but he opened the door wider to admit Banks. There was no hallway; the door opened directly into a small living-room. The curtains were half-closed, cutting out most of the light, and the air felt hot and cloying. From what Banks could see, the place wasn't dirty, but it wasn't exactly clean, either. A grey-haired old woman with a blanket over her knees sat in a wheelchair by the empty grate. She looked around as he came in and gave him a blank smile.

"It's about our Cheryl," the man said, reaching for his pipe.

"I heard."

"Look, Mrs Duggan," Banks said, perching on the arm of the settee, "I know it's a long time ago, but something might have come up."

"You've found out who killed her?"

"It's possible. But I still don't know that she was killed. You'll have to help me."

The file was still fresh in his mind. Cheryl Duggan had been fished out of the River Cherwell not too far from Magdalen Bridge and St Hilda's College on a foggy November Sunday morning over six years ago. The coroner's inquest said that death was due to drowning, or so it appeared. Several odd bruises indicated that her head may have been held under the water until she drowned. She had had sexual intercourse shortly before death, and the stomach contents indicated that she had been drinking heavily the previous evening. In view of all this, an open verdict was recorded and a police investigation was ordered.

To complicate matters, Cheryl Duggan, according to Folley, had been a well-known local prostitute since the age of fifteen. She had been only seventeen when she died. The investigation, Folley admitted, had been cursory. This was due to other pressures—in particular the drug-related death of a peer's daughter, in which the heir to a brewery fortune was implicated as a pusher.

"It could have been an accident," Banks said.

"It warn't no accident, Mr Banks," Mrs Duggan insisted.

"There was water in the lungs," Banks countered weakly.

Mr Duggan snorted. "You'd think she were a mermaid, our Cheryl, the way she took to water."

"She'd been drinking."

"Yes, well, nobody's saying she was perfect."

"Did you ever hear her mention a man by the name of Stephen Collier?"

Mr Duggan shook his head slowly.

There was a sense of defeat about the Duggans that weighed heavily in the dim and stuffy room and made Banks feel sick. Their voices were flat, as if they had repeated their stories a hundred times and nobody had listened; their faces were parchment dry and drawn, the eyes wide and blank, with plenty of white showing between the lower lashes and the pupils. Dante's words came into Banks's mind: "Abandon all hope, ye who enter here." This was a house of defeat, a place without hope.

Banks lit a cigarette, which would at least give him a more concrete reason to feel sick and dizzy, and went on. "The other thing I'd like to know," he asked, "is if you hired anyone to look into Cheryl's death. I know you didn't think much of the police investigation."

Mr Duggan spat into the grate. His wife frowned at him. "Why does it matter?" she asked.

"It could be important."

"We did hire someone," she said. "A private investigator from London. We looked him up in the phone book at the library. We were desperate. The police hadn't done anything for more than a year, and they were saying such terrible things about Cheryl. We took out all our savings."

"What happened?"

"He came from London, this man, and he asked us about Cheryl—who her friends were, where she liked to go out and everything, then he said he'd try and find out what happened."

"He never came back," Mr Duggan cut in.

"You mean he ran off with your money?"

"Not all of it, Alf," Mrs Duggan said. "Only a retainer, that's all he'd take."

"He took off with the money, Jesse, let's face it. We were had. He never meant to do anything about our Cheryl, he just took us for what he could get. And we let him."

"What was his name?"

"Don't remember."

"Yes you do, Alf," said Mrs Duggan. "It was Raymond Addison. I haven't forgotten."

"So what did you do?"

"What could we do?" she said. "He'd got most of our money, so we couldn't hire anyone else. The police weren't interested. We just tried to forget, that's all." She pulled the tartan blanket up higher around her hips.

"Mr Addison didn't report back to you at all, then, after the first time you saw him?"

"No," Mr Duggan said. "We only saw him the once."

"Can you remember the date?"

The old man shook his head.

"I can't remember the exact day," his wife said, "but it was in February, about fifteen months after Cheryl was killed. The police seemed to have given up and we didn't know where to turn. We found him, and he let us down."

"If it's any consolation, Mrs Duggan, I don't think Mr Addison did let you down."

"What?"

"He was found killed himself, probably no more than a day or so after you saw him, up in Yorkshire. That's why you never heard from him again, not because he'd run off with your money."

"In Yorkshire? What was he doing there?"

"I think he did find out something about Cheryl's death. Something the police had missed. You've got to understand that we don't have enough time or men to devote ourselves full time to every single case, Mrs Duggan. I don't know the circumstances, but maybe the police here weren't as active as you think they should have been. It's only in books that policemen find the killer every time. But Mr Addison had only the one case. He must have visited every possible place Cheryl might have been that night, talked to everyone who knew her, and what he found out led him to a village in Yorkshire, and to his death."

Mrs Duggan bit her knuckles and began to cry silently. Her husband moved forward to comfort her.

"It never does any good raking up the past," he snapped at Banks. "Look how you've upset her."

"I can understand that you're angry, Mr Duggan," Banks said, "but if I'm right, then we know who killed your daughter."

Duggan looked away. "What's it matter now?"

"Maybe it doesn't, at least not to you. But I think it ought to mean something that Addison didn't let you down, didn't run off with your money. He found a lead, and instead of reporting in, he set off while the trail was hot. I think you owe his memory some kind of apology if you've been blaming him and thinking ill of him all these years."

"Maybe so," Duggan admitted. "But what use is it now? Two people dead. What use?"

"More than two," Banks said. "He had to kill again to cover his tracks. First Addison, then someone else."

"All over our Cheryl?" Mrs Duggan said, wiping her eyes.

Banks nodded. "It looks like that's where it started. Is there anything else you can tell me? Did Cheryl ever talk about anyone at all she knew from Yorkshire? A student she was seeing, perhaps?"

They both shook their heads, then Mrs Duggan laughed bitterly. "She said she was going to marry a student one day, a lord's son, or a prime minister's. She was very determined, our Cheryl. But she'd too much imagination. She was too flighty. If only she'd done as I said and stuck to her station."

"Did she hang around with students much?"

"She went to the same pubs as they did," Mr Duggan said.

"The police said she was a prostitute, Mr Banks, that she sold herself to men. We didn't know nothing about that. I still can't believe it. I know she liked to tart herself up a bit when she went out, but what girl doesn't? And she wasn't really old enough to drink, but what can you do ...? You can't keep them prisoners, can you? She was always talking about what fun the students were, how she was sure to meet a nice young man soon. What were we to do? We believed her. Our Cheryl could make you believe she could do anything if she set her mind to it. Every day she woke up with a smile on her face, and that's no lie. Happiest soul I've ever known. What did we do wrong?"

Banks had no answer. He dropped his cigarette in the grate and walked to the door. "If you think of anything, let the local police know," he said.

"Wait a minute." Mrs Duggan turned to him. "Aren't you going to tell us?"

"Tell you what?"

"Who did it. Who killed our Cheryl."

"It doesn't matter now," Banks said. "It looks like he's dead himself." And he closed the door on their hopelessness and emptiness.

IV

"I'm sorry, Alan," Ted Folley said when he'd heard the story. "I told you it wasn't much of an investigation. We looked into it, but we got nowhere. We were sure the girl drowned. She'd been drinking, and there was water in her lungs. The bruises could have been caused by a customer; it's a rough trade she was in. She didn't have a ponce, so we'd no-one we could jump on right from the start."

Banks nodded and blew smoke rings. "We got nowhere with the Addison case, either," he said. "There was nothing to link him with Oxford, and we couldn't find out why he was in Swainshead. Not until now, anyway. What on earth could he have found out?"

"Anything," Folley said. "Maybe he found the last pub she'd been in, tracked down a pusher who'd run a mile if he even smelled police."

"Was she on drugs?"

"Not when she died, no. But there had been trouble. Nothing serious, just pills mostly. If Addison trailed around all her haunts and talked to everyone who knew her, showed a photo, flashed a bit of money . . . You know as well as I do, Alan, these blokes who operate outside the law have a better chance. He must have picked up your man's name somewhere and set off to question him."

"Yes. It's just a damn shame he wasn't more efficient."

"What do you mean?"

"If he'd gone back and told the Duggans what he'd found before rushing off to Yorkshire. If he'd just filed some kind of report . . ."

"He must have been keen," Folley said. "Some of them are, you know."

At that moment, Sergeant Hatchley came in from Woodstock. "Bloody waste of time," he grumbled, slouching in a chair and fumbling for a cigarette.

"Nothing?" Banks asked.

"Nowt. But judging by the expression on your face, you're that cat that got the cream. Am I right?"

"You are." He told Hatchley about his interview with the Duggans.

"So that's it, then?"

"Looks like it. Stephen Collier must've met up with this young girl, Cheryl Duggan, gone drinking with her then taken her to the meadows by the riverside for sex. It was unusually warm for that time of year. He got a bit rough, they fought, and he drowned her. Or she fell in and he tried to save her. It could have been an accident, but it was a situation he couldn't afford to be associated with. Maybe he was on drugs; we'll never know. He might not even have been responsible for the bruising and the rough sexual treatment she'd received. That could have been a previous customer. Collier might even have been comforting her, trying to persuade her back onto the straight and narrow. I suppose the version will vary according to what kind of person you think Stephen was. One mistake—one terrible mistake—and three deaths have to follow. Christ, it could even have been some silly student prank."

"Do you think he killed himself?"

Banks shook his head. "I don't know. In his state of mind, if he'd been carrying the guilt all this time and feeling the pressure build, suicide and accidental death might have been much the same thing. It didn't matter any more, so he just got careless. Katie Greenock said he was planning to leave Swainshead, and I guess he didn't much mind how he went."

"What do we do now?" Hatchley asked.

Banks looked at his watch. "It's three-thirty," he said. "I suggest we go pay Stephen's old tutor a visit and see if we can find out whether he was in the habit of taking up with young prostitutes. We might find some clue as to what really happened, who was responsible for what. Then we'll head back home. We should be able to make it before nine if we're on the road soon." He turned to Folley and held out his hand. "Thanks again, Ted. We appreciate all you've done. If I can ever return the favour . . ."

Folley laughed. "In Swainsdale? You must be joking. But you're welcome. And do pay us a social call sometime. A few days boating on the Thames Valley would be just the ticket for the wife and kids."

"I will," Banks said. "Come on, Jim lad, time to hit the road again."

Hatchley dragged himself to his feet, said goodbye to Folley and followed Banks out onto St Aldates.

"There you are," Banks said, near Blackwell's on Broad Street. "Caps and gowns."

True enough, students were all over the place: walking, cycling, standing to chat outside the bookshops.

"Bloody poofdahs," Hatchley said.

They got past the porter, crossed the quadrangle, and found Dr Barber in his office at Stephen's old college.

"Sherry, gentlemen?" he asked, after they had introduced themselves.

Banks accepted because he liked dry sherry; Hatchley took one because he had never been known to refuse a free drink.

Barber's study was cluttered with books, journals and papers. A student essay titled "The Dissolution of the Monasteries: Evidence of Contemporary Accounts" lay on the desk, but it didn't quite obscure an old green-covered Penguin crime paperback. Banks tilted his head and glanced sideways at the title: *The Moving Toyshop*, by Edmund Crispin. He had never heard of it, but it wasn't quite the reading material he'd have expected to find in the office of an Oxford don.

While Dr Barber poured, Banks stood by the window and looked over the neat, clipped quadrangle at the light stone façades of the college.

Barber passed them their drinks and lit his pipe. Its smoke sweetened the air. In deference to his guests, he opened the window a little, and a draught of fresh air sucked the smoke out. In appearance, Barber had the air of an aged cleric, and he smelled of Pears soap. He reminded Banks of the actor Wilfrid Hyde-White.

"It was a long time ago," Barber said, when Banks had asked him about Collier. "Let me check my files. I've got records going back over twenty years, you know. It pays to know whom one has had pass through these hallowed halls. As a historian myself, I place great value on documentation. Now, let me see ... Stephen Collier, yes. Braughtmore School, Yorkshire. Is that the one? Yes? I remember him. Not terribly distinguished academically, but a pleasant enough fellow. What's he been up to?"

"That's what we're trying to find out," Banks said. "He died a few days ago and we want to know why."

Barber sat down and picked up his sherry. "Good Lord! He wasn't murdered, was he?"

"Why would you think that?"

Barber shrugged. "One doesn't usually get a visit from the Yorkshire police over nothing. One doesn't usually get visits from the police at all."

"We don't know," Banks said. "It could have been accidental, or it could have been suicide."

"Suicide? Oh dear. Collier was a rather serious young man —a bit too much so, if I remember him clearly. But suicide?"

"Possibly."

"A lot can change in a few years," Barber said. He frowned and relit his pipe. Banks remembered his own struggles with the infernal engines, and the broken pipe that now hung on his wall in Eastvale CID Headquarters. "As I said," Barber went on, "Collier seemed a sober, sensible kind of fellow. Still, who can fathom the mysteries of the human heart? *Fronti nulla fides*."

"There's no real type for suicide," Banks said. "Anyone, pushed far enough—"

"I suppose you're the kind of policeman who thinks anyone can become a murderer, too, given the circumstances?"

Banks nodded.

"I'm afraid I can't go along with that," Barber said. "I'm no psychologist, but I'd say it takes a special type. Take me, for example, I could never conceive of doing such a thing. The thought of jail, for a start, would deter me. And I should think that everyone would notice my guilt. As a child, I once stole a lemon tart from the school tuck-shop while Mrs Wiggins was in the back, and I felt myself turn red from head to toe. No, Chief Inspector, I'd never make a murderer."

"I'm thankful for that," Banks said. "I don't need to ask you for an alibi now, I suppose."

Barber looked at him for a moment, unsure what to do, then laughed.

"Stephen Collier," Banks said.

"Yes, yes. Forgive me. I'm getting old; I tend to ramble. But it's coming back. He was the kind who really did have to work hard to do well. So many others have a natural ability —they can dash off a good essay the night before. But you'd always find Collier in the library all week before a major piece of work was due. Conscientious."

"How did he get on with the other students?"

"Well enough, as far as I know. Collier was a bit of a loner, though. Kept himself to himself. I hardly need to tell you, Chief Inspector, that quite a number of young lads around these parts go in for high jinks. It's always been like that, ever since students started coming here in the thirteenth century. And there's always been a bit of a running battle between university authorities and the people of the city: town and gown, as we say. The students aren't vindictive, you realize, just high spirited. Sometimes they cause more damage than they intend."

"And Collier?"

"I'm sure he didn't go in for that kind of thing. If there had been any incidents of an unsavoury nature, they would have appeared in my assessment file."

"Did he drink much?"

"Never had any trouble with him."

"Drugs?"

"Chief Inspector Banks," Barber said slowly, "I do realize that the university has been getting a bad reputation lately for drugs and the like, and no doubt such things do happen. But if you take the word of the media, you'd be seriously misled. I don't think Stephen Collier was involved in drugs at all. I remember that we did have some trouble with one student selling cannabis around that time—most distressing —but there was a full investigation, and at no point was Stephen Collier implicated."

"So as far as you can say, Collier was a model student, if not quite as brilliant as some of his fellows?"

"I know it sounds hard to believe, but yes, he was. Most of the time you'd hardly have known he was here. I'm having great difficulty trying to guess what you're after. You say that Stephen Collier's death might have been suicide or it might have been an accident, but, if you don't mind my saying so, the questions you're asking seem preoccupied with unearthing evidence that Collier himself was some kind of hell-raiser."

Banks frowned and looked out of the window again. The shadow of a cloud passed over the quadrangle. He drained his sherry and lit a cigarette. Sergeant Hatchley, quietly smoking in a chair in the corner, had emptied his glass a while ago and sat fidgeting with it as if he hoped Barber would notice and offer a refill. He did, and both policemen accepted. Banks liked the way the dry liquid puckered his taste-buds.

"He's a suspect," Banks said. "And I'm afraid that's all I can tell you. We have no proof that Collier was guilty of anything, but there's a strong possibility."

"Does it matter," Barber asked, "now that he's dead?"

"Yes, it does. If he was guilty, then the case is closed. If not, we still have a criminal to catch."

"Yes. I see. Well I'm afraid I can't offer you any evidence at all. Seemed a thoroughly pleasant, hard-working, nondescript fellow to me as far as I can remember."

"What about six years ago? It would have been his third year, his last. Did anything unusual happen then, around early November?"

Barber frowned and pursed his lips. "I can't recall anything. . . . Wait a minute . . ." He walked back over to his ancient filing cabinet and riffled through the papers. "Yes, yes, I thought so," he announced finally. "Stephen Collier didn't finish his degree."

"What?"

"He didn't finish. Decided history wasn't for him and left after two years. Went to run a business, as far as I know. I can confirm with the registrar's office, of course, but my own records are quite thorough."

"Are you saying that Stephen Collier wasn't here, that he wasn't in Oxford in November six years ago?"

"That's right. Could it be you've got him mixed up with his brother, Nicholas? He would have just been starting his second year then, you know, and I certainly remember him, now I cast my mind back. Nicholas Collier was a different kettle of fish, a different kettle of fish entirely."

14

I

Katie stared at her reflection in the dark kitchen window as she washed the crystal glasses she couldn't put in the machine. The transistor radio on the table played soothing classical music, quiet enough that she could even hear the beck at the bottom of the back garden rippling over its stones.

Now that Stephen was dead and she had unburdened herself to Banks, she felt empty. None of her grandmother's maxims floated around her mind, as they had been doing lately, and that tightness in her chest that had seemed to squeeze at her very heart itself had relaxed. She even noticed a half-smile on her face, a very odd one she'd not seen before. Nothing hurt now; she felt numb, just like her mouth always did after an injection at the dentist's.

Chief Inspector Banks had told her that if she remembered anything else, she should get in touch with him. Try as she might, though, she couldn't remember a thing. Looking back over the years in Swainshead, she had noticed hints that all wasn't well, that some things were going on about which she knew nothing. But there was no coherent narrative, just a series of unlinked events. She thought of Sam's behaviour when Raymond Addison first appeared. She hadn't heard their conversation, but Sam had immediately left everything to her and gone running off across the street to the Collier house. Later, Addison had gone for a walk and never returned. When they found out the man had been murdered, Sam had been unusually pale and quiet for some days.

She remembered watching Bernie pause and glance towards the Collier house before going on his way the morning he left. She had also seen him call there one evening shortly after he'd arrived and thought it odd because of the way he usually went on about them being so rich and privileged.

None of it had meant very much at the time. Katie wasn't the kind of woman to look for bad in anyone but herself. She had had far more pressing matters to deal with and soon forgot the suspicious little things she'd noticed. Even now, she couldn't put it all together. When she told Banks that she had killed Bernie and Stephen, she meant it. She hadn't physically murdered them, but she knew she was responsible.

The things she remembered often seemed as if they had happened to someone else. She could view again, dispassionately, Bernard Allen sating himself on her impassive body, as if she were watching a silent film from the ceiling. And Stephen's chaste kiss left no trace of ice or fire on her lips. Sam had taken her roughly the previous evening, but instead of fear and loathing, she had felt a kind of power in her subservience. It wasn't pleasure; it was something new, and she felt that if she could only be patient enough it would make itself known to her eventually. It was as if he had possessed her body, but not her soul. She had kept her soul pure and untainted, and now it was revealing itself to her. Somehow, these new feelings were all connected with her sense of responsibility for the deaths of Bernie and Stephen. She had blood on her hands; she had grown up.

The future still felt very uncertain. Life would go on, she supposed, much as it had done. She would clean the rooms, cook the meals, submit to Sam in bed, do what she was told, and try to avoid making him angry. Everything would continue just as it had done, except for the new feelings that were growing in her. If she stayed patient, change would come in its own time. She wouldn't have to do anything until she knew exactly *what* to do.

For the moment, nothing touched her; nothing ruffled the calm and glassy surface of her mind. Caught up in her dark reflection, she dropped one of a set of six expensive crystal glasses. It shattered on the linoleum. But even that didn't matter. Katie looked down at the shards with an indulgent, pitying expression on her face and went to fetch the brush and dustpan.

As she moved, she heard a sound out back. Hurrying to the window, she peered through her own reflection and glimpsed a shadow slipping past her gate. A moment later—before she could get to the unlocked door—she heard a cursory tap. The door opened and Nicholas Collier popped his head around and smiled: "Hello, Katie. I've come to visit."

II

The sun was a swollen red ball low on the western horizon. It oozed its eerie light over the South Yorkshire landscape, silhouetted motionless pit-wheels and made the slag-heaps glow. On the cassette, Nick Drake was singing the haunting "Northern Sky."

Much of the way, the two had sat in silence, thinking things out and deciding what to do. Finally, Hatchley could stand it no longer: "How can we nail the bastard?" he asked.

"I don't know," Banks answered. "We don't have much of a case."

Hatchley grunted. "We might if we hauled him in and you and me had a go at him."

"He's clever, Jim," Banks said. The sergeant's first name didn't feel so strange to his lips after the first few times. "Look how he's kept out of it so long. He's not going to break down just because you and me play good cop-bad cop with him. That'll be a sign of our weakness to him. He'll know we need a confession to make anything stick, so it only strengthens his position. No, Nicholas Collier's a cool one. And don't forget, he's got pull around Swainsdale. We'd no sooner get started than some fancy lawyer would waltz in and gum up the works."

"What I'd give for a bloody good try, though!" Hatchley thumped the dashboard. "Sorry. No damage done. It just makes me angry, a stuck-up bastard like Nicholas Collier getting away with it. How many people has he killed?"

"Three, maybe four if we count Stephen. And he hasn't got away with it yet. The trouble is, we don't know if he killed anyone apart from the girl, Cheryl Duggan. We can't even prove that he killed her. Just because Dr Barber told us he had a reputation for pestering the town's working girls doesn't make him guilty. It certainly doesn't give us grounds for a conviction."

"But it was Cheryl Duggan's death that sent Addison up to Swainshead."

"Yes. But even that's circumstantial."

"Who do you think killed Addison and Allen?"

"At a guess, I'd say Stephen. He'd do it to protect his little brother and his family's reputation. But we don't know, and we never will if Nicholas doesn't talk. I'll bet, for all his cleverness, Nicholas is weak. I doubt he has the stomach for cold-blooded murder. They might both have been at the scene—certainly neither had a good alibi—but I'd say Stephen did the killing."

"What do you think happened with the Duggan girl?"

Banks shifted lanes to overtake a lorry. "I think he picked her up in a pub and took her down by the river. She was just a prostitute, a working-class kid, and he was from a prominent family, so what the hell did it matter to him what he did? I think he got over-excited, hurt her perhaps, and she started to protest, threatened to scream or tell the police. So he panicked and drowned her. Either that or he did it because he enjoyed it."

The tape finished. Banks lit a cigarette and felt around in the dark for another cassette. Without looking at the title, he slipped in the first one he got hold of. It was the sixties anthology tape he'd taken to Toronto with him. Traffic came on singing "No Face, No Name and No Number."

"I think Addison was a conscientious investigator," Banks went on. "He more than earned his money, poor sod. He did all the legwork the police didn't do and found a connection between Cheryl Duggan and Nicholas Collier. Maybe they'd been seen leaving a pub together, or perhaps her friends told him Collier had been with her before. Anyway, Addison prised the name out of someone, or bought the information, and instead of reporting in he set off for Swainshead. That was his first mistake.

"His second was to ask Sam Greenock about Nicholas Collier. Greenock was anxious to get in with the local gentry, and he was a bit suspicious of this stranger asking questions, so he stalled Addison and took the first opportunity to run over the bridge and tell Collier about it. There must have been real panic in the Collier house that evening. Remember, it was about fifteen months after the girl's death, and the Colliers must've thought all was well. I don't know the details. Maybe Sam arranged for Addison to go over to the house when the village was quiet, or maybe he even arranged for the Colliers to go up to Addison's room and kill him there. I don't know how it happened, but I think it was Stephen who struck the blow. That would explain the state he was in when he met Anne Ralston later that night."

"What about Bernard Allen?" Hatchley asked.

"At first I thought he was just unlucky," Banks said. "He told Katie Greenock that he knew Anne Ralston in Toronto. She told Sam, who did his usual town-crier routine. Not that it mattered this time, if Allen was intent on blackmail. Stephen Collier was an odd kind of bloke, from what I can make out—a real combination of opposites. When he'd killed Addison, he had to unburden himself to his girlfriend, but I'm sure he soon regretted it. He must have had a few sleepless nights after Anne first disappeared. Anyway, Bernard Allen knew that Stephen was involved in Addison's murder and that it was something to do with an incident back in Oxford. He obviously assumed that if the police knew that they could put the whole thing together. Which we did, rather too late."

"You said you thought Allen was unlucky at first," Hatchley said. "What about now?"

"I think he was going to blackmail the Colliers. I've not had time to tell you much about Toronto, but I met a few people there who said that Bernard Allen really wanted to come home to Swainshead. His sister mentioned it, too, but the others all played it down. He'd even let on to Katie Greenock that he'd send for her when he got back to Canada. That was because she wanted to escape Swainsdale and he wanted to get into her pants.

"I wondered why I was getting so many conflicting pictures of Allen's state of mind, so many contradictions. But that was his motive. He was blackmailing the Colliers to get himself home. A job at the school, money in the bank—I don't know what he'd asked for, but I'm certain that was his reason. And it got him killed. I doubt that whoever said 'you can't go home again' meant it as literally as that. Anyway, the Colliers decided they couldn't live with the threat, so one or both of them waited for him in the hanging valley that morning. They knew he'd be there because he'd often talked about it and he was heading that way."

"And what happened to Stephen? Why would Nicholas kill him, if he did?"

"Stephen was getting too jittery. Nicholas knew it was just a matter of time before his brother broke down completely, and he couldn't allow him to remain alive when I got back from Toronto after talking to Anne Ralston. Stephen must have told his brother that he didn't give anything away to Anne about the Oxford business, but that he'd made a serious mistake in hinting at his own involvement in Addison's killing. Nicholas knew that what Anne had to tell me would give me enough grounds to bring Stephen in, and he couldn't trust his brother to stand up under questioning. If we could discover the motive behind Addison's murder, then we'd know everything. Nicholas couldn't allow that.

"What he did was risky, but there was a lot at stake—not just the family name, now, but Nicholas's own freedom, his home, his career. He had to kill his own brother to survive. And if he succeeded, it would look like the accidental death of a disturbed man or the suicide of a guilty one."

It was dark when Banks negotiated the tricky connections onto the A1 east of Leeds. Cream were singing "Strange Brew" on the tape and Hatchley had fallen silent.

Banks still didn't understand it all. Stephen had killed to preserve what was important to him, but Nicholas Collier remained something of an enigma. In all likelihood, he had drowned Cheryl Duggan, but what bothered Banks was why. Had he done it from pleasure, accident or desperation? And was he also responsible for the bruising and marks of sexual abuse found on her body? Dr Barber had said that Nicholas had been in trouble once or twice over consorting with prostitutes and offering Oxford factory girls money for sex. Banks wondered why. Nicholas had all the advantages. Why hadn't he hung around with his own set, girls of his own social class?

"Let's call in at the station first," Banks said. "Something might have turned up." They were approaching the turn-off onto a minor road that would take them over the moors to Helmthorpe and the main valley road. "We can always drive to Swainshead later if there's nothing new." He looked at his watch. "It's not late, only nineish."

Hatchley nodded and Banks drove past the exit ramp and on to the Eastvale road.

The station was quiet. There had been no serious crimes while Banks and Hatchley had been gone. There was, however, a message from John Fletcher timed at five o'clock that evening asking them if they would call and see him as soon as possible. He said it was important—something to do with Stephen Collier's death—and he would be at home all evening.

There was also a copy of Dr Glendenning's preliminary post-mortem report on Stephen Collier. The doctor had found the equivalent of about five capsules of Nembutal in Collier's system—not enough in itself to cause death, but potentially lethal when mixed with alcohol. And his alcohol level had been far higher than the amount five or six pints would account for. It looked as if Banks was right and Collier had been slipped vodka in the pub and more drinks back at the house.

"Should we go to see Fletcher tonight?" Banks asked Hatchley. "Or leave it until tomorrow?"

Under normal circumstances he would have expected Hatchley to take any opportunity to get off work for a pint or a session on the sofa with Carol Ellis, but this time the sergeant was angry.

"Let's go," he said. "Maybe Fletcher's got the answer. I wouldn't want to leave it till he went and got himself killed, too. And I wouldn't mind paying a call on Nicholas bloody Collier either."

III

"Go away!" Katie said, rushing forward and trying to close the door.

But Nicholas had his foot wedged in. "Let me in, Katie," he said. "I want to talk to you about Stephen. He was very fond of you, you know."

"He's dead," Katie said, still pushing at the door with her shoulder. But Nicholas was too strong for her and the door knocked her backwards against the kitchen table as he entered. He shut the door behind him and walked towards her.

"I won't hurt you," he said. "I know you were talking to Stephen the day before he died. I just wondered if he'd been saying anything silly. He wasn't well, you know." He reached out and grabbed Katie's arm as she tried to slip away. "There's no need to be afraid of me," he said, relaxing his grip a little. "No need to run away. I won't hurt you. I just want to talk to you."

"I don't know what you mean," Katie said. "There was nothing wrong with Stephen."

"He was upset. He might have said things he didn't mean."

"What things?"

"I don't know. That's what I'm asking you, you stupid bitch," Nicholas shouted, then lowered his voice again. "Just tell me what you talked about. Aren't you going to offer me a drink?"

"I don't have anything."

"Liar." Nicholas opened Sam's liquor cabinet and poured a large shot of gin. "I've been here before, remember? With Sam." He held out the glass. "Go on, have some. You like gin, don't you?"

Katie shook her head. Nicholas hooked the back of her neck with one hand, put the glass to her closed lips, and tipped it forwards. The vile-smelling spirit spilled down Katie's chin and onto the front of her dress. It burned her throat and made her gag.

"Stop it!" she cried, spluttering and pushing him away.

Nicholas laughed, showing his yellowed teeth, and put the glass down. He went back to the cabinet and poured himself some Scotch.

"What did Stephen tell you?" he asked.

"Nothing." Katie coughed and rubbed at her lips with the back of her hand.

"He must have said something. He was quite a one for confiding in the wrong people, Stephen was—especially women. And I saw you talking to that policeman. Where is he now? What's he doing?"

"I don't know. I haven't seen him since yesterday."

"What did he ask you? What did you say to him?"

"Nothing. He doesn't know anything."

"Stop lying, Katie. Did you do it with him too, just like you do with all the others?"

Katie turned pale. "What do you mean?"

Nicholas grinned. The dark comma of hair had flopped over his brow and his cheeks were flushed. "You know what I mean. Just like you did with Stephen and everyone else. Did you let him do it to you, Katie, that policeman?"

"No!"

"Oh, don't be shy. You do it with everyone, don't you? You know you're nothing but a slut. A filthy whore. Tell me you're a filthy whore, Katie, say it."

"I'm not."

Katie rushed desperately for the connecting door, but Nicholas got there before her.

"There's no way out," he said. "All your guests are in the White Rose. I saw them. And Sam's off with his fancy women as usual."

"He's what?"

"Didn't you know? Oh, don't tell me you didn't know. All those times he goes off to see his friends in Leeds or Eastvale. It's women, Katie. Loose women. Can't you smell them on his skin when he comes home? Or do you like it when he comes straight from another woman and takes you? Do you like to smell other women on your husband's skin?"

Katie put her hands to her ears. "Stop it! Stop it!" she screamed. "You're evil."

Nicholas applauded quietly. "Oh, Katie, what an act."

Katie dropped her hands to her side. "What are you going to do?"

"Do? Why, I'm going to take you away from here. I don't trust you, Katie. There's no telling what you know and what you might say."

"I don't know anything."

"I think you do. Stephen told you, didn't he?"

"Told me what?"

"About Oxford."

Katie could think of nothing to say.

"Look at you blushing," Nicholas said, pointing at her. "You know, don't you? I can tell. Be sure your sins will find you out."

Suddenly, Katie realized what he meant and a terrible thought dawned on her.

"You killed him," she said quietly. "You killed Stephen."

Nicholas shrugged and spoke in a cold, passionless voice. "I couldn't trust him any more. He was falling apart on me."

Katie stiffened. She felt like a trapped animal. "What are you going to do?"

"I'm going to take you away, far away. What did he tell you about Oxford?"

"Nothing."

"Did he tell you about that girl, that stupid slut?"

Katie shook her head.

"He did, didn't he?"

"No! He told me nothing."

Nicholas leaned against the table. His bright eyes glittered and his breath came in short, sharp gasps. He looked like a madman to Katie. A wild, terrifying madman.

"She was nothing but a prostitute, Katie," he said. "A fallen woman. She sold herself to men. And when I . . . when I took her, she didn't . . . She told me I was too rough and she tried to make me stop. Me! Nicholas Collier. But I didn't. I couldn't. I knew that was the way she really wanted it. A common tart like her. Like you."

"No!" Katie said. "I'm not."

"Yes you are. I've had my eye on you. You do it with everyone. Do they pay you, Katie, or do you do it for nothing? I know you like to struggle. I'll pay you if you want."

"I don't know what you're talking about."

"I want you to say it for me. Say you're a filthy whore."

"I'm not."

"What's wrong? Why won't you say it? I bet you even let that policeman do it. I'm better than the lot of them, Katie. Say it."

"No! I won't."

He spoke very softly, so quiet she could hardly hear. "I want you to go down on your knees, Katie, and tell me you're a filthy whore and you want me to do it to you like an animal. Like a dog. I want you to lift your dress up and crawl, Katie."

He was moving towards her now, and his eyes held hers with a power that seemed to sap what little strength she had. She felt her shoulders hit the wall by the mantelpiece. There was nowhere else to go. But Nicholas kept coming closer, and when he was near enough he reached out and grabbed the front of her dress.

IV

Banks drove fast along the dark dale by the River Swain, passed through Helmthorpe and into the darker fell-shadowed landscape beyond. He turned sharp right at Swainshead, tires squealing, and carried on up the valley to Upper Head. He slowed down as they passed the Collier house, but the lights were out.

"I hope the bastard hasn't done a bunk," Hatchley said.

"No, he's too cool for that. We'll get him, don't worry."

The glimmer of light high on the fell-side about two miles north of the village came from Fletcher's isolated cottage. It was a difficult track to manage in the dark, but they finally pulled up outside the squat, solid house with its three-foot-thick walls. Fletcher had heard them coming and stood in the doorway. Again, they were ushered into the plain whitewashed room with its oak table and the photograph of Fletcher's glamorous ex-wife.

Fletcher was ill at ease. He avoided looking at them directly and fussed around with glasses for beer. Hatchley stood by the window looking out into the darkness. Banks sat at the table.

"What is it?" he asked, when Fletcher had sat down opposite him.

"It's about Stephen's death," Fletcher began hesitantly. "He was my friend. It's gone too far, now. Too far."

Banks nodded. "I know. I understand there was no love lost between you and Nicholas."

"You've heard about that? Well, it's true enough. I never had much time for him. But old Mr Walter was like a father to me, and I always felt like an older brother to Stephen."

Banks passed around the cigarettes.

"Saturday night," Fletcher burst out suddenly. "I thought nothing of it at the time—it was just the kind of silly trick Nicholas would play—but when he went to buy a round, I saw him pour a shot of clear spirits into Stephen's drink. As I said, I thought nothing of it. I knew Stephen was upset about something—what it was, I don't know—and he seemed to want to get drunk and forget his problems anyway. No point causing trouble, I thought, so I kept quiet.

"That family has a secret, Mr Banks, a dark secret. Stephen's hinted at it more than once, and I reckon it's something to do with Nicholas and the ladies, though ladies is too dignified a term. Did you know he once forced himself on Molly Stark from over Relton way?"

"No, I didn't."

"Aye. Well, it was hushed up, like most things Nicholas got up to. All neat and business-like."

"Wasn't there also some trouble with a servant-girl when his father was alive?" Banks asked.

"Aye," said Fletcher. "Got her in the family way. But money changed hands and shut mouths. It was all arranged for, no expense spared, and she did away with it. He had a lust for lasses below his station, as they used to say. Working-class girls, servants, factory-girls, milkmaids ... I even caught him mauling Katie Greenock at Stephen's party last week."

At last it made sense to Banks. Nicholas Collier couldn't keep away from women of a lower social class: Cheryl Duggan, Esther Haines, Katie Greenock, Anne Ralston, the servant-girl, Molly Stark—they were all beneath him socially. Although the term had lost a lot of its meaning over the past few years, they might still be called working-class women. Obviously it didn't matter who they were as individuals; that didn't interest Collier. He probably had some Victorian image of the working classes as a seething, gin-drinking, fornicating, procreating mass. He thrust himself on them and became violent when they objected. No doubt like most perverse sexual practices, his compulsion had a lot to do with power and humiliation.

"I knew something serious was up when we had those two murders here," Fletcher went on, refilling their beer glasses. "That detective and young Bernard Allen. I knew it, but I didn't know what. Whenever I asked, Stephen clammed up, told me to leave it be and I'd be better off not knowing." He took a sip of beer. "Maybe I should've pushed a bit harder.

Maybe Stephen would still be alive. . . . But I don't think he killed himself. That's what I wanted to tell you. I saw Nicholas putting something into his drink, and he was in a hell of a state at closing-time, worse than if he'd just had a few jars. And the next thing I hear, he's dead. An overdose, they said. I knew he took sleeping tablets, but an overdose . . . ?"

"Yes, barbiturates," Banks said. "Usually fatal, mixed with as much alcohol as Stephen Collier had in his system."

"So it's murder, isn't it? That bastard brother of his murdered him."

"It looks like it, Mr Fletcher, but we've got to tread carefully. We've got no evidence, no proof."

"I'll testify to what I saw. I'll help put him away, as God's my witness."

Banks shook his head. "It'll help, but it's not enough. What if Nicholas was putting vodka in his brother's beer? As you said, it could have been a simple prank, and that's exactly what he'll say. It's all circumstantial and theoretical. We need more solid evidence, or a confession."

"Then I'll bloody well beat it out of him," Fletcher said, grasping the table and rising to his feet.

"Sit down," said Banks. "That's not going to help at all."

"Then what are you going to do?"

"I honestly don't know yet," Banks said. "We might just be able to put together a case, especially if we bring in Anne Ralston, but I don't want to risk it. Even if we could convince the court it's worth a trial, I don't want to take the chance of him getting off, which he might well do on what we've got so far."

"I know I should've spoken up earlier," Fletcher said. "I knew there was something wrong. If I'd told you before you went to Toronto, you might have had something to push at Stephen with, and he just might have told you the truth. He was on the edge, Mr Banks. That's why Nicholas had to get rid of him, I suppose."

"I think you're right," Banks said. "But we still can't prove it. You shouldn't blame yourself, though. You might have thought you were going to get Stephen in trouble. I imagine you were protecting him?"

Fletcher nodded. "I suppose I was. Him and his father's memory."

"To get Nicholas, you'd have had to betray Stephen. He was protecting his brother, or his father, like you were."

"What'll happen to me? Will you prosecute?"

"For what?"

"Withholding evidence? Accessory after the fact?"

Banks laughed. "You have a very thin grasp of the law, Mr Fletcher. Sure, you could have spoken earlier, as could a number of other people around Stephen Collier. But he kept everyone just enough in the dark so there was nothing, really, to say—nothing but vague fears and suspicions. Believe me, few people come to us with those—they don't want to look silly."

"So nothing's going to happen to me?"

Banks stood up and gestured to Hatchley it was time to leave. "No. You've helped us. It's up to us now to put a case together, or set a trap."

"I'll do anything to help," Fletcher said. "Tell the bastard I know something and let him come and try to bump me off."

"I hope it doesn't come to that," Banks said, "but thanks for the offer."

They sat in the car for a few minutes and lit cigarettes. It was pitch black, and far down in the valley below, the lights of Swainshead glittered like an alley of stars.

"How hard should we push Collier?" Hatchley asked.

"We don't push," Banks said. "At least not the first time. I told you, he's clever. He'll see we're desperate."

"So what do we do?"

"We confront him with what we've got and try to trip him up. If he's too clever to fall for that, and I suspect he is, then we try again and keep trying." He started the engine and broke the fell-side silence.

"You can't help admiring the bastard's nerve, though, can you," Hatchley said. "What if Freddie Metcalfe and Richmond had remembered seeing him order vodka and pour it in Stephen's pints?"

"Then all he'd have had to say was that he played a practical joke, like Fletcher said. There's nothing illegal about chasers. As things stand, it's only Fletcher's word against his, and a good defence lawyer would soon prove that John Fletcher had more than just cause to want to incriminate Collier. They'd bring up the incident at the party, for a start. Could you imagine Katie Greenock on the stand?"

Hatchley shook his head. "That lass never seems to know whether she's coming or going."

For some reason, Banks began to feel uneasy at the thought of Katie. What if she really did know more than she was telling? And what if Nicholas Collier suspected she knew? He might easily have seen her talking to Stephen. And Katie was exactly the kind of woman to set off his violent sexual behaviour.

He turned on to the road and headed south for Swainshead. There was still no light on in Collier's house. Hatchley hammered at the door but got no answer.

"Let's try the pub," Banks suggested.

Hatchley brightened up at that. He hadn't completely forgotten his priorities in a burst of professional zeal.

"Well, if it isn't Chief Inspector Banks," Freddie Metcalfe greeted them. "And Sergeant Hatchley, isn't it? What can I do you for?"

Banks ordered two pints of Pedigree and lit a Silk Cut. Maybe a pint would calm down his jangling nerves. The hairs at the back of his neck were bristling.

"Seen Nicholas Collier tonight?" he asked.

"No, he's not been in," Freddie said. "Has tha got any further wi' t'murder?"

"We're getting there, we're getting there," Banks said.

"Aye, and pigs can fly," Freddie said, passing their drinks. "None of the usual lot been in tonight?"

"Nope. It's been as quiet as this since opening time," Freddie answered miserably and loped off to serve a youth in hiking boots.

"You know," Banks said, "I've been thinking about what

to do next, and there's someone else we might profit from leaning on in this case."

"Sam Greenock?" Hatchley said.

"Yes. Threaten him with arrest as an accessory, and we might just get him to open up. He's cocky, but I don't think he's as cool as Nicholas. Stephen Collier's dead now. If we can convince Sam that Nicholas will fall from grace with or without his help, we might be able to strike a bargain. After all, without gentry to suck up to, what's Sam going to get out of it? Nicholas might well have sawn off the branch he was sitting on by killing Stephen."

"It's an idea," Hatchley said.

"And Greenock's a bully," Banks said. "Bullies are the easiest of the lot to lean on, especially men who beat up their wives."

"I think I might be able to work up a bit of enthusiasm," Hatchley said, grinning.

"Good. Let's go."

"What? Now? But we haven't finished our drinks."

"I've just got a feeling, that's all. We can come back to them. Let's see if Sam's in."

They left the White Rose and crossed the bridge. There were no lights on in the front lower or upper rooms of the Greenock Guest House.

"He's not in," Hatchley said. "Let's go back to the pub and call again later."

"It looks like there's nobody in at all," Banks said. "That's odd." He couldn't explain why he felt disturbed by the dark silent house, but he couldn't ignore the feeling. "No," he said. "I'm going in."

Hatchley sighed and followed. "I'll bet the bloody door's locked."

Before they could close the gate behind them, they heard a car coming. It was Sam's Landrover. He parked near the pub across the narrow Swain, as there was no road on the Greenocks' side of the road, and came bounding over the bridge.

"Evening, gents," he called out. "And what can I do . . .

Oh, it's you."

"Don't sound so disappointed," Banks said. "We might be able to do something for you."

"Oh?" Sam's boyish face looked puzzled. He patted his curly hair. "All right. Never turn down a favour from a copper, that's me."

"Can we go in?"

"Of course. I'll get the missis to brew a pot of tea." He dug in his pocket for his keys, finally found the right one and stuck it in the lock, where he poked and twisted it for a while, then turned to Banks and frowned. "That's odd. It was already open. Katie usually locks up at ten sharp and the guests let themselves in with their own keys. And it's not usually as dark as this. She puts the hall light on for the guests. They're probably still in the pub, but I can't imagine where she is."

Banks and Hatchley followed him through the front door into the dark hall. Sam turned the light on. The guest book lay open on its varnished table by a stack of tourist guides, maps and brochures advertising local businesses and leisure pursuits. Automatically, Sam looked at himself in the mirror over the phone and patted his curly hair again.

"Katie!" Sam called.

No answer.

He went into the dining-room and flicked the light switch on. "Bloody hell!"

Banks followed him inside. "What is it?" All he could see was the room where he and Hatchley had eaten breakfast. The varnished tables gleamed darkly in the shaded light.

"She's not set the tables for the morning. She's not even put the bloody cloths on," Sam said. He sounded more angry than worried about why or where Katie might have gone.

They paused at the foot of the stairs, where Sam called again and got no answer. "It doesn't look like she's home," he said, puzzled. "I can't imagine where she'd be at this time."

"Maybe she's left you," Banks suggested.

"Don't be daft. Where would she go? Why would she do a thing like that anyway?"

They carried on to the door that separated the Greenocks' living-quarters from the rest of the house.

"Katie!" Sam called once more, hand on the knob.

Still no reply. The absolute silence in the house made Banks's hackles rise.

Sam opened the door and walked along the short, narrow corridor that linked the two parts of the house. Banks and Hatchley followed close behind. Coats on hooks on either side brushed against them as they walked in single file behind Sam. The only faint illumination was at the end of the passage.

"At least she's left this light on," Sam said.

The light came from the pane of frosted glass on the door that led into the Greenocks' living-room. Sam called his wife's name again but got no answer. He walked into the room and stopped dead in his tracks.

"Jesus Christ," he gasped, then stumbled backwards into Banks and started to slide slowly down the wall, hands over his eyes.

Banks regained his balance, pushed past Sam and went in, Hatchley close behind. They stopped in the doorway, awed and horrified by the scene before them. Banks heard Hatchley mutter a prayer or a curse.

There was blood all over the room: on the carpet, the sofa, the hearth, and even splashed like obscene hieroglyphs over the wall above the mantelpiece. Nothing moved. Nicholas Collier lay awkwardly, half on the sofa and half on the carpet, his head bashed in, his face a bloody pulp. He wouldn't even have been recognizable if it hadn't been for the prominent, yellowish teeth splintered and bared in agony and shock.

Katie sat on the arm of the settee still holding the heavy wooden cross of her granny's that had stood on the mantelpiece. Her beautiful brown eyes were looking at things nobody else could see. The front of her dress was ripped open at one side and a few drops of blood glistened against the pale skin of her blue-veined breast.

Peter Robinson

CAEDMON'S SONG

On a balmy June night, after a merry evening of pub-hopping and party-going, Kirsten, a young university student, strolls home through a silent moonlit park. Suddenly, giving in to a childish impulse, she leaps on top of a stone lion statue. But Kirsten's reverie is violently shattered by a swift and brutal hand. . . . When Kirsten awakens, she discovers she has been the victim of an attacker who has left her sexually abused and horribly disfigured. She has no memories of that evening, and she suspects it would be too painful to remember. But the attacker continues, leaving a trail of mutilated female corpses across the northeast of England. As the police and the locals seem only able to stand back in horror and wait for the next murder, Kirsten becomes convinced not only that she *can* remember, but that she *must*. Through fragments of nightmares, the details slowly reveal themsevles—two figures hovering over her, one in white and one in black; wisps of a strange and haunting song; the rough texture of a hand. . .

Meanwhile, Martha Browne arrives in the coastal town of Whitby, posing as an author doing research for a book. But her research is of a particularly macabre variety. Who is she hunting with such deadly determination? And why?

Peter Robinson, in his first non-Banks novel, has created a gripping psychological thriller, which skilfully weaves together the two stories and unites them in a startling, chilling conclusion.

Peter Robinson

GALLOW'S VIEW

Short-listed for the John Creasy Award

Chief Inspector Alan Banks of the Criminal Investigation Department has been recently transferred from London to Eastvale, a town in the Yorkshire Dales. His desire to escape the stress of city life appears to be satisfied by Eastvale's cobbled market square, its tree-shaded river and its picturesque castle ruins. But the village begins to show a more dangerous side . . .

As a Peeping Tom disturbs the peace of Eastvale women, police are accused of underestimating the seriousness of the crime. At the same time, Banks is also investigating the case of two local teenagers whose crimes are escalating from theft to violence. The two cases weave together as this tough, gritty novel of power and suspense reaches a terrifying and surprising climax.

"This is a first novel that will knock you over with its maturity."

Howard Engel

"Offers all the suspense and local colour that anyone could expect, plus a few surprises."

Toronto Star

"A Fast-moving, gripping mystery story."

Winnipeg Free Press

Peter Robinson

A DEDICATED MAN

Nominated for the Arthur Ellis Award

It was a perfect summer. The weather was unusually warm for the Dales, and Harry Steadman, who was preparing a book on the area, and his wife, Emma, enjoyed their holiday at the Ramsden Bed and Breakfast.

But ten years later the memories of that peaceful summer are shattered by Harry Steadman's brutal murder. Inspector Banks is back, and investigating a case just as confounding as his first. Who would kill the kindly scholar? Penny Cartwright, a beautiful woman with a disturbing past? Harry's editor or the shady land developer? And is it possible that young Sally Lumb, locked in her lover's arms the night of the murder, could unknowingly hold the key to the case?

"A perfect little portrait of a village in the Yorkshire dales. . . . First-rate stuff for the detective story buff."
Province (Vancouver)

"A cast of interesting, human characters—especially his wry and introspective hero."
Star Phoenix (Saskatoon)

"A first-class story. . . . One of the most completely realized detectives in Canadian crime fiction."
The Toronto Star

Peter Robinson

A NECESSARY END

One rainy March evening, an anti-nuclear demonstration outside the Eastvale Community Centre turns nasty: the mood of the crowd begins to darken as the weather worsens. Finally the police lose control and violence erupts, leaving one policeman dead and almost a hundred suspects.

Detective Chief Inspector Banks is back, investigating his third case in Yorkshire. But things are made difficult for Banks when Superintendent Richard "Dirty Dick" Burgess is sent from London, for political reasons, to lead the investigation. Sifting through a host of unusual suspects and disturbing discoveries about the police themselves, Banks is finally warned off the case. And the only way he can salvage his career is by beating Burgess to the killer. As the two head for a final confrontation, Banks pieces together the full story behind his most tragic case so far.

"A good mystery and a contemporary variation. ...With the publishing of *A Necessary End*, I think we can now be assured that we have a series that is going to be with us for a long time to come."
The Vancouver Sun

"Well-written, and with a rich and varied cast of believable characters, *A Necessary End* is Robinson's best novel to date."
The London Free Press

"Perceptive insights into the philosophies of police and protestors."
The Times (London)